Johnny Came Home

Tony Breeden

Second Edition.

Johnny Came Home Copyright © 2009, 2012 Tony Breeden

John Lazarus: Mann from Midwich excerpt. Copyright © 2012 Tony Breeden

All rights reserved. No portion of this book may be reproduced, stored in a retrieval system, or transmitted in any form or by any means—electronic, mechanical, recording, scanning, or other—except for brief quotations in critical reviews or articles, without the prior written permission of the author.

Author's Note: This novel is a work of fiction. Names, characters, places and incidents are either products of the author's imagination or used fictitiously. All characters are fictional, and any similarity to people living or dead is purely coincidental.

All other characters are © and ™ their respective owners.

Author may be contacted for interview requests at 304-993-4792.

ISBN-10: **1452845506**
ISBN-13: **978-1452845500**

To Jesus Christ, my Creator, Savior & King.

To my wife, best friend and soul mate, Angie.

CONTENTS

#	Title	Page	#	Title	Page
1	Johnny Came Home	p. 1	23	Roy	p. 97
2	Casting Stones	p. 6	24	Frequency	p. 99
3	That's What Friends Are For	p. 10	25	Pandora	p. 103
4	Comic Book Conversations	p. 16	26	Be Careful Little Eyes	p. 106
5	Checking Out	p. 22	27	Zombies	p. 110
6	Hostage Situations	p. 24	28	Swatting Flies	p. 114
7	Making New Friends	p. 29	29	Dwight	p. 120
8	Winners and Wusses	p. 34	30	Sabotage	p. 124
9	An Hour Ago	p. 38	31	Fallen	p. 126
10	Good Karma	p. 43	32	Jailbreak	p. 128
11	The Consultant	p. 49	33	Breach	p. 131
12	Puzzle Pieces	p. 56	34	Challenger	p. 133
13	Pawns and Crackpots	p. 59	35	The Inside Man	p. 136
14	Siege	p. 62	36	Trailing Sparks	p. 139
15	Calm Before the Storm	p. 66	37	Fight or Flight	p. 142
16	Showdown at Soul's Harbor	p. 69	38	Fireside Chat	p. 145
17	Duct Tape	p. 75	39	Parasol	p. 147
18	Mopping Up	p. 77	40	Ghost	p. 149
19	Bad Karma	p. 81	41	Shadow Man	p. 153
20	Ness	p. 85	42	The Night of the Fire	p. 157
21	Gifted	p. 88	43	Burning Man	p. 160
22	And Busybody Boggess Saw the Whole Thing	p. 92	44	We Need a Ride	p. 164

45	Titan Overthrown	p. 167		58	Rescue	p. 229
46	Kelly's Kegger	p. 170		59	At the End of the Countdown	p. 232
47	Welcome Wagon	p. 177		60	Saucer	p. 236
48	Gamma Lab	p. 182		61	Emily	p. 242
49	Flare	p. 189		62	Harper Plaza	p. 248
50	Last Chance	p. 192		63	Destiny	p. 264
51	Disruptor	p. 198		64	Wreck of a Mech	p. 274
52	Control Room	p. 201		65	Tower Fall	p. 276
53	Hangar	p. 206		66	The Fat Lady Sings	p. 280
54	Auditorium	p. 214		67	We All Have a Choice	p. 284
55	Escape	p. 220		68	Aftermath	p. 287
56	Balcony	p. 222		69	For Sale	p. 294
57	Somebody's Gonna Have To Do Something Stupid	p. 226		70	The Bravest One	p. 298

A Sneak Peek at John Lazarus: Mann from Midwich

1	MIA	p. 302		2	Full Moon	p. 310
	About the Author	p. 322				

ACKNOWLEDGMENTS

The writing process is something of a group event. I'd like to thank my amazing wife, Angie, and Tim Chaffey [midwestapologetics.org] for reading the final draft and making helpful editing suggestions. . I'd also like to thank fellow authors Pastor Buddy Helms, Steve Schwartz, Peter R. Stone and Allan Reini for additional comments and editing suggestions for this Second Edition.

My wife deserves special thanks for encouraging me through the entire writing process and to follow through with the publication of this, my first novel.

I also owe a debt to my late aunt Sharon, who helped me put together my very first book – a dinosaur book written and illustrated by yours truly – put together with brads and cardstock. As a boy, I was very proud of that book and I credit my aunt with giving me the writing bug.

Arguments used by Arthur Lazarus in Chapter 42 were adapted in part from arguments presented in *Meet the Skeptic: A Field Guide to Faith Conversations* by Bill Foster (Green Forest, AR: Master Books, © 2012). Used with permission. [meettheskeptic.com]

1 – Johnny Came Home

Johnny always said he'd rather die than come back to Midwich, but he'd never counted on having to make that very choice.

When it came down to it, he found himself driving his maroon 1987 Plymouth Reliant with its Mustard Yellow front passenger fender in the only direction that offered a chance at life. Eventually, he pulled off the interstate onto a paved country road. The two lane highway degenerated into a single lane of cracked, lumpy asphalt guaranteed to give you motion sickness. Only poor farms and the occasional house trailer broke the monotony of the drive. At long last, he came to an opening in the trees on a high ridge. Midwich appeared below on the banks of a wide river, an improbably mid-sized city with a prominent downtown. Johnny stopped briefly at a scenic overlook.

It was almost exactly as he remembered it. The city was laid out before him like a map, bisected by the river. Off to the right of his view, the river spilled from the locks of a local dam. The dam powered the city itself and the surrounding area. Kaukasos College was nestled on a hilltop on the banks of a man-made lake, also the result of the dam. Across the valley from the college, he could see Titan Biotech's imposing complex.

The locals thought Titan was a Godsend. Titan's charismatic CEO, Charles Huxley, had made good on his promise to transform the economy of once-rural Midwich. He built the research complex, the dam and the power station. Then he brought in Titan-owned businesses like Argus Information Systems, Mnemosyne Marketing, and Gaia Biofarms. These jobs attracted more jobs and investors – and the poor people of Appalachia practically worshipped jobs. Anyone who'd seen the commercials knew that Titan hoped to usher in a better tomorrow through aggressive research into green power, genetically-engineered crops, pharmaceuticals, gene therapies, and better healthcare.

Johnny sighed, took note of the fact that his passenger was still asleep, and decided not to wake him until later. Weasel would have a thousand questions that he wasn't prepared to answer just yet. He headed toward town.

Though he hadn't really intended to, he found himself passing through the downtown district. Maybe it was out of morbid curiosity. They'd only just broke ground for Titan Tower when he left. Now it reached into the heavens like Babel, lording over Founder's Plaza and every other building in Midwich. Its top floors were still under construction, including an unfinished steel-and-girder statue of Atlas holding the earth on his shoulders.

Titan's downtown blossomed with skyscrapers, but these economic changes were still too new for Midwich's original residents. As a result, the area was an uneasy conglomerate of metropolitan newcomers and redneck tradition.

He passed the old comics shop on his way out of Founder's Plaza. The very last time he'd seen Emily was at that shop. He'd wanted to tell her about the strange things that were happening to him, but then chickened out. Black Ear Comics was closed, abandoned.

He headed for his old neighborhood. When he came to Archer Lane, he slowed down to take everything in. Despite himself, he admired the massive columns of oak that stood sentry on either side. Serpentine roots churned up the sidewalks, forcing children to take their bikes and wagons to the streets. Arching branches formed a near-perfect cathedral overhead, except for a thin center line of cloud-strewn blue sky. The site filled him with an unbidden sense of nostalgia. He suppressed it immediately. His childhood was a lie.

The houses were nearly identical, save one.

Each two-story structure sported a different hue of pastel homogeneity. Powder blues. Pale greens. Faded citrus. Ghostly yellows. Mellencamp pinks. All had big picture windows, where you could see the family gathered around the dinner table each afternoon. Each sported a two-car garage with a basketball hoop between the doors, whether the owner had more than one vehicle or not. Not one lacked a spacious, inviting porch with the prerequisite porch swing and a pair of old rockers. All had well-trimmed front lawns bounded by darling picket fences and big backyards rimmed with tall privacy hedges. Each backyard was guaranteed to have a grand shade tree big enough to support a good-sized tree house or an old tire swing. A storage shed stood sentry over a rustic gate that led to a gravel alley. In short, they were all picture perfect.

Johnny hunched down in his seat a bit. He doubted anyone knew the car, but that made it all the more conspicuous, didn't it? These guys were like the Neighborhood Watch on steroids. They'd notice a strange vehicle instantly. An old car like his did stand out a little bit in this neighborhood. More importantly, he didn't want them to recognize the car's driver.

Not until he had a chance to see if the house was still there.

The K-car's other occupant stirred, grumbling to embittered awareness. "Where the blazes are we, Johnny?" he asked. He blinked against the sun. "And why is it so bright?" Despite the shade afforded by the Archer oaks, any amount of sun was too much for Weasel Hopkins. He'd proven nocturnal by habit, perhaps by nature. He swept a comic book off his chest and shifted around in his seat, trying to take in his surroundings with a minimum of effort. "Are you kidding me? Does Martha Stewart know we're coming?"

Johnny didn't answer. He was concentrating on the ninth house on the left. "Just like I left it."

If the other houses on Archer were dream homes, this one stood as a monument to every home owner's worst nightmare. A gaping hole in its roof exposed charred, blackened boards. Its windows were shattered and boarded. Its first story entrances were bandaged in police tape. Abandoned. Decrepit. Condemned.

"Just like you left what?" Weasel asked. He followed Johnny's gaze to the ruined house. He made a face. "Ugh! Seriously, where are we, dude?"

Johnny hesitated a moment before answering. "Midwich."

Weasel sat up straight at the name, a bit confused. His eyes darted back to the house. He made the connection. "Was that your house, man?"

Johnny nodded, peering at the surrounding houses to see if they'd been noticed. He also took note of the Halloween decorations. Tonight was Trick or Treat night. Busybody Boggess lived right across the street. When Johnny was a kid, his nosy old neighbor was always spying on him, sticking his nose where it didn't belong, telling his parents, getting him in trouble. Busybody Boggess' porch light was always dark on Halloween. He seemed to have it out for kids – Johnny in particular. His house and Widow Harper's on the corner were the only two childless homes on Archer. They couldn't have been more different. Nobody skipped Widow Harper's house on Trick or Treat Night. Her parties were the best. He didn't see any sign of Boggess, but that didn't mean he wasn't there, spying on him like usual.

Weasel snickered, noting the official statement on the door. "Dude, it's condemned."

"They didn't tear it down," Johnny said. He'd worried that it'd been bulldozed in the three years since he left. Perhaps that's what bothered him. Did they suspect he might return to the scene of the crime? Were they watching the place even now? Was it a trap?

"Yeah, well, I thought you said you were never, ever coming back here, man."

"I changed my mind."

Weasel scowled, but said nothing.

A car pulled onto Archer behind them, drawing Johnny's gaze to the rear view mirror. A police cruiser. He muttered an unintelligible curse under his breath and tapped the accelerator back up to the speed limit.

"What is it?" Weasel asked. He turned around and glanced behind them. He spotted the cruiser. "Great, Johnny."

"Relax, Weez. We're not breaking any laws."

"Won't matter. You know they're gonna take one look at us and just assume we did something."

Johnny glared at him out of the corner of his eye. It was true that a black man and a long-haired metal head tended to attract undue attention from local law enforcement, but it wasn't profiling he was worrying about. It was recognition. Still, he couldn't have Weasel panicking. "Just stay calm and act casual."

"Whatever that means." He fished his jean jacket pockets for his lighter and cigarettes.

"Really?" Johnny's eyes flashed as Weasel started to fire up his cigarette. "You're gonna do that now?"

"What? You said to stay calm. Smoking calms my nerves."

"It also causes cancer. It killed your grandma, Weez."

Weasel stared at him open-mouthed, indignant and offended. Still, he slid his cigarette back into the pack. "Your car. Your rules."

Johnny tried to see if he recognized the officer in the car behind them. Before the fire, his father had been the sheriff of Midwich, so he got to know the town's police force pretty well. If it was Slim, they had a chance. That donut-eating cliché would be too busy admiring holiday decorations to even notice them. Any of the others would already be running his plates. That wouldn't be good.

At the end of Archer stood a white-steepled church. He pulled into the parking lot. Some church-goers liked to park closer to the alley instead of the street, just to get out of the parking lot a bit quicker after services. Today was Friday. Only one car sat on the premises, probably the pastor's. Johnny efficiently crossed the lot and headed into the alley.

Though he knew he should hurry, in case the cop called in for backup and attempted to box him into the alley, he couldn't resist slowing down as they approached his back gate. He meant to check the back door to see how hard it would be to break in tonight.

He didn't expect to see Emily swinging on his old tire swing. Their eyes met for a single instant, but he knew she recognized him. That would complicate things.

Weasel needlessly urged him on. He sped out of the alleyway as fast as he dared.

The cruiser pulled into the alley after him just before he made it out of the street. A moment later, Emily stepped into the alley to stare after him, blocking the car from view.

Johnny turned onto the blacktop and headed to the river.

"That was close," Weasel said.

"Yeah." Johnny was more worried about Emily than the cop.

"What now?"

Johnny took a deep breath. "We need to talk."

2 – Casting Stones

Under the shadow of the bridge, a stare-down was in full effect.

Weasel Hopkins sat on the still warm hood of the Plymouth, his cigarette hanging precariously from the corner of his mouth. Though the stinging smoke curled irreverently into his left eye, he seemed determined not to blink. Johnny held his gaze with those unshakable amber eyes, waiting until the cigarette smoke forced the issue. "Are you in? Or not?" Johnny asked as Weasel blinked, taking advantage of the other's loss of face to push his point.

"No, no. Let's think this out a bit, shall we? You want to break into your old house – the house you burnt down, mind you! And, by the way, does anyone else know you're an arsonist?"

Johnny turned away, pretending to examine the graffiti tagged on the bridge's concrete pylons. One message, spray-painted in tall, hot pink letters, caught his eye instantly: "Titan Lies!" His dad had warned him about Titan Biotech the night of the fire. He couldn't help but wonder who else suspected there was something amiss up at Titan.

"Well?" Weasel asked.

Johnny picked up a rock and casually turned toward the river. His eyes darted self-consciously to the graffiti before responding. "No, everybody thinks I'm dead." He attempted to skip the stone across the waters. Plunk! Too bulky. He cast about for something more suitable.

"Yeah, what's up with that exactly? No offense, buddy, but you just burn your house down and what? Let everyone think you went up with it? You let them live with that while you just went off –"

"Nobody cared, alright." He knew that now. He was different and they hated him for it. It wasn't until shortly before the fire that he realized why. He'd thought it had something to do with the color of his skin, or that he'd been adopted by a white couple, or that his girlfriend was the prettiest, most popular white girl in town. But it was definitely more than skin deep. You hate what you fear. You fear what you can't control. He blinked away the past, forcing himself to concentrate on the present. The ice shield slipped back over his eyes. "Just trust me on that one."

"Fine, I'm sure you had a perfectly good reason for burning down your house. Some of us would've liked to have had a big house to burn down. Burning down a real nice trailer home just doesn't have the same ring to it."

Johnny tried to suppress a grin. He flicked a rock towards the river. It skipped twice before it dove beneath the surface. Encouraged by his success, he looked around for a better stone to throw.

"But if nobody cared, why come back at all? And this better not have anything to do with that fortune teller we saw last night, dude."

"It's hard to explain, Weez."

Johnny had let Weasel know some of his story over the years. He'd told him about the house and the fire, how he'd lost his folks. He'd clued him in on the fact that the town was pretty much Big Brother. And given the effort he took to assure that they stayed off the grid, Weasel probably at least suspected that not everyone thought Johnny was dead. It looked like Weasel was beginning to resent being on a need-to-know basis. Yet how did one go about explaining that he'd made certain decisions in his life, ever since the night of the fire, based simply on a gut feeling that choosing otherwise would result in his untimely death? Call them premonitions, all he knew is that sometimes he came to a crossroads and when he considered one option against another, he could see his own death in one of them. These death visions came in quick, stabbing flashes, much too intense to ignore. How did one explain that from the moment he'd visited that fortune teller last night, he'd known he had to come to Midwich or die?

"So try me," Weasel said. "Use little words if you have to, but at least tell your best friend – your future accessory to breaking and entering, for crying out loud – what the devil is going on."

Johnny shook his head. "First, it's my house, so it's not breaking and entering. It's not even trespassing. Not really. Second, the less you know the better."

Weasel held his gaze for a few moments, then flicked his cigarette into the river and hopped off the hood of the Plymouth. The K-car's hood buckled back into shape with a metallic snap. "Fine. Be that way. You wanna shut me out? You got it." He started walking down the river bank.

"Wait."

Weasel stopped, but didn't look back.

"You really wanna know what's going on?"

Weasel turned around.

"Because what I'm about to tell you has consequences. Once you know, you're in. There's no turning back. You can't un-learn it. You can't go back and change your mind. You can't pretend you don't know. My enemies become your enemies," Johnny said. "And I know things that people will kill for. And once they find out I've told you –"

"Stop! I get it!" Weasel said. "Just shut up already. Are you like a spy or something?" He immediately dismissed the idea. "A teen spy. This isn't a movie. What am I talking about? Look, I'm in. Whatever. You didn't kill anybody, did you?"

"No. Well, not on purpose."

Weasel took a few cautious steps backward.

"I'm not a murderer or anything. It was an accident. Self-defense. I didn't know what I was doing," he said. He knew he was explaining badly and making himself look like a lying criminal in the process, but he honestly wasn't sure how much he should tell. His enemies had ways of getting information out of you. He'd evaded them for the last few years by being very careful. He'd never shared what he knew with anyone. He'd even been careful not to try to find out anything else about it. Internet searches, your library check-outs, medical records, purchases… they could track you down through any of that stuff.

But he needed Weasel's help. He needed someone he could trust to watch his back. Someone who wasn't connected with Midwich. Trust works both ways.

"Fine, we'll do it like this. The only way you're gonna believe me is if I just show you. Just promise not to freak out," Johnny said. "Pick up that rock, the big one right there."

"And do what with it?"

"You wanna know what's going on or not?"

"OK, OK, don't get your britches in a bunch. I'm doing it already." Weasel bent down and picked up the stone. It was pretty heavy and as big as his head. "Now what?"

"Skip it across the river."

"Are you kidding me with this? You seriously think I can skip this big chunk of rock, like, at all?"

"What have you got to lose?"

"Fine, but this better be going somewhere." Whirling around, he heaved the rock in a rather clumsy imitation of a discus thrower. He knew from the moment it left his hands that his weak toss wasn't even gonna reach the water. It landed with a slightly gross schlunk on the muddy bank of the river.

Weasel stared at it expectantly. Nothing happened.

Johnny grinned.

"OK," Weasel asked, "what exactly was that supposed to prove?"

"What did you think was going to happen?"

"I dunno. I mean, I thought I would at least get it in the water, but did I think it was actually gonna skip across the river? Well, no, if that's what you're asking."

"Let me try."

"Dude, you couldn't even skip some of the little ones."

Johnny ignored him. He walked over to Weasel's rock and hefted it. "Ready?"

Weasel smirked. "Good luck, dude."

Johnny whirled about and let fly.

Weasel stared transfixed as the stone skipped perfectly and impossibly across the river. At the other bank, it bounded out of the water and crashed into some bushes. "I don't believe it. I mean, I saw it, but that's impossible! I mean..." He sputtered to a stop, turning to John Lazarus with a mixture of fear and curiosity, confusion and amazement.

Instead of answering Weasel, Johnny pointed to a cabbage-sized stone nearby, causing it to levitate off the ground at eye level. While his friend gaped, he sent it spinning, faster and faster, then let fly. This rock also skipped across the river to land next to the first one.

Weasel turned to Johnny, eyes wide. "How?"

"Let's drive. I'll tell you on the way."

3 – That's What Friends Are For

"He's back." She blurted it out, unable to hold it in any longer.

Heather had been going on and on about her chronically "ex"-boyfriend Brad for almost the last two hours. He was her boyfriend as of last Thursday, but their relationship was off again and on again at a moment's notice. Personally, Emily thought Brad was a dumb jock and a prejudiced bully, but you couldn't say a bad word about him when they were together; and you didn't dare say anything when they were on the outs because inevitably they got back together and then you found yourself having to make a full retraction! Emily hadn't really been listening on this particular occasion or her friend's prattle wouldn't have gone on so long. Her mind was still on Johnny.

She'd been sitting in Johnny's old tire swing one last time. The tire swing's motion had become a metaphor for Emily's life. Back and forth. Up and down. Going nowhere despite all her efforts.

And the house.

The back door to the kitchen was still adorned with familiar curtains and a sun catcher Johnny had made when he was much younger. As she swung, she stared at it, through it, past it to a time when it wasn't just a reminder of a stillborn future. Emily was always welcome at the Lazarus family table. She remembered sitting on the front porch swing on hot summer nights, talking eagerly about hopes and dreams that the treacherous house would eventually extinguish. Or snuggling deeply into a soft sofa, wrapped in blankets and the smell of hot cocoa after a deliriously frenzied snowball fight, basking in the prophetic glow of the fireplace.

She remembered the last time she was together with them. Johnny's mom waved her in when Emily's face appeared in the back door window. The sun catcher clattered against the window in protest as the door swung open.

"Johnny should be down any minute now," Mrs. Lazarus said as Emily shut the door behind her. "Pancakes?"

Emily nodded thankfully and slipped into her usual chair. As always, a plate was set out for her.

Mr. Lazarus was reading his Bible, pen in hand. She always thought it funny that he hated it when he found marks or notes in a book at a flea market, yard sale or such, but he was always jotting down things in the Book he prized above all others. He took a sip of his coffee. Sometimes, he got so wrapped up in the Scriptures that he didn't notice her until he needed a refill on his coffee. An empty coffee cup always brought him back to them, even if only long enough to remedy the situation.

Mrs. Lazarus rolled her eyes, smiling at her husband's absent-mindedness. "Arthur, aren't you going to say Hi?"

He blinked. "What, Kate? Oh, Hi Emily. How's your mother?"

Mr. Lazarus always asked after her family and always seemed interested in her response. "OK, I guess," she said. She didn't really like talking about her family since her parents had recently divorced. To be polite, she offered him something. "She's got an interview Monday."

"Oh? Where at?"

"It's for the new Titan building they're gonna build downtown. Receptionist."

"I know some folks at Titan. Want me to put in a good word for her?" he asked.

"That'd be great." She straightened her fork and knife as she changed the subject. "You looked like you were pretty into it today." She motioned toward the Bible. "Whatcha reading this time?"

"I'm actually teaching Sunday school tomorrow. We're studying the first chapter of the book of Romans."

"Oh yeah?" She wrinkled her nose. "Sounds stuffy."

"I used to think so. A lot of folks think the Bible's a stuffy, pre-scientific rulebook. Paul disagreed. He described the Word of God as quick and powerful, sharper than any two-edged sword, able to discern the thoughts and intents of the heart. He saw the Gospel much the same way, telling the Roman believers that he's not ashamed of the Gospel because it has the power to save everyone who believes. Of course, some folks think that faith is a cop-out, so you'll hear things like *religion is a crutch* or arguments that pit faith against reason or science, but Paul argued that there is so much evidence to believe in God that the world is without excuse."

"Then why doesn't everyone believe?" Emily asked. As much as she loved and respected Johnny's parents, they were still the first people she'd ever met who actually lived like they believed the Bible. Most of the people she knew claimed to be Christians and a lot of them even went to church on a regular basis, but many of those same people were the most judgmental gossips she'd ever heard of. She'd suffered a lot of heartbreak over the things people said concerning her mom's adultery and later divorce. She tried to be polite, but she was still skeptical about their beliefs, even if Mr. and Mrs. Lazarus held them sincerely.

"Good question," he said as Mrs. Lazarus stacked Emily's plate with pancakes. "In the passage I'm reading Paul says that people basically suppress the truth in unrighteousness. They're really just exchanging the truth for a lie, which is foolish, though, of course, they think they're very smart to do so." He took a brief sip of his coffee, a well-known sign that he was just getting warmed up. Emily had heard Mrs. Lazarus call him a coffee-powered windmill under her breath once. "Elsewhere in the Bible, Peter warned that in the last days, men would be scoffers, believing that 'all things continue as they were from the beginning of creation,' an idea very much like uniformitarianism, which you probably learned in school as 'the present is the key to the past.' Unfortunately, this idea had been wed to pure naturalism, so it fails to account for the actions of a supernatural God. Peter foretold that men would use this idea to justify their willful ignorance of the fact that God created the world by His Word and judged it with a worldwide Flood in the days of Noah by that same Word. Their ignorance of the true history of the universe leaves them without a foundational basis for making sense of the Gospel."

Johnny plodded down the stairs and landed in the seat next to his father's. "Sounds a bit heavy for breakfast, dad," he said. "Didn't we talk about this?"

Arthur winked. "Your proposed 'No Bible studies before breakfast' rule was vetoed in committee."

"So mom's in on this, too, then?" Johnny's smile never reached his eyes.

His mother loaded his plate with pancakes and kissed him on the head. "Together till the end."

Emily wished her parents were more like Mr. and Mrs. Lazarus, whatever their beliefs. Maybe then they'd still be together. But right now their happiness made her a little bit miserable. She exchanged a glance with Johnny. It was obvious that both of them were dying to get out of there. "You wanna head down to the comic shop today?" she asked.

Johnny shrugged.

"Something bothering you?" she mouthed across the table when she was sure his parents weren't looking.

He nodded almost imperceptibly. "Later."

Whatever it was, he'd never gotten around to telling her.

"Who's back?" Heather asked, forcing Emily back to the present.

Emily hesitated, instantly sorry that she'd let anything slip. "Never mind. You were saying?" She smiled airily, hoping Heather would blithely return to the vapid world of Brad, Brad, Brad. No such luck.

"No, no. Something's got you all bound up. And I totally knew something was eating you the second you came through the door. Spill it."

Emily hesitated at first, but she didn't want to hold it in. She had to talk about this with someone, anyone, before she exploded! "Johnny's back."

Heather looked more alarmed than skeptical, so Emily pushed on before she could interject. "I was at the house."

"Em, you know you shouldn't be going to that place. You have to let go."

Even after the funeral, Emily had held out hope that Johnny was still alive. After all, they'd never found his body. Everyone told her to move on, but she couldn't. She took to wearing Johnny's old jacket, retrieved from his locker at school, as a visible sign of her unwavering allegiance. She'd even grafftied an overpass with the words "Johnny Lives!" And almost every night, she found herself sitting on the front porch of the condemned house or swinging lazily from the tire swing, staring up at Johnny's bedroom window, trying to connect with him in some way.

Eventually the anger cooled into embers of depression. Emily exchanged her sun dress for dark clothing, her blond hair and pink nails for jet black hair and nail polish. As Goth as her mother would allow. Her friends started calling her Emo behind her back.

Grief had its way with her, but it wasn't who she was. So she began to reach out for the comforts of her old life, trying to find things that she loved that weren't associated with Johnny and the house. She continued her vigil, but soon it was a duty, then a guilt-driven chore. She began to feel chained to the Lazarus house. It was like she couldn't lay Johnny to rest while the house remained. Her visits became more infrequent. It was the steady, monotonous rhythm of the tire swing with its inescapable message of pointless movement that convinced her it was time to let go.

"That's what I was doing," Emily said. "I came to say good-bye, but instead it was like hello. I mean, I looked into the alley because I could hear a car coming and there he was. It was Johnny."

Heather still looked skeptical, but since she didn't interrupt, Emily took that as the benefit of the doubt. "Anyway I ran out to the alley to make sure and

Johnson nearly ran me over."

She still remembered the squeal of the squad car's brakes and the sudden crunch of gravel at her heels as it stopped, barely in time. With heat of the car's engine on her calves, she spun in startled terror. She recognized Deputy Johnson instantly. Her expression was torn between bewilderment and accusation. Johnson's eyes were hidden behind sunglasses, but she could read his expression all-too-well. He looked like he wasn't altogether sure he'd made the right decision by stopping.

Heather gasped. "He could've killed you, Em."

"I'm kind of surprised he stopped at all," Emily said.

"Did he at least apologize?"

"No, he just yelled for me to get out of the way."

"What did you do?"

"Well, I got out of the way."

Heather shook her head. "I do not know what your mom sees in that man or why she ever left your father for his sorry rear end."

"Forget Jerry Johnson. Didn't you hear me? Johnny's back. He's not dead. He's back!"

Heather looked at the floor, clearly searching for the right words. Squaring her shoulders, she looked her friend in the eye and said, "Emily, I know you loved him, but this is not healthy. It's time to let go."

Emily started to get off the couch.

"Emily. No, listen to me, Em. I love you. I'm your friend and I care about you, but it's time to admit it: Johnny's dead and he's never coming back."

"Heather, shut up. Stop talking. I know what I saw."

"Em–"

"No. You know what? Never mind. Forget I told you anything. In fact, forget I ever told you anything about anything!" She rose to leave.

"Emily, wait. Where are you going?"

Emily hesitated.

"You think he'll come back tonight, don't you?"

Emily's internal alarms went off. Heather wasn't exactly a model of discretion. "Listen, you can't tell anyone."

"I'm going with you," Heather said.

"What?"

"You're planning on meeting him tonight. I'm going with you. It'll be like a stakeout, right?"

"You don't need to do that."

"Why not? You did see him, right?"

"Yes." Emily was confident that Johnny had recognized her as well.

"And you're sure he's coming back tonight?"

"Y-yes."

"Then it's a date," Heather said. "Just promise me one thing."

"What's that?"

"Just promise me if he doesn't show, that you'll finally put Johnny behind you."

Emily started to scold her, but as she looked into her eyes she saw genuine concern. "OK, I promise, but you can't tell anyone else."

"Not a soul." Heather crossed her heart. "What time you wanna do this?"

Emily tried to put herself in Johnny's shoes. He'd want to avoid being seen. He'd want to choose a time when there was plenty of distraction. "Tonight's Trick or Treat. He'll blend in with the crowds."

"Won't he be a little old for a Trick-or-Treater?" Heather asked.

"I'm not saying he'll be in costume," Emily said, "but you know that Brad and his drunk jock friends will be dressed up. Probably stealing little kids' candy and scaring everybody, like usual."

"Boys will be boys," Heather sang. "OK. Then it's agreed. We'll meet at 6 o'clock and head over to Johnny's old house."

4 – Comic Book Conversations

Weasel leaned hard against the passenger door, one hand on the door handle, just in case he needed to make a hasty exit. He still wasn't completely sure why he'd agreed to get in the car. Curiosity had overwhelmed him, he supposed. Fat lot of good it did this stray cat now.

He couldn't believe Johnny had managed to keep this big of a secret from him for the past few years, but some things were starting to make more sense now.

They'd met working together for a lawn service. As luck would have it, they started the same day. Worked their butts off, in fact! The sun was hotter than an oven and he lost count of how many yards they did each day. They worked every day unless it rained. It didn't rain for the first three weeks. Lenny was the type who paid you under the table, still but made you work three weeks before he paid you for the first week. He liked to brag that even though he paid less than minimum wage, his workers technically got more take-home pay than those stiffs who got gouged with government taxes on every paycheck. Weasel wasn't sure if any of that was true. He knew it sounded good when he signed up, but anything sounded better than living in his Mom's trailer.

Payday came around, but Lenny said everyone would have to wait until they did a few more jobs. He didn't have the money. The other guys weren't getting paid either, though Weasel was pretty sure that the biggest fellow, a man with a big mouth, a bigger temper and enough missing teeth to advertise a certain disposition toward brawling, got paid something. Probably got paid in beer. Some of the guys quit. They never did get paid. Others needed the money too badly, so they stuck it out for another week. Weasel was mad at Lenny for stiffing him, but too busy and too tired to find other employment.

At month's end, Lenny still wouldn't pay them. There were rumors that he was drinking it all, that he had a gambling problem or that he was just planning on skipping town. As much as he wanted the money he'd worked so hard for, Weasel Hopkins was flat broke. He needed a job that actually paid. There was a fair bit of grumbling over what to do. Some suggested a strike, but no one took that seriously. Everyone knew Lenny would just pack up his lawn mowers in the middle of the night and hire a brand new crew. He might've been planning something like that anyway.

Then Johnny spoke the first words Weasel would ever heard him utter. He was so quiet that some had started to assume he was a mute. So it got everyone's attention when he said those two little words.

"That's it."

Johnny walked into the large shed that housed Lenny's lawn mowers and shut the door behind him. Now that he thought back on it, the big door shut, but he wasn't entirely sure it didn't shut by itself. All he knew was that overgrown, gap-toothed monster they worked with tried to go in after him, but couldn't budge the door. A few minutes later, Lenny emerged with handfuls of cash for everyone. Weasel remembered now how he kept looking at Johnny out of the corner of his eye, how he licked his lips and laughed nervously like he was trying to please the Devil himself. At the time, Weasel and everybody else just assumed that, whatever happened in that shed, Lenny got what was coming to him. But he hadn't laid a hand on him that anyone could tell.

Johnny, Weasel and, to hear tell of it, most of the rest quit that very night. Lenny didn't argue. He paid what he owed them. He seemed glad to be rid of them. They probably could have asked him for extra! Particularly Johnny.

Weasel asked Johnny once what he'd done to change Lenny's mind. He shrugged and said, "I gave him a suggestion." At the time, it'd seemed pretty funny. It seemed pretty ominous at the moment.

"So what are you exactly?" Weasel asked.

"Someone looking for answers," Johnny said.

"No, I mean, what are you? I ain't never seen nobody ever do anything like that before."

"Ever been to a magic show? They tell you they can pull a rabbit out of the hat or make someone disappear, but it's all sleight of hand. It's all just a trick of the mind. Smoke and mirrors. Misdirection and deception. I remember reading about Uri Geller, the mentalist, how he could bend spoons and keys, stop clocks and read hidden messages, that kind of stuff, all supposedly with his mind. I asked my dad about it. He said Geller was a fraud. Said he'd been on the *Tonight Show* back when Johnny Carson hosted it and completely choked. Said he begged off that he didn't feel strong enough that night. He claimed to be a psychic too, but he wasn't psychic enough to realize he'd lose lawsuits against the people who said he was a fraud."

"What are you trying to say? It was a trick?"

"What do you think?"

"I saw you skip the rock across the river. The rock splashed when it hit the water, made ripples, the whole bit."

"That's impossible," Johnny said. "The rock was all wrong. Too heavy, too bulky, not even the right shape. Even if it had been the right kind of rock, who could skip it across the river?"

"I dunno. An Olympic discus thrower –"

"The world record for a discus throw is 243 feet, Weez. That river's at least 3 times that across. Do I look like an Olympic discus thrower?"

"Fine, there's no natural explanation, so how do you fake something like that?"

"I didn't say I faked it. I didn't fake it."

"What then? It was all in my head? You hypnotized me somehow?"

"I didn't hypnotize you."

"So you say."

Johnny took a different tack. "Where's that comic book I gave you? *Mann from Midwich?*"

Weasel reached a hand down to the floorboard and picked up the comic. The cover had a nice big footprint on it and was nearly torn off from being kicked around. "Sorry," Weasel said. "Here's your comic. I read it. You're saying that Hugh Mann, the guy who stumbled out of the woods with superpowers, that's you? You're the hero of the plot?"

"Of course not. Hugh destroyed most of Midwich in that comic. This Midwich is still standing. And, hello, he died at the end of that comic. Weez, do I look dead to you?"

"I get it. So what then?"

"So where do comic book heroes get their powers?" Johnny asked.

"Well, there's obviously radiation, chemicals, genetic mutation…" He threw up his hands. "…and why are we playing this game? You tell me."

"Fine. When it comes down to it, there are only a handful of comic book causes for super powers: radiation, chemicals, genetic manipulation, untapped human potential, alien physiology, alien artifacts, alien symbiosis, advanced technology, magic, evolution… That's pretty much it in a nutshell. So ask yourself, where did I get my powers?"

Weasel blurted out the question that'd been plaguing him since Johnny showed him his powers. "Are you an alien?"

"Do I look like an alien?"

"I don't know. What does an alien look like?" Weasel asked. "What if they look just like us? A lot of comic book heroes come from alien worlds where everyone looks like your average Earthling. How would we tell them apart from anyone else, aside from the powers I mean? You could even be an alien hybrid!"

"Try not to drool on yourself, Weez," Johnny said. His friend was obviously hopeful about the possibility that the alien angle could be true. "My blood test came back normal."

"Fine, so you're probably not an alien or a hybrid." He was reluctant to completely give up on the idea. "I'm guessing you don't ride around on a broomstick in your spare time."

"No, but notice where Hugh gets his powers in that comic: from a chip in his head. From a company called Titan. In a town called, hello, Midwich. And do you know what company overlooks this pretty little town, Weasel?"

"I'm guessing it's gonna be Titan."

"Exactly. Whoever wrote that comic knows what's going on around here. My guess is that they wrote it to get the word out to other people like me and Hugh Mann to point us in the right direction."

"Johnny, somebody probably wrote that comic to lure people like you down here so they could nab them and use them as lab rats or super soldiers or whatever."

"Maybe."

"How long have you known about these powers? I mean, were you like a super baby?"

"I was completely normal until a few years ago. I was too freaked out to tell anyone," Johnny said. "When I got my head straight, I realized that somewhere out there might just be someone who had developed, if not exactly like me, maybe in a similar way. I mean, we hear about people who can read minds, bend spoons and heal people with just a word or a thought. I just knew there had to be a shred of truth to it. There are other people out there like me: people who can do extraordinary things. People who'd like to remain anonymous, because, frankly they know there are people out there who'd just dissect them or force them into positions they don't want to be in. Think about it. What would the Mob do with a real, live psychic? What would the military do with someone who could move things with his mind? So the real McCoys hide. Some of them are mixed in with the magic acts and snake-oil peddlers. People just assume they're fake like the others."

"Did you ever find anybody else?"

"Do you remember that faith healer we met?"

"Brother Joel? Yeah, that dude was about as real as professional wrestling."

Johnny shook his head.

"You're kidding me?"

Unbidden, the face of the Reverend JC Darling came to mind. Fans of the self-styled faith healer called him Brother Joel. Johnny had signed them up as local labor to help put up Brother Joel's big tent. It was hard work, but it was a unique experience. In some ways, it was almost magical. Until they had to flood the tent with more folding chairs than he'd ever seen in his entire life!

The first night's performance lived up to his crass expectations. It was a spectacle packed with flash, glitter and surprises. It was clear that more than half the audience was made up of bona fide fans and true-believers. The rest were skeptics, curiosity seekers and reporters desperate for a story. They could smell blood, but they could never spot it. The event was an odd mixture of rock and roll and gospel music. The performances were polished. The music was rollicking. The jokes were perfectly timed. The offerings were plenty and often.

When the audience was pumped and primed, the man of the hour came forth, delivering a carefully choreographed string of anecdotes and product advertisements, followed by a 20-minute Power Point presentation, and then the main event itself: the healing service.

There was a jarring metallic noise of displaced folding chairs as everyone got to their feet to get a better view. JC Darling called forth person after person, naming their ailments with supernatural accuracy and promising them instantaneous healing if only their faith was strong enough. The healings themselves were done with all the showmanship of any good stage show. People fell to the floor, supposedly struck down by the power of God at the end of his bold, shouted prayers. Such was his alleged power that he had to be careful where he pointed lest he strike people senseless in their seats by what Weasel had come to think of as Brother Joel's "fickle finger of fate." As the show continued, Brother Joel displayed his power over everything from broken hearts and homes to broken bones. A man walked away carrying his crutches. A woman left with her white cane resting casually upon her shoulder, smiling at everyone she met. Weasel left wholly convinced that the man and his show were equally fake.

"Sorry, I just can't buy that," he said. "What I don't get is what any of this has to do with breaking into your old house? Why not just go straight to Titan and find out if they put a chip in your head?"

Johnny pulled into a parking space at the local SuperBig Mart in one of Midwich's more redneck areas. "I'll tell you after we do a little shopping."

5 – Checking Out

Weasel Hopkins tried not to look toward the front doors of the department store. He really resented being sent in alone like some little errand boy, but he could see Johnny's point. Somebody might recognize him in such a public place and, since John Lazarus was supposed to be dead, well, it would be awkward.

Some part of him wondered why Johnny hadn't simply picked up these items before they hit town. He also found it hard to believe that his pal had some sort of super voodoo mind powers, but couldn't use them to do his own shopping. He had seen Johnny skip that rock, right?

He was careful not to make eye contact with anyone, just like he was told. He got everything on the list, paid cash and walked out of the store. He looked across the parking lot and nearly dropped his bags. The Plymouth was gone!

Uncertain what to do, he just started walking, searching the parking lot, hoping Johnny had just moved the K-car. But it was nowhere in sight. Had the cops nabbed him? Had he just sent Weasel in alone to ditch him? He'd only been in the store for about 15 to 20 minutes at most, but that was plenty of time for Johnny to put some distance between them if he wanted to. But why do that after practically begging him to come along? It didn't make sense.

He reached the end of the parking lot. He glanced back, hoping against hope that the car would materialize. No Johnny. Where was he?

Despite his initial panic, he was pretty sure Johnny wouldn't ditch him without a good reason. Weasel spotted an approaching police car. He'd forgotten that the cops had already eyeballed the Plymouth once. Its mismatched fender made it hard to miss.

He kept his eyes on his feet, watching the squad car out of the corner of his eye as it passed. He thought the cop looked at him, but he wasn't sure. Experience had taught him that a lot of cops, particularly the good ol' boys, liked to harass metal heads simply for bothering to exist. It didn't matter if you were just passing through, minding your own business. It didn't matter if you weren't actually causing trouble and had no intentions of finding any. They took his very presence in their redneck fishbowl as a personal insult and practically tripped over themselves to be the one who got to drawl, "You lost, hippie?" or "You ain't from around here, are ya?" Hadn't they ever seen that first Rambo movie?

He followed the cruiser with his eyes. It looked as if he might have escaped notice, when suddenly the car made a U-turn, flashed its lights and headed back his way. Panicking, he bolted, heading down an alleyway between two storefronts facing the main road. He ran as fast as he could until he reached a dumpster near its end. Chest heaving, he ducked behind it and peered around the side to see if there was any sign of pursuit.

He needn't have worried. The cruiser was on other business.

While relieved that he wasn't being pursued and a little chagrined at having panicked, he was still reluctant to head back out of the alley the way he'd came. Just in case. The alley was a *cul de sac*, but there was a narrow pedestrian pass between two buildings in the direction of the SuperBig Mart.

Unfortunately, the narrow ended in a chained gate. Frustrated, he kicked the gate, listened to its rattle, and headed back toward the alley. He'd nearly reached it when he heard voices.

6 – Hostage Situations

Johnny peeled around the turn as fast and hard as the Plymouth and the laws of physics would allow, hoping to convince his passenger that he truly was doing everything in his power to lose their pursuers. Truth be told, he was seriously considering just letting the nice policemen catch them. He could always bust out of jail later and still make his rendezvous at the old house on Archer Lane. Maybe.

Everything had been going according to plan until about 15 minutes ago.

He'd been waiting in the SuperBig Mart parking lot for Weasel to return with his shopping list. He'd chosen a spot that afforded a good vantage of both the main road and the front doors of the department store.

Well, it did, until some half-drunk redneck in baggy blue overalls, a red ball cap with a frayed bill and an ill-fitting, grease-stained wife beater pulled up in the ugliest pickup Johnny had ever laid eyes on. The ancient oil burner might have been fire engine red at one time, but generous patches of rust and pink body putty had rendered it a mottled mess. Perversely, this metal beast belched out rowdy country music at a volume that rattled its windows and blasted fresh chunks of rust off its rocker panels. Johnny had always wondered why anyone would abuse a perfectly good radio with country music in the first place. It just didn't seem civilized.

To add insult to injury, the good ol' boy at the wheel fancied himself quite the vocalist. He sang with a gusto and enthusiasm that was conversely matched with his mastery of tone and pitch. As the song ended, he tossed back the last foam of his lukewarm beer, sloshed out of the truck and staggered off in the general direction of the store.

Johnny hunched down when he finally got a good look at the karaoke king of Midwich. This guy lived somewhere on Archer Lane, too. Was he Wacky Jackie's dad? Johnny watched until the big lout disappeared into the SuperBig Mart.

Suddenly the passenger door jerked open and a gun entered the cab, wielded by a wiry young man in a rubber mask.

"Hands where I can see them," the carjacker said. "And don't try anything funny."

Johnny's first instinct was to fling this misguided criminal right back out the door like he'd skipped that rock across the river, but at the very moment he considered that action, he saw his own death, immediate and brutal. He scowled much the same way he used to when he'd find himself at a dead end in one of those choose-your-own-fate books he loved reading as a kid. There was nothing to do but choose the other path and hope it played out better.

So instead of using his powers, Johnny did as he was told. The carjacker's voice was distorted somehow, but it definitely belonged to a man. The stranger ducked into the car, keeping the weapon trained on the driver. He was wearing a rubber mask that bore a vague resemblance to Hillary Clinton.

Johnny tried to remain calm, to keep control of the situation. He couldn't believe he was being car-jacked! He concentrated on finding the criminal's eyes, hoping this simple connection might establish him as a fellow human being and not just as a mark. The folds and shadows of the mask's eye slits thwarted his attempts. Too bad. If he could've made eye contact and held it, he might've been able to–

"Oh, no you don't! Eyes straight ahead. Do it now!"

"Look, my wallet's in my back right pocket," Johnny said. "You can have it. The debit card's maxed out, but I have about $60 cash."

"We don't want your money, John Lazarus. We want you."

Despite the gunman's warning, Johnny's head snapped around to face his abductor. "Who are you? How do you know my name?"

The gun went off.

Johnny saw the flash, saw the bullet racing toward him. Impossibly, it stopped in mid-air, hovering about three inches from his face, still spinning on its way toward him, right between his eyes. But Johnny hadn't stopped it. His eyes found his tormentor's. Green eyes leered at him mockingly from behind Hillary Clinton's face.

The bullet dropped, bouncing off the seat cushion between them.

"You're like me," Johnny said.

"In your wildest dreams. Now turn around and drive nice like a good little *boy*, Johnny, or I promise you I won't stop the next one until just after it stops your heart."

Johnny bristled at the racist way his abductor said the word "boy." Still, it wouldn't do to antagonize the masked man until he had a better idea what was going on.

"Sure. Whatever you say," Johnny said. He stole a glance at the store entrance without making it too obvious. There was no sign of his friend. Hoping he'd be able to reunite with Weasel later somehow, he started the car and pulled out of the parking lot.

"What are you going to do to me?"

"Just drive," Hillary said. "Make a right onto the main drive. I'll tell you where to go from there."

He did as he was told, wondering how he was going to get out of this mess.

"You said, we. *We want you*. Who are working for? Titan?"

"No more questions."

"At least, tell me how you found me so fast." As he distracted his abductor with questions, he mentally pushed the car's cigarette lighter.

"I said – No!" A police car had pulled onto the road ahead and was driving toward them. "No. No, no, no. Drive casually." He pressed the gun into Johnny's side. "Keep your eyes on the road. Do not attempt to make eye contact. And don't even think about trying anything *Twilight Zone*. Got it?"

Johnny glanced at his tormentor, who'd jabbed the gun into his side at the end of each sentence to emphasize his point. He swallowed his rage and nodded tightly. "I got it." He stole a peek at the cigarette lighter. It wasn't ready yet.

The squad car approached. Johnny glanced at the driver, despite himself.

"Eyes front." Hillary's warning was punctuated with a fresh dig of the pistol.

The police car passed them without incident. Hillary watched the cop's progress in the passenger side mirror, keeping the gun planted in his hostage's side. The lighter finally popped up, but Johnny couldn't use it with the gun trained on him.

"Well done. Turn here. We're getting off the main road."

At that moment, the cop car made a sharp U-turn, flipped on its siren and roared down the road after them.

"What did you do?" Hillary roared. He nudged the gun deeper into Johnny's side this time. Johnny gasped and struggled to keep the car under control through the pain. His assailant seemed singularly unconcerned about the extreme danger he was putting them in.

"Nothing. I swear," Johnny said. "The police saw us earlier, but we lost them. Must be looking for the car." Truth be told, Johnny had recognized the cop and he was pretty sure everyone still knew what the late Sheriff Lazarus' only son looked like. Of course, telling Hillary that would probably be disastrous, so he didn't mention it.

Hillary looked unconvinced. Johnny saw it in his eyes. This psycho wanted a reason to just shoot him and be done with it. What was holding him back?

"Besides," Johnny said, "you are wearing a mask."

"On Halloween!"

"Tell that to them."

"You've got to be kidding me. Floor it! Lose this pork chop. Head for the river."

Of course, rather than losing their police tail, they'd actually gained a pursuer since that moment. Johnny was as desperate not to be caught as his passenger; unfortunately, Hillary was insisting on calling the shots and he'd made a series of very bad decisions, thus far.

Johnny mentally pushed in the car's lighter again, hoping for another opportunity.

"They're gonna box us in," Johnny said. "The bridge." A third police vehicle was racing across the bridge to intercept them.

"I can see that! Just step on it!"

"We're not going to make it!" Johnny stomped down on the accelerator anyway.

As the Plymouth roared down the road, the temperature gauge caught his eye. Something was seriously wrong, like the heat gauge was trying to race the speedometer. He suppressed a grin, knowing Hillary wasn't going to like the next surprise at all. Something under the hood popped and steam blasted out from under the seams until neither Johnny nor the masked gunman could see anything.

"What did you do?" came the roared, if predictable accusation.

"It's an old car, moron!" The lighter popped up and he sent it flying into his opponent's face. His would-be kidnapper screamed, ripping at the mask. Johnny smelled burning latex and acrid radiator fluid as he swerved over into the high grass beside the road.

He slammed the brakes hard. With no seat belt to hold him back, Hillary flew through the front windshield like a cannonball. Johnny thought to use his powers as a makeshift airbag, but the steering wheel rushed at him much faster than he'd expected, delivered a haymaker that nearly broke his nose and had him seeing stars. He correctly guessed later that Hillary had been trying to pull him out of the vehicle with him kinetically.

In the movies, the hero's car always blows up after such a wreck. Dimly recalling this factoid, Johnny shouldered the door open and staggered out of the car. He blinked hard, shaking his head against the pain and increasing dizziness. Something warm trickled down his scalp. He only made it a few steps before vertigo dropped him to his knees.

"Hands above your head!" an officer barked. "Don't move!"

Johnny raised his hands weakly, looking about for some sign of Hillary. It appeared to be just him and the cops at present.

He needed medical attention. Everything was swimming. He felt curiously weightless. Then earth met sky, as he slammed into the ground, though he had the curious sensation that the ground slammed into him instead. He felt the itchy tickle of grass blades on his cheek, but he could feel nothing else. Weasel was going to be really mad, he realized. Then he felt nothing at all.

7 – Making New Friends

Even by daylight, there was something about this particular alley that reminded Weasel of one of those survival horror video games. Just add nightfall. Under the occasional glare of insufficient light, these alleys could hide just about anything. The corridors were always this improbable length. At the outset, they seemed too long, yawning on with dread possibility. You knew that as you kept walking, maybe even right as you were just about to peer around the corner, something would suddenly leap out at you. Perversely, the alleys were also too short to see trouble until it was right up on you, giving you little hope of making a run for it. If you did make it to the end of the alley without incident or cardiac arrest, your sigh of relief was bludgeoned to death by the merciless sight of yet another alley of improbable length. And you knew if you'd escaped incident in the last one, something was definitely gonna getcha in this one! The whole effect was edge-of-your-seat claustrophobia and horror-fueled dread designed to rob you of restful sleep for weeks to come. The only reason you continued on was that there were no other exits and you knew there'd be no sleeping until you beat this stupid game anyway!

He was being paranoid, of course. This wasn't a video game. And it was still daylight, thank heavens.

Though no zombies roamed these alleys, there was still something terrifying about being lost in a strange town. He didn't know anyone here besides Johnny, though it was plain to see that they weren't his kind of people. Johnny's old neighborhood was kind of money, but the problem now was that he was a lone heavy metal intruder in a back alley on the redneck side of town. Weasel knew from experience that good ol' boys rarely left him alone. And some of them had chosen this particular alley to stroll down.

Hugging the dirty brick wall of the narrow, he peered sidelong into the alley and listened intently. There were three of them, from the sound of it, all young rednecks judging from their accents. He couldn't make out everything they were saying, at first, but he definitely recognized the unmistakable sing-song tones of "Come out, come out, wherever you are."

There was literally nowhere to run and no place to hide. He didn't want to fight these guys. He wasn't a total wuss, but he wasn't a kung fu master either. Three guys was about two too many.

"C'mon, we just wanna talk to you," one of the thugs said. Cold sweat beaded Weasel's face. The voice came from much closer than he expected. He cast about for a potential weapon, but it was a lost cause. The only thing even remotely suitable was an empty bottle of liquor, which he picked up just in case. It was pretty much the most disgusting thing he'd ever touched. Maybe he should just make a run for it and try to climb over the gate.

"Yeah," another said. "You're being ridiculous. Where are you going?"

"He's right." The third redneck sounded a bit more confident than the others. This one had to be the leader. The others were along for the ride. "There's nowhere to go. You know that. You can't hide from us."

There was an ominous pause. Weasel knew he was busted. Glancing back longingly at the chained gate, he nonetheless recognized the truth of what they said. They had him and continuing this farce of hiding would only make him look like a world-class coward. He took a deep breath, mustered his resolve and started to step into the alley, the very picture of nonchalance, a fellow who just happened to be passing through their alley. *Never mind me and the locked gate behind me, boys. If you'll just pardon me, I'll let you get back to your business.*

"Gotcha!" One of the thugs burst into view. Weasel jumped despite himself.

There would've been no way to save face, except that the redneck punk wasn't even looking at him. They'd converged on the dumpster, clearly thinking their prey was hiding on the other side. The thug looked back to the leader with a disappointed shrug.

"Inside," thug number two mouthed, pointing with exaggeration at the dumpster. With a wicked grin, both thugs got on either side of the dumpster lid, while one of the biggest dudes Weasel had ever laid eyes on came to stand triumphantly before it. Even given the leader's size, the image of these hicks surrounding a filthy dumpster with obvious enthusiasm was just more than Weasel could stand.

He suppressed a laugh, though not well.

"I'm over here, guys," Weasel said.

"What?!" Their leader rounded on him, startled. His face was a picture of confused annoyance. He was a redneck's redneck. His bulldog head seemed to sit directly upon shoulders that belonged to a linebacker. His chest was barely contained in a seriously over-sized football jersey, while the rest of him was stuffed like a fat sausage into a pair of dirty jean overalls. He worked his massive jaws in annoyance and scowled at Weasel with hooded beady eyes.

Weasel grinned, though he was now pretty sure that Beef, or whatever his redneck friends called a fellow like this, possessed not the merest wisp of a genuine sense of humor or goodwill. "Seriously, dudes, don't waste your time. I would never hide in a dumpster."

"Who are you?" Beef asked. It was more of a demand.

For the first time, Weasel realized that they were never looking for him. They were after someone else.

"You lost or something?" one of the toadies chimed in cruelly.

"No, not lost. Just…" He glanced down at the bottle in his hands. "Just looking for a quiet place for a drink." They stared at the bottle dumbly. Weasel realized that these rednecks were actually too bright for this trick to work. "And, well, it looks I need to keep looking, don't it?"

There was no human kindness in Beef's expression.

"Right. OK. I can see you guys are busy, so I'll just be on my way." He took a step forward.

Beef took a step to block him. "That bottle's empty."

"I, I, yes, I know. It is empty." He nodded gravely, mentally calculating the thick-headed line backer's probable top speed against his own certain lack of physical fitness. "But I thank you for pointing that out. Very courteous. I need a new one." He was careful not to make eye contact or any sudden moves. "At the store."

"What's in the bags?"

Weasel had forgotten about the SuperBig Mart bags. He blinked at them in genuine surprise. "Um, just some stuff I got… at the store." He muttered the last three words under his breath.

Beef stepped toward him and snatched the bottle and the bags from his hands. He tossed the bags to one of his toadies for inspection, then glanced down at the empty bottle and sniffed it. "You found this bottle back there."

"Found it? What? No, please. I would never drink something I just found on the ground. That would be disgusting… and just… unsanitary." Beef wasn't buying it. And why should he? These were the worst lies ever uttered in the history of bad, obvious crap lies. Beef was going to pound him and his thugs were going to stomp on whatever was left of him afterward. "So if you'll just do me a favor and toss that one in the dumpster and give me back the rest of my stuff, I'll just —"

One of Beef's toadies found something he liked in the SuperBig Mart bag. "Hey! Night vision goggles. Awesome!"

"Hey, be careful. Those aren't mine."

The other toady snatched one of the bags from his friend. "Cool! What else's he got in there?"

"Just put the stuff back in the bags," Weasel said. "That's enough!"

Beef took another step. Now he was definitely violating his personal space. He sniffed at Weasel's face.

Weasel blinked. "OK, that was–"

"You're not drunk."

Weasel smiled weakly. "I'd like to be." This was going nowhere fast. Weasel squared his jaw. It was obvious that these goons had been looking forward to a bit of mean-spirited Halloween hijinks and they weren't about to let it slip away when Weasel would serve as an opportune substitute for their intended victim. So he was going down. The big one was easily more than he could handle. But he wasn't going down without a fight. His fear melted as a mocking mask of metal head bravado slipped over his features. "Look, I don't want any trouble, but neither do you. So are you going to get out of my way or not?"

Beef was faster than he looked. And apparently he wasn't into any sort of pre-fight trash talk. He waded into Weasel like a tsunami, carrying him effortlessly down the length of the narrow. Weasel was actually relieved when his back slammed into the metal mesh of the fence. They bounced off it slightly, but Beef planted himself against the recoil and commenced pounding his victim with meaty ham fists. Each cruel blow landed methodically in a perfect sledgehammer rhythm. Beef was a machine; Weasel had to give him that. He tried several times to hit his opponent back, but the blows landed with such cruel surety that he was soon forced to just put his arms over his head and hope the brute didn't give him brain damage.

He was just about to pass out when something went thunk! And Beef stopped hitting him. Turning slowly and angrily around, the thug nonetheless held onto one fist-full of Weasel's shirt, no doubt hoping to continue his work. Thunk!

Though one eye was now swelled shut, Weasel distinctly saw the big redneck's head bob down from the blow. Shaking his thick skull angrily, Beef let go of Weasel and turned to face his newest opponent. Bonk! This blow, to the front of Beef's skull, knocked him backward a bit. Weasel curled into a protective ball, fearing the behemoth would accidentally step or fall on him. The living tank recovered quickly and went charging down the narrow with a bull roar after his next victim.

Weasel blinked through blood and bruises, staring after his tormentor until he'd turned the corner, heading out of the alley toward the main road. Breathing heavily, gasping against pains that advertised themselves at the slightest movement, he managed to get into a sitting position. He listened for any sign of his enemies or his anonymous savior, but all he could hear were his own coughing gasps for air and the rush of his madly beating heart. Still, nothing seemed broken, except possibly his nose.

He wiped his bloody nose on his jacket sleeve and fished in his pocket for his cigarettes. The pack was smashed, but by some small miracle one of his cigarettes was whole and intact. He lit it up and sat there enveloped in smoke, chuckling with dark humor.

Several minutes passed by as he finished his cigarette. Not quite ready to get up yet, he fished around for another survivor, but the rest were smashed and torn near the butt. Johnny would tell him it was a sign from heaven that he should just give these things up. Johnny was probably right, but they did call it addiction for a reason.

Realizing he'd have to get moving, if for no other reason than he needed more smokes, he wobbled to his feet. It was probably best if he got out of here before Beef or his boys came back. That and he didn't want to see what else might haunt this alley after dark. He leaned against the gate for support for a moment, taking note of the deepening shadows. Spitting blood from a split lip onto the filthy pavement, he staggered down the length of the narrow.

It was just like one of those survival horror video games, he noted, except now he looked like the zombie, not the hero.

8 – Winners and Wusses

Brad Farley flexed his massive chest muscles and gratuitously kissed his own coconut-sized biceps in turn. It was good to be him. Some might say he was just a bully, that he only picked on people smaller than himself. He said to those wusses, What choice did he have? Everybody was smaller than he was.

It wasn't always this way. When he was a kid, he was pretty average-sized. He went out for sports, like his old man wanted, but he wasn't that good. Nevertheless, his coaches recognized that Brad was a scrapper, a fighter, somebody who'd take a hit for the team. He was all about the team. Well, that was only partly true. He was all about the winning team.

Life was full of winners and wusses. Brad was a winner. They could talk about him all they wanted, but they couldn't beat him and that was all that mattered.

Last year, things changed. For the better. He'd finally bulked up like he'd always dreamed of; better than he'd dreamed actually. He was strong as an ox and as wide as two linebackers. Coach Trager finally saw him for more than just a team player. Things were going really great. He was winning football games and winning friends and admirers just as fast. Every game, they chanted his name. He was their golden warrior. Freight Train Farley. The one-man offense. Eventually, he realized it was more like he'd become a one-man team.

The other teams were jealous. They accused him of unnecessary roughness, of using drugs, steroids mostly. But he was a winner and they were just whiners. They were jealous of his power.

Then Trager turned on him. He should've seen it coming. Coach was always telling him to tone it down, to rein it back, preaching about how everybody was an important part of the team. Then, he hurt that Freeman kid, the Crusaders' star running back, the one who nearly cost the Midwich High Titans a win with his fancy moves and crazy speed. He couldn't stand the little jumping bean stealing his thunder. Nobody could touch the little jackrabbit with the annoying grin. They were going to lose if Freeman kept running circles around them. It was up to Brad. He had to take a hit for the team.

Coach benched him. That wasn't the call, wasn't the play. He'd gone maverick, zeroing in on the little punk. Chased him down and plowed him into the earth. Well after the play at that. But they won the game.

With Freight Train on suspension, the Titans lost the next two games. People started criticizing Trager for punishing a player for playing a game where people got hurt. Some parents lobbied to get him back in the game. Other parents wanted him benched permanently. When the Freeman kid got hurt, rumors of locker room rages and bullying surfaced. 'Roid rage. Everybody wanted him tested for drugs. His daddy made a point of reminding everybody that both Coach Trager and that Freeman kid were black; he was convinced it was racially motivated.

In the end, they blamed it on his grades, but everybody knew the real reason. He was off the team. He knew better than to try out this year.

He found other things to occupy his time, like getting wasted, going mudding and hanging with his old teammates. Most of them thought it was just stupid how they'd dumped him. People got hurt playing ball all the time. Wasn't that why everyone wore pads and helmets? They were just picking on him because he was big, because if he really wanted to he could just crush someone, and they knew it. They were afraid of him.

Well, not everyone. Kaukasos College was willing to offer him a sports scholarship, despite his dubious reputation and the Freeman incident in particular. They saw his potential and, like the recruiter said, they wanted to help him fulfill it. They just asked that he keep his nose clean until graduation.

But it was Halloween night and he deserved the day off for being so good lately.

Right now, he was heading back to his place on Archer Lane with his two best buds, Dwayne and Tater. The day had started off kind of aimless until their favorite black cat crossed their path. Jackie was an uppity Goth girl with a razor tongue. She liked to smart him off in the high school hallways. Tater called her the Defender of Nerds and the Geek Avenger. Most people just called her Wacky Jackie. She thought she was too good for good ol' boys.

She lost them back in that alley where they'd beat up that stupid headbanger. *Banged his head alright.* They'd nabbed some cool night vision goggles off the guy, but the rest of his bags were just junk. They'd chucked everything but the goggles and two plastic serial killer hockey masks. Of course, it wasn't nighttime yet, so they couldn't really use the glasses, but it gave them something to look forward to.

Besides, just like Dwayne pointed out, Trick or Treat hadn't even started yet and they'd already scored some loot.

Brad's cellphone rang. He snickered as he recognized the ring tone and answered. "Heather." He winked at Tater, who stifled a tell-tale guffaw. "What's up?" Heather was Brad's back-burner babe. He kept her simmering, but he wasn't exactly a one-woman man. There was just too much love to go around.

She said nothing was up, which he knew was a lie. She was just being polite. He rolled his eyes. She never said what she meant and she always caved to whatever he wanted. She asked him what he was doing.

"Nothing yet. Whatcha doing tonight? Going to Kelly's kegger?"

Heather said that she wanted to, but her killjoy friend Emily wanted to stake out the old Lazarus place. That genuinely intrigued him. Not Emo Emily. He used to think she was hot until she went all freak-girl over Johnny. Personally, Brad had never cared for Johnny, but neither had anyone else. Brad didn't consider himself prejudiced or anything, but the guy didn't know his place. It wasn't just that he was uppity; no, Johnny clearly thought he was better than everybody else or something. Everybody tolerated him because of Emily. Emily the cheerleader, the honor student, the class president, the most likely to succeed. Now Emily the suicidal head case. Well, not everybody. Brad's daddy didn't make a secret of the fact that he didn't exactly approve of Emily dating a "darkie." Dad said it wasn't natural, that even the Bible said them people had dark skin because of the 'curse of Ham' (whatever that was), and that God had judged the Jews for allowing interracial marriage. Brad didn't know if that stuff was true or not – and he certainly didn't care what the Bible said; Dad sure liked to quote it, but it's not like he lived it. He didn't even go to church except at funerals and weddings. But like his dad, Brad used to think folks should stick to dating their own kind. Nowadays, he wasn't quite so sure.

"Why would she wanna do that? She needs to let go." Everybody knew she was always mooning over that old house all the time. Just pathetic.

Heather agreed enthusiastically, just as he knew she would when he told her exactly what she wanted to hear. The crazy thing was that Emily thought she'd seen her Johnny at his old place today. Except everybody knew Johnny was a ghost. *And tonight is Halloween.* This had some genuine potential for fun.

He sighed with pretended disappointment. "Sorry to hear that. I really wanted to see you tonight."

She faltered, suggesting that maybe she could break it off. *Lapdog.*

"No, no, she shouldn't go to that old house alone," Brad said. "Me and the boys got some things to do anyway, but maybe I could call you and hook up later tonight?"

She got off the phone praising him for being so wonderful and understanding, promising her undying love and that she'd try to find a way out to Kelly's afterward before it got too late.

Brad was thinking it'd be a shame if Johnny's ghost didn't make an appearance. He reckoned he could make sure Emily didn't wait around for nothing.

9 – An Hour Ago

Three police officers were strewn like rag dolls across the crime scene. His chief suspect was as elusive as the motive for the crime. Why would John Lazarus do this? Even given their history, it didn't make sense for Johnny to become a cop killer. It didn't fit his profile. True, he'd been MIA for the last few years, but it seemed inconceivable that he could change so drastically.

An hour ago, local high school football coach Mike Trager had stepped into his Victory Red Hum-V, balancing his briefcase, a travel mug and the local Sports section. He had a busy night ahead of him and his mind was already trying to nail down every detail of his punishing schedule. Efficiency was the name of the game, whether you called it football or corporate management. No one could survive without it. In fact, Mike was convinced that the secret to a happy and relatively stress-free life was the never ending quest for optimal efficiency. What he called "Efficiency Prime" or just "E Prime" for short. His kids were a bit gun shy of big-sounding words. Jocks liked memorable little buzz phrases they could chant to psych themselves up.

The radio came on as he brought the Hummer to life. Count Bassie. Nice.

Tonight, he was handing out candy while Mary took the girls out trick-or-treating, immediately after which he had to hustle over to the ball field for tonight's game against the Vikings. He'd tried to get out of candy duty this year, considering Halloween fell on a game night, but Mary was big on holiday traditions. As a compromise and a concession to reality, he would be cutting it short tonight to allow time to get ready for the game.

It was an uneventful drive home. He loved the tree-lined streets and the neighborhood in general. He wasn't especially fond of Cecil Boggess, though he smiled and nodded at the old codger as he passed by anyway. He had a feeling that this show of pleasantry actually offended Cecil on some level.

His cell phone rang as he pulled into the drive. Mike frowned as he glanced at the number on the screen. It was his boss. His real boss.

There were moments when Mike Trager found himself so immersed in the fishbowl that he forgot it wasn't the ocean. Or to put it another way, there were times that his fake day-to-day life seemed so real that the reality of the situation almost seemed like a dream. It was easy to think of himself as just a football coach with a small, but happy family and a comfortable house. It was easy to forget that he worked for a biotech firm that had stumbled on a way to develop human beings with extraordinary abilities, that was even now watching and cultivating its research project. The double life he led was the stuff of comic books and science fiction. Frankly, if his wife and kids had any idea what some of the people who lived in this town – even some on this very street – were capable of, they'd be scared out of their minds. All of the abilities that had manifested were amazing, but some held frightening potential.

Trager was someone they called to take care of situations that were starting to get out of hand, things that Titan's plants within the local law enforcement or city government couldn't or wouldn't handle themselves. More accurately, those guys basically kept a lid on things, while Trager handled the rest.

He answered the phone with a scowl. He did not have time for this tonight, but Charles Huxley was not in the habit of making courtesy calls. If Titan's Director was bothering to contact him at all, it had to be pretty serious.

"We have a situation."

"I'm listening."

"John Lazarus has returned," Huxley said.

Mike didn't respond for a few seconds. Truth be told, he was stunned. "You're sure?"

"His chip went green, right here in town."

"How long ago?" He put the Hum-V in reverse and headed back onto the street.

"About ten minutes ago."

"Ten minutes? Why didn't Zim catch it?" Trager asked. Few things slipped past their top technogeek.

"Not sure yet. He suspects someone tampered with the system, someone who wants to catch Johnny first."

"Right. Do we know where Johnny is now?"

"He spiked near the south bank of the river in the vicinity of the bridge."

"On my way."

He'd driven all of half a minute when his cell phone buzzed anew.

"Trager," he answered.

"Honey, where are you?" his wife asked. "The neighbors say they saw you pull in and drive right off. Is everything OK?"

"I'm fine, Mary. I just got a call from the school. One of my kids. Shouldn't take long."

"Is everything alright?" she asked.

"I dunno. Um, listen, traffic's... I need to get off the phone."

"OK, but what about Trick or Treat? You're not going to bail on me, are you, Michael Thomas Trager?"

"I'll be there. I gotta go."

"Bye. I love you."

Trager smiled. "Love you, too."

As he hung up, he wondered how he was going to manage any of what he'd promised with John Lazarus in town. He was kidding himself. There'd be no rest tonight. He should probably just call the Assistant Coach now and tell him he wasn't coming. No, he decided, there was still time for this to be wrapped up pretty quickly. Maybe. In any case, he could always call Coach Carson a little later. As for candy duty... Mary was going to be very disappointed. He'd deal with that unpleasantness later. Right now, he needed to focus entirely on John Lazarus.

He needed more intel. Cursing himself for leaving his i84 back at the office, he speed-dialed Daniel Zim.

"Mr. Trager, right on schedule. I was expecting your call."

"Where is he?"

"Question of the day, bud. I could use Argus," Zim said, referring to the satellite Titan kept in geosynchronous orbit over Midwich, "but I need some idea where to point it. I think I have a lead though. Cops reported a suspicious vehicle on Archer earlier today. A maroon Plymouth Reliant with a yellow fender on the front passenger side. They weren't able to get the plates."

"John Lazarus was on my street? Do we watch this town at all?"

"Relax," Zim said. "Or don't. He really didn't do anything. He just drove by his old house. Either way, know that we reviewed the feeds from the street cams and managed to snag a Bigfoot quality video of the vehicle's occupants."

"You said occupants, plural. He's not alone?"

"Want me to send the clip to your '84?" Every high-level field agent at

Titan had an i84, a specialized communications device that tapped into the city's grid and gave them access to Titan's ultra-secure mainframe. Designed by Arthur Lazarus himself, the i84 linked into every camera in Midwich. The device also gave people like Trager access to classified information that Titan would never dare let anyone else have access to. It was called the i84 because, while Arthur found it a necessary evil to thus invade people's privacy to protect them, there was something undeniably Orwellian about such a device. He'd irreverently named his creation after Orwell's *1984* as a tangible reminder of the possible misuse of such technology.

"I left it back at the office."

"You what? Trager, this is exactly the sort of situation the '84 was designed for."

"I realize that. Have somebody pick it up for me. In the meantime, where'd Johnny go?"

"We're still reviewing the city feeds. He picked a good spot to hang out, incidentally. We don't really have anything pointed in that area."

"None of our surveillance cams cover the bridge?" Trager asked.

"The bridge itself? Yes. The area around it? No. We have cameras we can point down there if we need to, but it's not really a hot spot, so... Look, the enigma of good surveillance is that no one can watch a million cameras at once. You know this, Trager, so I don't want to hear it. You find a better way to do this, you let me kn–Oh, would you look at this? Police are currently in pursuit of our Plymouth. Somebody must like you, Mikey."

"Or somebody hates John Lazarus. Where is he?"

"On Main, heading toward the river."

"Get Argus pointed at him and don't lose him. And don't call me Mikey. Ever again."

He turned off the radio and flipped on the police scanner, listening to the chatter. Two cruisers were pursuing the Plymouth, while another was trying to intercept them at the bridge. As he listened, he heard them note that something was wrong with the car. Steam or smoke was rolling out of it. It left the road and slammed to a sudden stop.

Trager cursed, speeding across town, but he knew he'd be too late now. Titan would have to rely on their sleeper operatives in law enforcement or possibly even the local hospital to extract Johnny, if he'd survived.

His cell phone rang at that moment, distracting him, so that he didn't catch everything they said. He glanced at it with annoyance, then blinked in surprise when he saw the name on the caller ID. What the blazes was Ed Blyth calling him for? He considered hitting the Ignore button.

Then there were screams of pain and panic on the police scanner, followed by ominous silence.

The phone was ringing insistently. Trager answered numbly as the dispatcher tried to get a response from any of the officers. "Hello?"

"Tell Titan they're too late," Ed Blyth said.

"What?" Trager asked. His attention was still on the scanner. None of the officers responded. The dispatcher sent a call for all cars to assist, warning them to use extreme caution.

"Tell Titan they're too late. We have him now."

"What? Who's we?" Trager asked, but the line went abruptly dead. He tried calling him back, but there was no answer.

By the time Trager arrived at the bridge, cops, emergency personnel and news media were swarming over the crime scene, but a detective on Titan's payroll let him know everything he needed to hear. All three responding officers were dead. Their cruisers were crushed into metal spheres. Neither of the Plymouth's occupants could be accounted for.

He had to find Ed Blyth.

10 – Good Karma

Atop the fire escape, she watched Brad Farley and his ever-present clown cronies as they left the alley and headed out of sight. She'd eluded them again, but she had to admit she'd been lucky this time. Ducking into that *cul de sac* had been a bonehead move. They could have trapped her in there and had their sweet way with her. She shuddered to think what that thug trio was capable of if they thought they could get away with it, especially that overgrown human tank. Brad thought he could take whatever he wanted.

When she was sure they were long gone, she turned her attention back to her knight in shining armor. Well, a knight in a bloodied jean jacket anyway. Come to think of it, he wasn't much of a knight either. Frankly, if she hadn't bailed him out, he'd be dead by now.

She graciously decided he had at least distracted them long enough for her to get the jump on her hated enemies.

Weasel Hopkins stumbled out of the pedestrian narrow leading into the alley, pausing to see if anyone was waiting to take a shot at him. He was pretty much past caring at this point. Each step brought more pains from injuries that he hadn't known he had. Apparently, his attacker had beaten him into a state of physical shock. His senses were now returning with a vengeance.

"I would kill for another cigarette right now," he said.

"You know those things are gonna kill you someday if your mouth doesn't first," she joked by way of introduction. "You should quit while you're ahead."

"Who said that?" Weasel asked. He looked partly panicked, but also really aggravated at the same time. She couldn't blame the guy. He had been pushed a bit far tonight, even if it was his own fault that he'd got his butt handed to him like that.

"I'm up here," she said, "on the fire escape."

"So I see..."

There was a female figure up there alright, but he couldn't make out her face or features. It was as if she were distorted somehow. The effect brought to mind that old alien horror adventure film starring Arnold Schwarzenegger. The aliens in that film hunted humans using some sort of electrical camouflage that bent light around them. They could only be seen if you were looking carefully. What he was looking at was a bit like that, except the distorted silhouette was easier to pick out. "What the – Who are you? How are you doing that?"

"It's a long story," she said. "Are you OK?"

"Me? I'm fine. You should see the other guy." Weasel chuckled dryly, recovering quickly. He was staring at the girl, what he could see of her anyway, making small talk while he worked this out in his head. "Big as a dump truck. Not a mark on him. You see which way he went?" Good, he thought. Keep it light. And try not to freak out.

She laughed at his dark humor. "He went in that general direction," she said, pointing.

Weasel squinted, then admitted, "I can't really see you that well. I have no idea where you're pointing. Maybe this would easier if you... Are you ever more visible? Like me? Without the blood. Dude, I loved this jacket."

"Sorry," she said, interrupting her camouflage field. In just a few seconds, a dark-haired Goth girl with thick mascara and torn striped leggings appeared in place of the shadow on the fire escape landing. "This better?" she asked.

"Much," Weasel said, admiring the view. She was much less creepy now that he could plainly see her. And cute. Goth chick meets metal head in hick town. Fate? He certainly hoped so. Then again, he had problems maintaining a relationship with a normal chick, so maybe he should just cut his losses. "Which way was it now?"

"What? Oh, that way."

"I see. Thank you, um..?"

She hesitated. Her peers called her many names, ranging from the annoyingly ridiculous like Wacky Jackie to things that were vile and designed to punish her for daring to exist outside the lines. Brad's thugs even gave her mocking titles, like the Geek Avenger, to belittle her for defending his favorite victims: those who couldn't fight back.

She could fight back. She possessed abilities that no one suspected. As an outsider, she had few friends or family who might stumble onto her little secret. Of course, it didn't hurt that she was vastly more intelligent than the cookie cutter culture clones at her school. She'd even gained an academic scholarship from Kaukasos College. She'd wanted to get out of town for college, maybe even go somewhere cool like New York, but she couldn't pass up a scholarship. She could always study abroad later.

Besides blending in with her surroundings, Jackie could generate an electrical field for other uses, like magnetism or delivering painful shocks. So far, she couldn't shoot lightning bolts or anything crazycool like that. In fact, she had to be in physical contact to make it work. She could magnetize forks to a metal table or reverse the polarity and make them float a few inches off the surface. And while it would've been killer to be able to fry Brad and his bullies from a distance, she took a certain satisfaction in knowing that her blows packed an extra punch, shocking them on each impact.

The down-side was that prolonged use of her ability exhausted her. In fact, the more tired she felt, the less electricity she had at her disposal. She wasn't sure how her bio-electric field had mutated, transforming her into a comic book hero, but neither did she care to look a gift horse in the mouth. She knew better than to advertise it, too, for as any comic book fan could tell you, making your secret identity known would pretty much guarantee your loved ones would be placed in grave danger. At the very least, a criminal could use them as leverage against any would-be heroes. And that's if people didn't see you as just plain dangerous and sic the military on you, like they did to Hugh in *Mann from Midwich*! She'd been especially careful to hide her abilities from her arch-nemesis, Brad Farley. So far, he just thought she could hit really well for a girl. If he had any idea that there was some extra juice behind that punch or that she could blend in with her surroundings right under his nose, she was sure he'd find some way to expose her to the authorities.

On the other hand, it'd been absolutely driving her crazy that nobody knew about this but her. She knew that was supposed to be the price of being a super-powered heroine, but frankly the isolation sucked way worse than the comics let on.

When she was a kid she'd had an imaginary friend. She'd shared everything with him. Her father was an alcoholic, though he hadn't always been that way. It was when mom left that the drinking started. Anyway, her imaginary friend was all she had. As she grew up, she remained an outsider. She wouldn't change who she was just to fit in. It just wasn't in her nature. But nobody was meant to be alone.

Maybe that's why she'd chosen to reveal herself to this half-dead non-knight in a bloodied jean jacket. But she wasn't ready to give him the name of her mild-mannered alter ego just yet.

"Karma," she replied at last.

"Karma," he repeated. He stared at her again, transfixed. He tried to remind himself that he was probably being stupid here. He didn't know her. All he knew was her name and that she could go close to invisible. And that she was hot. "Weasel, by the way," he said. "Weasel Hopkins."

"Weasel? Is that your real name?"

"Is Karma yours? It's OK if it is. I understand. My mom was a hippie."

She smiled demurely but didn't answer.

"Gotcha. Karma it is. And which way were you going from here, Karma?" he asked.

She grinned, then with a wink she pointed in a slightly different direction.

"That's what I was hoping you'd say. Listen, I'm a little lost." The moment he said it, common sense began giving him a third degree lecture inside his thick skull. What was he doing? He was playing with fire here. He shouldn't be flirting with this super powered mutant. For that matter, he shouldn't be grocery shopping for the other one.

"Do tell?" She dove off the landing head first, using her magnetic abilities to coast gently along the metal fire escape, until she could somersault to the ground. The practiced move was graceful and gave the impression that she was flying.

"Wow," Weasel said.

She blushed, despite herself.

"I know a guy who can skip boulders across a river." Why was he telling her this? Of course, he knew why. He was desperate to impress her.

"What? Really?"

"Well, big rocks anyway. Big as my head," he said. "He can make them hover in midair, too."

"You're saying there are others like me?" she asked.

"Maybe. I dunno. Until today, I only ran across this stuff in the comics section. Now I've met two people that can do things nobody should be able to do, all in the same day in the very same town. Coincidence?" he asked.

Now it was Jackie's turn to be stunned. "Wow."

They stared at each other, excited, awkward, not knowing how to proceed from there, looking for an excuse to keep the moment going.

"Anyway I rode into town with my buddy, but we got separated," Weasel said, "and I don't really know my way around so I was hoping you could maybe tell me how to get back to Archer Lane."

"Archer Lane? That's my street. Who do you know on Archer?"

"This just keeps getting weirder and weirder," Weasel said. "Look, I'd rather not – that is, I don't know if he'd want me to tell you. There are people after us and, I dunno, maybe they got him. Maybe he won't even be there. But I have to get to Archer Lane tonight."

She considered him for a long, slow moment, realizing for the first time that she might've made a mistake in showing this stranger her powers. It sounded like he and his friend were up to no good. She might've just shown her hand to the bad guys. All the more reason to play along, she decided. As the saying went, Keep your friends close and your enemies closer.

"This friend you have to meet," she asked, "he the one with the abilities?"

Weasel hesitated and then nodded.

"I'll do it," she said, "but on one condition."

"Which is?"

"I get to meet him."

"Agreed."

"Good." She flashed him a charming grin. "And now for the bad news."

"Oh?"

"We'll now be going in the same direction as the sentimental fool who just kicked your butt."

Weasel groaned. "You're kidding me. That overgrown ogre lives on Archer, too?"

"Must be something in the water," she quipped, but as she and Weasel walked out of the alley, arm in arm, she had a thought that had never before occurred to her. Was there something about Archer Lane itself? Were there others on her street, secretly hiding these kinds of abilities from each other? That seemed far-fetched, but it would explain Brad Farley's sudden, over-muscled growth spurt. What if it was something in the water? What if it was something else?

11 – The Consultant

Ed Blyth couldn't help staring at John Lazarus' prone form. This was Kate and Arthur's son, the subject of many prayer requests from his devoted parents. The last time he'd seen Johnny's face had been in the form of an over-sized photo at the boy's very own funeral. There'd been no body recovered from that fire; now he knew why. The only real questions were why had he faked his own death to begin with, and why was he here now in Ed's church of all places?

He glanced up at the delivery boy, a red-headed 16- or 17-year-old with a nasty circular burn mark at his left cheekbone and singed eyebrows. It looked like some of his hair had been flame kissed as well. His chest was heaving and he was lathered in sweat. That one radiated reckless, more immediate danger. And it wasn't just the gun in his hand. He seemed confused, agitated and desperately angry at his package, even though he'd taken the pains to bring him here. He didn't recognize the gunman. His first thought was that he must be from out of town.

He'd burst through his church door a few minutes ago, calling for help. Seeing both boys' condition, Ed had started to call for an ambulance on his cell phone. Then he remembered that he'd lost that phone about a week ago. Just as well. A moment later, the conscious one had whipped out the pistol and barked out a terse warning to keep his hands in plain sight.

"Is he OK? Will he live?" the gunman asked.

Ed sighed nervously. "I'm not a doctor."

"Doesn't the church sign say, 'Soul's Harbor Church, Doc-tor Edward J. Blyth, Pastor?'"

"I'm not a medical doctor. I have a doctorate in religious philosophy. You didn't bring him here because you thought I could treat him, did you?"

The dangerous young man's face twitched a bit, but he stared at Ed with such hate that the pastor decided to drop the question. The patient moaned, giving him a convenient excuse to look away from his captor. "Looks like he's coming around," Blyth said. "What happened to him?"

"That's none of your business, doc-tor," the other said.

"At least tell me why you've brought him to me."

"Because those were my orders."

Ed shot the young man a scathing look. "Orders? Orders from who?"

The young man didn't answer, just grinned. It was not a pleasant expression.

The patient coughed and opened his eyes. He startled when he saw Ed Blyth, his suspicious golden eyes shooting down to the pastor's hands. Ed backed off instinctively. "Easy now. I'm not going to hurt you, but you've been injured and–"

"I heal quickly. What do you want?" Johnny asked, trying to make sense of his surroundings. He was in a church sanctuary. Front pew. He recognized the older man who'd been talking to him as his dad's old pastor. He'd thought at first that the minister might be his abductor, but the man held no gun and his eyes were the wrong color. He looked further. A younger man sat irreverently upon the altar, a familiar weapon trained on him. He took note of the circular burn mark on his cheek. He sighed wearily, deciding to sit up. "Or should I ask him? Hillary Clinton, I presume?" he asked.

The gunman nodded.

The events of the recent past flooded into his mind. The carjacking. Being taken hostage at gunpoint by this clown in a Halloween mask. Being chased by the cops. Burning his assailant with the Plymouth's cigarette lighter. Slamming on the brakes. Watching his abductor fly through the windshield just prior to slamming his own head against the steering wheel. Staggering out of the smoking car, surrounded by policemen. Fading to black.

"How did we get here?" Johnny asked. "How did we escape the cops?"

Ed's blood ran cold at that particular question.

Hillary's expression faltered for a moment. His hands were shaking noticeably. In fact, now that Blyth noticed it, it was apparent that the young man was suffering increasing episodes of nervous ticks. "I – I killed them," he said.

"You what?" Johnny asked.

"I killed them," Hillary said, more evenly this time.

"Great, you're a cop killer now. And my guess is that they'll think I helped. Do you have any idea what cops do to cop killers in small towns, Hillary?"

"Shut up," Hillary threatened. His face twitched hard.

"Are you OK, young man?" Ed asked.

"What?" Hillary trained his gun on the pastor.

Ed raised his hands defensively. "Wait. Please. You're just twitching like I've never seen before. And you have your finger on that trigger–"

"Back off," Hillary said, waving [with the gun] toward two chairs on the stage. "Over there. Sit down, both of you."

Johnny groaned and grimaced as he eased himself off the pew. Ed helped him hobble laboriously over to the designated chairs. Hillary rose from the altar, following their progress, and then sat down on the front pew. To their surprise, he laid the gun down on the seat next to him.

Johnny glanced at the clock over the church doors at the other end of the sanctuary. His eyes narrowed.

"Is that clock right?" he asked Ed.

Ed followed his gaze. "It's five minutes fast."

Johnny leveled his gaze upon their captor. "How'd we get here so fast, Hillary?" he asked.

Hillary grinned mockingly, arrogant despite the nervous ticks that continued to wrack his body. "You're right, doc," he said. "It's just nerves. I'm used to it. It happens every time I do this, but it always passes after a few minutes."

"It happens every time after you do what?" Ed asked.

"I carried him here. I ran the whole way."

"We were clear across town," Johnny said. "No one can run that fast."

"Clear across town?" Ed asked. "Really?"

"We were over at the bridge a few minutes ago," Johnny said.

"I'm that fast," Hillary said, answering their unspoken question.

Ed caught his breath, beginning to realize just what he was dealing with here.

Titan.

They'd cut him a few checks as a metaphysical consultant for their clandestine research over the years. Until they'd approached him, Ed had never even heard of a metaphysical consultant. They asked a lot of weird questions. Things like, did he think angels or demons could be detected scientifically? Did he think that such supernatural creatures could really be a primitive understanding of inter-dimensional beings? Did he think faith healings were authentic? Or prophecy? ESP? Did Elijah use pyrokinesis? Since Pharaoh's magicians duplicated some of the feats performed by Moses, was magic real? Did he think magic could be a force of will? Did he believe in mind powers? Jesus could read or sense the thoughts of others; could anyone else?

There were endless questions like that. He'd had to stop and ask them if they were serious after the first 15 minutes or so. It was patently bizarre, but they seemed to take everything he said completely seriously. The impression he got was that they supposed that such powers might spring from the mind rather than directly from God. He'd been forced to qualify some of his responses, noting that he felt they were making some rather non-Biblical and, in some cases, perhaps even blasphemous suggestions.

His panel of interviewers, a group he now thought of as the Titan Inquisition, had coldly told him they'd take it under advisement.

Further interviews, all conducted with a mandatory nondisclosure agreement, suggested that they were trying to find scientific, specifically neurological or biological, explanations for supernatural and paranormal phenomena. They consulted him often in the beginning of their secretive relationship, but less so as time went on. Yet the later sessions were the most interesting. They were more specific, giving him a better clue as to what exactly they'd been hatching up there on the hill at the Titan research complex. Unfortunately, it also became increasingly apparent that at least two members of the Inquisition felt that the metaphysical angle was a dead end, useful perhaps as background information as to what might be potentially possible.

It was the last session that stood out in his mind. It was short. All of the questions had centered around the concept of "faith moving mountains." They wanted to know if he thought faith itself were a force any human could wield, if it was all hypnotic suggestion or a psychological placebo effect, or if it was dependent upon an Almighty God. In effect, they wanted to know if it was subject to scientific manipulation and exploitation, whether it was bunk or whether it was beyond the control and study of science. There was no simple blanket answer. The truth was that a good number of cases of faith healing were demonstrably bunk. People had put their faith in a "man of God" and trusted that he spoke for God when he said that they'd been healed. If the condition returned, the "faith healer" had a handy basket of excuses for this "reversal" of their healing: unconfessed sin, a lack of adequate faith on the victim's part, the allowance of people who were openly doubtful, negative or skeptically cautious into their sphere of influence or the ever-popular decree that God was simply testing the sincerity or tenacity of their faith. These guys, mostly televangelists who'd confused God with money in his opinion, were predatory frauds. Did they use hypnosis? He didn't think so. He thought instead that they preyed upon a combination of social pressures within the church and the victim's personal hopes and expectations. It was complex, but, no, he didn't think they were all hypnotists. He stated unapologetically that he leaned toward the latter answer that true faith healing was the province of God, while temporary placebo effects might be accomplished by human delusion. No, he didn't think of faith as sufficiently focused delusion. And so on…

A few days later, the tragedy of the Lazarus fire created a more-than-adequate level of pastoral business to drive all thoughts of mad scientists and their Frankenstein complex out of his mind. If police funerals weren't a big enough affair to begin with, everyone in Midwich and the surrounding county seemed to know Arthur Lazarus.

Eventually things settled down and curiosity got the better of him. He knew better than to ask Titan directly and he had a feeling that he should be careful how he conducted his investigation, considering the plethora of non-disclosure statements that'd been forced under his pen. He did a little digging. Every clue led to two more questions. After a series of false starts and frustrating dead ends, he'd nearly given up on prying open Titan's hermetically sealed lid.

Then one day out of the blue, he'd received an email from someone calling himself Malak.

"Pandora's Box has been opened, but Hope has flown. Prometheus seeks to bring forbidden fire. The Titans must be stopped. This is the will of the gods. The dead walk, for Lazarus is alive. Look for the survivor of Prometheus' flame."

The message struck him as nonsense, rather like a jabberwocky based on a mixture of Greek myths and New Testament references. He'd almost deleted it as spam. He wished now that he had, but three words caught his attention: Titans, Prometheus and Lazarus. Prometheus was a Titan punished by the gods for bringing fire down to man from Mount Olympus. For his crime, he was bound to one of the four pillars of the Earth where he had his liver devoured every day by an eagle, only to have it grow again the next day, and so on and so forth. In a certain light, the cryptic message seemed to be saying that Titan was somehow responsible for the Lazarus fire, but that there had been a survivor. Of course, only one candidate came to mind, since the only body that wasn't recovered from the ashes was that of the son, John Lazarus.

"You're an Indigo, aren't you?" Ed asked Hillary.

"A what?"

"You have special abilities," Ed said.

"Yeah, but I ain't never been called no *Indigo* before," the red-head said.

"It's not my term. I didn't make it up. It's what Titan calls people like you."

"What do you know about Titan?" Johnny asked.

"They used me as a consultant over the years," he admitted.

"Do you work for them now?"

"No, and frankly if I knew then what I know now, I wouldn't have gotten involved with them at all, money or no money."

"And what exactly do you know?" Johnny asked.

Ed Blyth started to respond, but paused, noting how intently both boys were gazing at him. "Um, look," he said, "before I tell you anything, I gotta know the answer to two questions, OK?"

They didn't object.

"First, is Titan looking for you two?" he asked.

Johnny glanced at Hillary, who shrugged and chuckled darkly. Johnny shot his captor a withering stare before turning back to Ed. "Probably," Johnny said.

"Thank you. One more question." He licked his lips. "Johnny, I need to know. Are you an Indigo?"

"I really don't like that name," Johnny said.

"Me neither," Hillary agreed. "It has a certain pansy quality to it."

"Please, just answer the question. We may not have much time."

Johnny sized him up, trying to decide whether he could trust Ed with his biggest secret. There certainly wasn't much risk in letting the cat out of the bag in this case. No one would likely believe him anyway, except Titan, who already knew. The question was there any benefit to revealing the truth to this preacher? At the very least, he decided, a person who learns a secret feels a certain obligation to reveal their own. Human beings have this intrinsic need for fairness in their lives. So the best way to get Ed to spill what he knew about Titan was to make him privy to a secret he already pretty much knew.

"Yes."

12 – Puzzle Pieces

"I don't care what you're seeing on that end," Zim said. "Unless he's found a way to keep the brain chip from broadcasting when he uses his powers, which isn't even theoretically possible, he didn't destroy those police cruisers."

"And I'm telling you," Trager said, "he crushed three police cruisers into metal balls. From what I'm looking at here, he used them as ballistics on the officers in question."

"I'm not disputing that an Indigo was involved. I'm saying it wasn't Johnny," Zim said.

"Fine," Trager asked, "who spiked then?"

"That's the problem. No one spiked. No one at all."

Zim finally had his full attention. "That's not possible. If they use their powers, the chips broadcast. I'm definitely looking at the work of an Indigo here, so…"

"You're not listening," Daniel Zim said. Trager glared at the offending cellphone. If that pencil-necked geek had been talking to him face to face, he'd never have had the temerity to interrupt him like this. "I mean, you're right to a point. If they use their abilities, they spike; however, that only applies to Indigos with Titan chips in their heads. No chip, no spike."

"So whoever is responsible for this mess doesn't have a chip in their brain."

"Or has someone else's chip in their brain. We've always suspected we might have rivals in this area of research. Titan probably wouldn't be able to detect spikes from a foreign chip. We're only set to watch for ours."

Trager nodded. Titan certainly had rivals. One company in particular sprang to mind: Parasol Limited, their chief competitor for government military contracts. "Fine, we know Johnny wasn't alone. We'll have to assume we're dealing with more than one Indigo and that this unknown has no problem using his powers to kill people."

"There's another problem," Zim said. "A transmission was sent out from our system when John Lazarus' chip went green."

"Who sent it?"

"No one. It was sent out automatically. Someone embedded a program in our system to alert them whenever this Lazarus kid went green and to alert us a full ten minutes later. It's a really old program. Not sure how we didn't notice it before. But get this: the program was written by Hope Holloway."

"You're sure?" Trager asked. "You do know you're talking Pandora here?"

"I'm aware. That transmission also provided her with the time and location of his spike."

"So she knows he's here," Trager said.

"Begging your pardon, but what's her interest in John Lazarus?" Zim asked.

"I'm not sure yet. It's not like he's not valuable. She could be working with someone else. Parasol maybe. Have you got a lock on where Johnny went after–" He glanced around him, searching for a word that might adequately sum up the bizarre horror of the crime scene. He finally settled on "–here?"

"We didn't get a camera oriented on that area in time to catch the incident, but I think I've found them. I added that grainy image we got of Johnny earlier today to our facial recognition system and told the software to use it as a template to age Johnny accordingly. The scanners just registered a match."

"OK. Where is he?"

"Archer Lane. We're tracking them live now."

"Arch – That's my street again!"

"That's not even the best part," Zim said. "Looks like our rogue cop killer can run faster than an Olympic medalist, and that's even when he's carrying Johnny."

"He's carrying Johnny?"

"You could see for yourself if you had your i84."

"Don't rub it in."

"I'm just saying. OK, looks like our boys have stopped running and you are not gonna believe this, Trager," Zim said. "They just ducked inside Soul's Harbor."

"Ed Blyth's church. This is a trap."

"That's what I was just thinking. How do you want to handle this?"

"We catch them in their own trap," Trager decided. "I need three full teams to meet me down there ASAP. I want snipers in place to secure the perimeter. Nothing goes in or out until I get there. Tranq guns with live ammunition as a fall back option only. I want him alive."

"You sure you wanna try to take him alive? Wouldn't it be safer to–"

"I owe it to Arthur Lazarus to try," Trager said.

13 – Pawns and Crackpots

"Oh, we really have to go now," the preacher said.

"Nobody's going anywhere," Hillary said. He picked up the gun to remind them who was in charge. His hand looked much steadier now, perhaps fueled by his new resolve. "My orders were to keep you here."

"For what?" Johnny asked.

"It doesn't matter," Ed said. "Titan will be here at any minute. I'm sure of it. And whatever you had planned for us will go up in smoke when they come busting down the church door."

"It does matter. Who's giving the orders?" Johnny asked. "Who are you working for?"

"I can take care of Titan," Hillary told Ed. "They have no idea what they're up against, what I'm capable of or even what we have planned for them."

"Young man, I assure you that you are severely underestimating the opposition," Ed said. "This isn't your average gaggle of lab coats. I've been investigating them over the last few years and I have to tell you, this is the stuff of spy movies and conspiracy theories! They're watching everything. They're even watching each other. I'm guessing that three-quarters of this town actually works undercover for the company, but only about a quarter that number is actually aware of just how vast the conspiracy stretches."

"Paranoid much?" Hillary asked.

"I know how it sounds. This is Hoover's Red Scare in miniature. They're everywhere, hiding in plain sight: our friends, co-workers and neighbors, maybe even people in our own family. Sleeper agents, all of them! Except in this case, it happens to be true." Ed rubbed the back of his neck. "I used to think how could you ever hide something like that? Somebody would eventually slip up, right? But think about it: even if someone let the cat out of the bag or just put two and two together, like I did, who'd believe them? You keep second guessing yourself, which is the beauty of it. The Big Lie you're presented with just seems so real and the truth seems too far out to be true. And who would you tell?" he asked. "If you're right, they control the media and maybe even the police, so you can't tell them. If you try to tell anyone else, they'll make you look like a crackpot conspiracy nut – if you don't do it for them."

"Wow. Why even tell us?" Hillary asked.

Ed knew the kid was mocking him but under the circumstances he'd never been more confident of his theory. "Because you represent undeniable proof of the veracity of my claim. Your abilities are something big enough, important enough to justify the level of conspiracy this humble crackpot is suggesting. By definition, you are completely inconceivable and, rationally speaking, the fact that you undeniably exist makes the possibility that the aforementioned conspiracy does not exist equally inconceivable," he said.

"That was a mouthful," Hillary said.

"Yeah, it sounds like you've given this a lot of thought, but this is getting us nowhere," Johnny said. He turned to his abductor. "Look, I don't know who you work for, Hillary; I know enough to strongly suspect it's not Titan. I think Ed here is right. They're on their way. I don't know what you're plan was, but I know Titan well enough to be certain that they're not going to give you the fight you think you're gonna get. We're too dangerous. They'll try to take us down with minimal contact."

"Say again?"

"He means they'll use gas or tranquilizers. They'll knock you out before you can use your abilities on them," Ed said. "When you wake up, they'll have you pumped so full of drugs you won't be able to bat an eyelash without their help."

"My orders were to keep you here."

"To what purpose?" Johnny demanded.

The scared puppy look that flashed across Hillary's face said it all.

"They didn't tell you. You have no idea. You're just a pawn."

Hillary leapt to his feet. "I am not a pawn."

"Keep telling yourself that," Johnny said.

Hillary leveled the gun at Johnny. "Watch it."

"Why do you even need that gun?"

Hillary shrugged, leering at him. "Because it works. If it ain't broke, don't fix it, right?"

Ed rolled his eyes. "That's lovely. Even if you're not a pawn, even if you're more of a knight or rook, the point is you can still be sacrificed for the 'greater good.'"

Hillary's eyes narrowed. "You're just trying to– No. She wouldn't do that. You don't know her. Titan sacrifices the little guy. Titan treats people like human cattle! Titan is the bad guy here! She's not like them! She's going to stop them."

"No matter what it costs?" Ed asked. They were wasting their time talking to this one. Hillary fully intended to carry out his marching orders. Ed had come to the realization that he was probably going to die. Even if he survived the impending confrontation between Titan and the Indigo pair, considering what he knew it was unlikely that they'd let him live. "Listen, there are some things I need you to know, just in case I don't survive this." He eyed Johnny in particular. "I have been receiving emails from an unknown benefactor who goes by the name Malak."

Johnny repeated the name, committing it to memory.

"I think it's a pseudonym because it literally means 'messenger' or 'angel'," Ed said. "Anyway, he's been giving me leads and hints into Titan's secrets, particularly concerning the Prometheus Initiative, which is all about young people like you with your special abilities. By the way, that college up on the hill, Kaukasos, it's named for one of the pillars of the world, the very one the mythical Prometheus was chained to for the sin of giving fire to men, and I don't think that's a coincidence. I'm not sure how it ties in to all of this but, apparently, they've been watching you Indigos–" He noted their defensive scowls at that term "– or whatever you care to call yourselves – your entire lives. My question is what kind of returns are they expecting from that investment?"

Hillary held up a hand for silence. "Hush! Listen."

They could hear the sound of sirens rapidly approaching.

"They're here," Johnny said.

14 – Siege

Four squad cars escorted a pair of black vans into the parking lot of Soul's Harbor, blocking both the street and the alley. Trager arrived shortly after the police formed their perimeter. The Titan-paid cops gave him a glance of recognition and let him through, a favor they would allow no one else.

Trager stepped out of the vehicle, using a headset now instead of his cell phone. "Where are my snipers, Zim?" He watched as Titan agents in hi-tech gear and Kevlar armor spilled out of the unmarked vans. One in particular caught his attention, both because he recognized him and because he was waving Trager's i84.

"Gage," he said as the Titan agent passed him his i84, "I see you completely ignored your uncle Ness' advice. How is old Quatermain?"

"Grouchy and old."

"You tell him yet?" Ness had quit Titan years ago back during the whole Pandora debacle. He'd threatened to disown his great-nephew if he ever got a job with the company.

"I'm still working on it."

Trager scoffed and placed his thumb on the i84's scan plate.

"Gimme a break," Gage said. "He never misses, for crying out loud." Ness' skill with a rifle was matched only by his irritable disposition.

"Which is why you need to tell him before he finds out on his own."

"I know, I know."

Zim reported over Trager's commset. "We have snipers at the tree line at the back of the church and on the rooftops of nearby homes."

Trager was already using the i84 to confirm they were in place. "Good. Alpha and Bravo team have the Archer street exits pretty well covered, but our targets could try to cut across yards."

Carter Munroe's voice cut through his headset. "Charlie team is in place. The perimeter is secured."

Mike Trager frowned at Carter's overconfidence, but declined to comment. He didn't exactly get along with Charlie Company's team leader. Carter was ex-military, a good soldier through and through, and a company man to boot. Unfortunately, he thought of Indigos as over-glorified weapons. He took a low opinion of dangerous and unpredictable "weapons" like Trager being in command. And he'd made no secret of that view.

Shrugging off his irritation, Trager brought his focus back to the present. He peered at the front doors of the church structure, pulling himself together before the inevitable fire fight. Stained glass windows prevented any view of the building's interior. He tried to pull up the cameras they had installed in the church on his i84. All he got for his efforts were a few irrelevant shots of the church offices and hallways. The sanctuary cameras were ominously blank.

"Why don't we have eyes inside that building?" he asked.

"Some of our surveillance cameras have been disabled," Zim said.

Trager grimaced at the news. They'd embedded cameras in nearly every structure in town, especially on this street. If Ed Blyth had discovered and destroyed a few of them, he was likely aware he was being watched. That would make things more difficult.

"Why didn't we notice this before?" he asked.

"We have a million eyes all over this town. Loads of them go blank from time to time. The church cams were scheduled for repairs, but it wasn't exactly a high priority. We've seen church on TV before."

"Everything on Archer is a high priority," Trager said, tapping furiously on his i84. "OK, it looks like we do have their heat signatures on satellite." He allowed himself a relieved sigh. The Argus satellite maintained geosynchronous orbit over Midwich, giving them an eye in the sky. He hadn't been relishing the idea of going in there completely blind.

"Our targets are at the front of the sanctuary near the altar," Zim said. "The rest of the building appears empty, but keep your eyes open."

"You think?" He stared at the thermal images from the church's interior on his i84. One of the figures inside was definitely holding a gun on the other two, who were sitting down. "Something's not right here," he said. "Ed called me before that whole bridge business. He said he had Johnny. I figured the cop killer was just the delivery boy."

"You wanted to spring this trap, remember?"

"Don't remind me," Trager said.

"How do you want to do this?" Alpha Team Leader asked him over his commset.

"Alpha, cover the front entrance. Bravo, cover the rear," he said. "Do not engage until I give the order. Tranqs only. Live ammo is only to be used as a last resort. This is to be a live capture. We are in pursuit of two, I repeat, two Indigos and one older male. The older gentleman is known to many of you as the pastor of this church, Ed Blyth. We need to detain the good reverend for questioning in a matter vital to Titan's interests." He took a deep breath before continuing.

"You all should have been briefed on one John Lazarus, a local teen involved in a rather infamous arson case a few years ago, presumed dead until today. He is a high level kinetic with razor-sharp intelligence and uncharted abilities. The other Indigo is a black box. All we know is that he can turn police cruisers into cannonballs. Obviously, these Indigos are to be presumed hostile and extremely dangerous. I do not need to remind you of the sort of damage these two could do to this community if they are allowed. They have already demonstrated their willingness to use lethal force."

"Sir, why don't we just take them down, sir?" Bravo Team Leader asked.

"John Lazarus represents a sizable investment to your employers. While potentially dangerous, his abilities are exactly what Titan has been trying to cultivate. The unknown may represent a rival company's investment."

"You mean he might not be one of ours?" Alpha Team Leader asked.

"Affirmative. Now, I want tear gas and flash grenades ready to launch through those windows on my mark. Let's stay on our toes. I will enter the building first to try and negotiate a peaceful surrender. If that fails, Alpha will storm that building. Bravo will make sure no one gets in or out until you receive the all clear. Charlie will maintain the perimeter as a fail safe."

"You sure you don't just want me to take care of this for you, Trager?" Carter Munroe asked. There was no mistaking the condescension in his voice.

"We'll do this my way, Charlie."

"With all due respect, Trager, your way usually involves a lot of collateral damage."

"You have your orders."

There was a moment of silence on the other end of the comm, followed by a dry, humorless laugh. "Charlie team standing by to mop up your mess."

Trager ignored the jibe.

Gage didn't. "Could we at least pretend like we're on the same team?"

Carter didn't respond. Trager knew he was fuming at the young man's temerity.

"Sir, do you think it's wise to go in there alone?" Bravo Team Leader asked.

"Well, I wouldn't suggest that any of you do it," Trager said. "Look alive, gentlemen." He glanced once more at the church door, considering it again. "OK, show time."

He walked stealthily to the front doors. He took a moment to make sure his teams were in place, then checked the doorknob. Unlocked.

As quietly as he could, he cracked the door open and glanced into the foyer. He could see a coat rack topped with a shelf for worshipers' hats and extra Bibles. They also stored the offering plates up there between services. Another set of doors led into the sanctuary. Each door sported a narrow window which the usher could use to see if it was a convenient time to let late-comers in. It wouldn't do to have someone shuffling to their seat during the prayer, after all.

Saying a prayer of his own, Mike Trager slipped in quickly, shutting the door behind him. He kept himself crouched to the ground to avoid being seen through those door windows. He crept across the cozy foyer in a duck walk and put his ear to the door to listen.

His targets were in a spirited argument. Good, they'd be distracted enough for him to get the drop on them. He intended to take out the gunman with a tranq dart and try to use that goodwill rescue as leverage to get the others to surrender. That was the plan anyway.

He slid silently to a standing position beside the door window, glancing in surreptitiously to get a lock on his targets' exact position, especially the gunman. Taking a deep, calming breath, he burst into the sanctuary.

15 – Calm Before the Storm

"How can you listen to that noise?" Weasel asked. "I thought you were supposed to be this Goth chick." They were bouncing around in the bed of an old and ugly pickup truck that might've been red once beneath the duct tape, rust and body putty. Their too-obviously-drunk driver was belching out the lyrics of his favorite country tunes in between slugs of beer. Weasel had no love for rednecks, especially not after his most recent brush with a paragon of the breed.

"What? I like this song," she said. "Besides, I don't think music should define who you are, and I don't think that who you are or who you hang with should determine your musical tastes. Or aren't you into individuality?" she asked.

Weasel shook his head. "No such thing, but don't let me bring you down. I'm sure you're special just like everybody else."

"You don't think I'm special?" she asked.

Her sly grin and perfectly arched eyebrow disarmed him. "No, no, I –"

She feigned disappointment. "No?"

"That's not what I–" He stopped talking, realizing she was just messing with him, maybe even flirting. He tried to regain his cool. "You know what I meant."

He watched, entranced, as she wiped a fluttering strand of hair out of her eyes. The chill wind kept gusting around them as they bounced down the road. The road, he noted, was reasonably smooth. The shocks on this rusted beast must be shot to Hick's Heaven.

She banged on the glass with the flat of her hand. "Curtis! You're gonna miss the street!"

The driver's red ball cap bobbed up and down in acknowledgment and suddenly the ancient truck lurched to the right, throwing Karma into Weasel's arms. He was so stunned by this unexpected answer to his prayers that he was able to ignore the sharp pain in his back as he also slammed into the side of the pickup bed. Still, he wasn't able to suppress a gasp of pain.

Hearing him, she said, "Easy, Tiger."

He blushed again, wishing he had something witty to say in return.

The truck lurched to a stop. "We're home, Sissy!" Without further ado, her dad belched and staggered into the house.

Weasel stared after him in awestruck wonder, rather like a man entranced by a massive train wreck. "I still can't believe that's your dad," he said.

"That's very sweet of you to say. I had been wondering if you have a girlfriend."

"Oh? Really?" He tried not to sound too pleased.

"Yeah, but with your mouth, I'm just wondering if you've ever had one." She turned to hide a grin.

"Oh, so it's like that. Fine. Tell ya what. Thanks for the ride. I got something I gotta do." He began walking down the sidewalk.

"I'm kidding!" she said. "Come back here, you wuss."

He spun around, partly annoyed and enthralled at the same time. "You really are maddening," he said.

"I get that sometimes."

At that moment he became aware of police sirens wailing for him in the distance. A sinking feeling formed in the pit of his stomach as the sound grew louder, closer.

"What is it?" Karma asked. Fear was clearly etched into his face.

"They're after me," he said. He regretted the slip the moment he uttered the words.

"They're after you?" she asked. An instant later, the light of revelation hit her and she turned on him, suddenly quite animated. "The cops?" She began backing away from him.

"Yes. I mean, no! Not really. They're after Johnny. They only want me because I'm with him."

"What did you do?" Her eyes were flashing – and not just from anger. Karma was definitely experiencing a surge of electricity.

"Nothing. Well, I think Johnny burned down his house, but that was before I met him. Years ago."

"Johnny burned down his house? Would that be a house on this very street? Are you talking about John Lazarus? Because he's dead, man."

"He gets that a lot," Weasel said. "Look, the only thing I knew until today was that this was his hometown, a place that he was allegedly never ever under any circumstances coming back to *ever* because of whatever happened to him here. Then suddenly, I wake up and he's driven us here and he says he burned down his own house and that he's killed people, but not on purpose, and that, since I'm clearly not freaked out enough, he has some kind of super powers! And now there's you, whom I would desperately like to get to know better under much better circumstances, and your twenty questions, and the cops in this town, who just seem to know your every tiny move, and–"

"I get it. I trust you. Stop talking and move." She dashed for the front porch, beckoning him to follow.

Several squad cars rushed onto Archer Lane, spurring Weasel into panicked flight. He nearly beat Karma to the front door of her house. Slipping inside, they slammed the door shut behind them. Karma locked it quickly, while Weasel peered cautiously out the window.

He was genuinely surprised when the cruisers passed the house. They didn't even slow down.

"They must not be after you," she said.

"Oh no," he said.

"What?"

"They're after Johnny."

16 – Showdown at Soul's Harbor

It all happened rather quickly. Johnny and Ed saw the sanctuary doors burst open. Hillary saw the looks on their faces. As recognition dawned, Hillary spun about, ducking instinctively. A tranquilizer dart whizzed by his head. Both Johnny and Hillary watched its progress with preternatural senses. The world seemed to slow down, though in reality it was they who had sped past its usual pace.

Hillary batted the second dart out of the way, slapping the ineffectual weapon contemptuously. He mentally stopped the third – and final – dart in midair, spun it around, and sent it back at the shooter.

Trager's itchy trigger finger had sent the third dart even though he'd realized it was futile. The moment he'd fired the third shot, he'd tossed the tranq gun aside and ducked behind a pew, reaching for his other weapon. The redirected dart shot back across the room and then sharply dove. It would've sank into his thigh had he not moved his leg at the last instant.

"We can do this the easy way," Trager said. "Or I can just put you in the hurt locker like I planned all along."

"Do you have any idea who you're dealing with?" Hillary asked. With a gesture, he caused a wooden pew to levitate, ripping it off the ground even though it had been bolted to the floor. Hillary sent the pew sailing across the room until it was above Mike Trager. Predictably, he dropped it, trying to crush his enemy.

Amateur. Mike was already crawling out of harm's way. He fired under the pews. Bullets shattered Hillary's left ankle, dropping him to the floor. He writhed in agony, howling wordless fury at Trager.

"I know exactly what I'm dealing with," Trager said. "We make people like you. We've studied you for years. We probably know how your abilities work better than you do. That's beside the point. Right now, you just need to decide whether we'll bring you in dead or alive."

Hillary laughed despite his pain. "You people are so naïve. So predictable. Such perfect pawns."

"Is that a yes or a no?"

The rogue Indigo sneered. "Take your best shot, old man."

Trager frowned momentarily, glanced at Johnny, then fired off a few more rounds. As he'd feared, the Indigo was prepared for him now. The bullets all stopped a few inches from Hillary's triumphant face and dropped to the ground harmlessly.

"Plan B." He sent his teams the electronic signal to attack.

Canisters burst through the stained glass windows on either side of the sanctuary. Flash bombs and tear gas, intended to punish and disorient the besieged, went off efficiently. But there was no noise or smoke, no flash and bang. Everything was strangely muted because the projectiles were already on their way back out the windows, where they momentarily distracted the invaders.

Trager hopped to his feet, trying to run for safety.

Hillary snatched him up with kinetic power and bashed him into a wall.

Alpha team burst into the church and the sanctuary was suddenly swarming with tranq darts. Once again, the world seemed to slow down in the eyes of the two Indigos. Irritated, Hillary swept up a good number of them and flung the swarm at a single foe. The Titan agent dropped, dead from an overdose of tranquilizers. Johnny altered the paths of the darts that came near him to protect himself and Ed.

It was at that point that Ed Blyth began asking himself why Johnny was neither joining the fight, nor attempting to flee. He was just watching. "Shouldn't we be leaving about now?"

John Lazarus looked like someone who'd just been interrupted in the middle of their favorite show. "You're right. It's not safe for you here."

Suddenly, every pew in Soul's Harbor was ripped out of the flooring, hovering over everyone's heads. Some of Alpha team had the presence of mind to switch to live rounds at that moment, but it did them no good. Closing his outstretched hand into a fist, Hillary caused each pew to implode into a ball of wood and splinters the size of a television set. He bashed his enemies with these wooden bludgeons from unexpected directions. In seconds, they were all down, either dead or unconscious.

Hillary laughed, coughing from the exertion, surveying the damage. "Was that it? Was that all they had?"

Ed stared horror-struck at the splinter-strewn war zone his sanctuary had been transformed into. Forget a pew fund. He was going to need another building fund if the action continued much more.

"We need to leave now," Johnny said.

"What? Did you not just see that?" Hillary asked. "We're gods! They can't hold a candle to us."

"Don't get cocky. This place is probably surrounded. How do you intend to fight them once they've worn you down to the point of exhaustion? They've already got you doubled over coughing."

"You're right. It is time for me to go. But you two aren't going anywhere. She wants you captured by Titan."

"You can't beat me. Don't try. Save your energy for our escape," Johnny said.

"I can take care of myself, you arrogant little jerk."

"I don't know," Mike Trager said, standing to his feet as casually as if he'd simply been tying his shoes and had now risen. "I'd be tempted to listen to him. After all, Johnny actually escaped us once."

Hillary stared at him hatefully yet with newfound respect. "Wow. I'm really impressed. You're actually still standing after all that."

"I'm hard to kill."

Hillary frowned. "I'll make it easy for you."

"Really?" Trager asked. "Didn't it strike you as even a little bit odd that I knew what you were, what you and Johnny both are, and still came in alone?" He shook his head sadly at their oversight.

A shadow of fear and uncertainty flashed across Hillary's face. "What's your point, old man?"

"My point is that my patience is wearing thin. Will you surrender peaceably or not?"

"Have you been paying attention, old man? Look around! You're in no position to be giving ultimatums. You're out of your mind!"

"Johnny, can't you talk some sense into your friend here?" Trager asked.

"Actually, he was my kidnapper," Johnny said.

"That makes sense." He turned his attention back to Hillary. "Some guys always gotta learn the hard way. So be it." With an eager grin, he whipped his gun up again.

"This again?" Hillary asked.

But when Mike Trager squeezed off rounds this time, the bullets didn't travel in a straight line. Instead, they seemed to swarm out of the gun at odd angles, arcing back toward their target. Since they came from nearly every direction, the young Indigo found himself hard pressed to stop them all. It was easy enough to concentrate on a single line of bullets traveling along one trajectory. It was a testament to his video gaming skills that he was able to keep track of each one and stop its momentum cold. Sweating from the exertion, he glared up at his assailant. "Nice trick."

"I'm just warming up," Trager said, whipping out a second handgun. He pressed both triggers, while Hillary steeled himself for another hail swarm of bullets. This time, Trager threw both guns away from himself. Amazingly, the guns continued to fire as they moved away from him. In fact, they hovered off the floor at the same height he'd held them at. In effect, Hillary had bullets flying at him from a 120 degree arc. Meanwhile, Trager was pointing at the ceiling fans, bringing both of them down and sending them spinning at Hillary with kinetic energy.

"Time to go," Johnny hissed to Ed. "Out the back!"

But at that moment, Bravo team, having carefully navigated the church's back hallways, burst through a door at the back of the pulpit stage. One agent knelt to fire while another fired over his shoulder.

Irritated, Johnny swatted the tranq darts away and sent the door swinging back into their faces. Ed was surprised to hear the lock click into place.

"That won't hold them for long," Johnny said. "Any suggestions?"

"The baptistery!"

As if reading his mind, Titan agents burst through the access doors on either side of the small baptismal pool. Perhaps inspired by the mural behind the baptistery depicting Moses crossing the Red Sea, Johnny chopped the air in front of him. It was as if a bomb went off in the baptistery. The water halved with tremendous force, smashing into Titan guards with the power of a tidal wave.

"Whoa! Now what?" Ed asked.

Both exits were now blocked. Through the holes in the stained glass windows, they could see that a good number of Titan agents waited for them outside. They were boxed in.

Johnny glanced at the pews in the choir loft, the only pews remaining in the church. Concentrating, he used his gift to rip the entire choir loft away from its moorings in one piece and sent it hurtling through the walls and stained glass.

Gage watched the battle with rapt interest. He'd often wondered what it would have been like to see his great-uncle Ness and folks like Trager in action. He had to admit it was a bit more terrifying than he'd imagined.

Thus far, he and everyone else outside had heard huge crashes and gunfire tearing up the place, but none one really had a good view of the actual fight.

Then suddenly, the entire side of the church exploded under the impact of a wooden wrecking ball the size of a bus. The projectile smashed into one of their black vans, caving in one side and sending it tumbling. The wrecking ball also swept a few unlucky agents along in its path. Gage picked himself off the ground, gasping from the near miss. He couldn't believe how fast it happened. If he'd been standing just a few feet to his left he'd be dead now.

The structural integrity of the building was now severely compromised. With the wall torn away on that side, the roof began to cave in. Hillary was understandably distracted by Johnny's escape attempt, especially with the ceiling coming down on him. Mike Trager took advantage of the moment to close the distance between them. Clapping down both hands on Hillary, he delivered an electric shock that zapped the younger man unconscious.

Johnny and Ed bolted through the huge hole the choir loft had made in the side of Soul's Harbor. Johnny leapt through with preternatural grace, carrying the older man along around the waist. Landing, he sprinted as fast as he could, trying to make it through the lot to the fenced backyards that bordered it.

It didn't take the Titan agents long to recover from their initial shock. Tranquilizer darts filled the air, cutting off their escape. Johnny rallied a brief counter attack, sending the tranq darts flying back at his opponents. As they scrambled for cover, an idea came to him.

"Where's your car?"

Ed pointed mutely to a small station wagon partially buried in debris from the rubble.

"Let's go!" Johnny shouted. At that moment, a tranq dart hit Ed in his still out-stretched forearm. He slumped into Johnny's arms, already losing consciousness. Still holding Ed up, the Indigo whirled around to punish the offending gunman. He mentally followed the projectile's flight path, preternaturally discovering the sniper on a nearby rooftop. Through his scope, the sniper saw Johnny look directly at him and grin cruelly. A moment later, the sniper found himself sailing through the air into the branches of a nearby tree.

John Lazarus ran to Ed's car, yanked open the passenger door and shoved the pastor inside. Opportunistic tranquilizer darts zipped in to take him down, but he deflected them with a mental wall of force. Jumping over the car, he opened the driver's side door and slipped behind the wheel.

He didn't have the keys. He glanced at Ed. The unconscious pastor wasn't going to be any help. There wasn't time to search him for the keys either, he decided. On a whim, he said a little prayer and put his finger to the ignition, willing the engine to life with a spark of bio-electric energy. Despite the situation, he laughed with relief as the car roared to life. He really hadn't expected it to work.

Seeing he was safe from their darts, the Titan goons switched to live fire. Johnny managed to back up and put the car into drive before they shot out his tires. Ignoring the sound of shredding rubber, he pressed the accelerator down hard, heading toward the alley behind Archer Lane. A cruiser blocked his exit.

Grinning savagely, he concentrated anew. Incredibly, the car left the ground, sailing over the cruiser. It took too much effort to keep the vehicle aloft, but he managed to clear the obstructing vehicle. Mostly. He did scrape the police car's light bar off.

Tearing down the alley as fast as the damaged car would allow, he nonetheless stole a glance at his old house in passing. So close. It would have to wait. He couldn't have half the town on his tail when he was searching the place. He wondered now if he'd ever get the chance.

17 – Duct Tape

"Curtis!"

Her father ignored her shriek of protest. Instead, he continued pressing the double barrel of a sawed off shotgun against the nape of Weasel's neck. "Don't move, don't blink, don't even think," he said.

Her father had never been the over-protective type. None of the friends she'd brought home had ever even caused him to raise an eyebrow. He loved her and there was always food on the table and money in the bank, but she got the feeling that they were more roommates than family. Live and let live, so long as she never complained about his near-continual pickled state. And where in blazes had he pulled that gun from?

"Sissy, I need you to go in the kitchen and get me the duct tape, and I need you to do it now." He was still slurring some of his speech. "I need you to trust me. Just do it."

"Curtis, this is crazy," she said. "Even for you!"

He ignored her, keeping his focus on the boy. He looked like he was sobering fast. "Now, why are the nice policemen after you, rock star?" he asked.

"You wouldn't believe me if I told you," Weasel said.

"Try me."

"Curtis, I'm warning you," Karma said.

"Sissy, kitchen!" His face was purple with anger. She'd never seen him like this. The assault had been swift and sudden. She couldn't believe how fast he had Weasel mashed against a wall with one arm pulled up behind him at a painful angle and a shotgun pressed firmly to his head.

She backed away instinctively.

He rounded on Weasel again. "Rock star, tell me!"

"They're not after him. They're after–" She looked at Weasel, faltering, not sure if she should betray his confidence.

Weasel sighed, closed his eyes and made a decision. "They're after Johnny," he said. "John Lazarus."

The pressure on the back of his neck eased for a moment as Curtis Holloway considered this new information. Yet just as Weasel was thinking it might be over, the pressure returned. "How do you know the Lazarus kid?"

"F-friends," Weasel said. "Look, I don't know anything."

"I bet you know more than you think, rock star," Curtis said. "Sissy, duct tape!"

"That's enough, Curtis!" she said. "Let him go!"

"Jackie, you shut that pie-hole of yours and do as yer told. Now!"

She shook her head. "I can't let you do this, Daddy."

He turned his head to look at her. "You don't understand what you're getting into, Sissy. You need to trust me on this one."

"No, Dad," she said, "you don't understand." She stretched out her hand, allowing electricity to crackle between her fingers.

She'd always wondered what his reaction might be if her dad ever found out what she could do. She'd expected fear, amazement, anger at being kept in the dark, or even drunken indifference. She never expected him to laugh.

"Sissy… Sissy, why do you think I'm wearing rubber boots?"

She looked down and, sure enough, he was wearing his ducks.

"You know what I can do? How long have you known?"

"All your life," he said. "Now, go get the duct tape."

"Can we do this without the duct tape?" Weasel asked. "I'm easy to get along with."

"I still can't let you do this," she told her father.

Curtis sighed. "Sissy, if he's with Johnny, he might know something about your mother."

She looked at Weasel suspiciously. "You know my mother?"

"Not the rock star," Curtis said. "The Lazarus boy."

"Please, don't do this," Weasel said.

She hesitated. Then she walked across the hardwood floor into the kitchen and opened a cabinet drawer.

18 – Mopping Up

"Zim, I need eyes," Trager said into his commset. "The primary target got away."

"Saw that," Daniel Zim said. "Tracking him on Argus."

A crowd of curious and alarmed people was growing just outside the police barricade. Trager looked up into the sky, hearing the chop of an approaching news helicopter. "Zim, I've got an audience. They need something to look at. Send in a fire truck and an ambulance. The official word is an explosion. We're still looking into the cause, but the police were investigating a tip on a possible meth lab."

Zim balked "In a church?"

"It explains the big, gaping hole in the church and gives us a reason to arrest Ed Blyth. We'll clear his name after we get a chance to interrogate him," Trager said. "We'll call it a gas leak."

His cell phone rang. He glanced at the caller ID. Charles Huxley. Trager groaned. Titan's director was the sort who only ever saw the storm cloud to every silver lining. The fact that they'd successfully nabbed the unknown Indigo wouldn't cut him any slack. He was sent in to retrieve all three targets. He'd failed to catch two of them, one being the primary and the other an unarmed civilian. Time to face the music. "I gotta take this, Zim. Keep an eye on Johnny. Make sure he doesn't leave town."

"You got it."

He answered the phone. "Trager."

"What happened?"

"The unknown was more adept than we anticipated. While I was busy with him, Johnny escaped with Blyth."

"Do tell? And where is he now?" Huxley asked.

"We have a lock on his car," Trager said. "I'll have him rounded up within the hour."

"John Lazarus is no longer your concern. Charlie team will handle things from here."

"What? You're taking me off the–"

"You will bring the unknown to Titan for interrogation immediately."

"I can do this!" Trager said. "You can't let Carter go after him. That's Arthur's kid." Carter Munroe wasn't about to give John Lazarus a fighting chance. This was an execution.

"I know that Carter and you have your differences, but he's a company man through and through. He has orders to take Johnny alive if he can."

"And if he can't?" Trager asked.

"You have *your* orders, Trager."

Putting his phone away, he stalked off to the surviving black van. He opened the back doors and peered inside. Three Titan agents looked back at him suspiciously. One of them already had his weapon up. They resumed their activities when they recognized him.

His prisoner was strapped down on a stretcher, an IV plugged into his arm. One of the agents had bandaged his injured foot. Unconscious, the kid was the picture of innocence. Pop culture references to Opie Taylor, the bewildered hero of Archie comics and half the cast of Happy Days made it difficult to take the young redhead seriously. He snorted at himself derisively for even considering the stereotype. The kid might not look like much, but he was a nasty fighter. With a little more training and experience, he'd be downright formidable.

"So who is he?" Gage asked as he walked up.

"Let's find out." He pressed a device no bigger than a television remote to the prisoner's fingers, scanning his prints, while another agent went through his personal effects.

Gage frowned at the scant items before the latter agent. "That all he had on him?"

"A wallet with small bills, a SuperBig Mart receipt and a prepaid phone card. No ID of any sort. He bought a candy bar at the SuperBig on Walnut Avenue not more than an hour ago," the agent said.

"What about his prints?" Gage asked Trager.

"Nothing so far. He's definitely not in Titan's database."

"Who do you think sent him?"

"I dunno. All we know is that he wasn't one of ours."

Gage looked at the ruined church and sighed. "That's a mess, that is."

Trager nodded, but his attention was really on his i84. His clearance level gave him access to far more information than most folks at Titan, which made the fact that he couldn't dredge up their prisoner's identity all the more disturbing. Who was this kid?

"I mean, why the church?"

"Maybe he has something against God."

"Maybe, but you think he would've picked one with, I dunno, a way out if things went south. I mean, look at this set up. He practically cornered himself. The street ends right here. There's no other way out except that alley. There's a million churches he could've picked if he wanted to make a statement."

"But only one on Archer Lane," Trager said, eyes widening in alarm.

"I don't get it. Why would he care whether the church was on Archer or not?"

"Because Archer is also my street. You were right. He was making a statement." Trager glanced at the other Titan agents. "Make sure we get some blood samples. We'll need a full DNA work up on this kid." He glanced at the Indigo one last time, recalling their explosive battle. "And make sure he stays sedated. Gage, walk with me."

As he stepped out of the back of the van, he spoke into his commset. "Zim!"

Daniel hissed through clenched teeth. "No need to yell. I can hear you just—"

"Sorry. Listen, I know we're all busy with this mess down here, but I've got a hunch. Has anyone else spiked in the last couple hours?"

"You mean like Pandora? We'd have been all over that, dude."

"No, she's too smart for that. I meant like anybody else."

"Oh." There a long minute of silence in which Mike Trager was treated to the sound of furious typing and incomprehensible muttering. "OK, the Holloway girl spiked a few times, but Brad Farley spiked right on top of her, so that's just their usual cat-and-mouse… Hold the phone. We did get a spike from an old friend, one we haven't heard from in a while: Ness."

Trager's heart skipped a beat as he thought on the implications. Ness, a veritable hermit now, had renounced his powers and moved up into an old cabin in the woods. All because of Pandora. He glanced at Gage and decided not to mention his great-uncle by name. "He spike at his place?"

"Yes, but–"

"I'm on my way."

"But you can't!" Zim said. "You have to bring the prisoner in for interrogation. I can send out a team to–"

Trager turned to Gage. "I need a favor."

"Sure, what?"

"I need you to escort our prisoner to Titan for me. Don't let him out of your sight. Make sure he's secured until I get there. Go now."

"I'm on it," Gage said, turning smartly on his heels.

"Problem solved," Trager said as he watched Gage board the Titan van.

"You're probably overreacting, you know," Zim said.

"Except Ness vowed never to use his powers again. Now when did he spike?" He began walking towards his Hummer.

"I'll have to advise the Director."

"Do that. Do it immediately," Trager said, hopping into his Hum-V. "I'm going. I owe him that. Just pray I'm not too late to save him."

"Fine, have it your way," Zim said. "Oh, by the way, we got a lead on the mystery passenger Johnny rode into town with. His face showed up on a SuperBig Mart store surveillance camera. I'm sending it to your i84."

Trager glanced at the image Daniel sent him, sizing up the long-haired rock star wannabe. The kid didn't match the description of anyone in their Indigo database. In fact, this Hopkins kid was listed as a runaway delinquent from Tennessee. Given today's events he couldn't rule out the possibility that he was dealing with a rival company's science project, but it didn't seem likely. What was this stranger's story? How did he fit into the big picture?

"Think it's another rogue Indigo?" Zim asked.

"My gut says no," Trager said, "but he may have information we can use. Give his image and description to the local police and tell them to bring him in for questioning. Once they nab him, send out a team to fetch him."

19 – Bad Karma

"I'm sorry," Karma said again.

"Sorry? You're sorry? Oh, I think we're well beyond sorry here. Sorry is I accidentally stepped on your foot. Sorry is I was late picking you up from school but I'll make it up to you." His expression turned dark. "You let your redneck daddy duct tape me to a chair!" He roared, struggling against his bonds.

Curtis snickered. "Relax, rock star. You cain't beat the duct tape."

"You suck," Weasel said. He looked past Curtis to Karma. "You both suck."

"Boy, you wanna leave with your teeth?" Curtis asked. "Cause it's all the same to me."

Weasel glared at him.

"Now that's more like it," Curtis said. "Let's get down to business. Why is John Lazarus back in town?"

Weasel shrugged.

Curtis whipped up the sawed-off shotgun, unamused.

Weasel swallowed. "We were going to sneak into his old house tonight, the one that's condemned."

"Why were you breaking into the Lazarus house tonight?" Curtis asked.

"He needed to get something. Something he left behind. I don't actually know. He wasn't all that specific."

"And you were still going with him?" He glanced at Karma. "Sissy, where do you dig up these strays?"

She shot him a warning look.

"Is there a point to all this?" Weasel asked.

Curtis ignored his bluster. "Where is Johnny now?"

"I don't know. I'd probably follow the sirens if I were you."

The shot gun pressed against his neck, urging him to be a bit more serious.

He obliged. "We got separated. He sent me into a store to get some stuff and when I came back out he was gone."

"Stuff?"

"Doesn't matter. A couple of much younger rednecks mugged me and took everything I had."

"Brad Farley and his ladies," Karma said. "Pretty much got his butt handed to him."

Weasel shot her a betrayed look.

Curtis laughed. And laughed. Every time he looked at Weasel, he started laughing again.

"I'm glad my misery causes you such amusement," he said. "Could someone let me up now, so I can leave this twisted redneck town before anything else happens to me?"

"No." Curtis forced himself back to a more sober frame of mind. "A few more questions."

"Make it quick, Curtis." Karma was already fishing around the kitchen drawers for a pair of scissors to remove Weasel's bonds.

"Have you ever heard the name Hope Holloway or Hope Darling before?"

"Sorry. Never."

Weasel noted that he was visibly upset not to have struck gold with this question.

"You're sure?" Karma asked.

"I'm sure, and I feel the need to point out that duct tape was not needed for that question."

"It would have been if the answer had been yes," Curtis said. "How long have you and Johnny been planning this break-in of yours?"

"Plan? What plan? He just drove us here in the middle of the night while I was asleep and told me when I woke up. Like out of the blue," he said. "But every time he talked about this place, he swore he'd never come back. And now I have a pretty good idea why he might feel that way." He struggled furiously against the duct tape again to make his point.

"What changed his mind?" Curtis asked, almost to himself. "Where were you last night, before he drove you here?"

Weasel shrugged. "Some small town carnival. We thought it might be fun to blow off some steam. You know, Ferris wheel, puke-a-whirl, a midway chock full of harmless scams for the occasional cheap plush toy. I'm telling you, the blasted pizza vendor was using ketchup for sauce. And they had this clown sitting over this dunk tank, the most annoying clown–"

Curtis nudged him roughly with the barrel of the shotgun. "I've been to a carnival before, rock star. I need to know if Johnny met up with anybody there. Maybe a woman?"

"Not unless you count the fortune teller. Madame Pandora Pandemonium. He always checks out the freaks and frauds and hucksters. That's his thing. We've scoped out everything from faith healers with neon crosses and star-shaped pulpits to guys who claim to be able to bend spoons and stop watches with their minds. I think now he was trying to find other people like himself. People with powers." He looked pointedly at Karma. "People like you."

"Would you recognize this fortune teller if you saw her again?"

"Yeah, sure."

The nervous excitement in Curtis' voice was unmistakable. "Sissy, go get the picture off the mantle. You know the one."

She dropped the scissors on the kitchen table and ran off to fetch the photo, eyes wide. She returned shortly, holding the picture almost reverently. He couldn't help but notice that the woman in the picture looked a lot like Karma. Weasel wasn't completely dense. He figured the woman in the photo had to be her mother. "The hair's a different color," he said, "but yeah that's her."

Karma and her father shouted in unison. "It's her!" They fell into each other's arms, hopping up and down with joy.

"Wait!" Karma said. "That carnival could be long gone by now. What town was it in?"

Weasel didn't answer immediately. Instead, he cleared his throat meaningfully and glared at the duct tape and then her.

"Oh! Right," she said. "The scissors."

"Wait," Curtis said.

"You've got to be kidding me!" Weasel said.

"Were you in the tent with Johnny the whole time?"

"Well, no." He glanced at Karma uncomfortably. "I left about halfway through actually."

"Why?"

"Um, how do I put this? This fortune teller had a very lovely apprentice and, um, she wanted to make sure she was getting the love potions just right, if you know what I mean."

Given his present situation, the look on Karma's face was priceless.

Curtis snorted. "Start cutting him out, Sissy. Lover boy's got places to go and people to see."

"W-where are we going?" Weasel asked.

Curtis shouldered the shotgun and walked out of the kitchen. "I'm low on ammo."

"Why does he need more ammo?" Weasel asked.

"I'm not sure," she said. A worried frown creased her brow. She ran after him. "Curtis!"

Weasel sighed, staring at the scissors on the table. They were quite out of reach, of course.

20 – Ness

It was magic hour, that moment between day and night where the sun flamed one last goodbye. It wasn't just the sunset. It was a mixture of blinding golden light and deep shadow that made it hard to make out details. It was much easier to see in either straight night or daylight.

And all Trager had were his eyes. He didn't even bother trying to bring up the embedded cameras in this area on his i84. Over the years, Ness had dutifully dismantled every camera Titan placed anywhere near his cabin and threatened to shoot anyone who tried to replace them. Given the fact that Ness never missed anything he was aiming at, Titan let him have his privacy.

In these deep contrasts, the log cabin with its picturesque trail of chimney smoke looked like something out of a child's storybook. But if you read your Grimm Brothers properly, the magical cottage in the woods was just as likely to hold robbers, monsters or witches as some temporarily disenfranchised princess. He was tempted to wait for better light, but something in his gut told him time was of the essence.

About fifty yards out from the cabin, a bullet whizzed by his ear. A warning shot. Ness never missed unless it was on purpose, a trait that had earned him the occasional nickname, Quatermain.

"That was your last warning! Go away!"

"Is that any way to treat an old friend?" Trager asked. He stepped out into the open, held both his hands skyward and purposely dropped his gun in plain sight of the cabin. Best to let Ness see his good intentions.

"Trager? Don't you have a ballgame to attend to?"

"Something came up."

"Why are you here, Mike?" Ness asked. "Titan send you?"

"Nobody sent me. I came up here on a hunch. Zim says you spiked."

"Never should've let 'em put that idiot thing in my head. OK, I spiked!"

Ness said. "Tell him I was out hunting and I cheated a bit 'cause I was too hungry to miss."

"Is that what happened?"

"What do you think?"

"I think you were never very good at lying," Trager said.

"Yeah, but you were, so go tell him what I said."

"OK, but before I do I need to know something, Ness. Did she come here?" Trager asked. There was no need to speak Pandora's name.

The cabin was silent for a while.

"Ness?"

"Yeah. She came. But I wouldn't let her in."

"Are you OK?"

"OK? Are you out of your mind, Mikey? She's back! And you know what that means."

"I don't know anything yet. And neither do you."

"Don't be a fool, Mikey," Ness said. "She's not who you think she is. She never was. I know you had feelings for her –"

"So did you," Mike Trager said. "She was like a daughter to you."

"– but if you see her, take my advice, and put a bullet in her head."

Trager could see this was going nowhere, but he threw out a shot in the dark. "She's not the only one who's come back, Ness. Arthur's boy rolled into town this morning."

"Little Johnny?"

"The same."

Ness was quiet for a moment. The silence was broken by a dry laugh. "Can't be a coincidence, her and Johnny coming on the same day. She wants to burn Titan to the ground, Mike," he said, "and she wanted to use me to do it. Maybe Johnny's come home to help her."

"Did you let her in?" Trager asked. Ness sounded a bit unhinged. Had she gotten to him? Was he already under her spell?

"No, she didn't get in, but she won't give up either. She'll be back. Or she'll send someone else to do it. Either way, she'll be back for her Ness."

"I have to get back to Titan," Mike said. If Pandora managed to destroy

Titan, no one would be safe.

"Don't try to reason with her," Ness said. "Hope is gone! Remember that!"

Trager was already running back down the drive, heading toward his Hummer.

21 – Gifted

Johnny glared into the forest, furious at his inability to change his fate. Ever since he'd left Soul's Harbor, he'd been fleeing premonition after deadly premonition. It seemed that any way he turned led to his death. It wasn't until he reached this spot overlooking Midwich that he realized the death flashes weren't connected with which direction he was fleeing in, but rather the very fact that he was fleeing. The very thing that had drawn him to Midwich was now preventing him from running away.

Ed Blyth was draped over the hood of the car beside him. The tranquilizer dart's effects should be wearing off anytime now. Johnny decided he couldn't wait any longer for the answers he needed. He delivered a mild bioelectric shock to the preacher and Ed gasped back into the realm of consciousness.

"Am I dead?"

"Not yet."

Ed sat up with a groan. "What did I miss?"

"Not much. Titan's still out there somewhere. They won't give up."

"So what now?"

"We need to talk. I met a faith healer named JC Darling while I was away." He watched Ed's face intently to see how he'd react. "Said you'd told him that if he found anybody out there with special abilities like mine that he should give them your calling card."

"And you recognized my name, remembered that I was the preacher of the church at the end of your street and what? Assumed I was part of Titan? That it?"

"Something like that."

"Honestly, I never expected that fishing expedition to pay off. God works in mysterious ways. His real name is Silas Darling. The whole JC thing – well, Joel Christopher gives him the same initials as Jesus Christ. I went to one of his meetings once upon a time. I think I had the zealous notion that I was gonna expose him for the fraud he was."

"Did he have the star-shaped pulpit back then?" Johnny asked.

"You know, he did. And a big, gaudy neon cross. I thought, *This guy's as fake as a four dollar bill. Why can't these people see it?* It was like he had them hypnotized or something."

"He did," Johnny said.

"You figured that out, did you?"

"It wasn't hard. He had this habit of looking deep into someone's eyes right before he 'healed' them."

"A lot of JC's healings had a tendency of reversing themselves."

"Yes, but some didn't. What about those, rev? I know he tricked some of them, but did he actually heal the others?"

"Well, technically, God healed them. Humans can't–"

"Have you been paying attention at all? Haven't you seen what I can do?"

Ed threw his hands up in surrender. "Now hold a minute. I just wanted to give you some perspective. I have been paying attention but, to be fair, what you're asking me to tell you is whether God happened to heal those folks despite that fake or whether Darling healed those folks by some power of his own, right?"

"Sort of. More like, is there some natural principle or force that has the power to heal if applied correctly? Like the power of suggestion or conviction or faith, but something that could be misused or used to one's own ends as easily as any other force." Noting the suspicion creeping across the pastor's face, he added, "Look, there are bad guys out there with abilities very much like mine. I need to know how this works."

"OK, for starters, let's keep in mind that not all of Darling's healings were permanent. To me, that suggests that Darling's power is limited somehow, dependent upon something else. That something could be the will of God."

"Or their level of credulity."

"Touché," the preacher said. "Of course, if that was the case, his power to heal would be dependent upon the faith of the person wanting healed. The hypnosis would serve to reinforce the buy-in required to begin the healing process, but if they didn't really believe or their faith wasn't potent enough, the cure would crumble after the hypnosis wore off. That said, I still believe it has more to do with the sovereign will of God."

"Really? Then how do you explain me and what I can do?" Johnny asked.

"I can't. Not yet. I would've said it was impossible at one time. I must be a poor student of history. Did you know there were men who railed from our country's pulpits that God would never allow a man to set foot on the moon because He'd judged them at Babel for trying to reach the heavens?"

"Babel? Seriously? Do you really think this is the time for Bible stories?"

"Maybe you'd prefer a comic book? Look, I know what you're thinking. You're wondering, Am I the next stage in human evolution?"

"What if I am?"

"So now you think you're what? More evolved than the rest of us? That it?" the preacher asked. "Johnny, you're still human, for crying out loud. I doubt you even qualify as a new species."

"So how would you explain somebody like me? How do you explain the things I'm able to do?"

"Kid, you might be able to do things we've only read about in myths and the lives of saints, but you're every bit as human as I am. In fact, that may be our first clue to this puzzle. The entire world has stories about people with unnatural abilities, just like we have a shared cross-cultural heritage of dragon legends, angelic beings, a world-wide flood and an event which confused the languages. We've always relegated these tales of amazing abilities to the realm of the occult, the supernatural or to primitive pre-scientific superstition. What if there were more to it?"

"I'm listening."

"Human beings only use the tiniest fraction of our brains. More correctly, I should say we only currently use the tiniest fraction. What if we once had the potential for much more? There's a lot of evidence for the early brilliance of man. Some things they did defy conventional explanation. Like how did they build the pyramids? What if the great stones of the pyramids and Stonehenge were moved with our minds? What if God instilled so much more in Adam and Eve than we presently manifest?"

"Problem. Where'd it all go?"

"Well, to be fair, according to our theory, it hasn't gone anywhere. Not completely. There have been manifestations in the recorded past, but it's more rare now, recessive," the preacher said. "Only eight people survived Noah's worldwide Flood and the Bible records that lifespans were dramatically shortened afterwards. Maybe there's something in that, the bottleneck effect, a sudden lack in the gene pool. Maybe there were other effects besides. Whatever occurred, it became infrequent. Maybe whenever it popped up, God in His sovereignty chose these gifted persons, like Moses perhaps or Sampson, to do His will."

"And witchcraft? Sorcery?"

"Yes, we mustn't forget that Pharaoh's magicians were able to duplicate the first few miracles and plagues which preceded the Exodus," Ed said. "Man has free will. People with great abilities and intelligence do evil everywhere you look. My guess is that witchcraft is just using the gift on the other face of the coin."

"So it's not the power of the devil?"

"I haven't got everything worked out. I just started on this. I can tell you that Satan is a separate entity with his own powers. I think demonic possession is a whole other issue, a possible complication which should only be pondered once we actually understand how these powers work."

Johnny didn't respond immediately. He thought he saw movement along the tree line back down the road they'd come. He trained his vision on the area. Just a raccoon.

22 – And Busybody Boggess Saw the Whole Thing

The moment he was free of the duct tape, Weasel Hopkins stormed out of the Holloway house and through the gate, the very picture of indignation. He could not believe the level of trouble he'd managed to land in on his very first – and if he had his way, his very last – day in this abominable freak town. Super powers and rednecks, back alley bullies and duct tape dispensing drunks. It was like he was in an episode of the *Twilight Zone* or the *Outer Limits*. Where in blazes was the remote? This channel sucked!

"Weasel!" Karma burst onto the porch, nearly in tears. "I said I was sorry!"

He whirled around to face her from the other side of her picket fence. "Sorry just doesn't cover it. We're well beyond sorry here."

"What do you want from me?"

"In a word: nothing. Just leave me alone. Forever. But, you know, thanks for the hospitality. I'll never forget you, but I will definitely try." He spun on his heel and walked away.

"Weasel!"

Weasel didn't respond. Nor did he look back when he heard Curtis say, "Get in the truck, Sissy. We have to hurry." His only thought was to put as much distance between himself and them as quickly as his feet could manage.

Unfortunately, he was so mad he didn't really pay attention to which direction he was huffing off in. It wasn't until he was passing by the condemned house that he realized that he needed to go the other way in order to escape Archer Lane.

He paused in front of the Lazarus house, glaring at it accusingly. What was it about this old dump? What was Johnny after? Was it even worth it?

He took a step toward the house on impulse, thinking he'd just go on in and find out. The dread weight of the house towered over him. It was Halloween night and, frankly, the abandoned house looked haunted. No such thing as ghosts, he reminded himself. No such thing as super powers, either. He stopped, glared up at the house, tried to figure out what he was doing there.

He and Johnny had done a little ghost busting in the past. In fact, they'd done a lot of weird stuff. Johnny was obsessed with mentalists, poltergeists, spiritualists, fortune tellers, prophets, magicians, faith healers, cryptozoology and crazy stuff like that. That old beat up Plymouth was like their own personal *Mystery Machine*. He only wished they'd picked up a Daphne or Velma along the way to keep them company. When Johnny wasn't talking, which was most of the time, it got pretty lonely sometimes. But it was never dull.

Something caught Weasel's eye, abruptly ending his trip down memory lane. Someone was staring at him from one of the second story windows. He back-pedaled, startled by the dark phantom. He looked back up, expecting it to be gone. Instead, the shadow remained there, staring at him calmly, then slowly turned away and walked out of view.

That decided it. No way was he going in that creepy old place, Scooby-Doo. Oh, he knew it wasn't a ghost, but with the exception of someone in an old William Shatner mask hoping to re-enact their favorite slasher flick, he couldn't imagine who would be lurking inside a condemned house on Halloween night.

As he turned to retreat, several people were returning from watching whatever was going on at the end of the street. Weasel's attention was drawn to a rather animated elderly fellow.

"I'm telling you, I know what I saw."

The equally elderly couple who'd been entertaining his notions were smiling politely, but nonetheless saying their goodbyes. Whatever he'd seen, they didn't appear to believe a word of it.

"Herb, you know me," the animated oldster said. "I've lived down the street from you for half your life. I'm not one to make up stories."

"Mr. Boggess," Herb's wife said, "I know what you think you saw, but there must be a logical explanation. People can't throw things around with their minds. It's..." She threw up her hands in defeat. "It's just impossible!"

"Now Susie, calm down," Herb said. "I'm sure he's just ribbing us. Aren't you, Cecil?"

"But I saw it," Cecil Boggess insisted. "Saw it with my own eyes!"

"A flying car and a bullet-proof boy? Just like you've been seeing black helicopters and UFOs for years, right?" Herb asked. "Seriously, Cecil, do you hear yourself?"

Herb muttered something to his wife that Weasel couldn't quite make out, but he distinctly heard the word, "medication." The implication was clear.

Cecil looked around helplessly, trying to find an advocate. "That bulletproof boy was little Johnny Lazarus. I'd recognize him anywhere."

"Honestly, Mr. Boggess! Now you're going too far." Susie turned to her husband for support. "Herbie."

"Cecil, that's enough," her husband said. He glanced at the condemned house. "The whole Lazarus family is dead, all of 'em. You know that. I'd say your little joke's gone far enough."

Weasel decided to intervene. "Hey, did you say you saw John Lazarus?" he asked. "Because I've been looking all over town for him."

Herb peered at Weasel, eyes narrowing. "Are you saying you know Johnny?"

"We rolled into town this morning, but we got separated," Weasel said. "What's going on?"

"That's what I'd like to know," Boggess said. "I nearly can't believe it myself. I saw this kid running past my porch faster I've ever seen anybody run before!" His eyes were alight. "Anyway, he's carrying somebody and, well, you don't see that every day, so I looked at who it might be and I nearly fell off the porch! It was Johnny he was carrying! Did you know he was supposed to be dead?" he asked.

"He mentioned that. Did you say someone was physically carrying Johnny?"

"They never did recover his body, which makes sense if you think about it," Cecil said. He appeared not to have heard Weasel's question.

This was too much for Susie. "Oh, really! Can we go, Herbie?"

"Certainly, dear." Herb glared at the other two for upsetting his wife. They stormed off without another word.

"Was Johnny hurt? Did you see where he went?" Weasel asked.

"They went inside the church at the end of the street," Cecil said. "After that, a swat team came blazing in and all Cain broke loose!" He whipped out a handkerchief and mopped his brow. "Kid, I don't know how well you know Johnny Lazarus, but I've just seen things I ain't never seen before. Flying cars! People moving stuff with their minds! Land's sake, I saw Johnny just wave off a bunch a bullets like he was shooing flies. Saw him pick a guy off a building 50 yards away and toss him into a tree just by looking at him."

Weasel didn't know how to respond to that. It was certainly more than skipping big rocks across the river.

Suddenly, Cecil seemed to realize that he had no idea who the boy standing in front of him was. "How was it you say you know Johnny?"

"He's a friend of mine. Met him a couple years ago."

"That'd be after the fire. Everybody thought he was dead. Well, I reckon they've lost him for good this time."

"Why's that?"

"Because I saw him take off in that preacher's car and fly away!" Cecil said. "An' I don't just mean he went real fast either. I mean his tires left the ground and he sailed off into the clouds! He's probably halfway to Saturn by now."

"That figures," Weasel said. "What's the quickest way out of this town?"

"Depends. Which way you headed?"

An official-sounding voice interrupted them. "Excuse me, young man. I'll need you to come downtown with me. You're wanted for questioning."

Weasel ran. The cop gave chase.

Weasel leaped over the Lazarus house's picket fence in one adrenaline-charged bound and ran for the side of the house. He hoped to cross the backyard into the alley and lose the cop somehow. The officer was a lot faster than he anticipated. He tackled Weasel in the backyard, knocking him to the ground.

"Let me go!" Weasel said. "I didn't do anything."

"Then why'd you run?" the cop asked, snapping metal cuffs onto Weasel's wrists. The officer jerked him to his feet.

Weasel fought to get away. Then he glanced at the house and saw the Shadow Man staring at him from the kitchen window. Weasel stopped struggling instantly. "You know what, I'm sorry," he said. "You have every right to question me. I'll cooperate, just so long as we leave *right now*."

"What's got you spooked?" the officer asked. He scanned the perimeter, but saw nothing out of the ordinary.

"Just get me out of here," Weasel said.

Moments later, he watched the world go by from the back of a police cruiser, wondering what he'd ever done to deserve this day. It was like a bad horror movie. Speaking of which, he reminded himself, he didn't dare breathe a word of truth to the authorities. Cops never believed you in the movies anyway. Not until it was too late.

As the car passed Karma's house, he looked for her involuntarily. She and her father were still in the driveway, apparently in the middle of a heated argument. They were both shouting at each other, but neither seemed to be listening to the other. Their argument ceased in mid-word as they gaped dumbfounded at the brave young man they'd so recently traumatized.

He seriously doubted he would ever buy or use duct tape again.

23 – Roy

He thundered into town on a motorcycle decked out in chrome and midnight. His file stated that his name was Roy McClane, but everyone called him the Anarchist. Roy just didn't have the same ring to it. Didn't fit his image.

He pulled into a gas station at the edge of town. Still seated, he reached over for the nozzle, having no intention of paying for the gas he was about to pump. The pump wouldn't turn on. He pressed the button. He pressed it harder. He pressed it a bunch of times in rapid succession. He glowered at the infernal machine, wondering if it was broken. Then he saw the sign, a big sticker with bold red letters that he'd somehow overlooked amongst all of the other drivel they printed on the gas pump: "Credit Card or Prepay Only." The Anarchist snarled at the offending sign, hopped off his bike and stalked into the store.

"Gas." The words came out in a low growl.

He startled the attendant, who'd been busy finishing up his dreaded and tedious cigarette count. He gaped stupidly, not yet comprehending the threat inherent in the ogre's very presence. He was too impressed with the spectacle before him to be afraid. Black leather jacket with an alien skull and crossed lightning bolts emblazoned on the back. Shaved head with an upside-down bullet-ridden American flag tattooed across the rear of this skull. Amish beard. No mustache. Steel-toed boots. Torn, faded blue jeans with holes patched together artfully with safety pins. A standard-issue black death metal T-shirt.

"You snuck up on me there," the attendant said. "Didn't see you come in. What can I do you for?"

"Gas."

"Right. How much?"

"Turn on the pumps."

"Um, I don't know where you're from there Easy Rider, but I cain't do that unless you pay first. Sorry, but that there's the way it works, pal."

"Turn. On. The. Pumps."

The attendant stood up a little taller. "Sir, I'm gonna have to ask you to pre-pay or I'm gonna have to call the—"

"NOW!!"

The hapless attendant was hurled backward by a blast of sound. All of his carefully counted cigarette packs flew in every direction. He himself slammed into the wall and slumped unconscious to the floor.

Turning toward the shelves and the glass cooler doors, the biker roared anew in wordless fury, blasting everything in sight. Quarts of oil, canned soup, soda bottles, bags of potato chips, candy bars and pretty much everything else flew through the store's front glass. His sonic rage shattered the coolers and anything made of glass. In fact, it destroyed nearly everything. When it was over, the store was lit by a solitary fluorescent bulb. Beer, liquor and orange juice, all once bottled in glass, swirled together and soaked the floor.

Roy McClane walked behind the counter, giving his unconscious victim a withering cursory glance, and turned on the pumps. All of them. He grabbed a liquor bottle that had somehow escaped the carnage off the shelf. He took a swig on his way back to his bike.

After he'd filled his tank, he locked all of the gas pump triggers into the ON position. They lay on the lot, writhing slowly, spewing amber fuel all over the place. Inevitably, he stuffed a rag into the neck of the liquor bottle and fired up his homemade Molotov cocktail with a butane lighter. Howling his pleasure, he tossed it over his shoulder as he roared off the lot on his bike.

The station went up in an orange ball of flame.

24 – Frequency

"Don't you think we ought to be looking for a more scientific answer?" Johnny asked.

"You're suggesting evolution again? Look, I don't want to argue about this right now. I doubt we have time. I don't buy evolution for a lot of very good reasons," the preacher said.

"You used to. My dad stopped going to your church for a while because you said that God could have used evolution and that the days of the Creation Week were really long ages."

"Well, yes, I did believe that, but I don't anymore. I believed those things were true because that's what I was taught in seminary by professors I respected and trusted… but it's simply not what the Bible teaches. But what about you?" Ed asked. "Last I heard from your father, you had rejected God, the Bible and religion in general because you couldn't reconcile science and history with Genesis."

"Well, I only believed the Bible because my parents told me to. If I had grown up in a Muslim country, I'd be a Muslim."

Ed scoffed. "Who told you that, Johnny? How does that even make sense? You grew up to reject the Bible despite your upbringing, and I know of lots of people in other countries who grew up in different faiths but are now Christians, even though it costs them dearly."

"Well, the point is I learned to think for myself."

"Did you? Or did you come to parrot someone else's views instead?"

"Look, even if God created man in His own image, well, Titan created freaks like me," Johnny said. "What's your Bible say about that, preacher?

"I have no idea what they did to you to make you like this. I don't work for Titan, no matter what you think. My gut tells me they just tinkered with something that was always potentially there, something they don't yet fully understand. I'm telling you, the kind of questions they were asking me when I consulted for them suggested that they were willing to consider anything and everything."

Johnny growled in frustration. Talking this thing to death wasn't getting him anywhere. "I have to go to Titan."

"As your current pastor I feel compelled to remind you that what you're considering is potentially suicide. Have you lost your mind?"

"I need more information."

"Why did you really come back, Johnny?" Ed asked.

"I can't tell you."

"Can't or won't?"

Johnny started to tell him about the premonitions right then and there, but something stopped him: namely, another death flash, a warning that telling Blyth about these warnings could prove fatal. Though he was beginning to realize that these "warnings" could simply be hypnotic suggestions to bring him to Midwich and keep him here, he wasn't quite brave enough to test that particular theory without being more certain. After all, if he was wrong, he'd be very, very dead. Conceivably, the hypnotist could have added a safeguard against telling anyone about the premonitions – in the form of another death flash, of course. So instead, Johnny related a secondary reason for why he came to Midwich. "What if I told you that someone tried to hypnotize me?"

"Brother Joel?" Ed asked.

"No. Someone else. Someone who tried to give me the suggestion to return to Titan and then burn the whole operation to the ground."

Ed gasped. "Someone sent you here as a weapon?"

"She knew a lot about me. She fed on my pain and suggested that I get revenge. That I wipe out the whole stinking town, every man, women and child. Especially Titan."

"Did it work?"

"No, but I let her think it did. I thought it might give me time to come up with a plan to stop her. Her assistant had my friend alone at the time. I was pretty sure if she thought I wasn't under her control or tried to stop her right there that she would've killed him."

"That still doesn't answer why you came back," Ed said.

Johnny nodded. "There's more. I don't think I'm the only one she's sent. It was just a hunch before, but then I ran into Hillary. There may be others."

"Hillary?"

"My kidnapper. He was wearing a Hillary Clinton mask when we first met."

"Oh, him. Why *did* he bring you to my church?" Ed asked. "If she thinks you're under her control… Unless she knows better!"

"That occurred to me as well," Johnny said. "The worst part is that I don't really know anything about this woman, except her intentions. She was just some fortune teller I met at a carnival last night. Madame Pandora Pandemonium."

Ed blinked. "Pandora, you say?"

"Yes. Why?"

"That Malak fellow I've been communicating with mentioned Pandora in his first email, one that also mentioned you, Titan and the Prometheus Initiative."

"What exactly did it say?" Johnny asked.

Ed quoted the email from memory. "Pandora's Box has opened and Hope has flown. Prometheus brings forbidden fire. Titan must be stopped. It is the will of the gods. Lazarus is alive. Seek the survivor of Prometheus' flame."

Johnny frowned, pondering the message. He made the connection between himself and the fire instantly. Who besides Titan knew that he'd survived it?

"I think there's a good bet that this carnival fortune teller and the Pandora that Malak mentions are one and the same," Ed said.

"You're probably right." Johnny scanned the perimeter. It was getting dark now. He shouldn't have stayed in one spot for so long, but he didn't really have a plan. He had to get his head together before he was caught for sure. "I need to try something, so I need you to watch my back."

"What are you gonna do?"

Johnny didn't answer. He was concentrating, blocking out every sensation except sound, narrowing his focus until all that remained were radio waves. They overlapped one another a bit and it took more concentration to sort them all out, especially since he was still intently ignoring more mundane noises, but he learned what he needed to know.

Titan was closing the net on him. "Snipers are almost in position."

Trager suspected an impending attack on Titan itself. "Pandora has returned. Lock everything down until I arrive."

He also heard something else, quite by mistake. "Hold the Hopkins boy until we can pick him up. Your officers are not to interrogate him. We'll see to that. As always, we appreciate your cooperation, Chief Whitcomb."

A sharp, involuntary intake of breath broke his concentration. "Weasel!"

"Huh?" Ed asked.

"We're surrounded, Titan's preparing itself for a siege and my best friend's in jail!" he said.

"What? How do you know?"

"I listened in on the radio frequencies."

"You listened in on th– Of course you did."

"I heard someone say they're coming to pick him up. The voice was electronically distorted, but I think we have to assume it was Pandora."

"What would they want with your friend? Does he have powers too?"

"No, but they could use him as leverage."

"Coercion," the preacher said. "There are other ways to get people to do your bidding besides hypnos– Did you say we're surrounded?"

Johnny didn't answer at first. He'd filtered out everything but the infrared spectrum in his vision and was busy scanning the surrounding woods. The snipers were in place, awaiting the order to open fire. "Get ready and stay down."

"They're here?"

Johnny nodded, already concentrating on the impending skirmish.

25 – Pandora

Destiny Pascalé hung up her Bluetooth device, then turned to her boss expectantly.

"So everything is in place?" Pandora asked.

"So far as we can know," Destiny said. Her boss seemed to have expectations of her gift that went well beyond what she could actually do. She wasn't a prophetess. And despite her codename, she wasn't much of an Oracle. There were too many variables for her to determine the future with absolute certainty. That would require omniscience.

"Meaning?"

"We still don't know if or when Jack's coming." Jack's gift defied technology, whether he wanted it to or not. They couldn't call him or even radio him. He was a walking dead zone. He could minimize the effect for short periods of time so that his field of disruption was only a few feet from his body, but the bottom line was that mobile communications were simply not an option. You couldn't even email the guy. He erased the hard drive on every computer he got near. Frankly, it must be frustrating, she supposed, to be so cut off from the Information Age. From human contact really, since anyone who got too near him passed out. "And you know how I feel about Roy."

"Jack will come," Pandora said. "Don't worry about that."

"How can you be so sure?"

She shrugged. "Because I asked him to. As for the Anarchist–"

"We shouldn't have brought him along. He's unpredictable." She meant the Anarchist, but she glanced involuntarily at the car's other occupant. He gave her the creeps.

"It was unavoidable," Pandora said. "Once he found out, we couldn't leave him behind. He would've come anyway. So let him have his fun. At least, this way you can factor him into your calculations. We proceed as planned." She peered out the window as they pulled into the back lot of the local television station. "It's time to recruit my army."

Destiny hurried to follow her as she exited the vehicle. The car's other occupant, a silent, stoic fellow, exited more deliberately.

Someone stumbled out the back door just as they reached it. The old fellow seemed completely shocked to see people waiting for him out back. He attempted to flee back inside, but he bumped the door shut by mistake. He tried the knob but it was locked.

"Stop," Pandora said.

He covered his face with his hands. "Wait! I'll get your money!"

The women glanced at each other. "I don't think we're who you think we are," Destiny said.

He uncovered his face. "Oh. Sorry about that. I thought you were... Well, nevermind that. I just came out for a bit of fresh air." He drew a cigarette from a pack at his breast pocket. Putting it in his mouth, he patted his other pockets absently. "Hang it all! Left it inside with my jacket. I don't suppose you ladies could give me a light?" he asked.

Pandora laughed, then turned to their silent, stoic companion. "Give the man a light," she said.

Her henchman held out his hand and caused a small blue flame to glow upon his palm.

"What in blazes?" The old fellow's cigarette fell from his lips. "How is he doing that?"

"That's not nearly as interesting as what he can do with it." Pandora signaled almost imperceptibly to the pyrokinetic. At her command, he caused the flame to violently jet into a yard high spurt.

The old fellow fell back in alarm. "What do you want?"

"You're going to let us inside. Give me your security card," Pandora said.

"You will do it," Destiny informed him with a sad look of resignation. "You don't really have a choice."

He kept his wide eyes on the pyro as he fished in his back pocket furiously, pulled out his wallet and tried to get the card. He couldn't seem to get the ID out with his fumbling fingers. Finally, he threw the wallet down in terror and ran with everything he had. "Just take it!"

The pyro sent twin jets of flame at his burly backside to speed him on his way.

Destiny considered the human flamethrower for a moment. Pandora hadn't ordered that final flourish. "Are you sure this thing is fully under your control?"

Pandora reached down and slipped the ID card out of the old man's wallet. "I control them, but they carry out my orders according to their... natural dispositions." She handed the ID card to Destiny. "Inform the others that Phase Two is about to begin. And tell Mr. Ridenour to meet us at Titan."

26 – Be Careful Little Eyes

Trager stared down at the unsuspecting town, courtesy of a bank of video monitors in Titan's control room. Daniel Zim was currently preoccupied with Carter Munroe's impending encounter with John Lazarus, but he'd put the city's camera feeds up on the main screens just in case anything else happened.

Trager only listened to the squawk absently. He should be paying a lot more attention, but all he could think of was Pandora. He'd known her first as Hope Darling. Hope, Ness, Cougar, Arthur and he were the original five members of what would become the Prometheus Initiative, the best and brightest of the adult subjects who were implanted with Titan's biochip and started manifesting abilities. They were brought from every corner of America and tested rigorously. Of course, they were all compensated beyond their wildest dreams. Titan had demonstrated that it would reward talent. The rewards grew with each progressive success. When Titan Biotech decided to begin implanting infants, they'd all been offered jobs with the company. Others had come and gone, but the first five had remained a rather exclusive club, spurring each other on to greater feats. Trager had dated Hope briefly, but in the end she'd settled for a local fellow with no powers.

He recalled the scandal that had ensued when Cougar had found out that Hope Holloway's father was a notorious faith healer. He'd tried to get her disqualified from the program on the basis that her talent might not be a result of Titan's biochip. Ephram Cougar was just jealous of her ability. And maybe just a tad bit afraid of it. Like her father, Silas, she could hypnotize individuals. Cougar never quite got over the indignity of being hypnotized into thinking he was a chicken for the space of several hours. No one had the heart to tell him that she'd also made him act like a donkey, a monkey and a pussycat. Ness thought it was the funniest thing he'd ever seen and never let "Cougar Cluck" live it down.

To say that Hope Holloway overreacted was an understatement. Her father could only hypnotize individuals one at a time. Hope could also mesmerize en masse; when she did so, her victims were like the drug-induced worker zombies of Haitian Vodou, human beings stripped of will and speech, bound to bidding of the sorcerous bokor who created them, rather than the rotting walking corpses of cinematic fame. She tried to take over Titan. The other four members of the Five were forced to try to stop her. Ness, their own personal Quatermain, the man who never missed, shot the daughter he never had. Arthur didn't agree with the order to terminate her. He used his kinetic gifts to alter the bullet's path, but by necessity he got there at the last second and Hope was still hit bad. Ness decided he couldn't finish her off and she escaped. Ephram Cougar was livid. Ness and Cougar got in shouting match that nearly turned into a pitched battle. Arthur was hurt, trying to separate them. Ness quit Titan and renounced his powers.

Ephram remained unapologetic to this day.

A developing situation on one of the monitors tore him away from his memories. A gas station had erupted into a huge fireball.

"What was that?" Zim asked.

"Could be her," Trager said. They reviewed the footage and found the culprit rather quickly. Daniel Zim froze the video at a point that framed the Anarchist's insane glee as he rode away from his handiwork.

"Who is he?" Trager asked.

"I'm running it against the database, but honestly who could forget a face like that?"

"What do you think? Pyro?" Pyrokinetics were rare, but their ability to summon and control flame made them formidable.

"Maybe." He scrolled the footage back and forth with practiced ease until he found what he was looking for. "No, see that? He used an incendiary. Molotov."

"Great. A Halloween vandal on top of everything else. Notify the police. Let them take care of this guy. We have bigger fish to fry. By the way, any word yet from Cougar? He should be here by now."

"He didn't report in."

"He didn't report? How long has he been out of contact?"

"Since some time the day before yesterday," Zim said. "Said he was going out of town to some fair or carnival. He was expected back this morning, but we haven't been able to reach him. Look, I'm not supposed to tell you, but I think we need to assume the worst here. We found his cell phone. His car was still in his driveway. None of his neighbors noticed anything unusual. He could be dead for all we know."

"Or Pandora might be planning to use him to burn Titan to the ground.

Ever think of that?"

"The thought did cross my mind."

Trager changed the subject. "Why hasn't she spiked yet?"

"Maybe she had the chip removed?"

"Can that be done?" Trager asked.

"By a really good neurosurgeon? Maybe. There'd be the risk of brain damage, to be sure. I was thinking more that someone like you could've done it."

Trager glared at him.

Zim rolled his eyes. "Not you specifically. Just someone like you. A good kinetic would probably make an excellent surgeon."

"Gage, report," Trager called on his commset. "How's our prisoner?"

"Secure as we can make him. When you planning on coming down here to relieve me?" Gage asked. "I'm starting to get hungry."

"Just a couple more minutes, I promise."

Some of the monitors fuzzed out.

Zim frowned. "That's odd."

"Somebody jamming us?" Trager asked.

"No. I dunno. It's back. Must've been a glitch." Then he noticed that some of the other cameras were going fuzzy instead. "Hey… Oh no, that is not good."

"Virus?" Trager asked.

"Can't be. It's following a straight line. The distortion is mobile."

"Try to point a long-range camera at the source of the disruption," Trager said.

Zim had a feed up in moments. They saw nothing out of the ordinary. Just a guy riding a bicycle. Except that everywhere he went the power went off and people passed out.

"How is he doing that?" Trager asked.

"Has to be electrokinetic. Like the Holloway girl."

"You've seen Curtis' kid do that?"

"Well, no, but what else could it be? I'm guessing his bioelectric field–" A warning flashed across his monitor. "Ephram just spiked."

Trager shot him an I-told-you-so look. "Where?"

"Gimme a second to lock it down."

Trager glanced around the control room, looking for something to occupy himself while Zim did his thing. "Are we still monitoring the news flap?"

Zim glanced up at the local television monitor. "Yeah. Oh look, they've got a piece on the gas station fire. They are totally abusing Occam's Razor, dude. They're blaming everything on a single 'terrorist.' I swear, I'm starting to think these guys all get their journalism degrees out of a gumball machine. Have at it. I can't watch anymore. TV rots your..." He trailed off as something caught his attention. "Trager, our girl's on camera. Pandora. I think she's making a statement. I'll turn it up–"

Trager felt a chill. Pandora on live television. An alarm went off on another monitor, letting them know someone else had just spiked. Trager didn't even have to look at it to know it was Hope Holloway.

"Don't look at the screen!"

But it was too late.

27 – Zombies

All she had to do was follow the zombies. With that thought, she began walking, determined to reclaim her husband.

A few minutes earlier, Susie Davis had been washing her dinner dishes while enjoying the sounds of a classical music station and the rich aroma of a freshly brewing pot of coffee. It'd been just herself and her husband tonight, but she'd still decked out the dinner table with Halloween confetti, candles and black paper napkins. The kids were grown with children of their own, but she'd still served their "bloody" punch with a few plastic ice cubes, the kind with fake bugs in them. It'd been a good supper, by and large, full of memories and laughs. She and Herb missed the noise and bustle of Halloween night with a houseful of kids. She fondly remembered making her children's costumes each year: pirates, hobos, clowns, sheeted ghosts, mummies, kings and monsters, oh my! They'd never had any sweet little princesses to dress up, but the boys made a startling menagerie of the heroic and the horrible, which they dutifully loaded into the back of the pickup each year to take out trick-or-treating. Each Halloween was full of magic, high adventure, treats and, eventually, the big party at the Harper house on Archer Lane. The Harpers were one of the town's founding families and had remained one of its chief benefactors over the years.

Herb was listening to the news, she realized. He was ever a creature of habit.

"Honey, it's starting in a half hour. Don't you think you ought to get ready?"

"I know. I know," he said. "Trying see what the weather's gonna be."

"It's gonna be cold with a strong chance of eggs and toilet paper if you don't get off your lazy old butt and get outside with that candy dish by the time those trick-or-treaters get here," she said.

"Just a second."

She sighed, but then laughed to herself. Everything was always "just a second" with her dear Herbie, even if it actually took him hours.

She rinsed the last dish, wiped her arthritic hands on a dish towel, put away her apron on its customary hook and peered out the kitchen window. She frowned. They'd missed the sunset. Too bad. She would've enjoyed sitting on the porch swing watching another day end with her life-long sweetheart.

She grinned impishly. They'd just have to make due with piping hot coffee and pumpkin pie on a chill, starry night instead, she decided. If she could wrench her Herbie away from the TV, that is.

Susie fished around in the refrigerator, found the pie and loaded up two plates. Herb always wanted his pumpkin pie heated up. She dutifully popped a plate into the microwave, set the timer and started pouring the coffee.

When she'd half-filled the second mug, she was startled by a loud boom. She dropped the cup and scalded herself a little in the process, but she didn't notice so much at first as she was transfixed by an orange fireball visible out her kitchen window.

"Herbie!"

He came bounding into the kitchen, her knight in rusting but still serviceable armor. He quickly took stock of the state of the kitchen – the shattered mug, the spilt coffee, his shaken wife – and was initially concerned that she might've suffered some sort of medical episode.

"What happened?" he asked.

She pointed wordlessly out the window.

"Oh my stars! I'd better call the fire department. Are you OK?" he asked.

"You didn't hear that?"

"TV."

"You need a hearing aid."

"Not now, Suze." He snatched the cordless phone and dialed the fire department. He frowned. "The line's busy."

"The phones are probably jammed with everyone calling about that." She gestured out the window. Sure enough, they both heard a fire engine wailing in the distance.

Hanging up the phone, Herb raced back to the living room. "Maybe there's something about it on TV."

Susie sighed, groaned at her scalded wrist and looked miserably at the mess on the floor. She fetched a broom and dust pan for the ceramic shards of the coffee mug.

"Susie, come here! There's something on the news about the fire. A gas station exploded!"

"Just a second," she said. She was disappointed that her plans had been spoiled and a little annoyed to be left cleaning up the spill with an injured hand while her husband gaped at the one-eyed monster like it was the Oracle of Delphi. Honestly! Didn't he always complain about how often the local news got everything completely wrong?

For example, there was their coverage of that alleged "car wreck" by the bridge earlier. Herb had gone about his usual routines today, ever the creature of habit, and had talked with his cronies down at the local mechanic's shop. One of the "usual suspects" was Dave Perkins, who owned a wrecker service. Dave said he'd been asked to tow those police cruisers away and that he'd been able to secure all three on his flatbed. Said they were crushed into big balls of metal, if you could believe it, so it must've been "some wreck." There was no wreck that could do that, they all agreed, but they were hard-pressed to figure out how it could've been done. On the other hand, they all swore they'd have been able to figure the whole mess out if the local news had managed to give them a few more facts.

"Oh my – Susie! Something's going on down at the TV station. Somebody just – They're taking over the station!"

"What?"

"You gotta see this! Terrorists in Midwich. This is crazy. Wait. Looks like they're gonna give a statement. Probably demands, ransom maybe."

Susie hurried into the living room with the dust pan still in her hand. There was nothing but static on the television. Herb wasn't in his usual chair. She heard the screen door slam. Through the front window, she caught a glimpse of her husband leaving.

"Herb?"

He ignored her and walked off the porch.

Now beside herself, Susie ran to the door and flung it wide. Herb was backing out of the driveway by the time she made it to the porch. She ran out into the yard after him, but he was already driving away. She wailed his name in terror and worry, wondering if he'd lost his mind. She didn't know what was going on.

People all up and down the street were shuffling out of their homes. Their movements were efficient and mechanical. All shared the same blank, listless expression, like their minds had been wiped clean. Like they were zombies. Some hopped into their cars and drove off in the direction Herb had gone. Others, lacking a vehicle, hopped onto their kids' bicycles or simply walked. Everyone was going in the same direction. Their unaffected loved ones tried to reason with them, to stop them somehow. Those who physically tried to impede their progress met with frightful resistance. The newly made zombies would not be deterred.

Susie Davis stared after the direction her husband had gone. She was out of her mind with terror and worry. She didn't know what had become of her husband or where he was going. She didn't have a car.

But she could still follow him.

All she had to do was follow the zombies.

28 - Swatting Flies

On Carter Munroe's mark, his carefully placed snipers fired as one. They had Johnny and Ed surrounded on all sides. There was no way the boy could block every shot with his powers. It was simply inconceivable.

Yet Johnny remained standing after the first salvo. A swarm of tranq darts buzzed around him like a hive of angry bees. He coaxed and commanded the swirling cloud of projectiles, letting his enemies get a good look at their utter ineffectualness. "Is this really how you wanna do this?" he asked.

Carter's jaw clenched at the taunt. The freak was mocking him. Toying with him. Making him look like a punk in front of the men. With that freak Trager listening in, no doubt, glorying in his helplessness.

"Give yourself up!" he said. "This is your last chance."

Johnny scoffed. At his mental command, the tranq hive seemed to detonate as he sent the darts zipping back from whence they'd come. Carter watched the whole thing via infrared night goggles. Some of the tranq darts had been sent to harry the general perimeter, but the biggest concentration had taken out the western side of his box. No one escaped on that side. Snipers who ducked behind trees found the projectiles following them round. Johnny now had a possible escape route.

Carter was livid. He tried to force himself to calm down. They were prepared for something like this, after all. Huxley had given him explicit instructions. He was to try to bring the young man in alive, as a professional courtesy to the late Arthur Lazarus. If a peaceable resolution failed, well, Johnny had already demonstrated that he was far too dangerous to be left to his own devices.

The kid had made his choice. "Switch to live fire. Fire at will! Bring up the M134s and cut that freak in half!"

The night forest erupted into an awful din of gunfire. Bullets fared no better than tranq darts. Each one stopped about a yard from the telekinetic and the preacher, hovering in place, awaiting Johnny's command.

"Where are those M134s?" Carter demanded.

One cue, three big SUVs came at Johnny from different directions. A Dillon Aero M134D was mounted to the bed of each vehicle. Spinning barrels hurled bullets at Johnny and the preacher at a rate of 3000 rounds per minute.

At the sound of these cannons, Johnny knew he was in trouble. The M134Ds were shooting bullets at him faster than he could reasonably manage. He didn't require a premonition to realize that if he missed even one single bullet, it could be fatal for either him or the pastor. The first time he'd ever seen one of these guns was in the movie *Predator,* where one of the characters had basically used it like an over-glorified weed eater to mow down the jungle. That was the movies. The real thing was much worse. He'd seen a video online showing the sort of damage these guns were capable of. He could have tossed the preacher's car into the line of fire, but the sheer number of bullets would've eaten through the car in no time flat and continued on to make manburger of their real objective.

He decided his best course of action was not to be there when the bullets arrived.

His entire assessment took place of the blink of an eye. His mind sped up, pushing his senses into overdrive and enabling him to watch the bullets racing toward him in slow motion. He grabbed the preacher by the back of his jacket and jumped skyward. As he rose, the cloud of bullets he'd assembled burst outward in all directions. Charlie team suffered significant losses from this bullet bomb. Notably, one of the M134D gunners slumped forward in his harness.

Johnny hated to kill anyone, but neither had he asked for a gunfight.

The other cannons continued firing, their bullet spray following Johnny into the air. The telekinetic's flight was a little awkward, since he was encumbered with the bulk and safety of Ed Blyth. He landed in a nearby tree, but immediately bounded away to keep them from zeroing in on him.

Behind him, the tree disintegrated under a hailstorm of bullets and – to his surprise – a rocket fired from a handheld launcher. Even in midair, Johnny's eagle eyes followed the flight path of this new threat. When he finally got a good look at Charlie Company's team leader, he was surprised to realize that he recognized Carter's Munroe's face. This man was there the night of the fire.

"You!"

Fueled by his rage, his gift manifested itself in an unexpected way. A wave of sonic power erupted from his mouth, flattening the grass and knocking down anything in front of him that lacked either strong roots or sufficient weight. Its force was actually such that it knocked Carter's men off their feet and deflected the bullet spray from the M134Ds. Pleased with the result, Johnny roared in earnest, coupling the sonic assault with his kinetic gifts to rip trees in half and send them hurtling into his foes. The SUVs were battered to pieces. The M134Ds were silenced.

Moments later, Johnny was the only thing left standing. Trees had been uprooted, knocked over and generally cleared away in a roughly circular acre-sized area around him. None of his foes stood before him. The battle had taken less than a minute.

He glanced down at Ed, who'd slipped unconscious under the sonic assault. The younger man checked the old preacher's pulse and, satisfied that he was still alive, stalked over to where he'd last seen Carter Munroe. He found him lying on his back, breathing raggedly. A good-sized tree lay across his chest, pinning him down. He was trying to push it off, to no avail. He didn't notice John Lazarus until his foe was standing over him. In panic, he tried to reach for his sidearm, but found he needed both hands to hold the relentless weight at bay.

"I remember you," Johnny said.

Carter couldn't draw enough breath to reply.

"You were there that night. My dad was trying to tell me something, something about Titan, about having a choice. I thought he'd be freaked out by what I could do," he said, "but he said he'd known all along. Then you came bursting through the door."

Carter stared up at him hatefully, defiantly unrepentant, though his eyes bulged and his muscles quivered with the effort of holding crushing suffocation at bay.

Despite his fury, Johnny realized that it was one thing to defend himself in the chaos of armed combat; it was another to watch a man die without lifting a finger to help him. Villains did that sort of thing – walking away while heroes or hostages were left in the clutches of some Diabolical Device of Doom. He might not be perfect, but he wasn't a villain. He might be superhuman, but he wasn't above humanity.

Using his ability, he lifted the log and tossed it a few yards away.

To repay his act of kindness, Carter jerked his firearm into play. Johnny deflected the one shot he managed to squeeze off, then used his gift to wrench the gun from the desperate man's grip. He mentally lifted Carter off the ground and held him in midair. Maybe this one didn't deserve to live. Maybe it was too dangerous to let him go free.

"What are you going to do with me?" Carter asked.

Johnny didn't immediately answer, mostly because he wasn't yet sure. He noticed that blood flecked the man's lips and nostrils. He didn't look like he could make it much longer without medical attention. Johnny took a moment to survey the destruction he'd just served up. The ravaged forest. The smoking wrecks of vehicles. The mangled remains of his victims. He'd never wanted to hurt anyone. He was just trying to defend himself. Maybe he was the one who was too dangerous…

"What are you going to do with me?" Carter asked again.

"I'm going to take you to the hospital," Johnny said. He'd had enough bloodshed for one day. With a thought, he lowered Carter to the ground.

That's when he heard the explosion.

The noise woke Ed Blyth. "What was that?" he asked.

"Something in town," Johnny said.

Ed peered at the fireball in the distance. "You think it's her?"

"Who else?"

"So what now?"

"I dunno. I didn't sign up for this," he said, indicating the dead Titan agents.

"You're not going to stop her?"

Johnny didn't meet his gaze. Some part of him still wasn't sure he shouldn't just let Pandora have her way with Titan. The company certainly deserved it. And it would finally get them off his back. There'd be no one left to track him. There'd be no more looking over his shoulder or forcing himself not to use his power, lest he give away his location. He could do as he pleased. No more running. No more jumping at shadows. No more living in deception.

Freedom.

"Stop who?" Carter asked.

"Pandora." Ed blurted artlessly.

Johnny shot him a scathing glare for leaking the news.

"Sorry," Ed said.

"How do you know about Pandora?" Carter Munroe asked, seeming to forget that he was the one being held prisoner.

"She sent me to destroy Titan," Johnny said. Despite himself, he enjoyed the look of sheer panic in Carter's eyes.

Carter stuck out his chin. "You won't succeed."

"Relax," Johnny said. "Her little mind tricks didn't work on me."

"But we think she may have sent others besides," Ed said. "Like the one who brought this young man to my church."

"The one they sent back to Titan." Carter frowned, half to himself, a new worry forming in the back of his mind. "Wait. You're saying that she tried to hypnotize you?"

Johnny nodded.

"And now you're here to stop her?" he asked.

"I dunno."

The preacher rounded on him. "Johnny, you can't seriously be thinking of walking away."

"Why not?" Johnny asked. Even the thought of running away resulted in a death flash of warning, but he vented his frustration anyway. "Don't you see? If I help Titan, they'll just make a lab rat out of me as a reward for my efforts. If I fight Pandora, more people will die. There's no point."

Carter laughed mirthlessly. "Of course people will die, Johnny. You guys are weapons. Weapons kill people."

"You shut up!" Johnny yelled. Without even thinking about it, Johnny swept up Carter in the kinetic chains of his anger. Once again, Carter was suspended in midair, but this time he felt himself being stretched apart. He screamed in agony, helpless against the Indigo's fury.

"Stop it! You're killing him!" Ed shouted.

Johnny ceased abruptly, realizing what he'd done. Carter dropped unceremoniously to the ground, further aggravating his injuries. Johnny felt sick, knowing he could have killed Carter. It would have been easy. And this time he couldn't make excuses that it was only self-defense. "I'm sorry," he said, unable to look Carter in the eye.

Carter lay on the ground, gasping for breath, fixing a weary gaze on Johnny. He coughed flecks of blood. "No, I had that coming," he said. "Ever since the night your daddy died, I've known you'd come for me."

"It's not like that."

"I need to call Titan," Carter said. He tapped his commset. "Zim, Charlie team has suffered heavy casualties. There's going to be an attack on Titan. I repeat, Pandora's going for Titan." He paused, frowning. There was no response. "Zim? Zim, do you read me?" He looked up at Johnny and Ed. "I'm not getting a response."

"Maybe your headset's fried?" Ed suggested.

Carter pulled it off his ear, checking it over. "No, doesn't look like it. Something's happened. We may already be too late."

"We've got our own problems. You need medical attention," Johnny said. "I can carry you." He glanced at Ed in apology. "I can't carry you both."

"And you can get there a lot quicker if you don't carry anyone," Carter said. "We don't have time for this. You have to warn them. You have to stop her. You don't know what she's capable of. She could've turned the entire town by now."

"What are you talking about?" Ed asked. "Turned the entire town?"

"She's a high level hypnotist. She doesn't just do individuals. She can make zombies of larger groups."

"You mean like people rising from their graves?"

"No, not that kind of zombie," Carter said. "She puts people in a trance. They become mindless slaves to her bidding. They're clumsier weapons, but well-nigh unstoppable. Unless she frees them herself, the only ways to wake one of her zombies are a lot of pain or electric shock. Anyway, you need to go now. There's a medic pack I can probably get to, if it survived this mess."

Johnny balked. "No, I can't leave you like this."

"Why? Because I might die?" Carter asked. "Look, I'm sorry if your conscience is bothering because you killed my men and likely me as well, but that's not my problem." Johnny's face flushed at the bluntness of the rebuke, but he didn't protest. Carter was right. "If you don't cowboy up and warn Titan, a lot more people are gonna die tonight."

"I was a chaplain long before I was a pastor, Johnny," Ed said. "I might be able to do something for him. But you need to go."

Johnny stared at them uncertainly, and then made his decision, nodding stiffly. If the premonitions were correct, he already knew that if he stayed here or tried to flee town, he was a dead man. He really didn't have much choice in the matter.

He looked resolutely down at the city below, hoping he wouldn't have to face a horde of innocent civilians turned into mindless zombie slaves. Taking a deep breath, he began bounding toward his objective with supernatural leaps.

But he wasn't heading for Titan. Not yet.

He had something else he needed to do first.

29 – Dwight

Curtis Holloway and his daughter walked into the police station with a mission: free Weasel Hopkins. They weren't sure how they were going to do it, but they were determined to give it their best shot.

It was his Sissy's idea. She felt they owed it to him. Curtis did feel a little guilty about the whole duct tape incident, so he was willing to entertain the notion so long as it wouldn't land either of them in jail alongside Weasel. She went into the building first.

As agreed, he waited five minutes before following. Each second felt like an hour. He kept expecting Titan agents to show up or the sounds of gunfire from within the station. At last, he took a deep breath and headed in after her.

Inside, there was no sign of his daughter. So far, so good. He glanced at one of the security cameras and headed for the charge desk. He greeted the desk sergeant with a wave. "Hi. They, uh, brought in a young fella just about a half hour ago. Said they needed him for questioning or something. The thing is: he's my nephew, visiting from out of town. I'm not sure what the mix-up is, but I wanted to see what we needed to do so that I can take him home."

The desk sergeant didn't even bother to look up. "Name?"

"His last name should be Hopkins."

The desk sergeant gave Curtis his full attention. "You're here for the Hopkins kid?""

"Yes, sir."

"And you are?"

"Curtis Holloway, what are you doing down here?" Deputy Jerry Johnson asked as he swaggered over. He walked right up to Curtis, invading his personal space a bit. "Are you giving our fine sergeant any trouble?"

"No trouble," Curtis said. "I'm just here to take my nephew home."

Deputy Johnson frowned. "Since when do you got a nephew, Curtis?"

"He says he's here for the Hopkins kid," the sergeant said.

"The Hopkins boy's your nephew?" Deputy Johnson asked. Before he'd sounded bemused. Now his voice was as cold as steel.

"Yeah, why?"

"He's wanted for questioning."

"That's what they told me."

"They tell you why?"

Curtis shook his head. "All I know is they brought him down here. He left my house to go check out that madness going down at the church at the end of my street. Next thing you know the neighbors are telling me the police picked him up. You guys even read him his rights?" he asked.

"Mr. Hopkins isn't being charged with anything... yet," the desk sergeant said.

Curtis didn't like the way the sergeant was looking at Johnson. "Then I'd like to see him."

The desk sergeant smiled. "Sure, no problem. Jerry, would you escort this poor worried fellow back to see his nephew?"

Jerry Johnson smiled back. There was something predatory in that grin. "My pleasure. This way, Curtis."

Curtis smiled at both officers, though he was pretty sure this was a trap. They were probably both on Titan's payroll. Almost everyone was.

They passed through a set of doors requiring a magnetic passkey for entry into a short hallway.

"So where is he?" Curtis asked.

"The interrogation room."

Curtis was wondering where his daughter was and how in Sam Hill he was going to get out of this mess when a half-camouflaged figure stepped out from the wall, slapped a hand on the officer's chest and delivered a strong electric shock. Johnson fell to his knees, stunned.

Jackie Holloway de-camouflaged and lifted Deputy Johnson's passkey from his pocket. With a nod of greeting to her father, she walked to a nearby door and swiped the card to gain entry. It prompted her for a password.

"Problem?" Curtis asked.

"He's in here," she said, "but I don't know the password."

"Then override it. A good shock ought to do it."

She wondered if it were that simple. It was worth a shot. She sent a surge of electricity into the card reader. The hallway lights went out.

"You blew the breaker," Curtis said.

She winced, but tested the door just to be sure. It opened slightly. With a thought, she made herself invisible and slipped into the room.

The emergency lights came on, bathing the room in a muted red glow. Weasel Hopkins was sitting on a chair at the center of the room, handcuffed to a metal table in the dark. He looked terrified. Then he saw Curtis in the doorway.

"What are you doing here?"

"We're getting you out of here," Jackie replied, still invisible.

"Karma!" He was surprised to find himself relieved to hear her voice. He felt her hug him tight, an odd feeling when you couldn't see someone do it. He heard her whisper "I'm sorry" directly into his ear. He found himself hugging her back. Weasel decided he could sort out his feelings later.

Noting that Sissy's rock star was handcuffed to the table, Curtis decided to search Johnson for the keys. As he turned toward the unconscious deputy's body, he felt the business end of a Sig-Sauer make contact with his temple.

"Stop right there," the desk sergeant said.

Two officers burst out of the door to the viewing room adjoining the interrogation chamber, their weapons drawn over flashlights. He realized belatedly that they'd probably witnessed their entire amateur jailbreak through the one-way mirror between the rooms.

He peered back into the interrogation room helplessly. To his surprise, both Jackie and Weasel were gone. It took him a second to realize that Jackie had simply extended her camouflage to Weasel. He tried to pick his jaw off the ground before they noticed. While he was piecing things together, they slammed him against the hallway wall, pulled his hands behind his head and slapped on a set of cuffs.

One of the officers from the viewing room shouldered past him and braced himself in the doorway, sweeping the room with his gun and flashlight. Another trained his weapon on Curtis so the desk sergeant could check Johnson's vitals.

"Just unconscious." Rising to his feet, he looked into the interrogation room. He saw the empty chair. "Where's Hopkins?" The desk sergeant peered back at Curtis.

Curtis clamped his mouth shut.

"Don't go in there, sir. There was something else was in that room with him," the cop in the doorway said. "Something unnatural."

"There's no such thing as ghosts," his partner said. Curtis couldn't really see his face, but it sounded like he was trying to convince himself.

"Something was in that room with him."

"Well where is he now?" the desk sergeant asked.

"He disappeared, sir. It touched the prisoner and he was just gone."

The desk sergeant frowned and trained his Sig-Sauer on the chair Weasel Hopkins had been sitting in. "People don't just disappear," he said. On a hunch, he shouted, "Show yourself or I'll fire!"

To their collective surprise, Weasel suddenly appeared in the chair. It was a testament to their training that they didn't shoot him out of panic.

"Keep your weapon trained on him," the desk sergeant ordered the others. "You guys said there was someone else in this room. Well, they got ten seconds to show themselves before I shoot the Hopkins kid."

He began counting.

30 – Sabotage

Mike Trager lunged for Daniel Zim. The latter had picked up the chair he was sitting in and begun bashing it against the console as hard as he could. The wiry surveillance technician hadn't torn his eyes away from the monitor in time. He'd stared deeply into Pandora's eyes as she wove her hypnotic spell and now Zim, like anyone else who'd watched that live news broadcast, was her zombie slave.

Trager had dealt with this version of her hypnosis before when she'd tried to take over Titan. Pandora's zombies were mindlessly driven and extremely strong. It was as if their minds primed their bodies for maximum efficiency. Maybe that's where the insane got their alleged superhuman strength. They had few weaknesses; only electric shock and extreme pain could bring the victims out of the trance. Right now, he was scheduling Zim for such a rude awakening.

He picked up the eerily blank-faced tech with his gift and slammed him hard into a wall. Zim never even lost his grip on the chair. Bolting to his feet, he continued to bash away at sensitive electronic equipment.

Trager drew his Glock and shot him in the leg. The bullet passed completely through the muscle. The zombie staggered for moment, then stood again despite his bleeding leg and shattered a few monitors, unhindered. Trager shot him again. This time the bullet shattered his femur. Zim dropped to the floor, howling in pain.

Trager surveyed the room grimly. Zim was back, but the zombie had done its job. The console was sparking, smoking, dented, mostly ruined. What was still operational was flashing with little red lights that he was pretty sure should never be blinking. He walked over to the wall to grab the medical kit.

"What happened?"

"Pandora used the TV station to turn you into a zombie."

"I did this?"

Trager nodded grimly.

"You shot me!"

"Extreme pain or electric shock. The only things that bring a zombie around."

"Well, next time shock me! Don't shoot me. It hurts."

"Can you fix this?" Mike Trager asked. He plunged a syringe of morphine into Zim's leg.

"I can't really see from down here on the floor."

Trager assisted him into a chair. Three monitors were still operational.

"Oh, I really knew what I was doing, Mike. The system is trashed along with most of the controls. I can fix it, but it'll take a few hours."

"We don't have a few hours. That broadcast zombified you and probably half the town. You know where they'll be headed."

"It can't be done," Zim said.

"Not your decision, I'm afraid," Trager said. "I need you to focus."

Zim groaned. "My leg really hurts."

"I know. I'm the one who shot you, but I need you to give us a fighting chance here. If Pandora gets her hands on this company's secrets, there's no hope for anybody. You know that."

"I know, I know. We need to give Huxley a heads-up."

"I'll take care of that," Trager said, walking toward the door. "You get the system back up."

"Where are you going?"

"To fortify this place. In case you fail."

"Good thinking," Daniel said. "Hey!"

Trager turned back around.

"Take one of the radios."

Trager nodded and picked up a commset on the way out the door.

31 – Fallen

Carter coughed blood. A lot of it.

Ed Blyth frowned. Carter wasn't going to make it. He needed medical attention badly and he simply wasn't going to get it in time.

"You shouldn't push yourself," the preacher said.

"Won't make no difference."

"You're not afraid of death?"

"Don't preach at me, preacher," Carter said. "Not until the funeral."

"It's my job, sir."

"Fine, say your piece. Won't make no difference," he repeated.

"If you met God today, and there's a good chance you might, and He asked you, 'Why should I let you into Heaven?' what would you tell Him?"

"I'd hope He grades on a curve."

"Do you know how good you would have to be?" the preacher asked. "The Bible says that all have sinned and come short of the glory of God. God is the standard we're measured against and He's holy. Perfect. It's like this: An Olympic long jump medalist can jump a lot farther than the rest of us, but if he's asked to jump across the Grand Canyon, he'll fail like the rest of us. No matter how good you were, and I'm betting you weren't all that much of a saint, it just won't measure up. That's the bad news."

"That is bad." It was hard to say whether he was taking Ed seriously or not.

"You know how you got that way?"

Carter drawled, half-seriously. "Cause I'm a bad, bad man?"

"Exactly," Ed said. "People get it backwards all the time. It's not sin that makes you a sinner. You sin because you're a sinner. It's hardwired into your system, ever since Adam disobeyed God. It's like spiritual genetics: a copy error that gets passed on and on. And this one's fatal. The Bible says that by one man sin entered into the world, and death by sin. But the good news is while the wages, or deserved earnings, of sin is death, the gift of God is eternal life through Jesus Christ. God so loved the world that He gave His only begotten Son that whosoever believes in Him should not perish but have eternal life instead."

Carter scoffed. "That's it?"

"If you confess the Lord Jesus with your mouth and believe in your heart that God has raised Him from the dead, you will be saved."

"You really think a foxhole conversion counts?"

"Jesus told the thief who repented on the cross beside Him, 'Today, you will be with me in Paradise.'"

Carter nodded, coughing and gasping for air. He grinned, despite it all. "You're awful pushy, but I think it's too late for me."

"Not while you draw breath."

No answer.

Ed sighed, realizing that Carter Munroe had spoken truly. He placed his hand over the departed's eyes and closed them reverently. He bowed his head for a moment, feeling completely defeated.

This morning's memory verse came to mind. "And let us not be weary in well-doing; for in due season we shall reap if we faint not."

Ed looked down on Midwich. He knew it was a fool's hope to think that the imminent super-powered confrontation at Titan wouldn't spill into the streets below. People were going to need help.

Ed began walking toward Midwich, already rolling up his sleeves.

32 – Jailbreak

Johnny bounded into town, using the rooftops for speed's sake. He was risking being seen, but time was of the essence. Besides, he figured any tales of a flying man on Halloween night would probably be dismissed as an urban legend.

While enroute, he noted that everywhere he looked the streets were oddly empty for trick-or-treat night.

He landed across the street from the police station. The building was dark, forbidding. Steeling himself, he walked across the street, up the steps and shoved the doors wide. By the dim glow of the emergency lights, he could see there was no one at the charge desk. In fact, the entire front lobby seemed oddly deserted. He hesitated. Was this a trap? Where was everyone? And why was the power off?

He peered into the adjoining waiting area. No one.

When he was a kid, his dad had taken him to the station plenty of times, which was just one of the perks of having a sheriff for your father. His memory was nearly flawless, so he knew where to go from here.

The door he needed was locked. Normally, he would've needed a passkey. With the power out, he could have simply pushed it open, but he wanted the element of surprise. Using his gift, he caused the metal door to crumple into a ball. It fell to the floor with a thud. A group of men were crowded in the hallway just outside the door to the interrogation room. With a sonic roar, he swept the hallway clean. Three officers and a man in handcuffs were blasted off their feet. They tumbled into a heap at the other end of the hall.

He intended to breeze past them to the cells, but as he passed by the interrogation room, he peered inside, mostly to make sure it was all clear. His objective was sitting in the middle of the room.

"Weasel!"

Weasel laughed when he saw him. "Johnny! It's about time. Get me outta here."

John Lazarus glanced down at the handcuffs. They clicked open and fell off Weasel's wrists.

Karma chose that moment to de-camouflage.

"Weasel, look out!" Startled, Johnny threw her up against the wall with his kinetic gifts.

"Wait! She's with me," Weasel said.

"Really?" Johnny released his hold on her, lowering her gently to the floor. He looked her over, realizing he recognized her. "You're Wacky Jackie. From down the street."

"You're John Lazarus. You're supposed to be dead. And it's just Jackie, thank you."

"Sorry, you surprised me. Didn't know you could–"

"My dad! He was in the hall."

"The guy in handcuffs?" Johnny asked, wincing.

She shot him a dark look and dashed into the hallway. He grimaced. He'd thought the big oaf looked familiar, but he'd been concentrating on neutralizing the police.

Johnny grinned at his friend. "You picked up Wacky Jackie? Dude, I know her."

"Gathered that. Don't care. Where have you been?"

"It's a long story. Short version: I was hijacked by someone like me, but I got away."

"That's it?" Weasel asked. "That's all you're going to tell me?"

"Later."

Fine, let's get out of here then."

Johnny nodded and headed into the hallway. Jackie had her handcuffed father on his feet, battered but conscious. "He OK?" he asked.

Curtis growled. "He's got a sawed off shotgun for you if you ever do that to him again."

Johnny ignored the threat. "You guys go on. I'll cover our escape."

The policemen were groaning, getting to their feet. John mentally tore their weapons from their grasp. That got their attention.

"I don't want to hurt you," Johnny said. He caused their guns to hover in front of them, aimed at them threateningly. "So I'd like you to go out the door behind you there, nice and quiet."

Exchanging a glance, they complied, not willing to call his bluff. The desk sergeant glared at him the entire time. The others were too busy dragging Deputy Johnson's unconscious body with them to show much animosity. Johnny warped the metal door once they were on the other side, jamming it shut, then hurried to catch up with the others.

As he burst out the front doors of the station, he saw Weasel and his friends dashing toward Curtis' eyesore of a pickup truck. As they piled in, a black van roared down the street and braked hard in front of the station. The side door opened and the biggest man Johnny had ever seen stepped out of the vehicle. And he was holding a rocket launcher.

That couldn't be good.

33 – Breach

So far, Mike Trager had found three other employees who had to be de-zombified. He was using Tasers now, something he wish he'd had at his disposal earlier with Zim.

Daniel had managed to get the building's internal security cameras up and running, but he only had three monitors on which to display any feeds, including feeds from the city. "Mike, we're almost completely blind here."

"You still have windows. Use them," Mike Trager said. "Open the blast shutters." The huge glass windows of the control room overlooked the front lawn and much of the valley below. Zim typically kept the metal shutters closed to block out annoying sunlight and the glare it cast across his monitors. They were designed to deflect mortar shells. At night, he usually left them closed. Zim was used to cubicles and claustrophobic server rooms. Those big windows just left him feeling dangerously exposed, especially at night.

Zim balked. "Won't that leave the control room vulnerable?"

"It's bulletproof. Pandora's zombies won't be able to get through it."

"Yeah, but if she's hypnotized someone like Johnny–"

"The blast shutters wouldn't stop him anyway. At least open you'll be able to see them coming."

"We should prep the *Grey* and initiate Final Protocol" Daniel said.

Trager hesitated. "Let me think about that, if you don't mind. That's not a light decision.

"Sure. Just think fast."

Trager sighed. He was alone, all that stood between Pandora and all of Titan's secrets. Maybe he should just order Zim to slag the servers now and set the silent countdown. Their data would be backed up in the Vault. They'd evacuated all non-essential staff.

The last time he'd faced her, she'd made zombies of a good number of Titan's staff, but Ness and Cougar had been there to watch his back. Arthur had interfered, but only to keep them from killing her. He'd never been on her side.

Now he was alone and she had an entire town of zombie slaves at her command, including a few possible Indigos, and he had absolutely zero back-up. What was he thinking?

Trager tried calling the Director. He was only a little surprised when he got a busy signal for his efforts. It didn't matter. He knew what had to be done. Everyone knew their Final Protocol. There wasn't anything else to do except wait and see if he'd have to blow this facility to Kingdom Come.

"Zim, how long until the *Grey*'s prepped?" he asked.

"Takes about twenty minutes, as always," the tech said. "Unless it gets buggy. Then it takes longer."

"As soon as it's ready, slag the servers and meet me in the Tunnel. I'm sending our remaining security to safeguard the *Grey*."

Daniel cheered. "Sounds like a plan."

It was certainly a better plan than waiting around for martyrdom. Now all he had to do was hold the fort long enough to see it through. Twenty minutes seemed like a long time right now.

"Do we have a camera pointed at the front gate?" he asked.

"Lemme check. Yes."

"Anybody there?"

"Not a soul."

"What about the camera we placed at the mouth of Corporate Drive?"

"Switching... OK, got it. Oh no, it's like zombie central out there, Trager. Must be half the town."

Trager sighed. "How long you think we've got?"

"It's gonna be close."

"We've got work to do," Trager said.

Grimly, he stood at the back of the lobby, awaiting the first assault.

34 – Challenger

Bantam stepped in front of the black van, dropped down on one knee and fired the rocket. If Johnny hadn't been standing there, it would have hit the police station. Since he *was* standing there, Johnny tossed out a wall of kinetic energy that met the rocket with sufficient force to deflect its course into a nearby parking garage.

Bantam rose to his feet. The vehicle's driver got out, shouldering a semi-automatic rifle. The scowl on her face broadcast annoyance, alarm and confusion. She and Bantam were supposed to level the police station as a precautionary measure. It was supposed to be a simple matter. Only now it wasn't. One of their own, someone with powers, was in the way.

Johnny stood at ready, waiting to see what they'd do next.

Jennifer Winters spoke into her headset. "Destiny, we have a problem. Please advise."

"Have you achieved your objective?"

"Negative," Winters said. "There is an unknown Indigo protecting the police station. He knocked our rocket out of the sky."

"Who are you guys?" John Lazarus asked. "Did Pandora send you? Or Titan?"

"He just asked us–"

"I heard," Destiny said over her commset. "Ask him to identify himself."

"Is he one of ours?"

"Just ask him."

"What's your name?" Winters called to the young man on the steps.

"I asked you first," he said. He glanced at his friends in the truck, hoping they'd have enough sense to just drive off quietly. But Curtis looked like he was itching for a fight. The dumb hick was just sitting there, idling his pickup, waiting to see what happened.

"My name is Jennifer Winters. This is Bantam. Now, your turn."

"Are you with Pandora?"

"What if we are?" she asked.

"Ask him if his name is John Lazarus," Destiny said.

"Are you John Lazarus?" Hadn't Pandora mentioned this guy? Wasn't he supposed to be on their side?

"Yes. Now tell Pandora I'm going to stop her."

"You hear that?" Winters asked. "Please advise."

There was a pause on the other end. Jennifer hated to be put on hold, especially at a time like this. Finally the order came and it wasn't from Destiny Pascalé. It was Pandora herself who spoke. "Neutralize him."

Bantam looked at her quizzically. Winters nodded. "Take him out."

Her partner tossed the rocket launcher aside and began charging toward Johnny.

Johnny steeled himself. Bantam looked like a human tank on steroids. Johnny roared, buffeting the giant muscle mutant back a little. Bantam stayed on his feet. Stunned, Johnny tried harder. Johnny's sustained roar slammed into the other super freak like a mighty wind. The ogre stepped backwards for a second, but then leaned into the sonic waves, walking steadily forward. Changing tactics, Johnny telekinetically lifted his foe into the air where he didn't have any traction and tossed him into a street lamp. Bantam's mass bent the metal light pole, but he got back up, no worse for the wear. Shaking himself, he jogged up for another go.

Meanwhile, Winters took careful aim at Johnny from over the hood of the van. She was none too surprised when a bullet whizzed past her ponytail. Pivoting around instinctively, she saw Curtis leaning out his window, weapon in hand. She made the connection instantly. Johnny had friends.

She opened fire. Curtis threw the pickup truck into motion, ducking behind the steering wheel as best he could.

Bantam was charging up the stairs like a juggernaut, intent on smashing Johnny into the pavement. Johnny waited until the last possible moment and then bounced skyward. Bantam missed him by inches, hitting the police doors like a battering ram. Unable to stop himself, he tumbled inside.

Johnny landed in the street in front of the black van. Winters, distracted by Curtis' approaching truck, saw him out of the corner of her eye. She turned to fire at him with preternatural quickness.

Curtis spat wordless curses as Johnny appeared in his path. He was about to swerve out of the way when Johnny did an impossibly high vertical flip and suddenly the way was clear again.

Winters adjusted her aim to track Johnny's flight, which was fortunate for those in Curtis' cab. If she had continued firing at the spot where Johnny had briefly stood in the road, she would have hit Jackie and Curtis. By following him up, she missed them entirely. A moment later, Johnny landed in the bed of the pickup beside Weasel. Winters dashed around the front of the van to fire after her hitchhiking target, but he deflected her bullets easily.

"Target is on the move," Winters barked into her commset. "Do you want me to pursue?" She couldn't believe Johnny had escaped them that easily. Her reflexes were absolutely unmatched, but somehow she'd had trouble following him in her sights. It was almost like he was bending the path of her bullets somehow.

"Don't let him escape," Pandora said.

Jennifer Winters looked askance at the police station, wondering if Bantam were OK. He burst through the front doors at the moment, looking madder than she'd ever seen him. It was frighteningly primal, conjuring up images of legendary heroes slaying lions with their bare hands, of Viking berserkers throwing themselves into the fray with no care for armor or even edged weapons. He stopped on the police station steps, glowering about for his foe.

Winters pointed after the beat up pickup. "That way." As he charged after John Lazarus on foot, she hopped into the van to follow him.

35 – The Inside Man

"Good news, Mikey," Zim said. "We're set to go. The *Grey* is prepped and hot!"

He heard Trager sigh over his radio. "About time we caught a break tonight. Take care of the servers. I'll meet you in the Tunnel. And stop calling me Mikey."

Daniel Zim was about to leave when Hillary burst into the room. They'd forgotten about the anonymous telekinetic from this morning's disaster at Soul's Harbor. It was an understandable oversight, considering everything else they were dealing with, but a costly one.

When Zombie Zim had trashed the control room, he'd interrupted Hillary's flow of sedatives. The captive woke up shortly thereafter, just like sweet Pandora had planned. Thanks to a little hypnosis, things he'd been commanded to forget until this moment came rushing back into his skull. He remembered the plan. He grinned, realizing he knew the layout of this facility intimately. He and Pandora had gone over it until it was thoroughly committed to memory.

The only unknowns in her plan were how much security would be left in the building. Right now, there were only two guards, both watching him from an observation booth. Hillary was strapped down in some kind of medical chair, but it would be child's play to break free. With a thought, he caused his restraints to break off and then hopped off his chair.

One of the guards burst from the booth, firing his weapon. Hillary sent the bullets back to their point of origin. The man slumped to the floor as the bullets slammed into his chest. He mentally plucked the man's gun from his hand as he fell as used it to kill the other guard. They never got the chance to sound the alarm.

Hillary exited the room, knowing that so long as he acted quickly and didn't encounter Trager or some other Indigo along the way, the rest ought to be a cinch. As he made his way down the hall, he heard the sound of a flushing toilet. He considered neutralizing the fellow as he left the restroom, but quickened his pace instead. Time was of the essence if he was to secure the control room before he was discovered.

Gage stepped out of the bathroom, wiping his hands on the back of his pants. Why couldn't the custodian ever stock enough paper towels? As he glanced toward the room they were holding the cop-killer in, he frowned. Why was the door open?

Drawing his weapon, he searched up and down the hall. His prisoner glanced at him over his shoulder, then turned right at a connecting hallway. Gage broke into a run, hoping to catch him. As he reached the T-intersection, he was tossed off his feet with enough force to knock him through the office door behind him.

Rolling to his feet, he scrambled out of the prisoner's line of sight. Ness had warned him what Indigos were capable of and, at the church, he'd seen firsthand what sort of damage they could deal, so he waited with his back to the wall, hoping the villain would move on.

Without warning, every door in the hallway was ripped off its hinges and sent hurtling toward him. The doors jammed themselves in the office doorway, trapping him inside.

Standing to his feet, Gage bit back a string of curses, realizing it would take him hours to dig out.

Hillary proceeded to Titan's command center and had oh-so-easily taken control from the lone tech that manned it. Pandora wanted this one alive, so he locked Daniel Zim in a mop closet for safe keeping. Unfortunately, Zim had managed to call out Trager's name into a radio before he'd subdued him.

Trager's voice called from the radio. "Zim! Zim, answer me."

Hillary pushed the radio button and answered in a perfect imitation of Daniel Zim's voice. "I'm here."

"What happened? Are you OK?"

"Yeah," Hillary as Zim said. "Sorry about that. Look, um, where are you right now?"

"I'm still in the lobby."

Hillary glanced about and spotted Trager on the monitor. "Perfect."

"Is everything alright? Are we still set to go?"

Hillary stalled. He'd fumbled badly by letting Zim get that warning off. "What? You're breaking up on me." He spotted the specs for the *Grey* up on one of the other two monitors. He snorted to himself, realizing what they'd been up to. After all, the *Grey* was their escape plan, too. Of course, if they'd bothered to prep it, they were executing their Final Protocol and Hillary couldn't allow that. Not yet. "Sorry. I just wanted to let you know the *Grey* is set to go. Are we ready to execute Final Protocol? I can't wait to get out of this place."

There was a slight pause. Was Trager on to him?

"Me neither," Trager said. "Set the countdown. I'll meet you in the Tunnel."

36 – Trailing Sparks

Curtis Holloway's beat up old pickup truck barreled down the street to the tune of some obnoxiously loud but somewhat appropriate country song.

"We got company!" Curtis said, catching a glimpse of Bantam in his rearview mirror. He stomped the accelerator into the floor. The charging juggernaut was roaring like a bull and gaining speed with every step. Curtis growled something unintelligible under his breath, then yelled, "Sissy, load my shotgun!"

Standing up in the bed of the truck, Johnny concentrated and tried to lift the muscle mutant and toss him away like he'd done before, but Bantam now had too much momentum going. The muscle mutant slammed into the back of the truck, buckling it badly and lifting it off the ground for a moment. Fortunately, he didn't get a good grip on it and the impact slowed him some, so he had to hurry to catch up again.

That gave Johnny an idea. Maybe he could slow the juggernaut down enough to get away. He telekinetically picked up a parked car as they passed it and tossed it at their pursuer. The human locomotive kept coming, but it did put a little more distance between them. He tossed another at Bantam, amazed that apart from a few scrapes and bruises the muscle mutant appeared unharmed by the bludgeoning. What would it take to stop this guy?

"Johnny, look out!" Curtis' sawed-off shotgun peaked out the back window of the pickup. Johnny dodged the barrel instinctively. Weasel dove to the floor of the pickup, sputtering in alarm and indignation. Curtis pulled the trigger. His head ringing from the shotgun blast, Johnny followed the bullet's path and saw that Jackie's crazy redneck father had been firing at Jennifer Winter's black van. She returned fire with a sidearm, driving with one hand.

To the tune of a bellowed command of "Sissy, reload!" and Curtis' rowdy country radio, Johnny arced the next parked car over Bantam's head, intending to stop the van. Winters barely dodged his first missile, swerving wildly. She was forced to ride up onto the sidewalk, shredding into a picket fence before she was able to get back onto the road. Johnny lobbed another one her way, convincing her to duck down a side street to avoid being crushed.

By then, Johnny was compelled to deal with Bantam again. This time, he sent a delivery truck into the monster's path. The vehicle fairly exploded as Bantam ripped through it, forcing Johnny to hide his face for a moment. Bantam kept coming.

The barrel of Curtis' shotgun poked out the back window again. He took a bead on the muscle mutant's forehead, grinned as he pulled the trigger. It didn't even seem to faze Bantam.

"Hang on!" Johnny screamed.

Bantam crashed into the back of the truck again. The truck lurched upward as the trailer buckled. Johnny and Weasel barely held on. Johnny thought for a moment that the muscle mutant was going to crush him against the cab and tear on through beyond, but Bantam reached his point of recoil. Every action has an equal and opposite reaction. He staggered in midair and lost his footing, tumbling away. He literally rolled into someone's living room.

The pickup truck pitched forward crazily until everyone was sure it was going to start rolling. Amazingly, it righted itself enough for a controlled stop. It helped that the truck's mangled pickup bed was dragging, showering the road with sparks. Heaven knows where the back wheel went.

They exited the relic hastily, fearing the wreck would blow up like in the movies. They stared at it from a distance, all the while scanning the perimeter for more attackers.

"This is crazy," Jackie said. "Did we lose them?"

"Dunno, but we lost our transportation," Curtis said. He stared at the ruined heap sadly. "That's totaled."

"I'm sure that'll buff out," Weasel said with a snicker.

Jackie intervened before her father could properly reward him for his smart mouth. "I'm sorry, Curtis."

He nodded. "Anyway, we best get outta here." He glanced at the old pickup one last time. Oddly, its radio was still belching forth some triumphantly rowdy hick tune. "You know, I was dead sure it was gonna blow up."

At that moment, it exploded, sending them all ducking for cover.

Curtis whistled from the ground. "If that don't beat all."

Lumber rattled as Bantam emerged from the rubble back down the road. Johnny hissed a warning to the others. "Quick! Hide! The big one's on his feet again."

They ducked down where they were, out of sight. The behemoth glanced up and down the street. When he spotted the burning pickup, he pumped his fists, uttered a victory shout and jogged over to bask in the warmth of the fire. He ignored the protests and accusations of the family whose house he'd ruined. Johnny and his friends willed themselves invisible, still hiding. Of course, Jackie actually succeeded.

Less than a minute later, the black van pulled up. Bantam lumbered inside.

"What happened?" Winters asked, nodding toward the burning pickup.

"Got 'em," Bantam said. "They're toast."

"Did you check for bodies?" she asked.

Bantam's face fell.

Rolling her eyes, Jennifer Winters hopped out of the van and got as close to the fire as she dared. Her eyes were better than most. The truck was empty. She quickly scanned the perimeter, but their targets were nowhere in sight. She returned to the van.

She tapped her commset. "Winters, reporting. Targets have eluded us."

Bantam growled.

She ignored him. "Do you want us to continue pursuit?" she asked.

"Regroup back at Titan," Destiny said. "Johnny will come to us."

Curtis and the others waited until the vehicle was out of sight.

"You hear that? They're expecting you, son," he said, getting to his feet and shouldering his shotgun.

Johnny nodded. "I did catch that."

"Well, I reckon we'll just have to make sure we don't disappoint them. Right, Sissy?"

Sissy didn't answer.

"Sissy?" An ugly suspicion crossed his mind.

Weasel groaned. "I don't think she's here, man."

Curtis stared down the road in the direction the van had gone. "Oh, no."

37 – Fight or Flight

Mike Trager watched as the Indigo he'd squared off against at Soul's Harbor stepped onto a metal platform three stories above him. The tunnel was immense and designed to look like an emergency pressure release for the dam. A tram and a couple golf carts were parked at the bottom of the stairs to help employees travel the length of the tunnel. Trager knew of several labs down here but he was generally kept in the dark as to project details.

What he did know was that the tunnel led to the hangar bay where he would not only find the *Grey,* but a row of oversized robotic combat suits and a weapons locker filled with gadgets specifically designed to take down Indigos. Unfortunately, it was too far away to be of any use right now.

Guns hovered in the air around Hillary, pointing this way and twitching that way, seeking out Trager's hiding spot. Judging by the way he kept two guns firmly clenched in his hands as he approached a metal stairwell to the catwalk below, Trager was pretty certain Hillary was taking this encounter a lot more seriously than their rumble at Soul's Harbor. Hillary hesitated at the edge of the platform.

Trager knew well enough to wait for the opportune moment. Besides, he needed to make sure this one was alone. He figured their prisoner had been released when Zombie Zim sabotaged their systems, but he needed to make sure he hadn't had a little help.

"Zim? That you?" Trager asked, throwing his voice.

Predictably, Hillary turned in the direction he thought the voice had come from. His back was now to Trager.

Zim's voice called worriedly from Hillary's lips. "Where are you?"

Mike's eyes narrowed. This kid was more talented than he'd suspected. He needed to proceed cautiously in case this twerp had some other, nastier tricks up his sleeve.

"Where's Pandora?" Trager asked. He picked a new direction to throw his voice from this time to keep his enemy off-balance.

"I dunno," the voice of Zim said, "but we need to get out of here before she arrives, don't you think?"

No answer.

Hillary sighed. "Fine, you're not buying it. Plan B is more fun anyway. Come out, come out, wherever you are."

Trager fired off three shots.

Hillary deflected the bullets easily and fired all of his weapons down in the direction the shots came from.

Fortunately, that gun wasn't in Trager's hand.

Hillary spotted the weapon hovering in the air at Trager's command and crushed it with a thought. "Nice trick," he said. "Just so you know, Pandora asked me to play nice and do the whole live capture thing. I think she wants to do you herself. Or maybe just make you a zombie like your old buddy Cougar."

It was Trager's turn to be surprised. If Pandora had really got inside Ephram Cougar's head, she'd made herself a very dangerous weapon. Pyrokinetics were rare. Most of them never learned to control their gifts properly and died horrible deaths. Titan had come to suspect that nearly all cases of spontaneous human combustion were latent talents that misfired, though the victim was unaware they possessed any such gift. Of course, they didn't think all cases of SHC were accidents for the excellent reason that they'd discovered that some were premeditated homicides by pyros who'd achieved mastery over their powers.

"I can hear you thinking it over," Hillary said. "Fight or flight? It's your evolutionary demi-urge. Survival of the fittest." He leapt over the rail the full three stories to the floor below.

Trager fired off two sniper rifles he'd had tucked away in separate corners of the tunnel, trying to take advantage of the situation. He'd hoped to catch the young man off-guard, while he was concentrating on cushioning his fall.

Hillary laughed as he swatted the bullets away, landing unharmed. "You know what your problem is, old man? No imagination." At that Hillary fired every weapon he had and even squeezed the triggers on Mike's guns. The ones he knew about anyway. He caught each bullet and drew it to himself as if he were a magnet. In moments, he was surrounded by a buzzing, swarming cloud of ammunition. "I'm really disappointed. I was really expecting more of a fight. Still, you can't hide forever."

He sent the swarm racing through the tunnel in front of him, trying to flush Mike Trager out. The bullets chewed through everything in their path. Fortunately, Trager was above the line of fire, hanging onto the understructure of an overhead catwalk.

"Oh, come on!" Hillary said. "I can do this all day. You, on the other hand… well, you need to make a move. Because when Pandora gets here, you're not gonna be able to take us all on at once."

Trager didn't answer. One of the intruder's guns was hovering within sight. If the other moved into view, he might be able to wrest mental control of them and turn the tables on his opponent.

"Oh c'mon, buddy. Where are you?" Heaving a mock sigh, Hillary tugged a walkie-talkie off his belt and spoke into it in a singsong voice. "I'm over here!"

Trager was so intent on getting control of the guns that he missed the significance of the intruder's actions, until the "I'm over here!" squawked from the walkie-talkie at his own belt. In that moment of realization, a grinning Hillary wrenched him from his hiding spot and slammed him to the floor. He mentally picked Trager up and hurled him into a wall for good measure. Trager lost consciousness.

38 – Fireside Chat

Curtis sniffed, staring at the burning wreck helplessly. "Well, we can't go in that."

"No, we can't," Johnny said. He was trying to plot out his next move. There were so many pieces on the board. It would be easy to miss something. And he couldn't be everywhere at once.

"OK, so now what? Off to Titan, I suppose."

Johnny nodded.

"That why you came back, Johnny? Titan?"

"No. I mean, I always planned on coming back eventually, for answers. I knew it would come to that. But I wanted to be ready first."

"Ready for what?"

"Well, it's not like they'd just let me walk away," Johnny said. "I'm an asset. A walking pile of money. You don't just let money walk out the door."

Curtis snorted, bemused. "Yeah, there's that. You were better off when they thought their money burned up with your house."

Johnny stared down the road. "They never thought I was dead. They knew I'd escaped. They just let everybody else think I was dead."

"What?"

Weasel snorted. "Dude, this town is totally messed up."

"It made things easier for Titan. If everybody thought I was dead, nobody'd be looking for me except them."

Curtis whistled. "Good thing they didn't find you, eh?"

"Not for lack of trying. They never gave up. Everywhere I went. I never had more than a month's peace. Always looking over my shoulder."

"And you'll always have to keep looking over your shoulder unless you settle this now," Curtis said. "I'm willing to help you, but I ain't got no funky comic book powers, so we're gonna have to make a little pit stop to get some weapons before we storm Titan's gates. And we're gonna need a vehicle."

"No offense, but you're not coming," Johnny said. He turned to Weasel. "In fact, you're getting out of Midwich. I never should have brought you here. Things have gotten way out of hand. It's too dangerous for you to stay."

"I can handle myself just fine," Weasel said.

"Weasel, I just rescued you from the police station. If it weren't for my powers and a stroke of pure luck, I wouldn't even have known they had you. You need to go before something worse happens."

Weasel started to protest, but Johnny cut him off, rounding on Curtis. "Do you wanna know how much good a weapon will do you against people like me, Curtis? Well, let me tell you. Before I got to the police station, I was attacked by a lot of men with really big guns and, you know what? They were all dead in less than a minute. They never stood a chance and neither would you."

"Says you," Weasel said. "I'm going."

"No, you're not." With a thought, he picked Weasel up and sat him down on the roof of a second-story home.

"Johnny!"

"This is for your own good, Weasel," Johnny said as he turned to leave.

"You gonna put me on a roof, too?" Curtis asked, squaring his jaw.

"Keep him safe, Curtis." Before the other could respond, he launched skyward, hopping from rooftop to rooftop.

Curtis watched him go, fuming at Johnny for basically sending him to the kid's table. If he wanted to risk his own neck, it was his business. Glaring up at Weasel, he asked. "Hey, Rock Star, you ready to help me find that fool daughter of mine?"

39 – Parasol

Dandridge Ridenour stared at his watch, unblinking. One look at this man and you were convinced. From the overpriced suit and designer glasses to his near perfect hair and impeccable tan, he simply screamed success. Dandridge was a businessman. A corporate executive who was going places, not some career yes-man. A fire-breathing dragon in a tailored suit. He glanced involuntarily at his other wrist at the handcuffs that secured him to a locked briefcase. A reminder that he still took orders from someone else. That he had yet one more rung to scale on success' ladder.

"Where is she?" he asked over the whine of the helicopter's rotors. "She's behind schedule."

An old man chuckled. "You expected everything to go according to your nice, neat little plan, did you?"

They were fast approaching Titan's facilities, but they'd yet to see the flare that indicated it was safe to approach and land. Dandridge spared the chopper's other occupants a glance. The black-clad soldiers were grim-faced and silent, ready for action. He looked out the side of the helicopter. The gates of Titan loomed ahead and below. It didn't look like anyone was minding the store, but neither were the gates open as planned. The access road was choked with Pandora's zombies, all intent on dismantling Titan, but there was no sign of Pandora herself. "Yes, that's exactly what I thought," he said.

"You're used to how things work in your corporate jungle," the old man said, eyeballing Dandridge's briefcase. "You say jump, they ask how high. Boss Man gives the orders, then knuckle-dragging Cubicle Man knocks himself out to make sure your unreasonable demands are carried out, that it?"

"Once again, yes, that's generally how it works," Dandridge said. "Kings and serfs. Pharaohs and slaves. It's how it's always worked."

"Well, this isn't your corporate world, Mr. Ridenour. This is a military operation. Nothing ever goes according to plan."

Dandridge clenched his jaw. "Why is she late?"

"No idea," the old man said with a shrug. "Maybe she decided to do a little sight-seeing. Check out her old haunts. See how the town has changed. She did used to live here, you know."

Their attention was drawn to a disturbance on the access road to Titan. The knot of zombified people were about halfway to the front gates when they began dropping to the ground on either side of the path, clearly disoriented. A man on a bicycle rode serenely between them. He seemed to be the cause.

A dark sedan followed several yards behind the Disruptor, safely out of range of his powers.

"Finally!" Dandridge said.

The old man smiled politely in return.

40 – Ghost

John Lazarus landed in the alley behind Archer Lane. Only the muffled crunch of gravel beneath his sneakers gave away his presence as he slipped down the alleyway. He reached the back gate of his old house. He didn't see anyone. He thought about dashing to the back door to see if the old house key was still under the loose step, but opted for a more careful approach.

When he was halfway across the yard, he heard voices approaching from the side of the house. Someone was coming around back! He leapt skyward and hid amongst the branches of the tree that dominated his yard. Two figures came into view.

Johnny recognized them instantly. Heather and...

Emily. For the second time in a day his heart skipped a beat. And for the second time today he didn't really have time for reunions. No matter how much he wanted to talk to her, to look into her eyes, to make her smile. No matter how much she deserved to hear him say, "I'm sorry," for leaving her behind, for letting her think he was dead, for simply not saying goodbye. Even if he thought he'd been protecting her.

So many things had been left unspoken between them. They'd spent most of their time together. She was a constant guest at his family's table. They were definitely closer than friends. In fact, everybody assumed they were officially an item. And all that came with a lot of assumptions, but they'd never just come right out and said how they felt. Would it have been so awful to just tell her that he could never be satisfied with just being her friend? He told himself he was always waiting for the right moment, as if he'd recognize it if it was staring him in the face.

And here he was, watching over her like her own personal guardian angel, so close he could smell her perfume, and he still couldn't bring himself to say... anything. He groaned inwardly, but told himself there wasn't time. But later...

As Emily placed herself on the old tire swing, Johnny made the preternatural jump across to his rooftop. The girls heard the noise as he hit the shingled roof, but he scurried over the other side before they could see him. He waited until he was sure their attention was elsewhere, then scampered to his old bedroom window, which jutted out of the rooftop. With practiced ease, he yanked the window open and tumbled inside.

Once inside, he took a moment to catch his bearings. The room was exactly as he left it. No one had so much as cleaned the place. The same old rock posters. The comics and gaming magazines. Clothes littering the floor. He may as well have stepped back into time. Aside from the dust and cobwebs anyway.

Not like it was in his nightmares. When he dreamt, the house was lit in flames of green and black that did not burn. Rather, they accused. *Murderer. You killed them. You were responsible for their death. Coward. You could have stopped them. You ran. You should have saved them, done something, at least turned yourself in. But you were afraid and out of control and your parents died for it.*

He shook his head, clearing it. He wasn't ready for this.

He took a tentative step back toward the window, but stopped himself. The time for running was over. He needed to face this thing. Steeling himself, he crossed the room, stepped out into the hall and looked down the stairwell.

He was a little surprised to see three guys waiting on the stairs. They were dressed in Halloween zombie makeup. They hadn't noticed him yet. Johnny couldn't believe someone was actually trying to haunt his own house.

"Can I help you gentlemen?"

As one, all three stared up at him in terror and shock. One of them was wearing a pair of infrared goggles, the kind he'd asked Weasel to pick up in the toy section of the local SuperBig Mart earlier today.

He recognized the biggest one. "Brad Farley, get your big ugly butt out of my house."

One of Brad's sidekicks wailed. "He knows your name!"

"Dwayne?" Johnny asked.

"He knows *my* name!" Dwayne tried bolting down the rest of the stairs, but Brad grabbed him by the back of the shirt.

"Wait!" Brad said. He frowned at Johnny. "You're supposed to be dead."

"Oh, I am dead and you're trespassing." He pointed his hand at a framed photo on the wall. It came loose and hovered in the middle of the stairwell in front of their eyes. He did the same thing to all of the other photos in the stairwell, until the trio of trespassers was surrounded. Dwayne wet himself and nearly fell down the stairs to get away from this apparition. Tater didn't run, but he did stand closer to Brad.

"I'm not afraid of you," Brad said. "How are you doing that? Where's the wire?"

"That's right, Brad. I'm not a ghost. I came back after all these years for no better reason than to stage a haunted house just for you."

"You better watch how you talk to me, boy!"

"And you'd better take care not to call me boy again," Johnny warned. "This ain't grade school, Farley. You have no idea what I'm capable of now."

Brad flexed his biceps. "You actually think you can take me?"

"I know I can," Johnny said.

"Only one way to find out." Setting his massive jaw, he charged up the stairs at Johnny.

Johnny almost didn't react in time, but going uphill slowed his would-be assailant down and he managed to catch the hulking jock with a wall of kinetic force. Oddly, it only rocked Brad back onto his heels. It did eventually stop him, but only after he'd managed to reach the top of the stairs. Johnny frowned. The muscle mutant from the police station had been able to resist his telekinetic push like this. Was Brad like Bantam?

Brad's piggish eyes narrowed. "How did you do that?"

"Forget this!" Tater yelled from below. Brad and Johnny watched him go.

"You should go with your friends," Johnny said.

"Listen here, you stupid n–"

Brad never finished his racist threat. Hit by a kinetic blast, he flew backwards, slammed against the wall and dropped onto the stairwell. He rolled to the bottom of the stairs with an avalanche of grunts and curses.

Emily and Heather appeared at the bottom of the stairwell, drawn by the commotion.

Heather recognized her boyfriend's impressive form at her feet, despite the zombie makeup. "Brad!? What are you doing here?"

Brad sighed and looked up at her. "I'm fine," he said as he rose to his feet. "Just fell down a flight of steps. Thanks for asking."

"You were coming here to scare us, weren't you? Weren't you??" Her face darkened.

"Gimme a break. It's Halloween." He glanced over his shoulder at Johnny. "Besides, I ain't the only spook haunting this house." He leered at Emily.

Emily clocked Brad with a vicious roundhouse.

Brad rubbed his nose and glared at her. "You hit like a girl."

"Brad!" Heather shouted.

Reading the look on Heather's face, he left via the kitchen door. Heather decided that wouldn't do. She chased after him, scolding the whole way.

Johnny was left standing at the top of the steps in Emily's cross-hairs.

Emily spoke first. "Johnny."

"Hi, Em."

She raced up the stairs into his arms, hugged him fiercely, unwilling to let him go. Her embrace fit him like a warm blanket and melted the darkness a little. He realized that he'd left a piece of himself here in Midwich. He hugged her back, drawing her closer still, until she gasped involuntarily. He eased off a bit. He hadn't meant to crush her.

She breathed into his chest. "I've missed you so much." She stepped back and looked up into his eyes. To his surprise, she erupted with a hard, angry slap. "How could you leave me? Where were you? We thought you were dead, Johnny. Dead! I watched them bury you! I cried for weeks! Did you even care?" she asked.

"You weren't even supposed to know I was here. You think I wanted to hurt you?"

"And thinking you were dead all this time didn't hurt?" she asked, blinking back tears. "You couldn't call or leave me a note?"

"I don't have time for this!"

"You don't have time? You just got here! Where you going, Johnny? What are you so busy doing that you can't take a moment?"

"There are people after me," he blurted, "people who'd like nothing better than to dissect me and see what makes me tick. And I have to save them and the rest of the town, because it turns out, well, they're the lesser of two evils."

"What are you talking about? Who's after you?" Her tone made it clear she didn't believe him.

"Well, if you really must know, dear girl," a new voice interjected, startling them both, "we are."

41 – Shadow Man

Johnny pushed Emily behind him protectively and watched a suited figure step out of his parents' bedroom. The newcomer wore a bowler atop his head and a business suit beneath his overcoat. He held a briefcase in his hands. Oddly, Johnny could see through him in spots. Other parts, like his face, were completely obscured in shadow.

"Who are you?" Johnny asked.

"I am, well, I'm Charles Huxley." The shadow fled from his face. "I'm Titan. I run it. And I've been watching you your entire life."

Johnny reacted instantly, tossing a blast of kinetic force at Titan's Director. The energy wave tore through Charles Huxley's form, disintegrating him. Yet a moment later, he reformed, completely unscathed and slightly bemused. Johnny thought he'd seen a small spherical shape where Huxley's heart should have been just before he came back together.

"What just happened?" Emily asked, eyes wide.

Ignoring her shock and confusion for the moment, Johnny addressed the Director. "You're not really here, are you?"

"Of course not," Huxley said. "What you're seeing is a holographic image. I'm not even in Midwich."

"What do you want?" Johnny asked. The hovering orb he'd glimpsed must be the source of the hologram. He wondered what other toys Titan had at its disposal.

"I want you to come back. I want you to join us. I don't want to dissect you. You're no use to us dead. We're willing to offer a salary, a job and a scholarship at Kaukasos College. A chance to stop running. To have a home, a normal life."

Just like that. The winning ticket. Everything he ever wanted all gift wrapped and topped with a bright red bow. A chance to start over. With Emily perhaps.

Except his parents would still be dead. His dad had taught him a few good lessons, one of which was if it sounded too good to be true, it probably was. Besides, who was he kidding?

"I'm not normal," Johnny said. "I can never have a normal life."

"Nonsense," Huxley said. "You're extraordinary, true, but people just like you have lived in this town with everyday jobs and everyday lives for a very long time. The question is: how badly do you want it?" They both ignored the bewilderment on Emily's face.

"I just want to be left alone."

"I think we both know that's simply not an option."

"I don't have time for this. I have to stop Pandora."

Huxley grinned. "Funny you should mention that, because that's part of the deal."

"Yeah, I saw that coming actually."

"Then we have an agreement?" Charles Huxley asked.

"I'll get back to you. Now, if you'll excuse me, I came here for a reason and you're in my way." He brushed past Titan's Director, distorting the image where they touched. Huxley's image nodded a smiling farewell and flickered out. Johnny and Emily watched the holosphere float out the window.

"What was that thing?" Emily asked.

"Some kind of hologram projector with, I'm guessing, some sort of antigravity drive."

"That's impossible. That's the kind of stuff they have in cheesy sci-fi movies. It doesn't exist in real life," she said.

"We have to go." Titan's Director might be gone, but he could easily double-cross him and relay Johnny's position (if the biochip hadn't already) to a Titan goon squad. Impatient, he tugged Emily along behind him.

Emily dug her heels in. "Wait! What's going on? What was all that? Are you in some kind of trouble?"

"All day long. Look. I'm sorry," he said, "for everything. And I'll explain all of this, I promise. I just need to get something I left here first."

She nodded, but looked skeptical.

He walked to the laundry room that adjoined the kitchen. Came to a door. Opened it and peered down into the darkness. His father's study was in the basement. Where the fire had started.

"Who's Pandora?" Emily asked.

"A very bad lady," he said. "She hypnotizes people and turns them into her little zombie slaves."

"Zombies??"

He read her thoughts correctly. "Not that kind of zombie. They're more like pod people really. Mindless drones that do her bidding."

"How is that better?"

"It's not as gross."

"And you're gonna stop them? I mean, can you?"

"Yup."

"Is that why Titan wants you? You hypnotize people?

"No, I'm… different," he said. He didn't want to freak her out. "I move things mostly."

"You move things? Like what you did back there with that holomajiggy?"

"Yeah, something like that."

"How?" she asked.

"I dunno. With my mind."

"How?" she repeated.

"I just do it. Here, watch this." The kitchen cabinets opened of their own accord. She jumped, startled.

"You did that?"

He nodded, a mischievous glint in his eye. Concentrating, he lifted her off the ground.

She protested, kicking her legs and trying to find something – anything – to grab onto.

He set her down gently.

"Have you always been able to do that?" she asked, her face flushed.

"No, it started about a week before the fire," he said.

"Why didn't you tell me?"

"I wanted to."

She stared down in to the darkness of the basement, sobering. "The fire started down there, didn't it?"

He nodded.

"Do you have to go in there?"

He nodded again. "I'm hoping my dad... I think he left something for me, but I have to hurry."

"It's dark," Emily said. "I can't see anything."

Johnny willed his eyes to see in the infrared. "I can. Do you want to wait up here?"

She didn't answer immediately.

Correctly reading her expression, he assured her. "I won't run off. Wait for me by the tire swing. I shouldn't be more than five to ten minutes, tops."

"Be careful."

42 – The Night of the Fire

He watched her head back out the kitchen door before he turned and walked carefully down into the basement. Where the fire damaged steps ended, he glided on down kinetically. He peered into the darkness with infrared vision.

There it was lying on his father's desk, a little singed, but miraculously intact. He searched about suspiciously. It seemed too easy.

He crossed the basement study and reverently picked up his father's Bible. He dusted off the soft leather cover. Dad had never let his Bible alone long enough for it to get dusty. He was always reading it, studying it, writing in it, talking about it. Other folks talked about sports or politics or the movies; Sheriff Lazarus liked to talk about the God and the Bible. He was easily as informed on the subject as the average sports fan was about their favorite team.

Johnny had largely rejected the Bible stories of his youth once he learned the facts of history and science in school, but he'd retained his general belief in God, mostly because of his father. If Arthur T. Lazarus could be so intelligent and down-to-earth yet still believe in God, he figured there must be something to it.

As he cracked open the familiar book, memories came rushing back.

The night of the fire, his father had told him that everything was going to be OK, that he knew about his abilities, that they needed to get far away. He said he'd already written his resignation and he'd be sending a copy of it to their Senator, in hopes that someone could intervene and provide them with protection. He no longer agreed with how Titan was handling things. There were people in the Company that wanted to exploit folks like Johnny, to turn them into weapons. They didn't see their potential to help humanity. They just wanted to maximize their profits.

Mike Trager showed up. Said that Titan was coming, that they were coming to take Johnny from him. They argued. His father asked Trager if he'd come to help Titan. Before Trager could answer, they were interrupted by a Titan security team. They burst into the basement study, led by Carter Munroe. His dad and Trager both shouted for the security team to stand down, but they had their orders. They'd figured out what Dad was up to. They weren't about to let him skip town with their investment. Tensions were high.

Somebody got an itchy trigger finger. That single misfire triggered a hailstorm of bullets.

For the first and final time, Johnny saw his father use his gift. To stop the bullets in midflight, to leave them hovering there in midair, threatening everyone in sight. His Dad could have killed everyone, then and there. Johnny could still recall the look of fear and desperation on his father's face.

But Trager intervened, quelled his dad's wrath.

That's when Cougar pounced. A man Johnny knew from family get-togethers and barbecues. His surrogate uncle. The guy who gave him his first pocketknife. Cougar was a pyro. He'd been hiding at the top of the stairs, well behind Carter's men. He jumped down the basement stairs, his face dark with murderous intent. Flames seemed to jet out of his hands and engulf Arthur Lazarus.

Trager threw Cougar back with a concussive blast, but it was too late. Arthur was too badly burned. He offered one last stricken, apologetic look at his horrified son and died.

All Cain broke loose. Something snapped inside of Johnny. A caged animal tore loose from his soul and exploded in vengeful fury. He was never really sure what had happened. The last thing he remembered was seeing Cougar's face as he got back to his feet and then Johnny's vision went red. When he came to, he was a good twenty miles out of town, his clothing singed and torn. He suffered minor burns and scrapes which healed in a matter of minutes. He learned about the fire and his alleged death later.

He began running.

He looked down at the Bible, which had opened to a familiar spot in John.

"In the beginning, was the Word and the Word was God and the Word was with God." Johnny read, skimming the chapter. "Without Him was not anything made that was made… and the Word was made flesh and dwelt among us." Johnny knew the passage spoke of Jesus Christ and recalled how his Dad was always quick to point out that it all tied back to the very first verse of the Bible. If the Bible was true, ultimately Jesus Christ was his Creator. But could he believe a Book that the mainstream intelligentsia had rejected as prescientific myth?

Arthur Lazarus had. He placed his absolute trust in the truth of God's Word, the Bible. Where others said that the all-natural explanation of science made supernatural claims unnecessary, Arthur would ask them how much faith was required to believe that nature could do miraculous things, since they believe that everything sprang from nothing or comic book multiverses, that life sprang from nonlife, and that a frog could become a prince after all… over millions of years. Where others had claimed that the Bible was full of contradictions, or full of prescientific myths and fables, or that it was written by flawed men, his father had asked them how we would recognize whether a book was really written by God. Then he would show them that the Bible is historically accurate, that any alleged Biblical errors or contradictions were simply misunderstandings, and that God's Word was supernaturally authenticated by both fulfilled Bible prophecy and the resurrection of Jesus Christ. In short, Arthur Lazarus was a true believer, but he believed because of the evidence, not in spite of it.

The question was: what did John Lazarus believe?

Closing the Book, he felt along its spine for a familiar lump. That's where his dad always kept the key. His father never suspected that he knew about it and the door it unlocked. Walking across the room, he shoved a bookshelf aside. It was on a track, hidden from view, so it moved with relative ease. Behind the shelf was a small door. He inserted the key in the lock.

Inside was a collection of currency and files in manila envelopes. One was labeled, "For Johnny." Intrigued, he opened it. Inside was another key on a chain necklace, a copy of his resignation addressed to their senator, and a short note, written in the event of his death. His Dad had apparently planned for everything, even his own demise. The key was for something at Titan. Something called the *Grey*. The note assured him that with the key he'd find all of his answers there. He slipped the keychain over his neck and stuffed the papers in his pocket.

The basement stairs creaked. He turned around, startled. Had Emily decided to come down after all?

Someone was coming down the stairs, but the legs belonged to a man. Johnny steeled himself as the other descended. Then he saw the newcomer's face, eerily framed in Johnny's infrared.

Ephram Cougar.

43 – Burning Man

The pyro's eyes searched the basement dark. Unable to penetrate the gloom, Cougar caused both his hands to ignite in flame. His twin torches illuminated the basement, exposing Johnny to view.

The sudden brilliance also hurt Johnny's eyes, temporarily blinding him, but he was already moving, knowing what Cougar had in store for him. Flames washed over the spot he'd just vacated, destroying the rest of the contents of his dad's locked box. Johnny reached out kinetically, picked his assailant off the stairs and threw him across the room.

Seemingly unconcerned, Ephram Cougar adjusted his aim and sent twin flamethrowers at Johnny even as he sailed through the air. The younger man threw himself backwards to avoid the fire jets. Cougar's assault was temporarily doused when he impacted with the far wall.

Johnny picked himself up and flew up the stairs. His assassin sent fire gushing up after him. Johnny exploded into the laundry room with a ball of flame at his back and sailed onward out the back door. Fortunately, the blast had thrown him clear of most of the fire. He landed in the cool grass of his backyard.

Emily, Heather and Brad stood staring at him in horror and wonderment. Getting to his feet, Johnny shouted, "Move! He's coming!"

"Who's coming?" Emily asked.

A moment ago she'd been absently listening to Brad and Heather's argument, when suddenly Johnny burst out of the back door silhouetted in flame.

Johnny pulled her along as he passed by her. "Just run!"

Brad and Heather hurried to catch up as fire began to engulf the rest of the house behind them, consuming it at a terrifying pace. The heat and Johnny's obvious terror forced them to make for the alleyway.

No, not terror, Emily realized. The look in Johnny's eyes confused her. It was intense, but he wasn't afraid. Not for himself. For them. For her, she realized. He seemed torn between saving them and turning around to face whoever he was protecting them from. Smoldering just below the surface was a rage that begged for release.

Suddenly, the house itself exploded. The brick garden shed that made up a portion of the backyard fence shielded them from the burning timbers. They couldn't help but stop and gape at the aftermath. A crater strewn with burning rubble was all that remained of the Lazarus home.

Brad turned to face Johnny. "What did you do? Is that why you came back? To finish your house off?"

Johnny shot him a withering glare.

"We need to call 911," Heather said. "It's catching the other houses on fire, too!" She drew her cell phone even as she spoke.

"What happened?" Emily asked, trying to make sense of the last several minutes.

Johnny didn't answer immediately. Instead he stared into the flames, watching intently. Then he saw what he was looking for. Purposeful movement. A figure engulfed in fire, but apparently unfazed by it. The Burning Man emerged from the fire and smoke. Looked right at Johnny. Began walking toward him.

"Run!" Johnny shouted as Cougar raised his arms and threw jets of flame at them. Once again, the brick shed took the brunt of the assault. They ran up the alleyway, cut through someone's backyard a few houses later and emerged onto Archer Lane.

"What was that thing?" Heather asked as she gasped for breath. "Did we lose it?"

"He's after me," Johnny said. "Brad, get the girls out of here. I'll lead him away."

"Wait!" Emily said. "That was your Uncle Ephram back there, Johnny. Why's he trying to kill you?"

"I'm more interested in why he's a human flamethrower," Heather said, trying not to hyperventilate.

"He killed my father the night of the fire," Johnny said, "but he was really after me."

Emily took a moment to assimilate that. "I think maybe we lost him."

The house behind them burst into flame.

"He found us. Coming?" Brad asked the girls.

Emily was reluctant, even given the circumstances.

"Go!" Johnny urged her. "He's after me, not you guys."

"I can't. I just got you back. What if he kills you?"

Brad started jogging away, tugging Heather behind him. "What if he kills *us*?"

"Go. I can take care of myself," Johnny said. "Please Emily. I just need to know that you're safe."

His eyes persuaded her more than what he said. She nodded. "What are you gonna do?"

"I'll lead him away."

"And then what?"

"And then I'm going to Titan to finish this. I'll find you when this is all over," he said. "So go with Brad already."

"I love you." Her face flushed red. She'd just blurted it out like an idiot. It probably wasn't the best timing, but she wanted him to know. Just in case.

He caught her eye, his unguarded expression a mixture of pleasure and surprise. "I love you, too." He grabbed her hand and pulled her close before the moment could slip away. Their kiss was fierce, desperate, an urgent release of what seemed like a lifetime of longing. It melted into something deeper, more tender and rhythmic.

"Johnny!" Brad's shout broke the moment.

Johnny stepped away from Emily and followed Brad's gaze. Ephram Cougar emerged from the fires, his entire focus on John Lazarus. "You have to go, Em," Johnny said.

"I know. Don't die, Johnny."

Johnny watched as Emily ran off to catch up to Brad and Heather, then turned to face his foe. He waited in the middle of the street for Ephram Cougar. The Burning Man barely spared Johnny's friends a glance. When he saw his target, Ephram began running toward him. Johnny backed up to put more room between them, sizing up his opponent.

"What do you want, Cougar?" he asked, hoping to stall him while he came up with a strategy.

The Burning Man didn't answer. He just kept running at Johnny. As he passed by, cars burst into fireballs, shrubs ignited, the Archer oaks began to burn.

Johnny blasted him backwards kinetically. Cougar got back to his feet and charged at him again. Fire crawled up the oaks on either side of the street, forming a cathedral of flame as it spread to the intertwined branches overhead. Johnny knocked Cougar on his back again. The pyrokinetic picked himself up more slowly this time. He stared at Johnny without emotion, but it was obvious that he was at least reassessing his strategy.

It took Johnny a moment to realize that he was staring at one of Pandora's zombies. Dead-eyed Cougar was under her control. So apparently she now wanted him dead. Zombie Cougar had no choice but to do everything he could to kill Johnny no matter who else got hurt along the way.

Johnny glanced over Ephram Cougar's shoulder. His friends had made it to the mouth of Archer Lane and were still running. Seeing that they were safely away, Johnny decided he needed to neutralize Cougar quickly. He couldn't bring himself to kill him. After all, he didn't really know what he was doing right now. But neither would it do to have a human flamethrower burning down the town while he was trying to deal with the one who was truly responsible.

It was starting to feel like he was inside a furnace. Like he was in hell. Unbidden, the Biblical tale of the rich man and Lazarus came to his mind. He understood the rich man's thirst. His thirst made him take note of the fire hydrants. With effort, he caused every hydrant to burst, sending cool water jetting skyward. For good measure, he used his power to redirect the streams at Cougar, violently dousing the Burning Man and sending him to the pavement hard. Even so, the heat became unbearable. Unable to take it any longer, Johnny launched skyward and burst through the burning branches into the cool autumn night beyond.

He would have to deal with Cougar later. He stared down at Archer, awash in smoke and blaze, as he reached the apex of his leap. He reminded himself that this was really Pandora's handiwork. Cougar was simply the weapon in her hands.

He directed his gaze toward Titan. Using his powers to break his fall, he launched skyward again, covering the ground to the Titan facility in incredible leaps.

44 – We Need a Ride

"Where's he going?" Brad asked.

"I don't know, Brad," Heather said. "I'm still trying to get past the fact he's flying."

"He's not flying. He's just jumping really high."

"Whatever."

"He's going to Titan," Emily said.

Brad stared up the mountain where the company's research complex was nestled. He was adding up the events of the day. He was never particularly good at math, but the answer to this one was pretty obvious. First of all, there was the fact that long-lost Johnny could jump like he was on the moon and move things with his mind. Comic book stuff. Secondly, Brad himself had beefed up recently. No, he was well beyond anything anyone would call merely "beefed." No one in his family was as big as he was. He was probably stronger than any comic book hero he could think of. Lastly, they'd just watched some guy torch practically every house on Archer Lane without the aid of so much as a matchstick.

And all this had something to do with Titan.

"We should follow him," he said. Emily looked stunned by his decision, but he could see it was what she wanted too.

"Aren't you at all concerned that your house is on fire, Brad?" Heather asked, glaring at her cellphone. "I cannot believe 911 just put me on hold!"

Brad gaped. It hadn't occurred to him for some reason that the wildfire had touched every home on Archer Lane. "My house! That guy burnt my house down!" He glared down the road at the man responsible. Ephram Cougar was gone. "Where'd he go?"

"I'm still on hold. Can you call my mom's cell?" Heather asked.

"Call her yourself," Emily said. "Nobody's coming."

"Says you," Brad said, pointing down the road at an approaching police truck. The black SUV had its lights flashing and its siren blazing. Brad tried to flag the vehicle down, but it whizzed on past. "What? Come back!"

The vehicle slammed on its brakes and backed toward them.

"Great, Brad!" Heather hissed.

Brad was looking for an exit, but he didn't think he could get away in time.

The SUV stopped in front of them and the black-tinted window rolled down. They were greeted with the unexpected face of Curtis Holloway. "What happened? My house! Is everyone OK?"

"Otis? I mean, Mr. Holloway?" Brad mentally cursed himself for uttering the nickname his dad habitually referred to Mr. Holloway by. Otis Campbell was the town drunk of *Andy Griffith*'s fictional Mayberry. Brad wasn't sure if Midwich's town drunk was even aware of the mean-spirited nickname, but Mr. Holloway didn't strike him as a man who would take kindly to it. For all his own strength, Brad wasn't entirely sure he could best the old drunk. "What are you doing in a squad car?" Frankly, if Curtis had been riding around in the back it wouldn't have surprised him so much. "Where are the cops?"

"Police station's been attacked. Abandoned. Found this vehicle back on Hickory. Tried the radio, but no one's answering." He stared mournfully at his house as it disintegrated in the flames. "What set the fire?"

Brad and Heather looked to Emily. "You're not going to believe us, sir," she said, "but we were at Johnny's house when this guy who was on fire–"

"Johnny was here?" a voice asked from the back seat of the police truck.

Brad peered suspiciously into the back of the vehicle. The tinted windows foiled all attempts to see within, but the voice sounded familiar. "Who's asking?"

"Nevermind him," Curtis said. "What were you doing in Johnny's house? Was he with you?"

"Yes, he was," Emily replied, hoping Curtis would have some information on Johnny.

Curtis spat and pounded the roof of the truck's cab. "Hang it! Where'd he go?"

"We think he went that way," Brad said, pointing. "To Titan."

"Of course he did. So he left you guys high and dry, too, eh?"

Emily bristled. "There was this guy who was on fire and he was chasing us. He led him away from us."

"Well, good for you, missy."

"I'm sorry, but you're not listening," Heather said. "A man on *fire* was chasing us, but he wasn't being burned!" Heather said.

"I heard you the first time."

Curtis' unsurprised reaction caught her off-guard. She stood with her mouth open, unsure how to respond.

"You're going after him, aren't you?" Brad asked.

Curtis blinked as if noticing him for the first time.

"Take me with you," Brad said.

Curtis shook his head. "This isn't a field trip, kid. You don't have any idea what's going on and you don't wanna neither. Trust me on that!" He reached down into the seat beside him and pulled a beer out of a case. "Anyway, it'll all be over by morning, I reckon." He snapped the pull tab and slugged back half the can. "One way or another," he said, wiping his mug with his sleeve. "So you just find yourself someplace safe to hide and ride it out, kids."

"Um, you really shouldn't drink and drive," Heather said.

"Wouldn't dream of it," Curtis assured her, tossing back the rest of the can. He crushed the empty can in a ham fist and tossed it into the passenger seat of the SUV. "See ya."

"Oh no, you don't," Brad said, grabbing the handle of the truck door. "You're taking us with you."

"Get your hand off the door, kid."

"Get in the truck, girls," Brad said, not letting go.

"This is for your own good, buddy," Curtis said. Without warning, he threw the SUV into drive and slammed the accelerator. Brad didn't let go immediately and found himself jerked off his feet. As he picked himself off the ground, he glared at the receding police vehicle. He looked down in his hand, momentarily surprised to find the handle still in his hand. He tossed the twisted bit of metal aside.

Heather gasped when she realized what he'd done. "Brad! How did you?" She stopped, eyes widening in terror. "You're like them! Nobody's that strong. You're like a mutant or something."

Brad just glared at her. "We need a ride," he said. Then he hit upon an idea. "Got it," he said, slapping the back of his hand into his other meaty mitt. "Kelly's kegger."

Putting thought into action, he began jogging. The girls looked at each other in bewilderment and hurried to catch up.

45 – Titan Overthrown

Daniel Zim tried to make sense of what was happening to him from the darkness of the broom closet. He'd fumbled around in the dark for the light switch, but as luck would have it, the bulb had blown when he flipped the switch. He just couldn't seem to catch a break today. First he was stuck here all day because of Johnny and Pandora and all that had happened, causing him to miss Trick or Treat with his young son. Then he'd been hypnotized and turned into a zombie, at which point he'd very efficiently made things as bad as he could possibly make them. He'd been awakened from his voodoo vandalism by gunshot. The wound still hurt and throbbed horribly. Pain medication and bandages only went so far. Then the Indigo they'd captured earlier had gotten the drop on him and shoved him into the aforementioned lightless closet.

There had been no sounds from the control room for some time. Not that it was much consolation. The door was securely locked. He was pretty sure the escaped Indigo had psionically done something to the lock to jam it, to boot. So he was stuck here with the old mops, cleaning solvents and brooms. He thought briefly about making some sort of weapon. That's what his TV heroes would've done. Then he figured he was just as likely to further injure himself in the dark. Besides, considering what he was up against, it would be like bringing a popgun to Armageddon.

When he'd first begun work at Titan he couldn't believe his luck. He was working alongside real-life comic book heroes. They could do things he'd only dreamt of. And most of them were just kids. Well, teenagers actually. Still, his job was to keep tabs on muscle mutants, human chameleons and living computers, amongst others. Titan had found a way to develop a bumper crop of super humans.

Not that the first generation was a bunch of slackers. The original Titan dream team had been comprised of a high-level hypnotist, a preternaturally accurate marksman, a human flamethrower and two guys who could juggle dump trucks with their minds. Of course, Arthur Lazarus was dead now and Pandora a fugitive. He'd met Ness a few times, but he refused to talk about any of it. That left Cougar and Trager, pyro and psionic knight respectively. Zim had found out pretty quickly that Ephram Cougar was an arrogant jerk and an outright bully. He was also a habitual liar. Mike Trager was pleasant enough, but it was clear that he carried around some pretty hefty baggage from the past and, like Ness, he didn't like talking about it. Everyone else either didn't know or wasn't saying.

So Daniel Zim had to content himself with rumors and those rare moments when someone let something slip. Oh, he knew the basics. He probably knew more about Pandora's defection and the Lazarus fire than anyone else who worked for the company – at least, more than anyone who wasn't actually involved in the incidents. His job description pretty much required them to brief him on those two events.

So now he knew just enough to be a danger to himself. Which was a little frustrating. Rival companies simply assumed he knew more than he did.

Without warning, light flooded into the dank closet. Daniel Zim was jerked unceremoniously out of darkness and pulled back into the control center. The rough treatment was agonizing on his injured leg.

The first thing that he noticed was there was no sign of Mike Trager, but the younger kinetic seemed smugly satisfied with himself. Hillary slammed him into a chair and spun him around to face…

"Pandora."

"Daniel Zim, I presume." When he didn't respond, she shrugged. "Well, you know who I am and you know what I can do. I need you to access the mainframes for me."

That's why they'd kept him in the closet and hadn't simply killed him, he realized. This was a robbery. Corporate espionage. Of course, once they were in, his fate was uncertain at best. "It won't do you any good," Zim said. "We've initiated the Final Protocol."

She snickered.

Supposing she didn't comprehend the full implications of what he'd just said, he elaborated. "That means the intel on the mainframes has been dumping into the Vault, so most of it" – he glancing at the clock on his monitor – "isn't there anymore and not even I know where the Vault is located, so you went to all this trouble for nothing."

"It's there," Pandora's assistant said.

"I'm sorry. Who are you?" Zim asked, annoyed at being contradicted.

"Destiny Pascalé," she said. "You're bluffing. Final Protocol assumes that you'll slag the mainframes after your company's files have been copied to the

Vault. It's still there."

"No more games," Pandora said. "We want everything. Do you understand?"

A moment later someone much more familiar to Daniel burst into the room with a squad of black-suited body-armored soldiers. Unlike the others, he was dressed in a business suit.

"Ridenour!"

"What? Oh, Daniel Zim, isn't it?" Dandridge Ridenour said. "You should've taken my offer."

"I'm not a crook."

"But you could've been rich. Too bad."

"Do you know what kind of scum you're working with?" Daniel asked Pandora.

"Oh, we're quite aware," the old man accompanying Dandridge said.

It took Zim a moment to recognize the old man as Pandora's father, Silas Darling. Now, he knew this was all much worse than they'd feared.

"We're on a schedule," Destiny reminded them, glancing at her watch pensively.

"Get us inside, Daniel," Pandora said. "You know it's pointless to resist me."

"I can try," he said.

"As you wish."

He felt his willpower melt under her gaze. Moments later, he was happily humming to himself, vaguely aware that his leg still hurt and that he shouldn't be helping these guys download all of Titan's files. But if you can't help your friends, what was the point?

46 – Kelly's Kegger

As far as keg parties go, it was a pretty typical mob. The party was really just getting started amongst the town's enclave of metal heads, punks, stoners and future bikers. Most of them were regulars. Very few of them had any idea what was going on in Midwich.

Kelly Harper was the black sheep of the town's founding family. He'd cultivated an outcast status by surrounding himself with the usual pariahs. Some thought he was dealing pot or coke, meth maybe, but his only real vice was supplying underage teens with alcohol. Everybody knew he did it. They even knew where. But he was from money and money has its privileges.

As Brad Farley approached the firelit revelries, he boxed back the phantom of glorious post-game parties amongst his jock friends. When Trager benched him and the rumors of steroid use surfaced, his popularity suffered almost overnight. You really found out who your friends were. The popular kids, even his teammates, turned on him, shunned him, shut him out. It wasn't long until he was reduced to slumming with Kelly's fan club of geeks, freaks, Goths and spazzes. It never occurred to Brad that other folks also thought of him as part of Kelly's gang of outcasts.

As he walked into the glow of the firelight, several party-goers turned to inspect him, then shrugged with recognition. Red plastic cups of beer graced nearly every hand. Most of them smoked as well. There were usually much more illegal things going around, but it was too early for any of that now.

The site wasn't exactly on a beeline to where they wanted to go; he'd had to veer about seven blocks off course, cross the tracks and climb over the earthen flood wall to reach the kegger, but he'd justified his decision under the assumption that he could make up lost time once he secured a ride. *Where was Dwayne?* At the top of the floodwall, he'd been greeted by the sight of a large bonfire surrounded by partiers and their vehicles, parked along a gravel service road. There were a few trees surrounding the scene, but none blocked their view of the river.

Out of habit, Brad scanned the area for Wacky Jackie. Kelly had made it abundantly clear that his turf was "Switzerland," his term for neutral ground. No fights. No bullying. Period. Have a good time or else. Unlike Brad, Kelly Harper didn't surround himself with useful thugs and minions; no, he liked to enforce his own rules personally. The little rich boy knew how to fight and he wasn't afraid to show it off. Those who came looking for a fight always found one. They never came back for seconds.

Wacky Jackie was nowhere to be found. But there was an unwelcome shock waiting for him.

"Brad! They told me you'd be here. Surprise!"

Alyshia lived in a neighboring town. A cheerleader from a rival high school. They'd met at a game. Things had gotten way too serious, but he'd always figured she lived so far away that no one would ever know he'd hooked up with an Oreo. His dad would kill him if he knew he'd been messing with a biracial girl. His pops still told folks that he'd nearly chucked his television when he saw the *Star Trek* episode where Kirk kisses Uhuru. Yet Brad couldn't deny that Alyshia was everything he'd wanted in a girl, except available whenever he wanted to see her… and white. Despite his racist upbringing, Brad hadn't been able to get her off his mind. He knew he was a hypocrite for treating Johnny the way he did for the color of his skin, while he secretly had the hots for Alyshia, but he was still working this out. Maybe dad was wrong. All he knew was that Alyshia spun him about like nobody else. He'd even fantasized about finding a way to see her again, but not like this and especially not with his backburner babe hot on his heels. He glanced over his shoulder to see if Heather and Emily had caught up with him yet. His luck was holding for the moment.

Licking his lips, he tried to feign happy surprise. "Leesha!" He realized then that he had no idea what to say. "Wow."

"I know, right? I mean it is alright, isn't it?" she asked. "You're happy to see me?"

"Y-yeah," Brad said. "I just – Look, there's no easy way to say this."

Alyshia's face fell. "You're breaking up with me," she said. "I'm so stupid."

"No, it's not like that," he said. "I'm not breaking up with you."

"You're not breaking up with *who*?" Heather asked. Her voice was cold enough to chill a polar bear. For all his size and strength, Brad Farley found himself unwilling to turn around to face his accuser. Heather zeroed in on Alyshia, brushed past Brad Farley and marched up to her very startled rival. She smiled sweetly, but without a trace of warmth in her eyes. "Hi, I'm Heather. And you are?"

"I'm Alyshia. Um, pleased to meet you."

"Are you? That's nice. How do you know ol' Freight Train Farley here?"

"Heather," Brad said.

"Shut up, Brad."

"Look," Alyshia said, "I'm not sure what's going on here and I don't want any trouble. I just came here to surprise my boyfriend." Her voice fell on the word "boyfriend," for it was at that moment that she looked to Brad for moral support and saw the truth of it in his eyes.

"Well, he is surprised. Isn't that right, Brad?"

Brad breathed a muffled curse, but he wasn't dumb enough to answer.

"I think I should go," Alyshia said, trying not to cry.

"But the party's just getting started," Heather said.

"Heather!" Emily scolded. "That's enough."

"Don't *Heather* me!" Heather said. She turned back to Alyshia. "Did you know about me?" She took a threatening step forward. "Did he tell you about us?"

"No! No, I thought he loved me. I thought…"

Which is when Heather realized that the girl standing in front of her with hot tears streaming down her face was just a much a victim in this situation as she was. "Yeah, I thought, too," she said. She shot a murderous glance at her ex-boyfriend. Turning back to Alyshia, she pitied her fellow sufferer. "I need a drink. You?"

Alyshia burst into tears. "I can't. The baby."

Heather turned on Brad, shooting him a look of such betrayal and fury that he wished he were a million miles away. He hadn't yet caught the full implication of what Alyshia was saying.

"What am I going to do?" Alyshia asked.

"Wait. You're pregnant?" Brad asked. The dual demons of his father's wrath and the unexpected responsibility of fatherhood threatened to steal the breath from him. "You're not saying it's mine?"

Alyshia nodded her head, not looking at him.

"But we just did it that one time. Are you sure? My dad's gonna murder me!"

"I've never been with anyone else," she replied.

"But I'm not ready to –"

"Shut your mouth, Brad Farley," Heather said, eyes smoldering. "Not another word." She took Alyshia by the arm, leading her gently away. "We'll figure this out. Come with me, girl."

Alyshia nodded mutely. Heather glared at Brad over her shoulder as they departed. Her face said it all. He had absolutely zero chance with Heather ever again. He wasn't sure about Alyshia.

Brad became aware that everyone was staring at him. Accusing him. Like they had after he'd stomped the Freeman kid. His face flushed beet red under their scrutiny. He knew what they were thinking. He was the bad guy. A womanizing bully. He bit back an angry rebuttal. It wouldn't do any good. He knew that.

Then he became aware that Emily was among those glaring at him. He turned to face her, knowing he had it coming. "Words fail me," she said. "How could you do that to her?" The bonfire seemed to flare hotter at her fury. "To either of them?"

"You wouldn't understand. My dad is gonna–"

"Your dad? Have you even called him to see if he's OK?" she asked.

"What?"

"Your house just burned to the ground, Brad. Have you called to see if he's OK? Because if you care so much about what your racist redneck father thinks, surely you're just dying to know whether he's dead or alive, right?"

Brad glared at her. Truth be told, he hadn't even thought to call his dad yet, but he assumed his pops was down at the bar, as he usually was this time of night. "I don't have to explain myself to you, Emo," he said. "And we don't have time for this. We came here for a reason: Titan, remember? That hasn't changed."

"I remember," she said. "You just remember who that baby's father is when this is all over.

"Are you still in or not?"

"We still need a ride."

Brad nodded and looked around for options. He saw Dwayne. Unfortunately, Dwayne had spotted him first, thanks to the scene Heather had made. Well aware he'd probably earned himself a thrashing for abandoning Brad back at Johnny's house, he'd bolted for his car and was already putting it into gear.

"Oh no, you don't," Brad said, sprinting him.

But Dwayne already had a good head start. He quickly put distance between himself and his pursuer, churning up gravel as he gunned down the service road.

For a moment, Brad despaired at the sight of his buddy's orange hotrod rapidly fading into distance and darkness, but Coach Trager hadn't trained his players to just give up. Freight Train Farley dug down deep and found the will to churn after Dwayne's Duster. His legs hammered the gravel like pistons as he focused on his goal to the exclusion of all else. To his surprise, he found himself closing the gap between them.

Dwayne gaped into his rear view mirror in horror. He'd never seen anyone run that fast before! He stomped the accelerator to the floor.

When he looked back at the road in front of him, he saw the Anarchist. There was no way he could stop in time. He steeled himself for impact. The biker roared and Dwayne found himself airborne, flipping end over end back the way he'd came.

The orange Duster came down with a sickening crunch, then rolled on down the road. Brad dropped to the gravel road as it bounced over him. It finally crashed into a stand of trees and exploded.

Stunned, Brad got to his feet, his eyes searching for the cause of Dwayne's freak accident. The Anarchist's bike came charging down the road, intent on running him down. Brad dove aside just in time. Getting back to his feet, he roared a challenge and took off after Dwayne's murderer.

Back at the bonfire, the noise of the crash and the Anarchist's motorcycle gained the partiers' attention. As they stared down the service road, trying to see what was going on, the Anarchist skidded sideways and came to a dramatic halt at the party's edge. The pagan leered at them, letting them get the full effect.

Which gave Brad the perfect opportunity to plow into him from behind. He knocked him off his bike and over the bonfire to land in the river. Shaking with fury, the stranger sloshed out of the water and glowered about for his assailant. Brad Farley stared at him from across the bonfire, ready for the next round.

Kelly Harper chose that moment to interject himself between the two. "That's enough," he said firmly, more to the Anarchist than anyone else. "You need to leave. Kelly Harper says no."

The stranger graced him with an ugly, savage grin, then roared with abandon. The resultant sound wave knocked Kelly off his feet and several bystanders to boot. Worse, it fanned the flames of the bonfire in Brad's direction. Helpless, he put up his hands to protect himself. To his surprise and relief, the flames washed around him but never touched him. It took him a moment to realize that Emily was behind him and that she had something to do with it, though she looked pretty well confused by the whole thing.

"How did you do that?" Brad asked her over his shoulder, hoping it might come in useful.

She shook her head mutely, too stunned to make sense of it. Her eyes found Heather's in the crowd. Her friend was staring at her the same way she'd looked at Brad when he'd ripped the handle off the police SUV.

Brad and the Anarchist stared one another down. "Well, if you figure it out," he said, "give me a hand, will ya?" He bent down in a familiar three-point stance and launched at his foe like he was blitzing the quarterback. He had to leap through the fire, but he barely felt the heat as he passed through. Just as he was about to make contact, the other let loose a sonic roar that swatted him away. Off-balance, he tumbled to the ground in a heap.

He rolled onto his back, trying to keep track of his enemy. The Anarchist's size 15 boot was about to come stomping down to squish his skull like a grape. Brad rolled to the right. The boot slammed into the earth next to him. The Anarchist reached down and grabbed him by the collar. Using his other hand to grab Brad's belt, he hoisted the disgraced football player above his head, intending to break his foe's back on his knee.

"Hey!" Emily yelled. "Let the loser go!"

Still holding a struggling Brad over his head, the Anarchist turned around to glare at the girl who'd called him out. He laughed when he saw her.

She wasn't laughing. She was concentrating, doing something she'd never suspected she could until few moments ago. At her will, the bonfire blazed skyward.

The Anarchist roared in defense, scattering the flame and knocking Emily backwards. Brad used the distraction. Struggling fiercely, he put the Anarchist off balance and sent them both toppling to the ground. Quickly, he scrambled away.

The biker got to his feet with a dark look. A ball of flame promptly slammed into his chest and knocked him back down. He struggled to get back to his feet, only be knocked down anew with burning punishment. Panicking, he got to his feet again, but this time in a retreat. Emily sent a fireball into his backside for good measure.

The Anarchist dove sizzling into the river. He emerged moments later. Notably, he didn't get out of the water, but glared at them from its relative safety.

Emily glanced around. The party was in a full rout. Every vehicle was churning up gravel in a hurry to flee the scene. Others were scrambling over the earthen flood wall in a panic. Heather and Alyshia were among the latter.

"I can't believe I just did that," Emily said, gasping for air. "Did I just do that?"

Brad nodded.

Emily concentrated again, forming a tongue of flame in the palm of her hand. "How is this possible?" she asked. "It doesn't even burn."

"We have to get moving." He nodded toward the water where the Anarchist glared at them.

She caused the flames to burn more intensely in her palm, glaring back at their foe. He quickly ducked under water. He emerged a few seconds later, further out.

"Now what?" she asked.

Brad didn't answer. He was staring at the Anarchist's bike with a wide grin.

Seconds later, he was roaring down the service road with Emily on the back of the motorcycle.

The Anarchist pouted impotently from the water.

47 - Welcome Wagon

Jackie was careful to remain utterly still as the pair exited the van. Her camouflage made it near impossible to see her when she was motionless, but you could see her blurred edges when she moved. As Bantam and Winters made their way across the parking lot, she crawled into the driver's seat and eased the door open. She slid outside and closed it gently.

She hurried after them, relying on her gift to hide her from sight. Only once did one of them turn around. Jackie froze. Jennifer Winters scanned the empty parking lot behind her suspiciously, but seeing nothing she hurried to catch up to Bantam.

They made it to the back door before Jackie. The door was locked. She could see Winters talking into her commset and moments later the door opened. Realizing they were slipping away, she did the only thing she could think of.

"Hey! Wait a second!" she yelled.

Both Bantam and Winters spun to face her. Winters had a gun out.

"Don't shoot," Jackie said. "I'll come quietly."

"Show yourself!"

"OK, but you have to promise not to shoot me. My name is Jackie Holloway," she said. "Pandora is my mother." She willed herself to materialize seemingly out of thin air, hands raised over her head.

Winters looked skeptical. Nevertheless, she called it in.

Jackie waited pensively, wondering if she even had a Plan B at this point. Finally the verdict came in.

"Come with me," Jennifer Winters said. "She wants to see you."

Jackie sighed with relief, then ran to join them. She noted that Winters kept her weapon trained on her.

Johnny bounded into a tall tree near the Titan complex. He hoped his chosen vantage might give him an idea of what kind of resistance he might expect. On the far side of the complex, two helicopters sat at ready, guarded by masked men in black body armor. The grounds were crawling with people. Some of them had crashed their vehicles into the building. Others were seemingly trying to tear it down with their bare hands or with whatever makeshift weapons they'd picked up along the way. With that kind of mindless determination, they'd find a way inside the building in no time.

Of course, these zombies were nothing compared to the Indigo he'd left behind on Archer Lane. He glanced back the way he'd come, searching for any sign of Cougar. Even though he didn't see his Uncle Ephram anywhere, he knew he was coming.

That whole mess back on Archer bothered him. Both Titan's Director and Pandora had known he was in town and that he'd be at his old house, but how? He supposed Titan probably had cameras stashed everywhere. They'd obviously been tracking his movements since he rolled into town. He suspected the Director had staked out his place via that hologram drone in the hopes that Johnny would visit it out of morbid curiosity or nostalgia or whatever. Pandora probably made a similar guess and sent Cougar to mop up after he'd been stupid enough to announce his intentions to stop her at the police station. But seriously, was he that predictable?

He launched skyward and landed on the roof of the complex to avoid the crowd of zombified townsfolk. He peeked over the rooftop to make sure he hadn't been noticed by those guarding the twin helicopters. Those below seemed oblivious to his presence. Realizing the established entrances were probably being monitored, he opted to make one of his own. He raised his hands above his head, calling upon his kinetic abilities to peel back the roof itself so he could slip inside.

He was more wary once he was inside. He didn't really know Pandora's exact whereabouts. Frankly, he figured she'd find him.

The intercom buzzed. "John Lazarus." He jumped, despite having expected something like this.

"Pandora."

"You're actually trying to stop me," she said. "Are you sure you're on the right side?"

"Pretty sure."

"You can't stop me, but you could benefit from this."

"Is that a bribe?" he asked, walking. If she was offering him a bribe instead of just finishing him off, she was in a weaker position than she let on. He wasn't sure where she was, but he'd just passed a sign telling him where the security control center was. That seemed like as good a place as any to start.

"A business proposition," Dandridge said, cutting in. "We'd like to hire your services. I compensate my people well."

"Who are you?" Johnny asked.

"Dandridge Ridenour. I represent a rival interest. Titan's superiors must've told you there would be others interested in employing your services?"

"I don't work for them."

"A free agent then. Even better. Perhaps you'd like to discuss terms. I'm sure we could come to a mutually beneficial arrangement."

"No. Let's just get this over with."

"I'm sorry you feel that way," Ridenour said, "but no hard feelings. Tell you what: if we both survive this night, the offer's still on the table."

The elevator at the end of the corridor chimed. A man stepped into the hallway.

"Trager," Johnny said.

Mike Trager stared at him blankly, hands at his side. He was unarmed.

"You're a zombie, aren't you?" Johnny asked.

The other didn't reply. He just stood there waiting for some unknown cue. Without warning, Trager sprang into action. Two pistols floated from behind his back, firing quickly.

Johnny kinetically ripped the doors off their hinges on either side of him and used them as a makeshift shield. He dove into the room on his left, someone's office. He mentally tossed a pair of metal filing cabinets out the door he'd just entered, even as he spotted another exit.

Dulled by the restraints of Pandora's spell, Trager barely avoided being crushed to death. As it was, he suffered a glancing blow from the first filing cabinet. Nonetheless, he sprang to his feet as if he'd merely tripped.

Johnny kept running, but the next room turned out to be a private restroom.

A fact Trager was all-too-aware of, since he knew the layout of this place intimately. He ripped the door off its hinges, like lifting a rock to see what squirmed and crawled beneath. He barely shielded himself from a porcelain sink Johnny tossed his way.

Johnny followed it up with a sonic roar, blasting Trager out of his path. He made a break for it.

Still getting to his feet, Mike Trager mentally pushed Johnny into a wall in mid-run. The younger man fell to the floor with a crash. Mike's guns fired as he got to his feet. Johnny attempted to alter their path and found another force resisting his. Still, the shots tore chunks out of the wall instead of his body.

Johnny caused the ceiling fan to fly at Trager as a distraction, allowing him a moment to stop the bullets in mid-flight and bolt for the door. Bullets dropped to the floor as Johnny kicked the door down and toppled into the hallway.

He barely had time to alter the path of a stream of bullets coming at him from the other end of the hall. Masked men like those guarding the helicopters outside emerged from the stairwell, at the opposite end of the hall from the elevator, firing at him with semi-automatic weapons. Stifling a surge of panic, he picked up one of the men at a distance and slammed him into a wall. The other two never stopped firing, even when their hapless comrade's body fell into their line of fire. Fortunately, friendly fire was met with Kevlar body armor.

More zombies, Johnny realized.

Johnny sent a surge of kinetic force plowing down the corridor like an invisible locomotive. The zombie soldiers were thrown down the stairwell like ragdolls. The young kinetic rode the backlash of that push to the elevator doors, which dented from the blow. Johnny cushioned himself somewhat with psionic energy, but the impact still rattled his teeth.

He pushed the elevator button. Trager stepped into the hall and began marching toward him like a machine. More masked zombies poured out of the stairwell at the opposite end of the corridor.

The elevator doors opened. Johnny dove in and pushed the Lobby button repeatedly.

Trager's pistols gave chase, firing the whole way. He ducked inside, out of the line of fire. The doors closed, but one of the guns slipped inside at the last second. Startled, Johnny fought to gain control of it. But struggle as he might, the gun kept turning toward him, firing all the while. One shot should've taken off the side of his face, but he arced the bullet's path away just enough. He followed suit with the next two shots, but the last shot was point blank.

Click. An empty chamber fired.

The elevator chimed. The doors opened into the lobby. Cautiously, he looked around for trouble. He was momentarily distracted by the sight of the townspeople beating on the bulletproof glass outside. When they got in, things were going to get enormously complicated. Seeing the way was clear, he stepped off the elevator.

He heard the locks on the front doors click. Zombies poured into the lobby.

Johnny retreated back into the elevator, pushing the Close Door button repeatedly.

The zombies spotted him and ran toward him quicker than he would've thought. These were no shuffling cinematic corpses! The elevator doors closed just before they reached him.

Without warning, the elevator dropped, its cable snapped from above. Johnny was jerked off his feet. Landing on his back, he did the only thing he could think of. He willed the elevator to stop. It stopped between floors. Carefully, he concentrated on making it come to rest on the floor below. The doors opened. He stepped through, still concentrating. Only then did he allow the elevator drop unceremoniously down to the bottom of the shaft.

48 – Gamma Lab

Jackie felt like she was going to leap right out of her skin. She'd hoped for, prayed for and dreamed of this day for a long time. Ever since her mother left. And now that it came to it, a host of conflicting emotions fought for dominance inside her head. Joy. She would finally see her mother. Worry. What if she didn't like her? An odd disquiet. Her mother turned people into mindless zombies. Excitement. Would her mother be surprised at what she could do? Resentment. How could her own mother just leave without saying goodbye. Hurt. Why? Anger. How dare she abandon them! Love. There was much too much to sort out now. All that mattered was that it was finally happening.

On the other hand, she wasn't a complete idiot. She knew what Curtis would say about all of this. She shouldn't be here. It wasn't safe. Yadda yadda. All true, but beside the point. When she'd heard Johnny mention Pandora – the woman Weasel had identified as her mother – to Bantam and Winters at the police station, she knew she had to come. Still, he would've warned her to have an exit in mind in case things went south.

Jackie glanced over her shoulder. Winters still had her weapon pointed stubbornly at the back of her head. Bantam took up nearly the entire width of the corridor behind her. The only way out was forward, which would afford Winters a convenient shooting gallery.

"Stop," Jennifer Winters ordered. "They want you to wait here."

Jackie glanced around in confusion. "Where's my mother?"

"I'll take it from here," a familiar voice said. "She wants you two to go on ahead. We're almost done here."

"Papaw Darling? What are you doing here?" Jackie asked. She rarely saw her grandfather, maybe once every couple years. Curtis didn't like him much and, well, the feeling was mutual with Silas Darling. Jackie had never been sure what their quarrel was about, but it ran deep. She presumed it had everything to do with her mother. But what did her grandfather have to do with all of this business at

Titan?

Silas glanced at his granddaughter. "One moment, dear child." He turned back to Winters. "You need to hurry. Jack will be covering our escape."

Winters nodded and hurried away. Bantam shrugged and turned to follow her.

"And now that business is out of the way, let's have a look at you," her grandfather said. He beamed from ear to ear as he appraised her. "You look so much like your mother did at your age. Simply beautiful."

"Where is she?"

"Busy with other matters at the moment, I'm afraid. And the less you know about all of that, the better."

"Where has she been?"

"I'm not sure I'm the best one to tell you. You've probably guessed as much, but she had a bit of a quarrel with Titan." He made a distasteful face. "They chased her out of town on a rail. Forced her to disappear. Speaking of which, Winters tells me you appeared out of thin air. Is that true?"

Jackie nodded.

"Fascinating. These gifts run in our family, you know. On your mother's side anyway, though I should say none of the rest of us can disappear."

"My mother seems to have managed," Jackie said.

"Ah, yes," he said. "Leaving you behind hurt her the most, I assure you. But if everything goes according to plan, you'll never have to worry about being separated again." He blinked distractedly, hearing something on his commset. "Ah! She's ready for you. Right this way." He took her arm and led her up the hallway.

They came to a door. Jackie beamed despite herself. Her elation was immediately chased by worry. "How do I look?"

"You'll be fine," he said as he opened the door and gestured for her to step inside.

Jackie's eyes swept the partially damaged control room, searching for her mother but taking in everything. There was a man in a business suit, several commando types, a young woman around her age, a techie who never once looked up from his computer screen and...

"Mom!"

Hope Holloway laughed, rushing across the room to sweep up her daughter in a fierce hug. "Jackie! Oh my baby girl," she said. "I've missed you so much. There's so much to tell you."

Jackie was enraptured. Her mother was here, as vibrant and close as if they'd never parted. And she still loved her. Both of them were crying tears of joy at their much longed-for reunion. It didn't seem real. It was more like a dream. And there was a part of her that simply couldn't pretend it was all better just because they were together again. She pushed her mother away. "You left me," she said, hot tears searing her cheeks.

"I'm sorry. I never wanted that. I couldn't stay in Midwich. Titan betrayed me."

"You could have taken me with you!"

"I wanted to. I tried. I really did. I'm so sorry," her mother said, forcing herself to wipe her eyes dry and regain her composure somewhat, "for everything, and I know you deserve a better explanation than this. When this is over, we can sit down and talk this out."

"When what is over? What are you even doing here? You're robbing Titan, turning people into zombies… How is any of this going to make anything better?"

Silas placed a hand on her arm, trying to calm her. "Now is not the time, dear child. She's doing this for you and for everyone else like us."

Jackie jerked her arm away and glared at him, but kept listening.

"The world isn't safe for people like us, Jackie," her grandfather said. "People fear us. They always have. Every dark legend finds its basis in us: vampires, witches, demons, wizards, people who could do things they shouldn't be able to. In the past, mankind was more superstitious. They came at us with pitchforks and torches, stakes through the heart, crucifixes and all the rest. But they came to kill us. Now they want to use us, dissect us, exploit us, make weapons of us." Noting that Ridenour was growing tense throughout his diatribe, he added, "There are those like Ridenour and Parasol Limited, people who are willing to compensate us for our voluntary service, but they are a rarity. Titan and all the rest want to control us. They see us as property. They're growing themselves a nice little bumper crop here in Midwich and I suspect this isn't the only science project they're running. The way they see it, they made us, they own us. If they can't control us, they'll destroy us because we're too dangerous to just let us go about our business."

"Let's say you're right," Jackie said. "You don't think this little stunt will just confirm their worst fears about us?"

Destiny spoke up. "It will, but it will also lead us down a path that will allow us to make it safe for all our kind."

"And you know this how?"

"Miss Pascalé sees the future, dear," Silas said.

"My men are almost in position," Ridenour reminded them.

"This will have to wait until later," Pandora said. "In the meantime, just trust me. I'm doing this for all of us."

Jackie was unconvinced, but it was clear the conversation was over. Pandora had already turned her attention to one of the few functional monitors. It took Jackie a moment to realize they were looking at John Lazarus.

The corridor he stepped into had windows on one side overlooking a laboratory. The lab was deserted. He couldn't quite make out what they were doing here, but he guessed it had something to do with the Titan's research. Several upright coffin-sized cylinders drew his attention. A red fluid obscured the shapes of the figures beheld through a window, but they were definitely human.

"Ah, there you are," Pandora said from the intercom. "I was afraid you'd gone down with the elevator."

Johnny scoffed. "I can sense your disappointment."

"You've found the laboratory," she said. "Good. There's something you need to see. Go ahead. Take your time. I want you to understand."

Johnny didn't answer. He was staring down at those pods, trying to make sense of the entire operation. Were they clones? Failed experiments? Alien hybrids? Just what was Titan doing down here. He heard a buzzing noise followed by a click. A door had just been unlocked.

Johnny dutifully opened the door and stepped into the lab. This could very well be walking into a trap, but he had to risk it. He had to know. "What am I looking at?" Johnny asked.

"Prometheus Stage 3."

"Explain."

"Titan's Prometheus Initiative. Once upon a time, Titan designed a biochip intended to monitor the development of neural pathways and brain functions, so that they could cure mental disorders and perhaps even boost intellectual potential. We were supposed to usher in a golden age of improved humanity. That's what they told us anyhow," she said. "They found us, studied us, and enhanced our abilities with the brain chip. That was all Stage 1: Prometheus Alpha."

185

Johnny stared into one of the coffin-like vats. The figure within was naked, obscured by the red fluid. This one was female. A young teenager.

"You and others like you are Stage Twos: Betas. You had the chip in from birth. They watched your talents develop. They found a way to make talents appear more often with the chip. It also makes you more powerful, more dangerous. You were spawned from the genes of alphas, our gift to the next stage of human evolution."

"If you say so." His conversation with the preacher had left him skeptical concerning evolution. He couldn't help but wonder why it was always the bad guys who invoked evolution as a justification for atrocities like racism, euthanasia, eugenics and genocide.

The pods held a strong fascination for him. Inside, each individual was connected to a series of leads, tubes and wires. Their mouth and nose were covered by a respirator. And they were so still, almost like they were statues. Or...

"Are they dead?" he asked.

"No. Death would be a mercy. They've spent almost their entire lives in there."

"What are these things?" he asked, examining a pod's controls.

"Growth accelerators."

"Why would you need to–? Titan's growing an army of super soldiers."

"Available to the highest bidder." She sounded pleased that he'd caught on so quickly

"Sounds familiar. Or isn't that what you do: sell yourself out to the highest bidder?"

He struck a nerve. "What I do for Parasol is a mutually beneficial business arrangement. Gammas are to be sold like cattle. Property. Merchandise. No rights. And they'll take the rest of us along with the gammas."

"Right," Johnny drawled slowly. "I, for one, would love to see them try it. And I'm betting the gammas will have something to say about their big, stupid plan, too."

"The gammas will do nothing of the sort. They won't be able to. Titan learned its lesson after they tangled with me. It was too late to do anything about you betas, but they modified the gamma chip to make them more controllable like my zombies. I'm told they also designed their little remote control chip with a self-destruct in case they don't do what they're told."

Johnny shuddered and found himself rubbing his temples involuntarily. He couldn't believe human beings were capable of such self-justifying evil. He was starting to see why his dad always used to say that original sin was the only scientifically verifiable doctrine of Christianity! "No. Human beings aren't property. People won't allow it. Once they find about this, they'll make Titan stop."

"You're so naïve, Johnny. *People won't allow it*." She mocked in a whiny imitation of his voice. "No, Johnny, people will demand it. Once they figure out how dangerous we are, they'll insist that we be tagged and regulated. For everyone's safety, of course. Never mind they should be serving us. We are the next stage of evolution."

"You keep saying that," Johnny said, "we're still only human."

"Only human? Johnny, compared to them, we're gods. Primitive tribes would have worshipped us. We've been here all along, evolving, waiting for our turn. The chip just accelerates the process."

"Or revives into something we lost long ago," he said, echoing Blyth.

"If you believe in myths like Adam and Eve."

Johnny blinked in surprise. How had she known he was thinking about Genesis? Why would she go straight there from his statement? Had she talked to Blyth before? Or maybe his father had voiced similar sentiments, he reasoned. Either way, Johnny was starting to see that it really did all come down to design versus chance, creation versus evolution, the Bible or the all-natural history of the world, and no one could avoid that conflict.

"Don't deny your destiny," Pandora said.

Johnny was pretty sure he'd just been handed a veiled ultimatum, but he simply couldn't buy her argument. "What destiny? Do you think you'll actually win? Better yet, do you think you're actually better than people without these powers? I mean, look at what you do with them. These powers certainly don't make us morally superior or wiser; they just make us stronger than the next guy, so it's really just might makes right."

"Or survival of the fittest."

"Yeah, Hitler had ideas like yours, and your racism is just as wrong as his was." The conclusion that evolution was an inherently racist theory had never occurred to him until he spoke those words. No, he didn't think that everyone who affirmed evolution was a racist, but the theory itself implied that some people groups were just more evolved than others. His father used to mention a man named Ota Benga, a pygmy who was once displayed in the Bronx Zoo's monkey house alongside an orangutan because men believed that people with darker skin were more ape than human. It was no longer politically or socially acceptable to voice such racist opinions, but no matter how you sliced it evolution still implied that some men were less evolved than others.

"Oh, that's right. Pull the race card."

He ignored her attempt to sideline his point. "Hitler used ideas like master races and survival of the fittest to justify the Holocaust and Germany's bid for world domination. I don't see how you're any different. If anyone's pulling the race card, it's you."

"Johnny, stop moralizing. This is just nature taking its course. Don't fight it. Don't fight your destiny."

"We're through talking," Johnny said.

Pandora hesitated before speaking. "Too bad. I could've used you."

He looked toward the exit. He could hear footsteps from the stairwell.

49 – Flare

Ephram Cougar walked up to the main access road to Titan. The gate yawned open before him, laid bare by the assault of Pandora's other zombies. She had mentioned the gate. It was imperative that he stop there, no matter what else was going on, and...

His gaze blank, he raised a fist in the air and shot a pyrokinetic flare skyward three times. Lowering his arm, he continued on his way.

Dandridge Ridenour snorted when he saw the flare light up the sky outside the control room windows. "That's a little late, don't you think? Isn't that the flare I was supposed to see before we landed the birds?"

Pandora glanced at her watch and arched her eyebrow in an unspoken question of Destiny.

Her assistant nodded. "Still within acceptable parameters."

"What's within acceptable parameters?" Dandridge asked.

"I told you," Silas Darling said. "This is a military operation. You have to plan for contingencies. Nevertheless, the mission overall is going according to plan."

Dandridge didn't reply. This whole operation felt wrong. His gut was telling him to get out and cut his losses.

Silas' little speech to his granddaughter and the intercom conversation between Pandora and Lazarus already had him on edge, though he'd been careful to keep his expressions masked. His superiors had warned him that Pandora was a manipulative little harpy, that she might be playing at her own game. They felt the risks were worth the possible payoff of acquiring Titan's wealth of research and information.

Parasol's own super soldier program, the Hive project, had already made great strides. With Pandora's cooperation, they'd been able to analyze the mechanism behind her hypnotic abilities. The information they'd gleaned had allowed them to make soldiers that single-mindedly carried out every order without regard for fear or danger. The black-suited zombie soldiers he'd brought with him were some of the best specimens they'd field tested. Hive drones had their drawbacks. Like Pandora's zombies, they were a bit slow and only as good as the limits of their abilities and training. That's why Pandora's mob was ineffectually beating their fists against the bulletproof lobby glass, while his government-trained drones could fly helicopters and operate expensive military hardware. All thanks to a revolutionary biochip implanted subcutaneously behind their left ear.

He glared at Pandora, silently vowing to make sure she got Hive-chipped as soon as this operation was over.

Ness walked out onto his porch, not really sure why he so strongly felt the urge to do so. Maybe it was the weather. He was usually in bed by now. He had the 4 a.m. shift, after all. Yet all of a sudden, he just needed to be on the porch.

Having little better to do, he looked up into the sky.

That's when he saw the flares.

It reminded him somehow of gaudy midway lights at a carnival. When had he last been to a carnival? When he was in high school maybe? No, it was just the other night. How had he forgotten? Carnivals weren't really his thing. In fact, he avoided people and public places in general, but he'd gone anyway. There was a reason. A good one. What was it?

His mind went back to the midway. He was determined. Grim-faced. A gun in his pocket. And a note from someone he'd thought dead. He didn't want to kill her, but he needed to stop her. Somehow.

He'd entered her tent.

How had he forgotten that? It didn't seem possible.

All of this he thought in the space between the first and second flares. On the third flare, he could only think of what the nice gypsy had told him to do. He didn't believe in fortune tellers, but this one seemed so familiar. It didn't matter. Nothing did. He needed to get in his truck and head to Titan.

But first, Ness grabbed his rifle.

Brad reveled both in the motorcycle's speed and in Emily's obvious discomfort with his near-reckless driving. Something big was going on at Titan and he didn't want to miss it. He got the feeling that it might be too late if he waited too much longer. He was also dimly aware of the fact that he was trying to put as much distance between himself and Alyshia as possible. Or maybe it was the baby and the responsibility of impending fatherhood. Or facing his racist father.

He skidded to a stop as he neared the paved circle that led to Titan's front doors and back out again, mostly to gape in disbelief and wonder. "What in Sam Hill?"

Dead-eyed townsfolk swarmed around the front of the building, desperately clambering to get inside. The lobby doors were open but a knot of them were trying to push through at once. None of them looked up at the pair on the bike. They had but one thought: Destroy Titan.

"We're not getting in that way," Emily said.

"There's always a back door." Brad turned toward the parking lot and a delivery road that led around the rear of the building. He slowed down as they approached, noting a familiar figure walking up to a back entrance.

"That's Cougar," Emily said.

"The dude that burnt my house down."

Cougar waited patiently by the door for a moment, then opened the door and entered. He left the door standing open.

Brad stopped the bike. "That's our way in. Hop off."

"That doesn't strike you as convenient? It could be a trap."

"That dude is completely zombified," Brad said. "He probably just forgot to shut the door behind him." Noting the pinched, unconvinced look on Emily's face, he added, "We'll be careful."

"Fine. You lead the way."

He made a sour face, then approached the building in a quick crouch. Emily shadowed him. He paused at the entryway, saying a silent prayer, then plunged ahead.

50 – Last Chance

Johnny was trapped. If the zombie soldiers shot out the observation windows, they'd effectively turn the lab into a shooting gallery with only one obvious target.

He ducked behind one of the coffin-like vats. Casting about the room, he located the security cameras and psionically crushed each one. It wouldn't do for Pandora to cheat and tell her goon squad where he was hiding. At this point, neither he nor the zombie soldiers could see each other, but that would change as they came closer. He needed to be able to see them before they got too close. And he needed to get out of here before Pandora could send Trager or some other super-powered lackey to finish him off.

He realized he could see the walkway above via the reflection in a nearby computer monitor. His foes were almost to the door. He got an idea. He concentrated, mentally lifting every desk, chair and computer he could locate. They assembled themselves before him, forming a shield his foes couldn't see through.

They began shooting almost instantly. No surprise.

He ran to the door, tugging along his shield of office furniture. He turned toward the ruined elevator shaft without stopping. The furniture followed him through the door, but then crashed to a stop, clogging up the hallway. The dead-eyed soldiers continued firing, chewing through the clog. Johnny ran to the elevator shaft, ducking as low as he could without slowing down too much. This was really tiring him out, but he wasn't about to just lie down and die. Besides, he was a phenomenally fast healer. He'd be fine if he could just catch his breath.

He reached the elevator doors. As he was willing them to open, he was knocked off his feet by the concussion of a grenade blast. The zombie soldiers trying to unclog the hallway had switched to a more effective tactic. A second later, they burst through the breach they'd created.

Johnny delivered a sonic roar that cleared the hallway from one end to the other. In doing so, he noticed an interesting side effect. He was momentarily able to see an image of the hallway and partly up the stairwell beyond, presumably by some sort of echolocation or sonar. He filed the information away for later, hoping the ability might come in handy.

Prying the elevator door open before his foes could recover, he slipped inside and bounded up the shaft. He glanced down, noting that the shaft ran so deep that he couldn't see the ruined elevator car that lay at the bottom. He stopped at the lobby, and willed the doors open a bit to peer out. It was empty. Pandora's servants had mindlessly torn apart the lobby, tossing furniture and smashing it to bits. They'd also strewn paper everywhere before hurrying onward to tear apart the offices and other areas beyond the lobby.

Johnny opened the elevator doors all the way and entered the lobby.

"Stop it, mother!" Jackie was unable to just sit by and watch what was going on any longer. "What are you doing? You're going to kill him."

They'd lost visual contact with what was going on down in the gamma labs when Johnny had crushed the cameras, but they'd picked up the action again on the hallway cams.

"Somebody get her out of here," Ridenour said.

"Johnny must be stopped," Pandora said. "He'll ruin everything."

"So you have to kill him?" Jackie asked.

"We're not going to kill him," Destiny said. "He's not that easy to kill. But we do have to slow him down somehow."

"It sure looks like you're gonna kill him to me."

"But we won't," Destiny said, treating her like she was simply overreacting.

"He's forcing us to defend ourselves," Pandora said. "He's determined to stop us. You heard him. He won't listen to reason."

Jackie blinked hard at her mother, biting back angry words. Truth be told, she'd found Johnny's logic much more convincing than her mother's. There had to be a way to save him. "Let me talk to him."

Pandora and Destiny exchanged glances. Destiny shrugged, but didn't look hopeful.

It was quiet, save for the sounds of offices being torn apart as if by wild animals. That was far enough away to be muted.

The security desk stood at the front of a grand double staircase leading up to the second floor on either side. Johnny heard a door open up there. Two zombie soldiers emerged onto the upper balcony, but they didn't fire.

"Johnny," Pandora said over the intercom. "One of your friends would like to talk to you."

A jolt of fear went through John Lazarus. Who were they holding hostage? Emily? Weasel? He was surprised when he heard Wacky Jackie's voice over the intercom.

"Johnny, can you hear me?"

He hesitated before answering. If she was on the intercom, Pandora was probably right there with her.

"I hear you. Are you OK? Did they hurt you?"

"Yeah. No, I'm OK. I'm not exactly a prisoner."

Johnny tensed, wary. "So you're on her side now?"

"No. It's not like that. She's my mom."

Johnny was rendered momentarily speechless by the revelation.

"Johnny, you have to call it off. They're going to kill you if you don't stop."

"And you're gonna help them? That it?" he asked.

"No, I don't want anyone to die here and I'm certainly not going to help anyone do it."

Pandora cut in. "Enough. My daughter has asked that we give you one last chance, and I have done that. Unfortunately we are on a very tight schedule here, so I need you to make a decision."

"I'm sorry, Jackie," Johnny said. "My gut says somebody has to stop this."

"Kill him."

The zombie soldiers didn't hesitate, but Johnny had anticipated the attack. He kinetically wrenched their weapons out of their hands after the first few shots and arced the path of those errant bullets away from him. Without ceremony, he banged their heads together. They bounced down to the stairwell and half-tumbled, half-slid to the bottom, quite unconscious.

Time to end this, Johnny decided. Taking the steps two at a time, he made his way to the second-floor balcony and peered through the ruined doorway to the corridor beyond.

To his utter shock and surprise, he saw Emily stepping out of a side room into the hallway. What was she doing at Titan?

"Look out!" she yelled to someone behind her and threw fire at him. He deflected the attack easily, but stared at her warily. He'd obviously startled her, but he couldn't say who was more surprised.

"How did you do that?" he demanded, hoping he wouldn't have to fight her.

"Oh my goodness! I'm so sorry, Johnny. Are you OK?" Emily asked. "I heard the noise and – You scared me."

"How long have you been a pyro?" Cougar was the only other pyrokinetic he'd ever met and, well, that wasn't exactly a good association.

"It just started happening. We went to Kelly's kegger to score a ride and this guy attacked us and it just... happened."

"Us?"

"She was with me," Brad said, stepping out the office. "She saved us all."

"What are you guys doing here anyway?"

"We followed Cougar up here. We came to help. And, well, I came for answers."

"You want to know about your powers, what Titan does, that sort of thing? Well, Titan put a chip in your head before you were born. It triggers the abilities."

"But it's different for everybody," Brad said.

Johnny nodded. He noticed a file in Brad's hand. "What's that?"

"It's to Titan from Kaukasos College."

"Johnny, didn't that Titan guy at your house mention a scholarship for Kaukasos?" Emily asked.

Johnny nodded.

"I have a scholarship for KC," Brad said.

Emily looked dubious. "Really?"

"Sports."

"I guess that makes sense."

"Can I see that?" Johnny asked. "I read over 7000 words a minute with comprehension."

Brad shrugged and handed it over.

Johnny scanned it quickly, flipping through the document at an abnormal pace.

"What does it say?" Brad asked.

Johnny summarized as best he could. "Kaukasos College confirmed that they'd nearly met their quota of beta candidates and wanted to know when Titan would have the gamma recruits ready."

"What's that supposed to mean?"

"People like you and me are betas," Johnny said. "We're sort of the prototypes, I think. Gammas are supposed to be more controllable. I saw some down in a lab. They're growing them in test tubes. My guess is that the chip in their head also allows Titan to control them remotely."

"Remote-controlled human beings…"

"Worse. Remote-controlled super-humans," Emily said.

"They want to turn us into weapons," Johnny said. "Just point and shoot. Worse, they've installed some kind of a kill switch into the gamma chip as a failsafe."

Emily shuddered. "So they can just kill them with the press of a button?"

"Pretty much."

"Can they do that to us?" Brad asked.

"I don't think so. Gammas have a new type of biochip. An upgrade." He glanced around until he found a fire escape map posted on the wall. One of the rooms on this floor was labeled, "Security Control Room." Johnny had never been in that room, but he knew there was a room from which Titan security watched all of the camera feeds. And Pandora had definitely been tracking him inside the building in a way that suggested she was in that room. "We need to get moving. I think Pandora's on this floor."

"Pandora?" Brad asked.

"The bad guy. She hypnotizes people," Emily said, remembering their conversation at Johnny's house.

"She can make you into a pod person with or without the gamma chip," Johnny warned.

Brad nodded.

"Where is everyone?" Johnny asked as he peered into the hallway. If Pandora was as close as he thought she was, this floor ought to be swarming with zombie soldiers and super-powered minions. And where were the zombies who'd breached the lobby? Surely some of them had reached this area. "Something's not right here. We need to be careful."

51 – Disruptor

Johnny peered down the hallway ahead before leading the others out of the room. Nothing. They turned the corner to more deserted hallway. This corridor seemed to stretch on forever. He kept expecting someone to jump out at them from the side doors, but nothing happened.

They came to the next intersection without incident.

"Which way?" Brad asked. Each path looked equally empty.

Johnny stopped, trying to remember how to get to the security control center. The fact that he was having any problems remembering bothered him. His memory was near photographic so he almost never got lost, but right now he wasn't real sure where he was. In fact, everything was starting to feel fuzzy. He couldn't remember what he was doing. Had he pushed himself too far? Was he suffering a stroke or something?

"Feeling a bit disoriented?" someone asked from the shadows. "Not sure which way is up? Yeah, I have that effect on people."

"I got this one," Brad said, jutting out his chin, but he was slurring whether he realized it or not. He brushed past Johnny, intent on knocking someone down, but dropped to the floor a few steps further, as if hit by a tranquilizer dart.

Johnny wasn't sure who he was dealing with, but he did know that he needed to get away from him. Instinctively, he backtracked, pulling Emily along behind him. He tried one of the doors he'd passed. Locked. He couldn't concentrate well enough to remedy the situation.

He broke into a run, checking doors at random. Finally, he hit pay dirt. He dashed through the unlocked door, locked it behind him. He was in a good-sized custodial closet. Mops, brooms, toilet paper. A low basin for the mop bucket. Various cleaning agents. Nothing he could use. There was a red metal ladder affixed to one wall. He followed the rungs upward with his eyes. It led to the roof!

Quickly, he scampered up it. The roof hatch was padlocked. He suppressed a growl of frustration. He knew it might be useless, but he concentrated with every ounce he was capable of on that lock, willing all of the tumblers inside to rise into the unlocked position.

Nothing. Worse, he felt dizzy. It would not pay to be high up on a ladder if he passed out. He climbed down as carefully and quietly as he could. He entertained the hope that the Disruptor would pass by so he could regain control of his powers. Perversely, his foe stopped right outside the door. How did he know he was in here?

He checked on Emily, who appeared to be unconscious.

There had to be another way out. He took in his surroundings more carefully, fighting off the constant vertigo. There was a cleaning cart. A lanyard hung from it. Keys! He struggled over to them hopefully. One of them was a Masterlock, same as the padlock above.

He snatched it up, turned to the ladder.

It was only by sheer force of will and perhaps dumb luck – Ed would have called it Providence – that he made it to the top of the ladder a second time. The key turned at his desperate, silent prayer. He thrust the hatch upwards and scrambled frantically onto the tarred roof.

As he crawled away from the hatch, he felt his powers returning.

As he recovered, he re-assessed his strategy. Thus far, his attempt to stop Pandora had been an absolute farce. He was running out of energy and he was just getting beat up for his efforts. Time for a more direct approach.

He got to his feet and forced himself to think this through. The guy in the hallway disrupted electrical power, apparently even enough to render people unconscious. It didn't sound like the type of power Pandora would want to risk being around when she was trying to download files. So she was probably on the move then, escaping, and this guy was the rearguard.

He turned back to the hatch, intending to mentally lift Emily out of the closet below, now that he was out of the Disruptor's range of influence. She was already crawling out.

"I think that guy, he went away," she said, standing to her feet. "I thought I was gonna pass out, but then the dizziness just kind of left."

He nodded grimly. "Pandora probably left him to guard her escape."

"What now?"

"Control room. We stick to the plan. She was able to see me from there. At the very least, I'll be able to see where she's headed."

"And then?"

He shrugged. "We stop her. Ready?"

She nodded again, steeling herself.

52 – Control Room

With Emily in tow, Johnny crept across the rooftop. They came to a row of skylights. Crouching down, they peered over the edge.

There was only one person in the control room. His attention was occupied by a computer screen. Johnny didn't recognize him.

"Looks safe enough," Johnny said.

"How do we get in?"

Johnny grabbed her hand. "Hold on tight," he said, then launched skyward. As he landed he shattered the skylights with a blast of concussive force and eased them down through the hole he'd made.

They scanned the room for hidden threats, but the computer technician really did appear to be the room's only occupant.

"Where did she go?" Johnny asked.

The man didn't answer. He just kept staring at his computer screen.

Johnny made the connection. "He's a zombie. We have to wake him. He might know where she went."

"How do we do that?"

He recalled Carter Munroe's warning about how to wake a zombie. "Extreme pain or electric shock."

"I'm not going to burn him," she said.

"Well, I don't have any way to shock him."

"No."

"Fine. What would you suggest?"

"I dunno. I mean, this is the security center. Don't they have Tasers or something?"

"That's an idea. Let's look around." He was trying to be patient with her, but every moment they wasted gave Pandora a bigger head start on them.

She'd only just begun her search when Zim's monitor caught her eye. "Um, Johnny, what's that?"

Johnny frowned. "It looks like a countdown. Twenty-six minutes."

"A countdown to what?"

"What else? Boom."

"We have to get out of here."

Johnny nodded, but he was thinking of Pandora's zombies, still wandering the complex. They were all going to die when that countdown stopped. This was exactly the sort of thing he'd always hated about comic book plots. The villain always seemed one step ahead of the hero. While he was busy saving the world or performing some critical Herculean task, the villain would get away or the hero's friends would be put in harm's way. And here he was, rounding up zombies bent to her nefarious will, while she got away with Titan's secrets.

How exactly was he going to stop all of those zombies? For all practical purposes, only Pandora herself could dispel the enchantment en masse.

"Johnny!" Emily had opened the closet to find a Taser when a body rolled out. "It's Jackie Holloway!"

Johnny hurried over to them. Jackie had suffered a nasty blow on her forehead. Someone had knocked her out and stuffed her in the closet, but she was alive.

Suddenly, Jackie bolted upright. "Mom!" Seeing Pandora was gone, her face fell.

"That was pretty stupid coming up here alone," Johnny said. "Are you alright?"

"I'm OK. I just wanted to talk to her," she said, "and I was afraid Curtis would try to stop me. She's my–"

"Your mom. I know. You told me," Johnny said. "It's OK. I get it. I probably would've done the same thing if it was my folks."

"What happened?" Emily asked. "Did she hurt you?"

Jackie shuddered. "No, but she was going to kill you, Johnny. I tried to stop her. Coach Trager – he's one of her zombies – he jumped me and slammed me against the wall. Knocked me out. You know the rest."

He was about to ask her if she knew where Pandora had went when he heard voices in the hall. Including one he hadn't heard in a while.

"Weasel?" Jackie said, choking. Her expression was something between relief and utter disbelief.

Johnny hushed her. "He might not be alone."

Emily held out her hand, ready to engulf the door in flames if necessary.

The door burst open. Weasel gave his best Viking yell, wielding a gun and waving it around like an idiot. He accidentally squeezed off a round at Johnny before he recognized his friend. Johnny deflected it easily and grinned.

"Johnny!" Weasel said. Then realizing he'd nearly shot his best friend, he added, "I almost shot you. Are you OK?"

"Of course." He didn't mention the fact that Weasel's shot would've taken his head off if he didn't have superpowers. All of those first-person shooter games were apparently paying off for his friend. "I thought I told you to skip town."

"You're kidding me, right?" Weasel said. "Tell me you're not glad to see me."

"OK, OK," Johnny said. "What took you so long? And where's Curtis?"

"He ditched me almost as soon as we got here," Weasel said. "I told the guy. When ya gotta go, ya gotta go. Nature calls. But does he wait? Anyway, I've been wandering around here looking for him or you or pretty much anybody else ever since. Then I found this jerk out in the hall," he said, as Brad walked into the room. "By the way, did I tell you this guy beat me up earlier today?" Weasel asked with casual malice.

"What?" Johnny asked, glaring at Brad.

"Yeah, this redneck thug and his little toadies jumped me in an alley and stole all the stuff you had me buy at the store."

"Is this true?" Johnny asked.

Brad didn't answer but he looked very uncomfortable.

"Johnny," Emily said, nodding toward the countdown clock, "we don't really have time for this."

Weasel seemed to notice her for the first time. "You must be Johnny's girl. Emily, right?"

Johnny turned away, hiding a blush. Emily looked after him with a smirk.

"Hey, Weez," Jackie said with a wan smile.

"Jackie?" His eyes went wide with alarm when he saw her injuries. "What happened? Are you OK?"

She waved him off, but grinned at the attention. "I'll be OK."

"Listen, we're on a tight schedule here," Johnny said. "Pandora set some sort of countdown and there are innocent people she hypnotized roaming all over this building. We think this guy might be able to help us, but he's been zombified. The only thing that can bring these zombies around is extreme pain or electric shock."

Without hesitation, Jackie hauled herself to her feet, walked over to the technician and shocked him. Daniel Zim found himself awake and painfully aware that he'd set Titan's Final Protocol in motion.

"Hey, Mr. Zim," Johnny said, reading his ID badge. "I need your full attention. I don't know if you can do anything about it, but there's a countdown–"

Zim groaned. "I know. She had me set it before she left for the *Grey*. I can't believe she got me twice in one night."

"I need you to focus, sir," Johnny said. "Is there any way to shut it down?"

Zim took a deep breath to clear his head. "No, there's no failsafe. The Final Protocol was designed to keep anyone from stealing Titan's secrets."

"Wouldn't Titan lose everything that way?" Emily asked.

"No. Everything's automatically backed up at the Vault when Final Protocol is set," he said. "Not even I know where the Vault is. Not that it matters. She had me download everything onto two discs before she and Ridenour took off."

"Ridenour?" Weasel asked.

"Ridenour is from Titan's rival, Parasol Limited. They've been developing a super solider version of Pandora's zombies," Zim said.

"I think I've already ran into a bunch of those," Johnny said.

"They call it the Hive program," Zim said. "Those Hive drones are stone cold killers. The Hive chip frees them of all fear, remorse or ethical entanglements. Just point and shoot."

Johnny looked at the clock. "We have 24 minutes, give or take, and we've got a lot of innocent people wandering the halls. Is there any way to get them out of the complex?"

Zim shook his head. "They're not wandering the halls anymore. Pandora sent them all to the auditorium before she left the control room."

"Why would she do that?" Emily asked, a bad feeling forming in the pit of her stomach.

Zim pulled up a feed from the auditorium. "A lot of our cameras are down, but that looks like all of them," he said.

"What are they doing?" Weasel asked. "I mean, they're all just sitting there staring at the stage. What are they waiting for?"

"The countdown," Brad said.

Jackie's face fell. "She's just gonna let those people die."

Johnny winced, thinking how awful it must feel to realize your mother was a mass murderer. Yet he could see Pandora's strategy. She was using the Gruber Gambit. In the original *Die Hard* movie, the fictional Hans Gruber had attempted to do something similar. Posing as a terrorist, he'd hoped to cover his robbery by blowing the roof off the Nakatomi Tower with his hostages. Gruber figured the authorities would be so busy sorting through the rubble for bodies that he'd be long gone before anyone realized he hadn't also perished in the blast!

"No, she's not, Jackie," Johnny said. "Not if you can help it. You and Weasel get down there. Shock 'em back to their senses and get them out of here."

"What about you?" Weasel asked.

"I'm going after Pandora."

"I'm going with you," Jackie said. "She's my mom. I can't just sit back and–"

"You're not going," Johnny said. "Nobody else can bring all those zombies around. You're the only one who can help them. It has to be you."

"But you'll kill her."

"Nobody's gonna kill anybody," Johnny said, hoping he could keep his promise, "but I do have to stop her, OK? Just like you have to save these people she's leaving here to blow up with the building. OK? You with me, Jackie?"

"I have your word? You won't kill her?"

"You have my word."

"Well, I'm going with you," Emily said. Johnny knew better than to argue.

"Me, too," Brad said.

"OK," Zim said, pulling up a schematic of the complex, "the auditorium is on the first floor. I'll talk you guys down there. Johnny, you need to get into the Tunnel. Pandora's going for the *Grey*." He pulled up an image of the craft.

"That's the *Grey*?" Johnny asked.

"It's a flying saucer," Weasel said.

Zim nodded, grinning despite their situation. "Ain't it cool?"

53 – Hangar

A trio of Parasol Hive drones waited with infinite patience for someone – anyone – to come down the stairwell after Pandora. Having already checked it out, they ignored the elevator behind them. The ruined elevator car had crashed to the bottom earlier, warping the doors slightly ajar but nothing could make it through the wreckage without gaining their attention.

Johnny glided silently down the shaft behind them, his shadow barely visible through the doors. His friends waited pensively from above. Using a surge of kinetic force, he blew the doors off. Two of the drones were swept off the metal platform with the doors. The third turned to fire at Johnny.

"I'll take that," Johnny said, ripping the man's semi-automatic assault rifle from his grasp with a thought. It flew into Johnny's hand of its own accord. The unarmed drone rushed at him. Johnny picked him up in mid-run and slammed him into a wall. He slumped to the floor, unconscious.

Taking a cautious sweep of the Tunnel beyond, he stepped back into the elevator shaft and mentally eased his comrades to the bottom. He noted that Emily looked nervous. "You OK?"

"I just prefer both feet on the ground. How much time are we looking at?"

"18 minutes," Daniel Zim said over their commsets.

"Which way do we go?" Emily asked, noting that the massive Tunnel extended in both directions.

"I can't see the balcony. Can you describe him?" Zim asked.

"Come again?" Johnny asked.

"Sorry. Wrong channel," Daniel Zim said. "Just descend the platform to the Tunnel floor and hang a left."

"That way," Johnny said with a thrust of his chin. "Be careful. Three of these zombie soldiers were waiting for us when I got down here. No telling what else she left behind."

"The cameras don't show anyone," Zim said, "but the *Grey*'s still there. A lot of my cameras are down, so Pandora could be hiding in one of my dead spots obviously. Sorry about that."

"She could've killed the cameras on purpose," Weasel said.

"This is a trap," Johnny said.

"What do you want to do about it?" Emily asked.

"What else can we do?" Johnny asked. "We spring the trap."

"Naturally," Weasel said, affecting martyrdom.

"Naturally." Johnny grinned back, but the humor never reached his eyes. Each of them knew how serious their situation was now. If they kept going, there would be no turning back. By silent consensus, they descended the ladder at the edge of the platform. Johnny waited topside until they were safely at the bottom. He glided down to join them, keeping his eyes peeled. He was looking for Trager and Cougar in particular.

"We should take those," Emily said, nodding toward a pair of golf carts. "It'll be faster than walking."

Johnny shook his head. "It's not far. We don't want them to hear us coming."

"Then you should probably do a better job of keeping your mouths shut," a voice hissed at them.

Johnny spun on his heel, gun at ready. Then he recognized Curtis Holloway at the top of the platform they'd just came down from. "Do you know how close you came to getting your head shot off?" Johnny asked. "Don't sneak up on me like that."

"You should be more worried about the fact that I was able to. I was beginning to get bored waiting down here for you."

"Hey, Zim. Where were you on that one?" Johnny asked. The techie was supposed to be watching out for them. They were lucky it was only Curtis. Somebody could've wiped them all out before they knew what hit them.

There was no answer.

"Zim?"

Worried, Emily tried her own commset. After a few tries, she shook her head.

"Something must've happened to him," Brad said. "What do we do now?"

"We keep going," Johnny said. "Those hostages are depending on us."

"Yeah. Anyway, anybody care to fill me in on the plan here?" Curtis asked "You do have a plan, right?"

Johnny grimaced. "Mostly. We stop Pandora before she blows this place to Kingdom Come. She's got a good lot of the town zombified, waiting to blow up with Titan if we don't get to her first. Your daughter's trying to get them out of here in case we fail." He said the last for Curtis' benefit.

"You sent her in alone?" he asked.

"Of course not. Weasel's with her."

Curtis did not look at all reassured. "How much time we got left?"

"15 minutes or less."

"No time," Curtis said, mostly to himself. "Reckon I'll just have to hope for the best. We better hop to it. You guys get going. I'll catch up."

Johnny and his comrades began jogging down the Tunnel, driven by a sense of urgency. True to his word, Curtis managed to not only catch up to them but also kept pace with them. Finally, they saw the *Grey*, a bona fide silver flying saucer. It arrested their attention for a moment, looking like a prop from a 1950s sci-fi flick.

Emily noticed it first. "She's not here."

"Are we too late?" Brad asked.

Johnny shook his head. He was very sure that Pandora intended to escape using the *Grey*. She could be inside it. He glanced at Curtis, who was likewise unconvinced that Pandora was gone.

"Well, somebody's been here." Johnny pointed out a few dead Titan guards lying nearby.

"Look alive everybody," Curtis said, raising his shotgun.

Johnny did likewise, scanning the crates, catwalks and sundry equipment that surrounded the saucer.

Pandora laughed. Black-armored drones appeared at the perimeter, taking cover behind crates and equipment, weapons at ready. Pandora herself appeared atop a catwalk control station. She was accompanied by Destiny, the Parasol executive, Hillary, Bantam and Winters.

"Give yourself up," Johnny said.

"You know I can't do that, Johnny," Pandora said.

"Hope!" Curtis called. "Hope, what are you doing?"

"Hope? No one's called me that for a long time. Do I know you?"

Curtis' eyes narrowed suspiciously. "What? I'm your husband, Curtis Holloway. You abandoned us. Ring any bells? Honestly, what are you playing at? Amnesia?"

"Curtis? What are you doing here?"

"What am I doing here? What are you doing here? I've been here, in Midwich, all this time. You abandoned us, remember? So where the Devil have you been all these years?"

"I did not abandon–"

Johnny was too intrigued the couple's melodrama to realize he should've been taking advantage of Pandora's obvious but unaccountable confusion. If he didn't know better, he'd say she was waking up from a dream. Did she really not know who her husband was? Who could ever forget they were saddled with Curtis Holloway?

"Do you know where our daughter is right now? She's upstairs trying to free those people you planned to blow up with this building," Curtis said. "She could be killed. You need to stop this, Hope. This has all gotten way out of hand."

"I've heard enough of my son-in-law for one day," Silas Darling said as he stepped out from behind Bantam, "as I suspect we all have. Don't listen to him," he said to his daughter. "He's a figment of your past, a bad memory easily forgotten. Daddy will take care of this."

She calmed down, staring at Curtis without recognition.

"Silas, what have you done to her?" Curtis asked.

Silas ignored his son-in-law and turned his attention to Johnny.

"Brother Joel," Johnny said, surprised to say the least.

"John Lazarus, we meet again, just as our Oracle said we would," he said, nodding toward Destiny Pascalé. "Of course, I was counting on that."

"You've hypnotized her," Curtis said. "Your own daughter!"

Silas Darling scoffed. "I'm allowing her to fulfill her destiny. All you ever did was to hold her back, you unevolved caveman. But she was meant for more. Much more." He walked over to stand behind his daughter. "I've helped her forget all about those mistakes, you miserable speed bump."

"We'll see about that," Curtis said, squeezing off a round. The bullet hit an invisible barrier.

"Trager." Johnny cast about for his foe. Trager stepped out from behind a tower of crates, strapped into the cockpit of a robotic battle suit twice Johnny's height. An array of various automatic weapons hovered at ready around the mech-suit at Trager's thought.

"Actually, that was me," Hillary said. "If anyone cares…"

"Now, if we're through beating our chests and rattling our sabers," Silas said, "it is quite time we were off. Daughter?"

Pandora pressed a button, causing the hangar doors to begin to open, then followed her father down a flight of metal stairs. As they descended, Silas said, "I had hopes once that you could join us, Johnny, but you turned out to be too much like your father. He too was afflicted with outdated notions of fair play and morality. But morality evolves with the human experience."

"That's just something people say when they want to justify something awful," Johnny said. "Morality doesn't evolve just because you drift away from it. You oughtta know that, *preacher*."

Silas glared at him.

Pandora, Winters and Bantam ascended into the saucer. Destiny Pascalé paused to make eye contact with Johnny before she vanished into the craft. He could've sworn she winked at him. Hillary waited for Silas to ascend the metal steps.

"What about Johnny?" Ridenour asked.

"Did you bring what we asked for?" Silas asked.

Ridenour grinned and held up the briefcase handcuffed to his wrist. He started to fish the key out of his pockets, when Silas nodded to Hillary.

"Allow me," Hillary said. The handcuffs fell off Ridenour's wrist and the briefcase floated into Silas' hands, where it unlocked and opened.

Silas inspected the contents with a satisfied grin. Snapping the lid shut, he tucked the briefcase under his arm and said, "A deal's a deal. He's all yours."

"You wish," Johnny said.

Silas considered him sadly. "Ness, shoot my son-in-law."

A rifle shot rang out instantly.

"No!" Johnny screamed. He automatically tried to arc the bullet's path away from Jackie's father, but Ness never missed. The elder marksman had already taken Johnny's abilities into account when he took aim. Curtis dropped, clutching his chest. He was still breathing, but raggedly. And he was bleeding a lot.

Johnny's thoughts turned murderous.

Silas sighed. "Ness, get ready to shoot the girlfriend."

An infrared dot appeared on Emily's forehead. Johnny followed the infrared beam to its source. Ness was crouched atop a loading crane high above where he could cover the entire hangar.

"Ness never misses."

Johnny remembered going with Ness and his father to a favored spot up an old mountain hollow where they'd set up a "poor man's firing range" of paint buckets and aluminum cans. As a kid, Johnny had just thought that Ness was a crack shot with a rifle. Now he'd guessed the truth of it. Ness never missed. Not even once. Nobody was that good or even that lucky. Old Quatermain was an Indigo.

"Now, now, don't go pretending as if you had any choice. Surrender or watch your friends die, one by one by one."

Johnny didn't want to hear it. He'd fought so hard, risked so much. He couldn't lose now. His mind raced for a solution to his dilemma. With every second, his anger and frustration level rose. The walls of the Tunnel began to vibrate.

"Yes, yes, bring down the walls on your enemies like Sampson of old, but you and your friends will still die."

Johnny blinked. He hadn't realized he was making everything shake. He looked at Emily. She looked terrified. He knew he was trapped. As much as he hated to admit it, this was defeat. The least he could do was get his friends out of this. He hung his head. "Let my friends go. I'll come peacefully."

Ridenour grinned savagely, then barked an order into his radio. In moments, one of the Parasol helicopters touched down. Hive drones unloaded a large container similar to the ones he'd seen down in Gamma Lab: a coffin-shaped pod with a window. Standing upright, it looked for all the world like a jukebox dressed up as a science fiction theater prop. The drones efficiently prepped the pod and opened it up.

Ridenour walked up to Johnny with a hypodermic needle.

"What's that for?"

"Something to make you more controllable."

"If I'm so dangerous, why not just kill me and get it over with?"

He scoffed. "You really don't get it, do you? You're not like everybody else. You're not even like them," he said, indicating the other Indigos. "You're the magnum opus. Everything the others can do, you can do. And you can do it better.

If they're gods, you're Zeus."

"You're so full of it," Johnny said. "Can we get on with it now?"

"You'll feel some disorientation. Try not to pass out."

Johnny steeled himself, then looked away from the needle. "Do it."

"Wait," Silas said, noticing the key hung round his neck. "What's that?" He glanced at Hillary, who kinetically lifted the keychain off Johnny's neck and sent it flying into Silas' hand. A quick inspection confirmed it was a *Grey* key. "How did you get this?"

Johnny refused to answer.

"No matter," Silas said. "Proceed."

Nodding, Ridenour injected something into Johnny's shoulder and then gave a nod to the Hive soldiers. One grabbed Johnny by the arm and led him into the pod.

"Wait!" Emily said. "Johnny, I love you!"

He studied her face, trying to imprint every detail into his memory. She seemed so hopeless and small right now. And here he was, her own personal Han Solo about to be frozen in carbonite. All that was missing was a howling Wookie.

He smiled wanly, beginning to slur. "Lub you, too, Em. Always hab... Alwayzh…" He slumped forward. The drones caught him before he hit the floor.

"Johnny? Johnny!"

Efficiently, the drones strapped Johnny's limp form into the harnesses, put a respirator mask over his mouth and nose, plugged him into the pod's medical monitoring system and slammed the door shut.

Emily prayed silently for a miracle as they hooked up several bulky canisters to Johnny's containment pod. She tried to catch his eyes through the pod's observation window, but whatever Ridenour had given him had knocked him out cold. A syrupy red liquid soon filled the pod.

Ridenour ran over to the pod as the drone soldiers removed the now empty canisters. He checked the controls and reported. "He's ready."

As he and the drones boarded the helicopter with their prize, Ridenour turned to Silas. "A pleasure doing business with you. We'll meet you at the rendezvous."

Silas watched him board the helicopter before turning to Emily. "I'm sorry you had to be a part of this," he said. "And I'm sorrier still that I can't let you live. Johnny shouldn't have dragged you into this. Ness and Trager will keep you company to make sure you stay put. It'll all be over in a few minutes." He smiled sadly, glancing at his watch. He glanced at Ness and Trager. "If they so much as move, kill them all."

He and Hillary climbed into the *Grey*. The stairs rose after them.

Emily watched bitterly as the helicopter lifted off and hovered near the mouth of the subterranean hangar. Less than a minute later, the *Grey* rose, leaving the hangar in a smooth glide. Parasol's helicopters escorted it away.

Leaving Johnny's friends standing under guard, waiting for the end of the countdown.

54 – Auditorium

"OK," Zim said, guiding Jackie and Weasel to Titan's auditorium, "Pandora hasn't left the hostages unguarded. Watch yourself. Looks like we got a Hive drone guarding the entrance to the auditorium."

"Right," Weasel said. "Any suggestions?"

"Don't die."

Weasel suppressed a growl of frustration, readied his weapon and stepped around the corner.

He ran smack into a drone, knocking them both to the ground.

Jackie reacted instantly, jerking him back around the corner to safety as bullets tore chunks out of the wall. A few seconds later, the drone rushed down the hallway in pursuit, unaware that they'd just passed the camouflaged couple pressed up against the wall.

De-camouflaging, Jackie directed them to a side room, a finger to her lips for silence. They waited there for a few pensive moments until they were sure they were unnoticed.

"Where were you on that one, Zim?" Weasel asked.

"He was in a blind spot."

"Well, be more careful next time."

"I'm on it," Daniel Zim said. "Aside from that one, I just see the one guarding the auditorium doors and another onstage, so far."

"Are you sure that's all?"

"That's all I can see. I'm not God, guys. I've got two teams to watch, more blind spots than cameras and only three monitors to watch everything on anyway. I'm sorry. That's just how it is."

"I'll scout it out," Jackie said, partly to mollify Weasel and partly because she didn't think it wise to just take Zim's word for it. "You stay here."

She slipped out the door, vanishing from sight. Weasel spent the next few minutes staring at the door and sneaking ever more nervous glances at his wristwatch. Where was she?

Suddenly, the door swung open and a black-suited Hive drone took aim at him. Weasel brought his weapon up sharply, but his foe already had him in his sights. Just when he thought he was a goner, the drone spasmed and slumped to the floor.

Jackie materialized in short order. The downed zombie soldier was smoking slightly. In her urgency, Jackie had shocked him with far more voltage than she'd intended.

"What did you find out?" Weasel asked.

Jackie spoke into the comm for Zim's benefit. "There's five bogies total: this one, one at the door, that guy you tripped over earlier, and another onstage like Zim said. There's one more up in the balcony," Jackie said. "He's not like the others. No armor. No weapons."

"Then he's probably an Indigo," Zim said.

"That's what I was afraid of."

"I can't see the balcony. Can you describe him?"

"Yeah, late forties. Balding, but built like a lumberjack. Oh, and he has one of those Hulk Hogan-looking mustaches."

Zim sighed audibly over the comm. "That sounds like Ephram Cougar. Cougar's a pyrokinetic, a human flamethrower."

Weasel winced. "We're toast."

"You'll have to sneak up on him," Zim said.

"Any ideas?" Jackie asked.

"No, but you'll need to neutralize him quickly. Can you use your invisibility to get close enough to him to zap him?"

"That kind of stealth takes time we don't have."

"You need a diversion."

"OK, but what?"

There was no answer.

"Zim?" Weasel asked, but there was still no response. "We're on our own."

"This one looks like he's about your size," Jackie said, indicating the downed drone.

"You want me to pretend to be one of these guys?" Weasel asked. "Haven't you ever seen a movie? This never works out."

"I'll be right there with you, you big baby. I just need them to be watching you for a second so I can sneak up on them. You know you can still see me a bit when I'm moving."

It took Weasel a precious minute or so to get changed. He was very self-conscious with Jackie right there in the room with him, but that couldn't be helped. Finally, he was ready. The clothes were a little loose, but they were a passable fit. "How do I look?"

"Scared witless." Her joke earned her a dark look. She smiled to disarm him. "Switch weapons with the other guard and give me your old one. All the other Hive soldiers are using rifles. We don't want you to stand out," she said. "Now listen to me. We need to take out the Indigo before he's wise to us. The others will be all over us the second they hear us, so we need to do this as quietly as possible."

"Stay quiet. Get the firestarter. Don't miss. Don't get dead," Weasel said. "Got it. Let's do this before I chuck."

Jackie blended into the scenery. She appeared as an odd smudge of movement against the background. If you weren't looking for her, she was really hard to spot. She slipped her hand into Weasel's. He wasn't sure if the electric jolt he felt at her touch was static or a deeper connection or something in between. Why did he continue to fall for the girl who'd let her father duct tape him to a kitchen chair?

She led him along imperceptibly. A Hive drone raised his weapon as they approached the auditorium doors, but relaxed a bit when he recognized the uniform. The drone trained his attention further down the hallway beyond Weasel. As Weasel drew nearer, the sentry's suspicious eyes darted back to him. Weasel saw his eyes widen in alarm. The drone's weapon swung round to blast the imposter away.

Jackie reached him before he got off a shot. She didn't shock him as bad as she had the first, but it was more than enough to put him on his back.

As the soldier rose to a sitting position, he groaned, holding his head with one hand. "What happened?" he asked. "Who are you?"

Weasel shushed him. "We're not in friendly territory," he said, pulling him away from the auditorium doorway. He mentally noted that Jackie remained invisible, indicating that she was being cautious.

"They're holding hostages in that auditorium. They used some kind of mind control on you and your buddies," Weasel said. "There's a bomb, set to go off in less than 10 minutes. You getting all of this?"

"Yup," he said, getting to his feet. He pointed his rifle at Weasel. "I just don't have any reason to believe you."

Weasel winced. "We're all gonna die."

The guard slumped to the floor, having received a far more powerful jolt of electricity this time. "We can't waste any more time. We need to neutralize that pyro and we need to do it now," Jackie said.

"I'm on it. Where is he?"

"Balcony. Careful, the other guard's onstage."

Weasel nodded.

The lights and monitors in the command center began to flicker.

"Uh oh," Zim said, recalling how the power had gone out and folks had passed out when the Disruptor walked through Midwich. It would be very bad to be asleep at the end of the countdown. Correctly guessing that his foe would use the front door, Zim hopped toward an emergency exit on his uninjured leg, already feeling groggy. It felt like the hardest thing he'd ever done, but somehow he fought his way across the room, praying the entire way. He shouldered the door open with the panic bar and fell through. He kicked it shut with his good leg from the ground and listened, barely holding on to consciousness.

Behind him, the command center went completely dark. The Disruptor peered inside, saw it was empty and moved on to his next appointment.

Weasel walked into the auditorium, forcing himself to ignore the fact that it was filled with people who sat staring straight ahead, like department store manikins. Or film footage of a picturesque 1950s neighborhood mockup filled with smiling, happy plastic dummies going about their stereotypical TV Land lives, oblivious to the fact that they'd only been propped up to show the effects of a nuclear blast on suburbia. He reminded himself that these weren't alien pod people. They were flesh-and-blood folk with real lives and real problems. And though they were apparently quite oblivious to the fact, they were all going to die in just a few short minutes if he didn't wake them up and get them out.

He stayed in the shadows and slipped up the stairwell at the back of the auditorium. It didn't appear the sentry on stage had noticed him.

He emerged onto the balcony and saw his target immediately. A large, muscular fellow in his mid to late forties. Balding. No beer gut. His back was turned to Weasel. His target turned his head slightly to glance at him as he stepped onto the balcony, but shrugged him off when he saw the uniform.

From his experience with the other sentry, Weasel realized that Pandora's zombies were a bit slow on the uptake, but not completely stupid. He figured that if he simply turned his weapon on the guy, the super zombie would incinerate him. So he decided to play it cool, like he'd just come up to inspect things. Weasel looked this way and that, always watching the Indigo out of the corner of his eye. Then he turned to walk back down the stairwell.

That's when he heard the gunshot. He jumped, startled, but he hadn't been hit. In fact, it had come from below and it was followed by several bursts from a semi-automatic interspersed with the original weapon's report. The sentry they'd fooled earlier must have returned, meaning he had very little time left. Weasel turned around quickly to shoot the super zombie.

He was forced to dive down the stairwell instead to escape a wave of flames. Searing heat washed his back. He was pretty sure he was actually on fire. He bounced off the wall at the mid-level landing, then pitched down the remaining stairs. There were going to be some serious bruises and burns, perhaps even some breaks. He rolled to a stop at the bottom of the stairs, just past the auditorium doors.

The doors burst open. A blur he knew to be Jackie raced up the balcony stairwell. She hadn't seen him. Moments later, the returning Hive drone also burst through the entrance.

Fortunately, the single-minded fellow ascended the stairs after Jackie without noticing him either.

Weasel got to his feet in a haze of pain. His head felt swollen and stuffy. Something warm trickled down his forehead. He was really banged up. Bleeding. As he attempted to rise, a wave of vertigo brought him back to his knees.

Jackie was up there alone with the zombie soldier and the pyro. There'd been shots fired earlier. Was she hurt? She needed his help. Determined to aid Jackie despite a probable concussion, he lifted his head, preparing to attempt to rise again. That's when he realized the drone onstage was aiming at something, preparing to fire. Hastily, he brought up his semi-automatic and rained bullets on the would-be sniper. Once again, a lifetime of first-person shooter games paid off. His opponent dropped to the stage and did not stir again.

Remembering Jackie, he turned back to the stairwell. Unable to get to his feet, he began laboriously crawling up the stairs.

55 – Escape

On the comm with his superiors at Parasol, Ridenour stared down at the shrinking Titan complex with a smile.

In retrospect, he couldn't believe how easy it'd been. He had a disc filled with Titan's secrets and John Lazarus to boot. He'd half-expected Johnny to put up some resistance. When Johnny had shaken the Tunnel, he'd genuinely been afraid the boy would inadvertently kill them all. That young man had no idea what he was, what he was truly capable of. Which made him all the more dangerous.

He glanced back at the gamma containment pod, where Johnny's face was visible through the port hole. His eyes were closed. He was no longer a threat.

"Yes, yes, we have the package," he said. "Safe and sound."

His boss asked the million dollar question.

"No, I think you were right about her. It's worse than we thought. She definitely has her own agenda. We have the boy and the disc. I say we cut our losses."

He waited while his boss deliberated. The answer came. Ridenour grinned as he disconnected the call and turned to speak to the pilot. "Turn this bird around. We have what we came for. When that saucer leaves the hangar, blow it to Kingdom Come."

"Target acquired," the drone pilot said.

Ridenour eagerly craned his neck to see the saucer as it emerged from the mountainside hangar. The *Grey* was moving slowly and majestically. He imagined the pilot was really savoring this epic moment.

"Blast them out of the sky!"

The drone pilots of both helicopters reacted without hesitation. Since Ridenour hadn't specified the exact method of destruction, they threw both missiles and a hailstorm of bullets at the unsuspecting craft below. The *Grey* bucked violently from the onslaught, nearly being thrown back into the mountainside at one point. Yet the craft suffered seemingly little damage for all the fury being heaped upon it. The bullets ricocheted. The missiles left charred dents in the hull.

An ominous crackling of ozone was the only warning Ridenour's escort chopper got before a great gout of green energy roared out of the saucer to engulf it. They watched as the other helicopter exploded.

Ridenour sputtered, aghast, but managed to spit out the order to retreat. Whatever else might occur this night, he had no intention of becoming a martyr for his company. He glanced over at Johnny's containment pod, wondering if one kid was really worth that much.

Johnny was staring back at him. The red liquid made him look like the devil himself. "He's awake!"

Johnny ripped the door of the containment pod off its hinges and sent it flying. The door swept the corporate shark out the open side of the helicopter. Slimy crimson fluid splattered everywhere, covering the helicopter's interior and its occupants. From the outside, it looked as if Ridenour had been shot out of the chopper in an explosion of red paint... or blood. He fell unconscious, knocked senseless by the containment hatch. He was struck dead on impact with the saucer below. He bounced off, lifeless, into the mountainside.

John Lazarus walked to the edge of the helicopter and looked down. His face waxed grim as he caught sight of the saucer rising toward them. The ozone crackled again. Johnny's eyes narrowed. Some sort of green energy was building up around its equator. Johnny had seen enough sci-fi movies to recognize it was probably a weapon of some sort.

Realizing he had no time, he dove off the helicopter. He aimed his free-fall at the saucer, reasoning that so long as the death ray missed him he'd stand a better chance of surviving the shorter fall to the *Grey*.

56 – Balcony

Jackie was halfway up the stairs when she heard booted feet in the hallway. Realizing the Hive drone they'd fooled was returning she turned back downstairs to intercept him. She didn't like leaving Weasel up there to face the pyro alone, but neither did she fancy being ambushed from behind.

No sooner had she exited the auditorium when she spotted the zombie soldier. He was closer than she thought. Hoping to drop him before he was even aware of the danger, she aimed her pistol and fired. Right in the chest. A perfect shot.

Caught by a bulletproof vest.

The drone fired his semi-automatic in the direction the shot had come from. Jackie bolted back to the auditorium, firing behind her wildly in the hope of slowing it down. The Hive drone launched headlong after his barely visible foe, heedless of the bullets she sent his way.

She was nearly up the balcony stairs when she realized she was racing straight into Ephram Cougar's burning clutches. Worse still, Weasel was up there and she was towing a drone in her wake. She'd unwittingly created the proverbial rock and a hard place.

"Weasel, look out!" she screamed, hoping to warn him of the new danger as she emerged from the stairwell. It was stupid. It was also mostly involuntary. Instinctive.

Ephram Cougar turned toward the sound, washing the area in flame. Jackie dove flat to the floor, and then scrambled to her feet when the wave retreated.

Where was Weasel? Had Cougar already burned him to a crisp? She forced these worries out of her head. She didn't have the time to think about it, not with that zombie Indigo hoping to roast her. Forcing herself to concentrate on neutralizing her opponent, she had an epiphany: the balcony chairs had metal frames. She used her electrokinesis to magnetize them. When Cougar attempted to fry her again, she leapt atop them and glided out of the way as if she were a human monorail. Well, technically it was more of a magnetic grid. She managed to elude him twice before she was distracted by more gunshots.

Out of the corner of her eye, she saw the drone she'd forgotten about drop to the stage, jerking with the impact of several shots before he fell. Who was her rescuer? She hoped against hope that Weasel was still in the game.

From Cougar's outstretched fingers, blinding cinders showered forth. Disoriented, Jackie put distance between herself and the pyrokinetic, sliding atop the chairs until she was at the other end of the balcony.

Into the waiting arms of the drone who'd been pursuing her. Or nearly.

As he leveled his semi-automatic at her, she vanished. This momentarily confused the Parasol Hive drone, who found himself electrocuted a second later for his hesitation.

This time, it was Jackie's turn to find herself surprised, for she hadn't touched the drone soldier. Electricity had arced off the balcony seats and blasted the hapless soldier at her thought.

The zombified pyro was unimpressed. Cougar tossed a trio of small fireballs at her. She darted quickly aside, dodged another quick succession of fireballs, then arced an electric bolt at her assailant. Cougar jerked violently as the current grabbed him, then slumped smoking to the balcony floor.

She heard someone behind her. Thinking it was another drone, she charged up her electromagnetic field and turned around.

To the sight of a near mirror image of herself. If she were a boy anyway.

"This is... unexpected," the young man said.

"Who are you?" she asked, fully prepared to make him ride the lightning if he so much as blinked at her the wrong way.

"Why aren't you falling down like everyone else?" he asked with an almost detached politeness.

"Why would I be falling down?"

"I have that effect on people. It's what I do. I generate an electrical field that disrupts everything around me. Lights. Internet connections. Brain synapses. Anything I want to really, so long as it has an electrical signature. People generally become disoriented and black out when I pass by. So the question is: how are you still conscious?"

"Maybe you're not trying hard enough."

"Perhaps." Suddenly, she felt a nearly overwhelming force, like someone trying to snuff out her consciousness. It was difficult to breathe. She just wanted to pass out.

Somehow, she rallied herself and...

"You pushed back," he said, grinning. "You can actually resist me. How?"

"You said you disrupt things with an electric field. Well, I'm generating one of my own." Electricity crackled off the balcony seats, warning him not to try that again.

"That makes sense, I guess. What's your name?"

"Look, no offense, but I'm on kind of a tight schedule here."

"What's the rush?"

"I've got to wake these people up and get them out of here before the entire complex blows up," she said.

"Oh, that." He made a face. He glanced at his watch, a wind-up timepiece. "Only a couple of minutes. You really think you can get everybody out of here with the time you have left?"

"I can try."

"I'm supposed to stop you, you know." He mentioned as if he were talking about the weather. "Of course, I have no intention of getting blown up myself in the process, so I'm also, as you put it, on a tight schedule. I'll tell you what: I'll knock off early if you tell me your name."

She stared at him evenly, trying to gauge whether he was serious. "Jackie Holloway."

His eyes were guarded. "A deal's a deal."

"So that's it? How do I know you won't just jump me when my back is turned?"

"Because we're both pressed for time." He turned to go, descending the stairs.

"Wait! Who are you?"

"I'm Jack," he called from the shadows of the stairwell. "Jack Holloway. Your brother..."

Stunned, she did nothing for a moment. Why didn't she remember a brother? Yet Jack looked exactly like her. A twin! *Her* twin. How? Her mind went back to her childhood. Was Jack her imaginary friend? More to the point, was her imaginary friend a phantom memory of her brother trying to break through her consciousness? Who had done this to her? Her mother? Papaw Darling? She was torn between chasing after him to demand answers to her questions and saving the people in the auditorium. The hero in her won over.

Arcing electricity off the balcony, she shocked the entire auditorium out of their night-long trance.

57 – Somebody's Gonna Have To Do Something Stupid

It was probably the worst situation she could have found herself in. Pandora couldn't have picked two more dangerous zombies to leave behind. Ness had a well-deserved reputation for marksmanship. He never missed. Ever. And right now he was aiming for Emily's skull. Trager was a more experienced version of Johnny and he was in a mech-suit surrounded by a swarm of automatic weapons. Of course, there was also the countdown to contend with and a handful of drone soldiers thrown in for good measure.

And Johnny wouldn't be able to save her now. He'd been captured. Had given himself up gallantly to save his friends. Because of her. Because he was afraid they'd kill her. Well, she was going die anyway. Whether they killed her or the impending explosion did her in, he wouldn't be able to save her. Once again, he'd left her and she had to deal with the fallout.

Self-pity wasn't buying her any more time or options. Pushing her resentment – and her abandonment issues – to the back of her mind for the moment, she ran a mental checklist of her options.

She couldn't talk her way out of this. Zombies and Hive drones couldn't be negotiated with, bribed, threatened, tricked or even reasoned with. So that was out.

If Ness never missed, it was obvious that she needed to keep him from firing at all. But in all likelihood, she wasn't going to be able to prevent that and Ness was going to shoot someone. Someone was literally going to have to bite the bullet to give the rest of them a fighting chance.

"One of us is gonna have to do something stupid," Curtis said.

"Quiet," Emily hissed. "They'll hear you."

Curtis spoke low so only Emily could hear him. "It needs to be me. I'm probably not going to live through this anyway." Given the amount of blood he'd already lost, she was stunned that he was still breathing, much less conscious.

Emily frowned, shaking her head slightly. "No. There's another way."

"Oh, really?" he asked, coughing up more blood. "Enlighten me, Sissy. We're out of time. If we think about this all night, we're all dead for sure."

"Speak for yourself," Brad said.

"Everyone calm down," Emily said. "Let me think."

"You heard him. There's no time for that anymore. This place could go up any second now. Time's up."

Emily was worried that Brad was about to do something rash and get her shot in the process, but she was more worried about Curtis. She was sure no one who'd lost that much blood could possibly be thinking straight. "Curtis, I don't know what you're thinking, but your daughter doesn't want to lose her daddy. Think of Jackie."

Curtis sighed. He seemed to shrink in defeat. Then he fired at Ness, quicker than she would've imagined possible in his shape.

Ness returned fire. Impossibly, their bullets collided in mid-air. Fused together, they fell to the floor.

The rest happened all-too-quickly. Brad Farley began a cowardly mad dash for the open hangar doors, drawing the fire of both the Hive drones and Trager. Curtis switched targets, firing at Trager. Ness fired at Curtis again. Emily sent a jet of fire out of one hand and a rain of bullets out of the gun in her other hand.

In her mind's eye, Emily could see it all playing out, like dominoes falling. Each step determined the next in an unstoppable drama that could only have one terminus. Bullets bounced off Brad like they were made of rubber. Like Bantam, his kinetically enhanced skin was a formidable natural armor. Seeing that he was a lost cause, Trager turned his attention back to the remaining targets.

Emily's fire washed over Hive drones. Her panic-driven flame was too intense to merely hurt them and bring them around. Instead, it incinerated them where they stood. Charred skeletons dropped to the concrete. Horrified at what she had done, what her gift was capable of, she nonetheless recognized that they probably died too quickly to have even slipped out of their trance.

Ness never missed. Curtis dropped like a stone. Emily screamed in outrage, turning her attention to Ness. Who now had her in his sights as well.

The bullets Curtis had sent Trager's way before he fell were deflected almost casually. Zombie Trager aimed his hovering guns at Emily.

And that's where she died.

That's how she thought it would end anyway, but then two things happened. Gage sent the hangar crane into action, causing Ness to fall from his perch and Johnny fell from the sky, skidding like a meteorite across the hangar bay.

58 – Rescue

Gage had been watching everything from the shadows, staying out of the action.

After digging himself out of that office, he'd been lucky enough to spot his prisoner, Pandora and the rest as they left the control center. He'd waited a few seconds after they'd gone before trying to follow them at a distance. He hid in the shadows when they stopped at the *Grey*.

When the action started, Gage climbed up into the hangar crane's control box and sneakily knocked Ness off-balance, causing the elderly zombie to fall to the hangar floor. In truth, he hadn't meant for his uncle to fall. Or maybe he had. His plan had been a little shaky, made up on the fly and he hadn't quite connected all the dots when he was forced to act. All he knew was that Uncle Ness would never forgive himself – or Gage – if he allowed the old cuss to kill these people in cold blood.

A few moments later, Johnny fell from the sky and Gage began climbing down from the control booth, desperate to join his uncle and make amends.

Less than a minute ago, Johnny had ended his carefully executed ruse. He'd been mentally suppressing the signals being sent to his gamma pod's medical readouts to make it appear as though he were actually unconscious, but all the while he'd been listening. The situation in the Tunnel was a bona fide stand-off that he was sure almost no one would've survived. By allowing himself to be captured and feigning unconsciousness, he'd hoped to turn the tables on his foes when he had better odds. He'd also hoped to get his friends out of harm's way obviously.

As for the tranquilizer, well, he hadn't been able to think up a way to avoid that, not with everyone watching. But by concentrating on the injection site, he'd been able to keep much of it contained. Once he was inside their containment pod, he forced the solution back out of his skin. A little of it had gotten into his system, but not enough to really have an effect on him.

When he realized that corporate brain trust Ridenour was actually fool enough to open fire on Pandora whilst she was in a flying saucer with unknown weapons capabilities, he'd made his escape. As it turned out, he'd dove from the helicopter none-too-soon. A bolt of green energy vaporized the craft on his very heels. He'd been aiming for the *Grey*, but the concussive blast sent him tumbling, which was how he came to land back in the Tunnel, extremely banged up but alive thanks to the cushioning effects of his kinetic powers.

As he got to his feet, it became apparent that he was in the middle of a super-powered Gunfight at the OK Corral. It took him all of a second to realize that Emily was in harm's way. Reacting hastily, he grabbed her with psionic energy and shoved her out the hangar doors. Surprisingly, she outpaced Brad until the latter got caught up in a tailwind off the blast. Both tumbled down the hill, out of control.

Deprived of his target, Zombie Trager trained his weapons on John Lazarus. Johnny dared to glance out the hangar doors at the *Grey*. It was still slowly rising. Pandora was getting away. His face hardened as he turned back to Trager. He had to end this quickly. That's when he got the idea to knock his feet out from beneath him. The bigger they are…

Trager was caught by surprise. Johnny glanced skyward again, a dangerous idea forming in his mind. He already knew he could leap great distances. Could he fly?

Drawing up a surge of psionic energy, he shot out of the Tunnel on a collision course with the *Grey*.

Mech-suited Trager did not take kindly to being put on his back. He flipped forward onto the balls of his metal feet, a little on the angry side for a zombie. He cast about for Johnny, eager to dispatch his mission. Ness rose to a sitting position, a bit more slowly. Trager looked skyward and caught sight of Johnny. He fired up his jetpack, intent on pursuing the young hero.

Ness took about half a second to realize that Trager was a Zombie. In the remaining portion of that second, he fired at his long-time friend's rocket pack. The jetpack ignited. The resultant explosion blasted Trager out the hangar doors and sent him tumbling down the hill after Brad and Emily.

Ness tried to get to his feet, hoping to see if Trager had survived, only to find that his leg had broken in the fall that woke him from Pandora's hypnosis. He managed to get his good leg underneath him, using his rifle as a makeshift crutch. He was still a bit addled from the fall and weary from all of his efforts as a zombie, but he did remember something about a doomsday countdown, so he knew he had to make tracks.

He had only taken a few steps when he heard Gage shout, "Look out behind you!"

59 – At the End of the Countdown

"C'mon! Move it! The whole complex is gonna blow!" Weasel yelled. "Get moving!"

Jackie was likewise occupied, herding bewildered, skeptical, sometimes belligerent townspeople safely out of the Titan complex. Most of them just wanted to find their loved ones. They were confused, panic-stricken and disoriented. After she brought Pandora's zombies to their senses, it had taken a few precious minutes to get everyone on the same page and moving out of the auditorium. None of them knew how they'd got there or had any memory of anything they'd done since Pandora had hypnotized them.

When the first Parasol helicopter exploded in a flash of alien green light and orange flame, everyone stopped to stare. They wondered what it was. Most of them had only half-witnessed it. Those who had seen it wondered what it meant for them. Seconds later, the second chopper exploded. Many of them came to their senses and began running, not wanting get in the middle of whatever warzone might be developing here.

Others were riveted to the spot either in fear or wonder. Some of them even had their cell phones out to try to record what was going on in the air above Titan.

"Dude, what was that?" a young man asked, gaping at the sky as he fished a digital camera out of his jacket pocket. "Some kind of crazy laser weapon?"

"Dunno," his friend said, wielding his own camera phone like a protective talisman, "but dude! I think somebody jumped from the second chopper right before it exploded!"

Jackie fumed. This was no time to be mooning over the pretty fireworks show. They were still too close to the complex. "We need everybody out now! Titan is going to explode! We have to go now!"

Ephram Cougar grabbed her by the arm as he passed by. "Leave them! We don't have time for this."

Jackie jerked free and glared at him in betrayal and outrage. Weasel had objected to his tagging along. It was Jackie who'd given him the benefit of the doubt, arguing that Cougar hadn't been himself when he tried to roast them.

"Unless you want to martyr yourself?"

Reluctantly, she nodded. "You heard him, people!" Jackie shouted, shouldering past Cougar without meeting his eyes. "Move it or lose it! Titan's gonna blow!"

Those within earshot reacted as one, fairly stampeding away from Titan. Those ahead of them were forced to quicken the pace to avoid being trampled. Jackie paused to pick up a young girl who'd either tripped or been knocked aside, then continued on as fast as she could. Weasel followed behind, keeping one eye on the Titan complex.

That's when they saw the flying saucer rising slowly and ominously from the other side of the complex. Screaming and wailing in mindless panic, the recently rescued mob ran down Corporate Drive as fast as their collective legs could carry them, thoughts of H.G. Well's *War of the Worlds* adding speed to their flight.

"Aliens! Black Choppers! Uncle Cecil was right!" the young man with the digital camera said as he ran past. "It's all true! It's all true! Run for your lives!"

His friend with the camera phone stayed behind, tempted by the prize of having exclusive feed of what would doubtless be the biggest news story of the century. Jackie couldn't help but note the guy was wearing a red shirt. That couldn't bode well.

"Keep moving!" she shouted to the straggler. "We're still too close."

He ignored her, mostly because something else had arrested his attention. "Oh! Oh! This is unreal! I'm not even sure what I'm looking at," he narrated to his camera. "First, that alien death ray toasted those black helicopters. Then, well, I mean that's a flying saucer, dude! We are not alone!" He hadn't yet noticed how far behind everyone else he was. "Wait, it's, like, snatched somebody up in a tractor beam or something. I dunno. I mean, it looks like they're dragging him but there's no visible support. No, wait! He's flying! Elvis has left the building!"

Jackie and Weasel looked back at the cellphone videographer, up at the flying man, then exchanged glances. Wordlessly, they agreed to keep moving, but both were thinking the same thing: it had to be Johnny.

The Tunnel hangar was a mess. Charred skeletons, twisted metal, emptied shells and broken bodies littered the area. It was all too much to handle. The only sane thing in view was the pre-dawn glow, visible through the open hangar bay door. Gage was drawn to it like a moth to the flame, desperate to get his great-uncle and himself out of the building.

Then he heard a miserable moan. "Help," Curtis Holloway said in a barely audible whisper.

As much as he wanted to get to his uncle, Gage couldn't just ignore him in his pitiable state. "Oh, man," he said, staring at Curtis' wounds. The battered redneck was lying in buckets of blood. "This is not good."

Curtis motioned for him to lean in closer. "Gotta get us out. Building's gonna 'splode soon. Countdown."

Eyes widening in alarm, Gage nodded mutely, picked up one of Curtis' burley arms and tried to sling him over his shoulder. The man was just too big.

"No," Curtis said. "Mech-suit. Carry." He managed to point breathlessly to a robotic mech-suit standing empty by the far wall.

Nodding comprehension, Gage dashed across the hangar, noting along the way that Ness too appeared to be breathing. The mech-suit was probably his only means of rescuing both injured men before the Tunnel blew. Taking the metal stairs to the pilot's catwalk two at a time, he frantically pulled open the mech-suit's cockpit and slipped inside. At first, he was worried that he wouldn't be able to find the ignition switch, but the moment he put his hands into the pilot's control gloves, the suit came to life. Walking and moving inside the suit was pretty much like walking anywhere else, thanks to the suit's mechanized servos, but his new size and weight took some getting used to. Nevertheless he managed to cross the floor, scooping up both Ness and Curtis along the way.

Gage was at the edge of the hangar tunnel when Titan exploded in a giant orange ball of flame.

Jackie, Weasel and the small child they'd rescued were all flung to the ground when Titan exploded. A moment later, they were pelted with a rain of debris and shrapnel, forcing them to cover their heads with their arms. Weasel winced as a familiar cellphone bounced in front of his face.

"Red shirt," Jackie said with a grimace.

"What?"

"Nothing. You OK?" she asked.

"Yeah, you?"

When she nodded, he glanced at the girl. The child nodded, wide-eyed and bit shell-shocked. Only then did he take in the smoking crater that used to be Titan. He looked at Jackie, realizing she must be worried about Curtis. And maybe even her mom a little. "I'm sure everybody made it out alive," he said.

She nodded, mostly to reward him for trying to be there for her, but dread and worry still nagged her. She turned away from Titan.

Those they'd rescued were being met at the security gate by those who'd followed their zombified loved ones up to the complex. One couple in particular caught their eye. A joyfully tearful old woman wrapped her arms around her bewildered Herbie and held him as if she'd just found half her soul, grateful that the long nightmare had ended.

60 – Saucer

Johnny showed up on the *Grey*'s radar shortly after he gave chase.

"Pandora," Jennifer Winters said from the pilot chair of the *Grey*, "something's just launched from Titan." She tried not to sound too alarmed. After all, this saucer had just taken a full battery of rockets from the Parasol helicopters with only minor dents to show for it. And the *Grey*'s primary weapon was simply unmatched. Nonetheless, she couldn't help wonder whether Titan had some kind of failsafe in place to prevent theft of its futuristic toy. Something like whatever was being tossed at them right now.

"Well, blast it out of the sky," Silas said.

Winters exchanged a glance with Pandora, wondering whether she or her father were really in charge here. Not for the first time either. Sometimes it seemed like Pandora was their leader. Other times it was undeniably Silas pulling the strings. And they both listened to the Oracle, no matter what.

The latter situation bothered her most. OK, Pandora's father clearly acted as her handler, but it was equally clear that he usually let her have her head. This whole Destiny business – how did they know when she was telling the truth? How did they know when following her instructions would lead to their promised future or when it would get her one step closer to her own agenda? They had to trust her, but what if she had other plans? Like earlier, when Pandora had given the order to destroy the helicopters: Destiny Pascalé had thrown a fit when she realized they were willing to kill Johnny in the process. She was certifiably obsessed with the Lazarus boy and, as far as Winters was concerned, that was one powerful conflict of interest they shouldn't ignore. If it came down to Johnny or their shared agenda, which would Destiny choose? And how would they know if she began betraying them?

In this case, Pandora nodded with the go-ahead to fire upon the unknown threat. Winters didn't hesitate. On the off chance that she was dealing with some sort of saucer-busting missile, she decided on overkill. Her target swerved aside to dodge a burst of green energy.

"We missed," Winters said. "Bogey took evasive maneuvers."

"Is it a missile?" Silas asked.

"I don't know, sir, but it's highly maneuverable and still in pursuit. Computer, I need a visual of that bogey." The craft's controls were partly familiar to her thanks to Pandora's pre-mission briefing, but if the *Grey* hadn't come with a user-friendly interface she'd be in the dark when it came to the flashier tools at her disposal.

"Visual established," the *Grey* intoned as its cameras zeroed in on Johnny. The saucer's occupants gaped at the flying Indigo for a moment, mouths open.

"You've got to be kidding me," Pandora said to no one in particular.

John Lazarus winged through the skies in pursuit of the flying saucer. Truth be told, he wasn't really flying per se. When he'd initially launched skyward, he'd been something akin to a slightly maneuverable human bullet. He could steer somewhat, but it was like sky-diving in reverse. Inevitably, he began to lose momentum, but just as he was slowing down he got the idea to psionically latch onto the *Grey* itself. Now he was telekinetically tethered to the saucer and it was dragging him through the heavens like a celestial Nantucket sleigh ride. It was a bit hard to steer, but with a bit of practice he was able to maneuver much as if he were water skiing.

Having narrowly avoided the death ray, Johnny rushed forward to close the distance between himself and the *Grey*. He needed to get near enough to the saucer that they couldn't effectively use that "alien" weapon. As of right now, he was in their kill box. He doubled his efforts to reach the craft.

"He's coming back around!" Winters said.

"How is he doing that?" Hillary asked. His jealousy was obvious.

"Does it matter?"

Destiny was unable to hide the hint of a smirk. "If you fight him, you'll lose."

"Oh, like we can trust you," Winters said. "You'll say anything to protect your precious crush."

Destiny shot her a hateful glare, but Pandora interrupted before she could retort.

"It doesn't take a psychic to comprehend that Johnny has grown much too powerful. Destiny's probably right. If we fight him, we risk everything. Get us out of here."

Nodding wordlessly, and biting her tongue, Jennifer Winters kicked in the afterburners.

Yet Johnny not only managed to hold on, he began to close the gap between them again.

"He's gaining on us!" Pandora said, eyes wide. "Do something!"

"You're gonna wanna strap yourselves in," their pilot warned.

Hurriedly, the *Grey*'s crew ran to their chairs and secured themselves into the safety harnesses. Winters confirmed they were safely tucked away with a quick glance, then suddenly hit the brakes and caused the saucer to shoot straight up into the sky.

Johnny was nearly shaken off by the sudden change in direction. Mentally latching onto the *Grey* was a bit like being attached by invisible webs. When the saucer stopped on a dime, he'd been sure he was about to hit its silver exterior like a bug on a windshield. A moment later, he was jerked straight upwards. The saucer was going impossibly fast and showed no signs of stopping. Johnny started to worry that the *Grey* was headed for outer space!

Fortunately, Winters wasn't completely sure her 1950s sci-fi movie saucer was actually built for the rigors of space. Frankly, they were approaching a couple Gs and everyone but Bantam was suffering for it. She brought the craft to a full stop, considering what to do next while she recovered from the climb.

"What were you doing?" Silas asked. "We're not astronauts, fool girl!"

"Yeah, I got that."

"Did we lose him?"

"Not yet." Without warning, she descended at an angle. Johnny overshot the *Grey*, then whipped around to follow her.

"Lose him in the clouds," Pandora said.

Nodding, Winters banked the saucer into the cloudscape. Dawn was fast approaching. Sunlight seemed to ignite mountaintops made of cloud in quick succession. Winters whipped through the cloud canyons, hoping to lose her pursuit. She even went through a few cumulonimbuses, but Johnny was tenacious. When nothing else worked, she dove into the clouds and, while obscured in the mist, changed direction suddenly to emerge through the bottom of the cloudscape.

"Did we lose him?" Pandora asked.

Johnny punched through a second later, eliciting howls and groans from the *Grey*'s cockpit.

"Why can't we shake him?" Silas asked. "Every way we go, he follows."

"I think he's attached to the ship somehow," Winters said. Testing her theory, she banked left and then sharply changed direction, keeping her eye on Johnny. Noting the way he whipped around like an airborne water skier, she said, "See! He's latched onto us somehow. That's how he's doing it."

"I don't care how he's doing it," Pandora said. "Get rid of him!"

"Maybe I can scrape him off," Winters said, diving back toward Midwich. She grinned savagely, noting how much her actions distressed Destiny. The saucer pilot made her approach from the river, a nasty plan forming in her mind. She dipped low enough to cause Johnny to skip off the water's surface a few times, then whipped up, hoping to catch him on the bridge.

Johnny gasped in horror when he realized that the *Grey* was coming in too low. His head snapped up as he saw the bridge fast approaching. Thinking quickly, he released his hold on the *Grey* in time to barely pass under the bridge. On the other side, he reached out and re-affixed himself to the saucer.

Winters pushed onward, heading for Midwich's downtown riverfront district. Tall steel-and-glass office buildings dotted a landscape of stolid stone structures that looked like they were built in the Roaring Twenties. The saucer climbed suddenly, jerking Johnny up into the sky, then dove toward downtown with a purpose. The *Grey* came in so low, that it was forced to turn sideways to fit between the buildings. It passed just over the tops of pedestrians, mowing down electrical power lines and traffic lights as it zipped along the street.

"Look out!" Pandora yelled, clinging to her seat desperately. "Are you crazy?"

Winters was paying more attention to what was behind her than where she was going. She took a moment longer than she should have to confirm that her plan was working. In that moment, she plowed through an ancient double-decker bus the citizens of Midwich knew affectionately as the *Murray*. The *Murray* was a minor tourist attraction and made regular runs of the downtown district to the tune of an oldies station. The driver, as much a historical treasure as the relict vehicle, was crossing the intersection, singing a duet with a Tony Bennett recording without a care in the world. Seconds later, the *Grey* hit the *Midwich Murray*, taking a chunk out of the top deck and sending the vehicle into a lateral roll. Only later would the battered bus driver realized he'd just survived a hit and run with a flying saucer.

Descending from on high, Johnny was forced to release his grip on the *Grey*. His invisible tether was too long. If he hadn't let go, he would have plowed into the street. Probably several feet under the pavement actually.

He used a blast of force to try to redirect his fall. He bounded off the top of a building, using kinetic energy to cushion the impact, but then crashed into a tall building behind it. He blasted through the steel and glass structure like a cannonball. Fortunately, the building was sparsely occupied due to the early hour. He punched through cubicles and desks on his way out the other side. When he realized he had enough momentum going to exit the building anyway, he built up a surge of energy and punched through with a purpose.

Johnny raced after the saucer, trying to get close enough to re-affix his kinetic tether. After the saucer hit the *Murray*, its pilot realized she needed to slow down a bit and proceed more cautiously as it continued to navigate through downtown flipped on its edge. But Johnny knew it was only a matter of time until it reached an area where it could allow it to right itself and soar away. In fact, the Harper Plaza traffic circle with its obligatory centerpiece statue of Midwich's founder and ample greenspace was only a few blocks away. Johnny doubled his efforts, chasing it along the rooftops, trying to close the space between them.

Having reached Harper Plaza, Winters righted the saucer. Spotting Johnny approaching by rooftop, she charged up the saucer's death ray.

Johnny barely leapt away in time as the green energy beam disintegrated the structure he'd just vacated and punched through the row of buildings beyond it.

"Nice shooting, Tex," Hillary said. "You missed!"

Winters turned to shoot him a look of warning. "I suppose you could do better?"

"Ignore him," Silas said. "Johnny is getting away!"

"Fine," Winters said, turning away from Hillary. Unfortunately, Johnny was nowhere in sight.

"I've lost him."

Hillary scoffed. "If you want something done right…"

"What do you mean, you've lost him?" Pandora asked. "*He's* chasing *us*! Where is he?"

"I don't know, but he can't have gone far. Computer?"

"Target located," the *Grey* intoned. The camera zoomed in on a water tower on a building bordering Harper Plaza.

"I don't see him," Silas said.

The screen went infrared. Rendered in warm reds, oranges and yellows against a cooler green and blue background, Johnny was suddenly visible next to the water tower.

"That's because he's invisible," Pandora said.

"How is he doing that?' Hillary asked for the second time.

Winters grinned. "He doesn't know we can see him. He'll never know what hit him."

Johnny chose that moment to attack. Bracing himself, he blasted the saucer with a sonic roar. The *Grey* was washed backwards on a sonic wave. Unable to compensate in time, the saucer smashed into Titan Tower.

Outraged, Winters returned fire. There wasn't time to power the *Grey*'s primary weapon, so she threw conventional artillery at him. Johnny mentally wrenched the water tower from its moorings and heaved it into the path of her rockets. The tower exploded. The resultant water bomb drenched the *Grey* momentarily. When the water sluiced clear of her cameras, Johnny occupied the center of her screen.

Panicking, she threw everything she had at him.

61 – Emily

She stopped running, her back to a tree. Her breath came in ragged gasps. She willed herself to calm down, to control her breathing lest Trager hear her.

After their unexpected fall from the hangar bay, Brad and Emily had taken an immediate wild tumble down the mountainside. They finally came to a halt, covered in scrapes and bruises. Brad came to rest about 50 yards away from Emily. As she got to her knees, she saw him stagger to his feet. He was immediately hit with a round from one of Trager's guns.

After his jetpack exploded, hurtling him out of the tunnel in their wake, Zombie Trager had immediately zeroed in on them. He'd lost the hovering arsenal of automatic weapons somewhere on his way downhill, but the mech-suit came with a really big gun, sized to fit in the suit's oversized gauntlets. Ignoring the fact that the mech-suit was smoking and its mechanics were operating stiffly, he continued his pursuit. Drawing the weapon from a back holster, he'd honed in on Brad first. The mech gun's bullet hit Brad in the thigh. It didn't penetrate his kinetically enhanced skin, but the high-powered rifle did give him one doozy of a bruise, making it difficult for him to run.

Enraged at the insult, Brad picked up a big rock and hurled it like a discus. It would have hit its intended target had not Trager stopped it in mid-flight and sent it back at him. Brad flung his arms above his head and turned away, catching the rock on his broad muscled back. The rock shattered. The muscle mutant did not fall, but neither did he throw any more rocks. Instead, he turned and ran into the trees. Even somewhat hobbled, he could still run faster than any normal man.

Not wanting to be left alone, Emily dashed after him.

Trager descended the hillside after them. Rocks and large branches were picked up by kinesis as he passed by, until the mech-suited zombie was accompanied by a wall of debris. Before he stepped into the woods, Trager sent his missiles flying, effectively bashing down a large swathe.

Emily only just managed to stay ahead of the damage path. There was no sign of Brad.

Trager marched methodically through the leveled section of forest, hoping to flush out his prey. He immediately saw the retreating muscle mutant bolt from cover. He took a few more shots at him, but his efforts became increasingly futile as Freight Train Farley picked up speed and began to put distance between them.

The girth of the tree Emily chose to hide behind allowed her to slip around the side unnoticed while Trager was distracted with Brad.

A twig snapped beneath her feet. Trager turned on instinct, his gun swiveling around to fulfill his deadly intent. With no other options, Emily blasted him with a stream of flame. She hated to do it, recalling all-too-well how she'd reduced the Parasol Hive drones to charred skeletons in the hangar tunnel. Trager attempted to deflect the fire stream with kinetic force, but he was too late. Searing heat blasted his cockpit windshield, which blackened under the intensity.

And broke his trance.

The de-zombified Trager used a kinetic blast to remove the ruined cockpit window so he could leap from the smoking hot ruins of the mech-suit. He lay moaning on the ground, badly injured.

Emily approached him hesitantly, palms facing them. He wasn't acting like a zombie anymore – he was mostly writhing around on the ground, moaning in pain – but she was ready to barbecue if it was some kind of trick.

Trager raised his head, agony tightening the features of his face. Yet his eyes gleamed with undeniable gratitude when they lighted on her. "Thank you. I can't believe you got the drop on me."

"Sorry."

"Don't be," Trager said, chuckling. "I'm a fast healer. Plus I believe in Jesus, so..." Emily watched as Trager concentrated on his own wounds. Miraculously, the raw burns began scabbing over. A few minutes later, the scabrous tissue fell off, revealing pink new skin. He sighed mock seriously, getting to his feet. "That always ruins my tan."

"That's amazing."

"What's amazing is how he forgets his friends once he's OK," Ness said from behind him.

Trager and Emily spun about to the sight of a towering mech-suit. Ness was riding shotgun on its shoulder. Trager grinned when he saw who was piloting the mech-suit. Gage picked Ness off his shoulder with giant metal hands and placed him gently on the ground.

Trager frowned. Ness was badly injured, having broken his leg in his earlier fall in the hangar bay. "I can pop it back into place, but that's gonna need a splint. And it's gonna hurt."

"It already hurts," the old man said. "Just shut up and do it, Captain Obviou– aaaaah!" Ness screamed as Trager popped the bone back into place kinetically.

"Shouldn't we get him to a hospital?" Emily said, wincing at the old man's histrionics.

Trager shook his head. "Not until we catch Pandora."

"But he's really hurt bad and she could be long gone by now."

"Or she's not," Ness said, scanning the horizon. He pointed off to downtown Midwich. The saucer was barely visible. Mostly they could tell where it was from the smoke and destruction around it. "I reckon Arthur's kid has something to do with that."

"Probably," Trager said with a groan. "We're gonna need a way down there if we don't want to miss the party. Let me see your commset, Emily."

"Who ya gonna call on that?" Ness asked, grimacing against his pain. "Zim? The command center went up with Titan."

"Yeah, but if I know Daniel Zim he's already switched to our redundant comms," he said, nodding toward an array of communications towers on a nearby ridge.

"He needs help," Emily reminded Trager, daring a quick look at Ness. The memory of bloodied bone jutting out of his leg still made her squeamish.

"He'll be fine," Trager said. "He heals a bit slower than the rest of us, that's all." Turning away, he called, "Zim, do you read me?"

"Loud and clear. Trager! I thought you blew up with Titan. Hey, it sucks being a zombie, doesn't it?"

"Where are you?" Trager asked. "We need a pick up. The *Grey* is engaged over downtown Midwich. If we hurry, we might still be able to stop Pandora."

"Really? OK, well, let me–"

Jackie Holloway cut in over the commset. "Zim, is that you?"

Zim laughed. "Jackie! Are you and Weasel OK? Did we get everyone out?"

"Banged up but alive. We managed to de-zombify everyone before Titan blew. Is my father with you?"

Trager looked at Ness and Gage askance. "You see Curtis Holloway on your way here?"

Ness frowned. "He was with us in the hangar. When the hangar blew, we went flying in all directions. Gage managed to keep ahold of me, but Curtis was thrown clear."

"We looked for him, but we couldn't find him," Gage said. "We came here because we heard voices. Thought it might be him."

Trager nodded. "He's not here," he said to Jackie.

"Did he escape Titan?" she asked.

"Looks like it. Look, if you wanna come up and here and look for him, be my guest, but I need you to clear this line. On the other hand, after the way you kids handled yourselves tonight, I could really use your help."

"What's going on?" Jackie asked.

Without warning, Cougar snatched the commset from Jackie. "Hey, Zim," he said. "It's Cougar. Forget these kids. Just come pick me up and we'll take care of this."

"We're coming," Jackie said, electricity crackling off her fingertips. Her dad could probably look after himself for a while longer. Meanwhile, her mother was on that ship and she had to stop her before she had the chance to hurt anyone else. In her mind's eye, she could still see that auditorium full of innocent hostages. They would have all perished if Pandora had her way.

Cougar shrugged, teasing her with a palm full of fire. "No offense, but you got lucky the first time. I'm a lot more than you can handle now that I'm back in the driver's seat."

"I liked you better as a zombie," Weasel said.

"What's your position, Jackie?" Zim asked. He knew that talking to Jackie instead of Cougar would only upset the big hothead, but he really didn't like Cougar that much.

"No offense," Cougar said, "but the last thing we need right now is to babysit a bunch of kids. Pandora is serious business. Just come and pick me up and we'll–"

"Those kids just rescued half the town while we were doing what?" Trager asked.

"Yeah, but—"

"This is my call, Cougar. I'm in charge here and I say the kids go with us. You want in or not?"

"Fine, but I am not responsible for what happens to them. If things go south, that's your problem. You deal with it." Handing the commset to Jackie, he said, "Just stay outta my way, alright?"

Zim cut in. "OK! If mom and dad are through fighting now, let's get this show on the road. Give me your positions and I'll pick you up."

"In what?" Trager asked.

"Oh, yeah. I hijacked that sweet Hum-V of yours. I couldn't stand the thought of letting it blow up with Titan."

"Well, thanks, I guess, but don't get too comfortable. I want it back."

Brad Farley ran through the woods like a juggernaut. Initially fueled by fear and panic, his aimless path found a compass as adrenaline flooded his system along with a maddening dose of testosterone. Enough hormones to kill a normal man actually. Like the Viking berserkers of old, his reason was slipping, giving way to passion.

Rage. Like the worst case of 'roid rage ever.

More experienced muscle mutants like Bantam had a measure of control over their passions, but Brad had never reached this stage before. All he knew was that he felt powerful, unstoppable, vengeful. And his enemies were worms compared to him. They would pay dearly for putting him to flight.

His father chief among them. Over the course of the night, he'd faced death several times. They say that when you have a close call, you realize what's important to you. Despite his initial shock, he'd come to admit to himself that Alyshia and that baby were very important to him. He just hoped she'd take him back. He was ashamed of how he'd tried to pretend she didn't exist, that nothing ever happened between them, simply because of his daddy's bigoted ideas. He was beginning to see his racism for what it was; he wasn't denying his own responsibility for being a racist himself, but he'd come to see that the root of his prejudice was that he'd been taught to hate and discriminate.

In his berserker state, the muscle mutant's thinking was a bit more visceral. In essence, all he could think of was punishing his father for training up his child to be a hater. He wasn't thinking of the fallout or what the consequences would be – all he could think of was that he wanted to pound the hate out of his father. His passion blinded him to the fact that the violent assault he was contemplating would likely land him in prison, forcing Alyshia and the baby to fend for themselves.

God provided another focus for his berserker fury.

When he came to a gap in the trees and saw the explosive destruction the saucer was wreaking in downtown Midwich, it resonated with his violent mood. He remembered Pandora was on board and that she was ultimately responsible for his earlier humiliation.

Having a focus for his fury, he bounded off in pursuit with a primal roar.

62 – Harper Plaza

It was at that moment when Johnny was suspended in midair across the street below, just before the *Grey's* death ray fired, that he heard the late Dandridge Ridenour whisper from his memories. *"You really don't get it, do you? You're not like everybody else. You're not even like them."*

Johnny slowed his world to bullet time, giving himself an opportunity to think instead of merely reacting. What had he meant by that? What made him so special? Parasol had taken him as their sole captive when they could've had all of the Indigos with Johnny as their prize. Something about him stood out to them.

"You're the magnum opus. Everything the others can do, you can do."

Was that true? Up until now, he'd simply assumed he was like Trager or Hillary. Was there more to it? Could he really do anything the other Indigos could do? Because it would be really convenient right now if he could just go invisible like Wacky Jackie. Yet what if he could? He'd never really tried.

Concentrating, he willed himself to become invisible. When he opened his eyes, he was just a barely perceptible smudge against the sky. Even he had a hard time making out his opaque reflection in the windows of the nearest building.

He dodged the death ray, grinning invisibly. This had possibilities.

As he reached Harper Plaza, he took stock of his situation from beneath the shadow of the water tower. If the *Grey* decided to fly straight up, he'd be back to square one. He needed to ground it somehow. Or anchor it down.

The ring of buildings surrounding the traffic circle gave him an idea. Titan Tower loomed directly behind the *Grey*, a half-constructed marvel of glass and steel intended as Titan Biotech's downtown corporate headquarters. The upper floors were still unfinished, but it was still all-too-recognizable by its distinctive architecture and the giant bronze Eye of Ra logo on its face. It was evident from the steel framing that Atlas, holding an enormous globe, would grace the building's summit. A smaller statue of Prometheus holding a torch stood sentry over the tower's entrance. Bracing himself, John Lazarus let loose a sonic roar. It was more effective than he'd hoped, lodging the saucer into the side of Titan Tower, at least temporarily.

The *Grey* retaliated by throwing swarms of missiles at him. It took him a moment to realize he was visible again. Apparently, he couldn't remain invisible and use his other powers at the same time. It simply required too much energy to maintain the electromagnetic field required to camouflage him.

Johnny tossed the water tower into the path of the missiles to intercept them, and then launched himself at his enemy. Not knowing how long it would take the saucer to wrench itself free of the building it was caught on, he hurried to press his advantage. He was forced to clear his path of a few stray missiles, one of which he lassoed mentally and pitched back at the *Grey* for spite.

"Stop him!" Silas yelled as Johnny bridged the impossible distance between them.

"Get us out of here!" Pandora said.

Winters tossed another salvo of missiles at Johnny while she lurched the craft forward, trying to free it.

Johnny crushed each rocket with a thought. He smiled when he finally set foot on the *Grey*'s shiny metal surface. He immediately reached down and charged up his electrokinetic field. Concentrating, he mimicked Jack the Disruptor's ability.

Inside the saucer, the lights went out. It was pitch black for a second, then the emergency lights came on.

"What happened?" Pandora asked.

"Some kind of electromagnetic pulse," Jennifer said. "Knocked out most of the systems."

"Why aren't we falling then?" Silas asked, though he was mightily relieved that they weren't crashing into the Plaza below.

"I dunno. There must be a failsafe."

"Can you fix it?"

Winters scoffed. "Yeah, sure. I went to Flying Saucer Repair School in case of just such an emergency. I have no idea how to get this thing up and running. Computer?"

There was no response from the *Grey*.

"That's just awesome. Pandora, you're supposed to be the expert here. I mean, you've actually flown on this thing before. Any ideas?" Winters asked.

"Arthur was the pilot. It was his ship. His design."

"Anything. Can you remember anything at all?" Winters asked.

"Stop badgering my daughter," Silas said.

"Don't tell me what to do, old man, unless you plan on telling me how to fix this ship! Maybe if you hadn't monkeyed around with your daughter's memories so much, she might be able to help us!"

"Enough! You're not helping the situation here," he said.

Pandora was looking at her father and the saucer pilot with growing confusion and agitation. Had her father really been tinkering around inside her head? Was she hearing this right? Why? And how *dare* he?

"What's she talking about?" Pandora asked. "Have you been hypnotizing me, dad? Your own daughter?"

"We don't have time for this now. John Lazarus is about to board this vessel even as we speak."

"Just answer the question!"

He forced himself regain his composure. "I think you already know the answer to that."

"How dare you?"

"How dare I? You asked me to do this, Hope. You wanted me to take away your pain. This was never my idea."

"I don't know if I can believe you."

"Well, I'm sorry you feel that way, but right now we don't have the luxury to sort this out."

A monitor beeped and a cursor appeared onscreen. "I've got something," Winters said.

Pandora stared at her father hard. He was telling the truth about one thing. They didn't have time for this little chat right now, but she wasn't going to let the matter drop forever. She turned her attention to Winters. "Right. What did you do?"

"Nothing. It looks like the *Grey* is trying to reboot itself."

"OK, that's a good thing. I do remember this: It takes the *Grey* about twenty minutes to prep from a cold start, but Arthur used to tell us it only took about five to reboot once it got going."

"Johnny cannot be allowed to board this ship," Silas said. He turned to Hillary. "You and Bantam keep Johnny busy until the ship reboots."

"C'mon, big fellow," Hillary said.

Bantam smiled.

Johnny stood to his feet after disrupting the ship's electrical systems. A wave of intense nausea and vertigo hit him like a ton of bricks. He gasped for air, sure he was going to fall off the saucer. He staggered to the metal deck, heaving. At first, he was afraid he was going to vomit. Then he sincerely wished he could just get it over with! Apparently, disruption took some getting used to. Still, his efforts were rewarded with a loud whining sound and a satisfying pop. The *Grey* bucked for a moment and Johnny worried that it was about to crash down into the Plaza; however, it remained hovering in place.

He immediately cast about for an access hatch. He knew that the moment they fixed whatever was wrong with the craft they'd do their best to extricate themselves from Titan Tower and shake him off. He had to act quickly to get inside. There was one evident hatch, off center, near where he presumed the "back" of the saucer was. But as he headed for it, the hatch burst open and someone shot out of it. Hillary touched down almost right on top of it.

"You again," Johnny said. "Haven't you done enough for one day?"

"You're not gonna mess this up. This is our chance to come out on top."

"And you're willing to do anything to make that happen, right? Face it: Pandora doesn't care who she has to hurt or kill to get it done." He waved his arm theatrically, indicating the city beyond. Midwich was a smoking, burning war zone.

"We're next level, Johnny. Those people down there are worms compared to us. You don't like what you're seeing, but nature's got no morality, bro. It's survival of the fittest. And nature is selecting those dinosaurs for extinction."

"And that's how you justify mass murder?"

Hillary scoffed. "Murder? Please. Have you ever considered how many worms and insects die every time we lay down the foundation for a new house? Is that murder? No, that's progress. And these humans are so far below us they might as well be bugs, Johnny, so–"

"Spare me the monologue and get out of my way."

Hillary clamped his jaw shut and glared at him hard.

"Whatsamatta? A second ago, you were talking survival of the fittest. Let's see it."

Hillary tried to blast Johnny off the saucer with a kinetic burst. Johnny planted himself firmly atop the craft, using his own powers to deflect the attack. He was about to respond in kind when Bantam emerged from the saucer's interior.

"Guess you drew the short straw again," Johnny said as Bantam stood to his full height.

He noted that the big guy was more wary up here, mindful of the long drop to the ground. Bantam took slow, solid steps toward him. He was unarmed. A wise choice, considering how often Johnny had used his foes' weapons against them. Almost thoughtlessly, he prepared to pick Bantam up telekinetically and toss him overboard. It wasn't like the muscle mutant probably wouldn't survive the fall. Johnny wasn't sure what it would take to kill something like Bantam, but he didn't think it was a few stories and gravity.

To his surprise, he couldn't pick Bantam up. That's when he noticed Bantam's odd footwear. Some kind of magnetic boots. With a nasty grin, the muscle mutant's plodding began to pick up. He chugged along, gaining momentum, clearly intending to crush Johnny in his path.

Johnny dodged him easily the first time. The ogre kept running, going over the edge of the saucer. But the boots kept him secured to the *Grey* even when he was completely upside-down on the bottom of the ship.

Not content to let Bantam have all the fun, Hillary dove off the saucer and vanished under the craft, too.

Johnny didn't like how this was playing out. He couldn't see either foe. Bantam was the more predictable of the two. But even Johnny was amazed at how fast the human juggernaut blazed into view. It was all he could do to get out of the way. Bantam roared past him and charged along the bottom of the *Grey* for another attempt.

Johnny waited expectantly for Hillary's attack. Logically, the other Indigo had kinetically tethered himself to the *Grey* and was merely sling-shotting around it, but he fully expected Hillary to shift direction – precisely because that's what he would've done. Though he anticipated the others strategy, he wasn't able to react in time to thwart it.

Hillary tossed a kinetic blast of force at him as he whipped around the craft. The attack simultaneously knocked Johnny off balance and recoiled to bounce Hillary onto a new pathway. As Johnny tried to recover, Bantam popped top-side. Johnny tossed out a hasty concussive wave, but it did little more than slow the ogre down. Bantam bashed him into open space.

This would have been a lot more effective on someone who couldn't fly. Johnny managed to anchor himself to the *Grey* firmly enough to bungee spring back toward the craft. Hillary intercepted him before his feet even touched the surface. Johnny was knocked into a wild spin. Bantam bowled into him again as he was pin-wheeling out of control.

And once again Johnny found himself tossed off the *Grey*. Shaking it off, he anchored himself to the ship again. As he bungeed in this time, he did a few quick calculations. Orbiting the craft once, he spotted Bantam and kinetically anchored himself to the muscle mutant. He gritted his teeth as he was whiplashed around in his wake.

Looking for Johnny, Hillary ignored Bantam as he charged about, except to stay out of his path. Not expecting Johnny to be right behind Bantam, Hillary was clotheslined right after they passed him. He slammed to the deck, flat on his back.

Johnny severed his connection with Bantam and landed on his feet at the other end of the *Grey*. As Hillary attempted to rise, Johnny swept him off the saucer with a concussive wave.

Spitting like a wet cat, Hillary recovered and leapt skyward, intending to whip around the saucer again. Johnny grabbed Hillary kinetically and jerked the other Indigo back to the deck. He landed in the path of Bantam. Unable and perhaps unwilling to stop, Bantam punted Hillary off the saucer.

Recovering again, Hillary bungeed back to meet his foe, roaring a wordless challenge. He drew his pistol in midflight and began firing. The bullets raced after Johnny like miniature homing missiles.

Johnny heard the shots. Bantam was nearly upon him, preparing to meet him with a thunderclap chop. Both of the muscle mutant's ham-fists were in motion, hoping to crush his head like a ripe cantaloupe. Concentrating intently, Johnny caused his world to come to him in bullet time. He altered his path slightly, so that he would pass on the left of Bantam, avoiding the thunderclap. He landed and twisted around the hulking figure in one deft move. Hillary's first bullet slammed into the ogre instead of Johnny. Johnny hooked his hands into the big guy's collar bone as Bantam passed him. Drawn forward by inertia, the muscle mutant dropped backwards. The several impacts of Hillary's bullets helped speed him to the metal beneath their feet.

Landing on the surface of the *Grey*, Hillary took more controlled aim. The gun dry-fired, its ammo spent. Tossing it away, he asked, "Why can't you just die?"

"You first," Johnny said, willing himself invisible.

"What the– Where are you? How are you doing that?"

Johnny didn't answer. He was already in motion.

Bantam was getting to his feet again, looking angrier and surlier than Hillary had yet seen him. He glared about accusingly, his small piggish eyes lighting on Hillary. "Where is he?" he asked.

"You tell me. He went invisible. He could be anywhere." Truth be told, Hillary was starting to get a bad feeling about this. How come Johnny could suddenly turn invisible? They'd told him it was possible, but he'd never been able to figure out the trick of it. Unbidden, his thoughts went back to his showdown with Trager inside the church. Maybe he had been holding back all this time. Certainly, Johnny had just sat back and let them duke it out for the biggest part. And, OK, Hillary himself had been holding back then, too. He'd let Trager win without making it too obvious, so they'd take him to Titan, like Pandora planned. But why would Johnny be holding back? What other tricks did he have up his sleeve?

Suddenly, Bantam spasmed and fell to the deck. Johnny materialized as the unconscious muscle mutant dropped. He'd traded his camouflage to neutralize the ogre via electric shock.

"Gotcha!" Hillary blasted Johnny with a wave of force.

Johnny was flung like a ragdoll into open space. For a moment, he sprawled above the Plaza below. Anchoring himself to the *Grey* again, he swung back to the saucer and clung to the bottom of the craft magnetically. Taking a deep breath to steady his nerves, he planned his next move.

Surveying the devastation from the shoulder of Gage's mech-suit, Ness asked himself, "Hope Holloway, what have you done?"

Against Trager's better judgment, he'd insisted that Gage continue to pilot the mech. Gage wasn't combat trained, but he could handle the mech-suit's controls well enough and he added to their numbers. Besides, Ness was determined not to let one of the last remaining family members that he actually liked out of his sight until the current threat was neutralized.

As the mech flew over the city via jetpack, they got a good look at the damage caused by Johnny's super powered battle across Midwich. Buildings had been reduced to rubble. Others were on fire, billowing smoke. Still others sported shattered glass and gaping holes. As they closed in on the saucer, a building collapsed before their very eyes, no longer able to sustain its structural integrity against the damage it'd taken.

Fortunately, it fell below them.

Trager's Hum-V flew beside them. Jackie and Weasel had been more than a little surprised, even given the general weirdness of recent events, when Trager's Hummer had come to pick them up, mostly because the vehicle was hovering several feet off the ground. After it'd landed, scattering panicked townspeople, they quickly boarded. Ephram boarded more slowly. Trager was flying the hovercraft, having assumed the driver's seat the moment Zim had picked him up.

Once underway, Weasel asked the obvious question of Trager. "So are you making this thing fly... with your mind?"

"No," he said, grinning despite himself, "though I suppose I could if I had to. The Hummer runs on the same technology that powers the *Grey*."

"Is the *Grey* alien technology?"

"What do you think?"

"Did you guys have something to do with Roswell?"

No answer.

"And your truck's been a hovercraft all this time?" Jackie asked.

"Company perk," Cougar said. "You ought to see how they tricked out my bike."

"It didn't seem extravagant, considering what I'm up against," Trager said. "Anyway the fuel cells only last a few hours, so it's not like I get to joyride or anything."

"Speak for yourself," Cougar said with a wry grin.

"But still," Weasel said. "A Hum-V hovercraft... that's pretty awesome, dude. Something this cool should have a name."

Trager rolled his eyes. "How about the company car?"

"I was thinking something more like the Hummercraft! Part Hummer, part hovercraft. Get it?"

"I get it." The smirk on his face made it clear that it was honestly one of the dumbest things he'd ever heard.

They were approaching the *Grey* as cautiously as possible, not wanting to draw fire from its formidable death ray. It soon became obvious that their caution was unnecessary. The *Grey* was inert and caught fast on the corner of Titan Tower.

"Some parking job," Weasel said.

"Looks like Johnny managed to slow them down," Trager said.

"Yeah, but where is he?" Jackie asked.

"Got him," Zim said. "Bottom of the saucer."

A human figure crawled along the bottom of the craft making his way back to top-side. "That's my best friend," Weasel said. "Did I mention that?"

"Yeah, yeah," Cougar said. "Your bud's a rock star. We get it."

Jackie's eyes and hands crackled with electricity, warning the older Indigo to back off. Cougar's eyes blazed in return, defying her to try anything.

"Hey!" Emily said, eyes smoldering a warning of her own. "Just back off."

Cougar blinked in genuine surprise. "Another burner. Interesting." He glanced at Trager. "Why didn't you tell me there was another?"

"You have access to the same files I do," Trager said. "We didn't know. She was supposed to be a dud."

"A what?!" Emily asked.

"Bad choice of words," Trager said. "Not everyone who's chipped ends up evidencing powers."

"You were a late bloomer," Cougar said.

Emily's eyes blazed and her cheeks flushed at the taunt.

Weasel had heard enough. He leaned toward Cougar, grinning like the devil. "You do know this is Johnny's girl, right?"

Cougar's eyes narrowed at the implied threat, but a moment later, a wolfish bravado slipped back over his features. He raised his hands in mock surrender. "OK, OK, I can see you guys can't take a joke."

Once Johnny reached the top of the craft again and no longer needed his magnetic abilities, he turned invisible again.

Hillary was waiting for him, standing atop the hatch protectively, but didn't appear to have spotted him yet. Bantam was missing. Johnny was understandably alarmed by the absence of the muscle mutant. Where had he gone? Back inside? Or was he lying in wait somewhere else? He scanned the nearby buildings worriedly.

Without warning, he felt himself being picked up and slammed toward the metal deck.

"Gotcha!" Hillary said.

Johnny didn't respond, concentrating instead on minimizing his impact. He was able to stop himself right before he made contact, but he was alarmed that Hillary had managed to spot him at all.

"Did you think I didn't see you crawling up here, you little cockroach? I saw you turn invisible."

Johnny got to his feet, appraising his foe. So Hillary had simply seen him before he camouflaged, but pretended otherwise to catch him off-guard. Clever. "So how do you wanna do this?" Johnny asked. "You want me to give you some time to make yourself a white flag or are you more informal about this kinda thing?"

"I'll crush you." It was more than a cliché. Johnny actually felt something pressing in upon him from everywhere at once, like he was being gripped inside a giant invisible fist. Hillary was trying to compact him like he'd done those police cruisers less than 24 hours ago. Johnny pushed back desperately. He couldn't believe how powerful Hillary was. The sheer amount of concentration his foe was putting into trying to murder him was unreal.

Fortunately, Hillary's focus was interrupted when he noted the approaching hovercraft. It took Johnny a moment to realize that he was looking at Mike Trager's Hummer. Johnny sighed in wordless frustration. He was doing well to simply fend off Hillary. He wasn't sure he could take on Pandora's super zombie at the same time.

For his part, Hillary appeared confused by what he was seeing. "Trager? Why aren't you dead?" he wondered aloud. Unlike Johnny, he put two and two together rather quickly. "Oh no. You broke Pandora's spell, didn't you?"

Acting quickly, he pushed Johnny backwards and then grabbed the approaching hovercraft psionically, attempting to shove it into one of the other buildings at the Plaza's edge.

Inside the flying vehicle, Trager pushed back, but the Hum-V still bounced off the corner of the building. "Who is this kid?" Trager asked as he righted the hovercraft.

Zim shrugged.

"Well, he's about to learn to choose his enemies more carefully," he said, gripping the steering wheel tightly. "Ness, get ready to take this guy down."

"Ready," Ness announced into the comm. Gage's mech-suit was clinging to the unfinished top of Titan Tower from Atlas' skeletal globe. Still perched on the mech's shoulder, Ness had a bird's-eye view of the saucer.

"You Indigos hang on and get ready to jump," Trager said.

"Jump?" Emily asked. "Couldn't we go a little lower first?"

Trager pushed a button, causing the doors of the Hum-V to pop off. The metal doors would've fallen to the Plaza below but Trager sent them zipping at Hillary for spite. Hillary deflected them easily. Trager was already circling Hillary with the Hummer, hoping to keep his attention so Ness could get a bead on him.

The ruse might have worked if Hillary hadn't caught site of the mech. Noting there was someone on the mech's shoulder, his eyes narrowed suspiciously, then widened in recognition. Pandora had briefed him on Quatermain. Neutralizing the sharpshooter had been critical to their plan.

Hillary reacted instantly, running for the end of the saucer that was lodged in Titan Tower. He quickly accelerated to the speed of a locomotive, hoping to escape into the structure's interior before Ness pulled the trigger.

An invisible Johnny clotheslined him before he could get away. Hillary slammed into the unforgiving metal deck hard enough to loosen his teeth. Johnny reeled in his catch psionically, his face grim.

Ness jerked his rifle up, stopping himself from taking the kill shot.

Trager brought his vehicle to hover over the *Grey* briefly so Jackie, Emily and Cougar could jump off. Once they were safely atop the saucer, Trager moved his hovercar to a spot nearby where he could keep an eye on things while he gave the wheel back to Zim.

Johnny held Hillary to the deck with kinetic force, glaring at his prize, trying to calm himself down. Hillary had nearly killed him; it was taking every ounce of self-control Johnny possessed to keep from returning the favor.

"Johnny, are you OK?" Emily asked as she came to join him.

He was glad for the diversion. "What are you guys doing here?"

"We thought you could use some help," Jackie said, "but it looks like you have everything well in hand."

"Not exactly. Your mom's still inside. We have to stop her before she gets the *Grey* up and running again.

"How'd you stop it to begin with?" Cougar asked.

Johnny's head snapped around, really noticing his Uncle Ephram for the first time. "You've got a lot of nerve coming to this party," he said. "I should kill you for everything you've done. You murdered my parents. You burned down my home."

Cougar stared at him open-mouthed for a moment. "Look, I'm sorry about your house, but in case you haven't noticed, I wasn't exactly myself tonight. And your folks, well, I never meant to kill them either. Things just got out of hand."

"You were trying to kill me."

"It's complicated. Tell ya what? I'll explain everything once this is all over. I owe you that much. But you're gonna need help bringing Pandora in. So once again, how did you stop the *Grey* the first time?"

"I disrupted the power flow."

"Can't you just do that again?" Emily asked.

"Maybe." He remembered the intense episode of nausea that followed that little trick. He'd already decided disruption was a measure of last resort. "If I have to."

Hillary chuckled darkly at Johnny's feet. "You'll never stop us."

"I don't know about that," Cougar said. "We stopped you just fine. How's the view from down there anyway?"

"You have no idea what you're dealing with."

"Do you ever stop talking?" Johnny asked.

"Allow me," Jackie said. Electricity crackled between her fingertips.

"No, I got it," Johnny said, delivering Hillary a shock that rendered their mouthy opponent unconscious.

Jackie blinked, genuinely surprised. "Wow. I didn't know you could do that."

"Yeah, it's new for me too."

"Now what?" Emily asked.

"That's our way in," he said, indicating the hatch.

"It's opening," Jackie said, bracing herself.

All four heroes stood at ready, wondering what Pandora would throw at them next.

Bantam glared down at his enemies from the unfinished top levels of Titan Tower. The wind whipped about him as he crouched low, eyes fixed on Trager's hovercraft as it slowly circled the saucer. He too was clinging to the skeletal globe atop Atlas' shoulders. Gage's mech-suit had its back to him.

Bantam's small piggish eyes flitted to Johnny and narrowed. The electric shock that little bug dished out earlier had knocked him out alright, but his kinetic resistance allowed him to shake it off rather quickly. At Hillary's suggestion, he'd leapt into the open side of the unfinished floors of Titan's downtown headquarters while Johnny was on the underside of the saucer. He'd been there waiting to ambush Johnny from above when the hovercraft and the mech-suit flew in. It was a stroke of luck that the mech chose Titan Tower for its perch. All Bantam had to do was hug the shadows, climb into position and wait for an opportunity.

Unfortunately, while he'd been waiting Johnny managed to put Hillary down. When the saucer hatch opened, Bantam realized that with everyone's focus on it, he finally had the perfect moment to attack.

Without warning, he knocked the mech-suit from its perch with a flying kick in the back. He rode the oversized metal man as it fell, noting that the old man on its shoulder managed to jump free and catch a ledge on the way down. He'd deal with that guy later.

As Bantam surfed the free-falling mech-suit, Weasel peered up through the sunroof to see what was blocking the light. Seeing the mech's silhouette against the sky, he shouted, "Look out!" but it was too late.

Gage's mech-suit smashed into the Hum-V in midair. Weighed down, the flying car descended sharply, pin-wheeling out of control. Gage bounced off and continued falling, but Bantam leapt free and held on tightly to the Hummer, ensuring it too would crash down.

Johnny and his friends heard the impact, which immediately drew their attention to the fact that a mech-suit and the spinning hovercraft were hurtling from the sky directly at them. Slowing the world to bullet time, Johnny dug in and kinetically stopped the mech-suit and Hum-V only a foot or so above their heads.

Bantam leapt away and landed heavily atop the saucer.

At that moment, Jennifer Winters poked her head out of the hatch, pointing a pair of automatic weapons their way. Jackie immediately grabbed Emily and went invisible, while Cougar dove to the deck, tossing fireballs in their foe's direction. Winters ducked behind the hatch door, using it as a shield against Cougar's attacks. She popped out a second later to fire at the pyrokinetic again. Still holding the hovercraft and Gage's mech-suit aloft, Johnny arced the bullet stream away from his Uncle Ephram.

While he was thus occupied, Bantam smashed into the already damaged Hummer and literally tore it in half, tossing either end aside with a savage grin. Surprised, Johnny lost his hold on both vehicles. The mech-suit landed on its large metal feet.

Still hurtling through the air, Bantam cocked back a hamfist to drive Johnny into the deck. Johnny barely had time to blast him away. The muscle mutant fell flat on his back only a few yards away. Gage lifted the mech-suit's oversized metal boot, intending on stomping the ogre. Bantam grabbed the offending foot, got to his feet and hurled the mech-suit away like a discus thrower. Gage landed atop the saucer, but his momentum caused him to slide off the edge.

Meanwhile, Trager was forced to use his powers to stop the front cab of the Hum-V from likewise going over the side of the saucer. Trager and Zim breathed a sigh of relief as they stopped just in time. That's when they remembered that Weasel had been in the back.

When Bantam tore the Hummer in half, Weasel was unceremoniously dumped out, rather like a yolk falling from a cracked eggshell to the frying pan. The landing was less than delicate. Bantam spotted Weasel as he let out a howl.

High above them, Quatermain had managed to pull himself securely up onto the ledge. He was already cursing himself for not checking out the top of the Tower before they chose their nest. He actually thought he'd seen something out of the corner of his eye while they were waiting for an opening on Hillary, but he'd been fool enough to dismiss his instincts. Looking down now and seeing his hulking assailant coming for the defenseless young man on the saucer deck, Ness shouldered his gun.

Laughing cruelly, Bantam raised his big metal-clad foot high to squash Weasel Hopkins. Johnny's friend rolled out of the way of the kick and scrambled away. Bantam chased after him, stomping down as Weasel continued rolling out of his path. Weasel was getting dangerously close to the saucer's edge.

Johnny was well aware of the peril Weasel was in, but was momentarily unable to do anything about it. Winters had tossed aside her conventional weaponry and brought up something from below that looked for all the world like a small bazooka. The hand cannon was a miniature version of the *Grey*'s death ray. The first salvo caught Cougar square in the chest, blasting him off the top of the saucer. Johnny reached out kinetically to catch him, but then Winters turned the hand cannon on him. Cougar plummeted like a comet, defiantly hurling flame at his foe until he crashed into the Plaza below. Unlike bullets and missiles, Johnny found the energy weapon's discharge was somehow slippery, harder to deal with. He didn't have anything tangible to grab or stop. He suffered a glancing blow from her first shot, which knocked him down. He did better with her next attempts, using concussive blasts of force as a clumsy shield.

Fortunately, Jackie and Emily weren't just content to hide. Without warning, Emily appeared at Winters' right, sending a gout of flame in her direction. Realizing she'd been outflanked, she dropped back down through the hatch.

Which finally gave Johnny the break he needed to attend to Weasel's rescue…

…only to discover that his friend didn't need his help this time.

Mostly out of sheer luck, Weasel had managed to dodge Bantam's attempts to crush him. Bantam took each lucky escape as a personal insult. Like a man gone mad after a fly that refused to succumb to the flyswatter, his attempts became more and more manic. The big lug was huge and powerful, but not that fast in close quarters. Part of his lack of speed likely had to do with his big metal magnet boots. The ones he was trying to stomp Weasel with. Still, he managed to maneuver Weasel to the edge of the saucer.

Ness fired a shot from his high-powered sniper rifle. He knew he had little chance of stopping bulletproof Bantam, but he had to at least distract the muscle mutant. Bantam's head jerked back as the bullet slammed into his thick skull. Bantam frowned, glaring up at Quatermain. The flattened slug fell off his forehead as he growled at the sniper's insult.

Hearing the whine of a mech-suit's jetpack, Bantam's head snapped up. Gage rose into view over the edge of the saucer. Ness' nephew grinned savagely from behind the cracked windshield of the mech's cockpit. His metal gauntlets held an over-sized rifle with which he fully intended to put Bantam on his ample posterior.

Weasel ducked into a fetal position and covered his head, sure he was about to be crushed, shot and otherwise killed in the crossfire. As the ogre raised his monstrous fist to bash the mech-suit, Freight Train Farley plowed into him from behind.

Once Brad reached downtown Midwich, he'd begun bounding higher and higher until he was stepping off rooftops like Johnny. He reveled in his new-found abilities, feeling more powerful than he'd ever felt before. The flying saucer would've been hard to miss. A tell-tale damage path led to Harper Plaza. The streets below were filled with frightened people, mostly running away from the action. When he reached the Plaza, he got a good look at the action going on atop the flying saucer.

John Lazarus was alive and emo boy was having a full-out brawl atop the space ship! As he watched, Winters blasted Cougar off the craft with some kind of alien ray gun. He watched her unlucky victim fall from the sky in a blaze of glory. There was nothing he could do for that guy, even if he wasn't still mad at him for burning down his house, so he returned his attention to the rumble atop the saucer.

When he saw Bantam going after Weasel, something deep inside him snapped. Racing around the rim of the Plaza atop the buildings, he launched himself at the other muscle mutant, driving home with everything he had. It was enough to break the hold of Bantam's magnetic boots. Both ogres fell off the saucer into the plaza below, sweeping the mech-suit along in their path. They tumbled earthward locked in combat, flailing at each other with punches and kicks all the way down.

63 – Destiny

"You OK?" Johnny called to a wide-eyed Weasel.

His friend nodded mutely. One second, Bantam there; the next moment, the monster was gone like a bad dream.

Trager and Zim exited the ruined cab of the Hum-V and hurried over to join John Lazarus.

Johnny could hardly look Trager in the eye. "Cougar fell. I tried to save him."

"You think a little fall like that kills a pyro?" Trager asked. "You have a lot to learn, kid. Do you know how burners like Cougar survive their own flames? Phenomenally fast healing abilities."

"So he actually survived that?" Weasel asked, glancing over the edge of the saucer.

"I'm not saying it didn't hurt," Trager said. "And I'm not saying he'll get up anytime soon, but, if I know Ephram, that loud-mouth will be back to his usual jerk self by tomorrow morning." He glanced back at Johnny, sizing him up. "You really did try to save him, didn't you? Good for you, kid."

"Now what?" Johnny asked, uncomfortable with this praise.

"Bringing the civilians was a mistake. I want everyone who doesn't have a super power to get into that building and get out of here," Trager said.

Zim nodded.

Weasel glared at him, offended.

"That means you, too. The people inside this saucer will have no qualms about killing you or using you as hostages. This is as much for our good as yours." Trager turned away from Weasel dismissively. "They'll be waiting for us down that hatch, Johnny. It'll be close quarters. I think you and I should go alone."

"What kind of chauvinistic garbage is this?" Emily asked. "I'm going."

"If she's going, I'm going, too," Weasel said.

"Look, I appreciate everything you've done so far, but all things considered… I've seen what a burner does in close quarters," Trager said. "So has Johnny. You're just as likely to get us killed."

She winced at the memory of Hive drones being reduced to blackened skeletons back in the Tunnel. "I get it. I'll go," she said. "Just Johnny, please be careful."

Johnny nodded, thanking her with his eyes.

Weasel looked as if he might be about to say something provocative, something Trager might be tempted to throw him overboard for. Johnny intervened smoothly. "You'll look after my girl, right?"

"I'll do it for you," he said. "Not because he says so."

"Where's the Holloway girl?" Trager asked, casting about for her.

"I don't know," Weasel said. "She goes... invisible."

"When the last time you remember seeing her?"

"Um," Johnny said, staring at the still open hatch.

"She went in alone, didn't she?" Weasel asked. "Why does she keep doing that?"

"Let's hope she didn't get herself killed," Trager said.

Beneath their feet, the *Grey* began to thrum with power.

"They're firing it up! Get out of here!" Trager shouted.

Weasel hesitated.

"You take care of my girl. I'll take care of yours," Johnny said. "Now go!"

Weasel nodded and took Emily's hand. As he led her along, Emily glanced over her shoulder, taking one last worried glance at John Lazarus. Then they dashed into Titan Tower.

"The hatch!" Trager warned. It was beginning to close. Mike Trager hurried to hold it open kinetically as Johnny and he dashed over to it. When they reached it, both glanced down the hatch and then at each other. "It's a trap," Trager warned as the *Grey* lurched forward, wrenching free of Titan Tower.

"Of course it is!" Johnny shouted above the saucer's increased humming. The *Grey* began to rise slowly out of the plaza. "But I think I know a way to find out what's waiting for us down there." Back in Gamma Lab, his sonic roar had somehow triggered a sonar effect. It was worth a shot. He roared into the hatch.

The sound waves bounced back to him, giving him a rather good image of all of the open spaces they'd traveled through.

"What was that all about?" Trager asked.

"Sonar. Winters is at the end of a corridor opposite the hatch, waiting to ambush us. Pandora's in the cockpit area with her father."

"Anybody else? The Holloway girl?"

"That's all I saw."

"Well, let's do this before this baby really takes off," Trager said, remembering how fast the saucer could accelerate. "Ready?"

Johnny nodded. Taking a deep breath, they both jumped down the hatch instead of using the ladder. Johnny threw a concussive wall of force as he descended. Jennifer Winters was apparently ready for something like this, for she ducked out of sight at blinding speed, then whipped back out, weapon blazing. He deflected the energy bursts from her futuristic ray gun, then crushed the weapon in her hands with a bit of concentration. She tossed the useless weapon away from her, partly fearing an explosion. In one smooth movement, she drew a twin set of automatic weapons, sweeping the corridor with a liberal spray of bullets. With little room to arc the bullets away from him or prevent them from just ricocheting back on him anyway, he opted for stopping the bullets in midair. Even before the bullets dropped to the floor, Winters tossed her guns away and produced a handful of metallic four-pointed shuriken. She dashed down the corridor, whipping them at Johnny. There wasn't room here to swarm objects around him. He barely had room to knock them aside.

Trager was forced to duck behind Johnny. He waited at ready, in case she managed to put Arthur's boy down.

To his consternation, Johnny found that every time he thought to dispatch her, he had his hands full deflecting shuriken or throwing spikes. She was constantly in motion, doing flips, bouncing off the walls, doing everything in her preternatural power to make herself a slippery target. In this manner she steadily advanced, closing the distance between them. And he remembered how formidable she could be in close quarters.

She drew a pair of knives, closing in for the kill. Her expression was cold, all business, no mercy. Suddenly Johnny grinned like the Cheshire cat. She faltered.

Johnny roared and a wall of sonic force slammed into her. This close to Johnny and in such tight quarters, she couldn't get out of its path, no matter how fast she was. The force wave carried her the entire length of the passage. She hit the opposite wall and slid to the floor. A born fighter, she managed to lift herself up to her knees. Trager picked her up mentally and pinned her to the wall. He walked up to her, preparing to finish her off. He didn't want to kill her, but he wasn't sure she was going to leave him a choice.

Jackie Holloway materialized next to him, nearly earning herself instant death from both Johnny and Trager.

"Easy, boys. I'm on your side, remember?" She touched Jennifer Winters and shocked her into unconsciousness. "See? Problem solved."

"Thanks," Johnny said.

"Wait. How did you slip past their guard?" Trager asked.

"Invisible girl, remember?" She phased out of sight briefly to make her point.

Trager considered her for a moment, then glanced down the adjoining corridor. "Cockpit's that way. Let's keep our wits about us."

"Wait," Johnny said. Something caught his eye near Winter's unconscious body. "What's that?"

It was a baseball-sized metal sphere with a camera lens on one face. Johnny picked it up. It was a lot like the holosphere he'd encountered back at his house. He immediately noticed the Argus Information Systems logo stamped on it. Titan owned Argus.

Trager frowned. "It's a hovercam, but what's it doing on board the *Grey*?"

"I think I shorted it out during the fight," Johnny said.

"It doesn't make sense. We use them for surveillance," Trager said, "but there's no reason to scope out the Grey. The saucer has its own security system."

"Are there a lot of those things?" Jackie asked.

Trager shrugged. "I can't say. That's Zim's area."

Suddenly, the hovercam hummed back to life and vanished.

"It can camouflage," Jackie said. "Like me."

"Which means these things could be anywhere, watching us," Johnny said.

"But why?" she asked. "And who's using them to watch us? My mother?"

"No, that's Titan tech," Trager said.

"Yeah, but mom used Mr. Zim to hack into Titan back in the control room," Jackie pointed out.

"You've never weaponized any of these creepy little things, have you?" Johnny asked, concentrating on his vision until he could see the hallway in terms of temperature.

"Not to my knowledge," Trager said. He didn't look particularly happy with that prospect.

Johnny nodded. He'd located the hovercam. He crushed it with a thought. It startled Trager and Jackie when it appeared in a shower of sparks and dropped unceremoniously to the floor. "Just in case," Johnny said.

They proceeded quickly but carefully, expecting an ambush at every moment. As they entered the cockpit, Pandora and Silas were waiting for them. Johnny wasn't sure what he was expecting at that moment. He'd had this fleeting image of having to fight his way through an army of ninja zombies. He'd at least expected them to have more hostages. He never thought he'd see them just standing there with their hands raised over their heads.

"Well, we surrender," Silas said "What are your terms?"

"Just like that?" Johnny asked.

"That really doesn't seem like you, Silas," Trager said.

"I'm not a fighter, Johnny," Silas said, ignoring Trager. "I'm an old man. I just want this over with. So why don't you just–"

"Stop talking," Johnny said, realizing with a start that Silas had intended to hypnotize him. He would have obeyed without even realizing it.

Silas opened his mouth to protest, then clamped it shut with a wry nod.

"We really should tell him," Pandora said. Her father rolled his eyes and shook his head.

"Tell me what?"

"Careful, Johnny," Trager said.

"There was a message for you when we used that control key we took off you," she teased. "From your father."

He knew he shouldn't be talking to them. He knew he should simply knock them both senseless before they could zombify him or hypnotically suggest he let them go or kill himself... or cluck like a chicken. But that control key had been left for him. The note that came with it had promised him his answers were on this saucer. "What did it say?"

"First let us go. That's the deal."

"I can't do that," Johnny said.

"Well, you can't arrest us," Silas said. "You're not a cop. Are you a killer?"

"No," Johnny said with a ghost of a smile, "I'm just here to save the day."

"You don't want to be a hero, boy," Silas said. Reaching into his jacket slowly, he procured a comic book and tossed it at Johnny's feet for effect. Johnny recognized the cover art immediately: *Mann from Midwich*. "Here in the real world, the hero dies. Worse, he dies unmourned. He's treated with hate, fear and mistrust by those he seeks to protect, because he's different. Special. Superior. And these talking monkeys you waste your talents on know our undeniable superiority can only mean one thing: their evolutionary replacements have arrived."

"Wow. Where do I sign up?"

"Don't take this lightly, Johnny," Silas said. "Our plans are fully in motion. They can't be stopped. This is our time. We will rule this miserable planet. You can either join us or... well, perhaps Destiny should be the one to tell you."

Johnny and Trager felt the cold barrel of a gun press into their respective necks. Each put his hands up. They'd forgotten about Pandora's assistant. Johnny's sonar hadn't shown her, of course, but it wouldn't have if she were behind a closed door. Trager looked like he was itching to do something stupid, but he was experienced enough to know he couldn't stop a bullet when the gun was pressed to his skin.

"Don't turn around, either of you," Destiny said. She held her pistols firmly to each man's nape. "Don't move. Don't even think. Just listen"

"You have my full attention," Johnny said. But he was already thinking about how to get out of here.

"Destiny's gift is rather rare, even compared to pyrokinesis," Silas said. "She deals in causality and probabilities and, I'll spare you the technical description, but let's just say she can nearly always predict the future by examining the variables in light of intuitive deduction."

"And that means what to me?"

"Well, it means she's the reason you're here."

Johnny glanced over his shoulder at his captor. "You're behind all this?"

"Of course not," Silas said. "But her gift of foresight did help us set things in motion that would almost inevitably lead us to this moment and onward to a future where *Homo excelsior* will rule by right of superior adaptation."

"*Homo excelsior*?? You sound like a bargain basement comic book villain.

You do realize that, right?"

"You cannot fight the future, Johnny," Silas said. "If you don't join us, you will suffer the consequences. I'm sure Destiny would be most upset if you chose poorly."

"If you don't join us tonight, you will die," Destiny said. "You will watch all of your friends and loved ones either die or live to betray you. You will die alone. You will be branded an enemy of the world. And the world will celebrate your death as a holiday."

"That sounds bad. But if I join you all that bad stuff just goes away, that it? Sounds a bit convenient. How do I know you're not just making all this up?"

"Why don't you believe me?" she asked.

"You are holding a Glock to his head, sweetheart," Trager said. When he'd glanced at Johnny earlier, he'd recognized the gun. He was already working out a plan.

"You may not believe me now," Destiny Pascalé said, "but you will. No matter which future you choose."

"What makes you say that?" Johnny asked.

"Because in the future, we're married. We have a child. We love each other."

"I don't even know you, lady." As if this night hadn't been crazy enough...

"Not yet," she purred.

"You guys are crazy."

"What's your decision, boy?" Silas asked.

"Somebody has to stop you people."

"*You* people?" Pandora mocked. "We are your people, Johnny. When are you going to stop pretending you are or ever were one of them?"

"Think about what you're saying. You really think you're better than everyone else just because we can do something other humans can't. What you're saying is no different than some people thinking they're better than others because they're better educated or they have more money or have a different skin color. In fact, that's all this really is: racism based on genetics."

"You will come to regret this moment," Pandora said.

"I'm already there."

"What are you going to do with us?" Trager asked.

Silas and Pandora stepped in front of Johnny and Trager respectively.

"You're going to hypnotize us," Johnny realized.

Pandora nodded.

"It's easier if you just relax," Silas said.

"Jackie, now," Johnny said.

Jackie Holloway appeared directly behind Destiny, instantly delivering a nasty shock. Knowing her ambush was imminent, Trager had concentrated on keeping Destiny's triggers from moving. Thanks to her Glock's safe action, the weapons could not be fired unless someone placed their fingers on the triggers and squeezed them. Destiny fell to the floor, out cold. The Glock slid out of her hands and flew into his.

Silas and Pandora backpedaled in alarm. Trager aimed his weapon at Pandora and squeezed off a round. To his consternation, the gun jammed.

"What are doing?" Jackie asked. "You can't kill them!"

"She's right, you know," Pandora said. "You *can't* kill me. You can't even hit me."

"What? No, the gun jammed," Trager said.

"Really?"

Mike Trager attempted to blast her into the wall with kinetic force. Nothing happened.

"I can't. I really can't."

"But I can," Jackie Holloway warned her mother.

"But you won't," she said. "You won't harm a member of your family any more than you will allow someone else to harm them. In fact, you're going to protect your family, aren't you?"

"Shut up!" Jackie said, her outrage rendering her immune to her mother's attempt to hypnotize her. "You left all those people at Titan to just die! My mom would never do something like that. So don't you dare talk to me about family."

"You watch your tone, young lady," Silas said.

"Or what, Papaw Darling? You'll brainwash me like you've done my mother?" she asked, electricity crackling off her fingertips dangerously.

"You'll do as you're told," he said, "or you'll never see your mother or your brother ever again." He paused, feigning surprise. "Oh yes. Did you know you had a twin brother?"

"Jack already introduced himself."

"You've met Jack?" Pandora asked. She sounded a little lost again. Johnny guessed that Silas' hold on her was weakening in the presence of her daughter.

"Who's Jack?" Silas asked with a cruel leer.

"What? Dad, Jack's my son. Your grandson," Pandora said.

He looked into her eyes steadily. "But you don't have a son, my dear. Jack was never real. He was just your daughter's childhood imaginary friend."

"Oh, that's right," Pandora said, smiling fondly at her daughter. "You had such an imagination, Jackie."

"Stop it, Silas," Johnny said. "Not another word."

"Or what?"

Johnny blasted him into the far wall with barely a thought. The villainous old man bounced off the futuristic equipment and slumped to the floor.

Johnny winced as he looked at Jackie. "Sorry."

"Don't be," she said, wiping tears from her eyes. "I am so gonna need therapy after this."

"Dad!" Pandora wailed, running to her father's side. "If you've killed him…"

"I promised Jackie not to kill anyone," Johnny said. "Don't make me break that promise. Give yourself up."

"You can't beat me, Johnny."

"Wanna bet?"

"Johnny, look out!" Jackie shouted as two figures rushed out of the corridor behind him.

Johnny and Trager spun around hastily as Hillary and Jennifer Winters attacked.

Forgotten atop the saucer, Hillary had awakened shortly after the *Grey*'s engines thrummed to life. As the ship began rising, he rose stiffly to his feet, trying to get his bearings. He was alone atop the saucer. He made his way to the hatch, using kinetic energy to anchor himself to the saucer. After mentally opening the hatch and lowering himself cautiously inside, he discovered the unconscious Winters. After he woke her, Winters had secured a pair of "alien" rifles out of a weapons locker before they made their way to the cockpit.

Jackie went invisible instantly, ducking low to keep out of harm's way.

Johnny had just enough warning to deflect the first salvo of green fire. The blaster fire ricocheted off Johnny's force wall and hit some important-looking computer equipment. A warning klaxon sounded as the saucer lurched to a standstill. Jennifer Winters rode out the turbulence with preternatural skill and fired another salvo at Johnny.

"Are you insane?" Trager asked, as her shot deflected away from Johnny again and destroyed yet more of the saucer's electrical systems. "Stop shooting!" He kinetically picked up Winters up and slammed her into the bulkhead. She slid to the floor, her finger still locked on the trigger. Unconscious, she managed to do more yet damage to the *Grey*'s cockpit.

The cockpit lights flickered, died, and were replaced by flashes of red emergency lighting. The ship lurched to one side, slipping into a dive momentarily before recovering.

Jackie Holloway materialized behind Hillary and tried to shock him, but he twisted away from her and tossed her aside with a telekinetic push.

Johnny took advantage of his foe's distraction. Without hesitation, he hoisted Hillary into the air and slammed him into the ceiling harder than was necessary to render him inert. He dropped the troublemaker to the floor like a ragdoll.

Pandora was already on the move. While everyone was occupied with Hillary and Winters, she'd hurriedly strapped herself into a chair. Before Johnny or Trager could react, the roof popped open above her chair and she jetted skyward. At that same moment, one of the cockpit consoles exploded, overwhelmed by the damage Winters had inflicted during her brief assault. The *Grey* pitched into a dive, knocking everyone off their feet. Still unconscious, Hillary, Winters, Silas and Destiny slid across the floor and landed in a jumbled heap. The rest caught themselves and held on with their gifts.

Johnny glanced at Trager, then at the hole Pandora had escaped through. The cockpit swirled with wind and noise.

Mike Trager shouted above the wind. "Well, don't just stand there. Stop her!"

Johnny nodded. Standing beneath the evacuation hole in the ceiling, he launched himself skyward.

"Wait! Hang it, kid. I meant take one of the evac pods."

64 – Wreck of a Mech

Still trading blows, the two muscle mutants fell to the plaza below, tumbling apart on impact. Brad plowed into a row of parked cars, smashing in windshields as he bounced and rolled to a stop. Bantam sailed on further, crashing through the glass front of a sandwich shop.

Gage had managed to break free from the pair with a lucky rifle shot, which he admittedly squeezed off in panic. He hastily activated his jetpack, hoping to break his fall. Unfortunately, he was nearly horizontal with his face to the sky when the rockets fired, so all he really managed to do was to sail out of the Harper Plaza via one the downtown streets. He plowed into the earth like a comet, ripping up two and a half blocks worth of asphalt before his jetpack exploded, sending him skyward. Gage screamed as he shot into the sky. Somewhere near the top of his arc, he realized he was going to land in the second or third story of a parking garage. There was a shower of concrete and rubble as he landed, smashing into a parked minivan. Car alarms began going off in the vicinity from the shock.

Inside the mech-suit, Gage was surprised to find himself anywhere near conscious. His heads-up display, splashed across the spiderweb-cracked interior of his cockpit window, was flashing all sorts of warnings at him, confusing the battered human pilot further. He heard a groaning sound and realized that the mech-suit was about to fall. Wearily, he moved the controls to hold on, but one arm was no longer working. As the mech-suit fell, its right arm snagged, ripping it from its metal socket. He managed to slow his fall with his remaining arm. He landed heavily on his metal feet.

He took a moment to find a switch that silenced the alarm that was telling him that – surprise! surprise! – his arm wasn't working, as well as another telling him that his jetpack was "malfunctioning." He assessed his situation. The mech-suit was still moving. He'd lost his big mech rifle and his robotic right arm was missing. Sighing regretfully, he used his left gauntlet to remove the impossibly cracked cockpit windshield, getting rid of the dead weight.

He'd always wondered what it would be like to fight alongside his great-uncle Ness. Despite the tight-lipped secrecy concerning the subject, Gage had figured out that something strange was going on in Midwich. He'd even traced everything back to Titan. Overheard conversations, snippets from family members' journals and some good old-fashioned nosing around finally convinced him that Ness' skill with a rifle was something more than natural ability. He'd confronted uncle Ness with what he'd discovered, but the old cuss had told him he was a fool to investigate Titan, neither confirming nor denying the allegation. Determined to get to the bottom of things, he'd got a job at Titan. He'd learned a lot more than he set out to, but at least now he could see why Ness was so leery of the company. All that remained was what to do with the knowledge he'd gained.

Of course, there was no real question. He and his uncle were cut from the same cloth. He really couldn't see turning his back and letting other people fight his battles for him, not when he had it within his power to do something. He might not come out of this alive, but he'd make sure they remembered him.

With grim determination, he set his sights back on Harper Plaza, where the fight was still raging.

65 – Tower Fall

Back in the Plaza, Freight Train Farley got to his feet groggily, still half-stunned that he'd survived the fall at all. He cast about for his foe.

The bigger muscle mutant charged out of the deli, roaring his outrage. A part of Brad realized that the other Indigo could seriously hurt him. This wasn't football. He didn't have the benefit of pads and referees. Neither was he obligated to meet this ogre head-to-head. Wrenching a lighting pole out of the ground, he swung it like a baseball bat. It caught Bantam in the chest, bending the pole and knocking both Indigos on their respective rears.

Bantam recovered first. He rushed at Brad, arm extended to clothesline him as he got up. Brad slammed into the pavement after pin-wheeling through the air from the impact. Bantam plucked him up before he could recover and tossed him into a storefront window.

Head reeling, Farley picked himself up and stared at the hole he'd come through. This wasn't going well. That ogre meant business! He couldn't *ever* remember being hit like that. For a moment, he seriously considered just hiding out until the other Indigo left, but a part of him wouldn't accept that. He'd ran before and kicked himself for it ever since. The world was filled with winners and wusses and the Freight Train was certainly not one of the latter!

With a Viking war cry, he stormed out of the building into the Plaza. Bantam was waiting for him with an expectant leer. It'd been a long time since Brad was unable to simply overpower his opponent, Wacky Jackie's cat-and-mouse notwithstanding, so it took him a moment to think it through. Before he'd bulked up, he'd often had to go toe-to-toe with guys twice his size on the football field. Coach Trager told him it boiled down to one thing: the other guy's center of gravity.

As Bantam closed in, Brad crouched down and launched into the others ribcage. Bantam's momentum caused him to flip unceremoniously over Brad's back. For his part, the smaller Indigo was knocked onto his back, swept up in the Bantam's inertia. Their tumbling flight ceased abruptly when they crashed into a van. Scrambling to his feet, Brad came out on top. Taking advantage of the moment, he punched the other repeatedly with jackhammer fists.

Growling in fury, Bantam kicked him away. Brad rolled across the Plaza, slamming to a stop at the base of the founder's statue at the center. When he picked himself up again, Bantam was already at full steam, intending to squash him against the statue's base. Hastily, Brad dove out of the way. Unable to stop himself, Bantam crashed into the statue, tearing up a shower of concrete and gouging a large chunk out of the monument's base.

Brad got to his feet, hammering the other ogre in the chest several times. Bantam rolled over and backhanded him to the lawn. Brad scrambled backwards hastily, trying to put distance between them. Bantam leapt into the air, intending to body slam his foe. Brad rolled away and got back to his feet.

"Brad!" Emily yelled from across the Plaza. "This way!"

Brad Farley's head snapped around at the sound of the voice. He spied Weasel and Emily coming out of Titan Tower. They were supporting Zim, who was still very much injured from his first de-zombification. Ness was walking under his own steam with a barely perceptible limp. Like Trager said, Ness healed a bit slower than some of the others, but it was still pretty quick by non-Indigo standards. Ness had begun heading downstairs the moment the saucer wrenched free from Titan Tower, leaving a jagged – and critical – hole in the building. When it'd torn itself free, the building's structural integrity had suffered heavily. It groaned under its own weight, ready to fall at any moment.

Hoping they could help him defeat Bantam, Brad ran in their direction.

As he approached, Brad saw Gage's one-armed mech bounding into the square. Gage made a bee line for Bantam. The ogre didn't bother slowing down or changing course, but he kept one eye on the approaching threat.

Taking on Bantam without a protective cockpit windshield between them was probably enormously stupid. After all, what prevented the monstrous Indigo from simply reaching into the exposed cockpit and crushing him to death? Gage had never thought that Sigourney Weaver should have survived her face-to-face encounter with the Alien queen in the second *Aliens* movie; after all, those lift loaders were just as exposed as he was now and were three times as clumsy. Of course, he wasn't exactly planning on taking on Bantam from the front. As Gage came up alongside him, he pushed Bantam hard in the back, slamming him down into the ground. Bantam growled as he got a mouthful of turf, before Gage tripped over him and they both went rolling. At some point in the tumbling heap, Bantam twisted around in the air and, while he was at the top of their arc, grabbed the mech-suit's remaining arm. Letting his momentum carry him over, he used his grip on the mech to hurl Gage over his shoulder and slam the mech into the ground. As Gage lay stunned on the turf, Bantam charged onward, as if nothing had happened.

Emily pointed behind him. "Brad, look out!"

Brad didn't bother. He knew what was back there. Digging in, he ran towards his friends with everything he could muster. Behind him, Bantam roared victoriously, confirming that he was much closer than Brad had suspected.

"Get down!" Emily shouted as he closed in. Seeing her hands outstretched and the fire in her eyes, Brad flattened himself to the ground. A wave of flame washed over his head. The fire blasted into Bantam, who howled in indignation. Momentarily blinded, he tripped over Brad's prone form.

Bantam kept coming, borne along by his own momentum. Everyone dove aside as the wrecking ball kept tumbling toward them. Ness brought his rifle up and fired. The bullet penetrated Bantam's left eye. He sailed past them, into the foyer of Titan Tower. As he smashed into the building, they heard a series of crashes, then a final, awful metallic groan.

"Run!" Weasel yelled.

They all fled as the tower came crashing down behind them in sheets of metal, stone and glass. The rumbling thunder of its destruction overwhelmed all other sound. The statue of Prometheus which stood sentry over the building's front doors was pulverized by the apocalyptic rain of stone and steel. Glass shattered at the heroes' heels as they ran as they'd never run before. Atlas' unfinished globe of steel girders wrenched free from its spot atop the tower.

Lying flat on his back, Gage tried to rise but found the mech-suit was now damaged beyond functionality. The suit jerked and sparked, but wasn't following his movements. Realizing he'd have to ditch, he tried to unbuckle his harness. It was jammed.

Glancing up at the falling steel globe, he began panicking, desperately clawing at his harness.

Ness' eagle eyes spotted his great-nephew in his dilemma. Intuitively, he knew that even if Gage freed himself of his restraints, the metal atlas would crush him before he could scramble away. So Quatermain shouldered his rifle and fired toward the mech. It was a one-in-a-million shot, impossibly lucky for anyone else, but his bullet hit the emergency ejection switch.

Gage found himself bursting free of the mech's chest like a more explosive, mechanized version of one of the *Aliens* he'd just been thinking about. At first, he was terrified that he would simply meet the metal sphere in midair, but he managed to pass by it. Great-uncle Ness never missed. At the apex of his flight, twin chutes opened up to float him to the earth. From that height, he had a good view of what was going on in the Plaza below.

The steel globe fell, bounced and rolled through Harper Plaza like an oversized wireframe bowling ball. The heroes hit the deck as it bounded over them. It caught between two buildings, stuck fast a story and a half over a street exiting the traffic circle. A wave of dust swept over their backs in the globe's wake and rushed to coat downtown in a dirty grey.

The heroes rose as the dust settled around them, coughing and brushing themselves off.

"I didn't expect that," Brad said, spitting to clear the dust from his teeth.

Weasel gaped wide-eyed at the rubble that was once Titan Tower. "We didn't just kill that guy," he said. "We buried him!"

Ness snorted. "You think that killed him?"

They all glanced at him in horror and disbelief.

"Just kidding," he said. "Oh! You should see the looks on your faces!"

"Yeah, yeah," Weasel said. "If it's all the same to you, I'd like to get out of here before he gets a chance to dig himself out."

66 – The Fat Lady Sings

"Can you stop it?" Jackie asked.

After Johnny left, Trager had jumped into the pilot chair and attempted to wrestle the controls back online. "She's fried everything!" he said. "There isn't time to fix it. We need to abandon ship!"

"OK. What do we do?"

Trager pointed to the passenger chairs lining the wall. "Strap in and hit the Eject button."

"What about the others?" Jackie asked. "We can't just leave them here to die."

Trager nodded. Maybe that was the most fundamental difference between people like Silas and Pandora and himself: that he saw the intrinsic value in human life. People weren't simply valuable for what they could do for you, but because they were made in the image of God. The rest of non-Indigo humanity wasn't his competition in some evolutionary arms race. That sort of Darwinian bigotry had led to Hitler's death camps and Margaret Sanger's equally monstrous sterilization crusade against racial minorities, the handicapped and those she considered "feeble-minded."

With a thought, Mike Trager picked Silas up and tossed him into a chair, then mentally caused the harnesses to strap into place. He did likewise with the others as Jackie strapped herself into another chair nearby. With a mental nudge of the ejection buttons, Trager sent each chair rocketing skyward with their unconscious occupants. Hopefully what was left of Titan could round them all up later.

He glanced at the forward viewscreen. The saucer had been climbing above Midwich again when Pandora pitched it into a dive. The ground was coming up pretty quickly. It looked like the *Grey* would overshoot the downtown district and crash land somewhere in a residential neighborhood. And there wasn't a thing he could do about it.

"Our turn!" Trager yelled above a baleful warning klaxon.

Jackie punched her ejection button and blasted off as he hopped into a chair and strapped himself in. Before he ejected, Mike spared one last glance at the viewscreen. In moments, they'd be crashing into a neighborhood of homes and small businesses. In a perfect world, he'd be able to minimize the collateral damage this crash was going to cause, but he was simply out of time, out of options. Sighing with regret, he punched the eject button.

Thrust high above the city of Midwich, Pandora watched the *Grey* begin its ominous slide earthward. If Arthur Lazarus were alive today, he'd kill them all for what they'd just done to his baby. Of course, if Arthur were still alive today none of this would be happening. They never could have infiltrated Titan with the late Mr. Lazarus around to guard it. Arthur was a master strategist, the kind of chess player that thought seven moves ahead – no, more like the kind who'd memorized the book and knew every possible outcome based on the first several moves alone! More to the point, if Arthur had survived, his brat kid wouldn't be involved in this fiasco. Or maybe he would. Maybe Titan would've recruited him by now. Offered him a job. He was certainly heads and shoulders above the other beta Indigos...

None of that mattered now. Johnny was still doggedly determined to bring her down. She glanced behind her at the saucer. Sure enough, an impossible human figure shot out of the top of the *Grey*. For a moment she was transfixed. Silhouetted against the morning sky, he looked so much like the hero he thought he was. She felt a twinge of jealousy. She could make people do anything she wanted to, but she couldn't do what they did. And once she was out of zombies, well, it wasn't like she had super strength or could move things with her mind or anything. She was as defenseless as any of... *them.*

Pandora shook her head, cleared it, and brought herself back to the present. She punched a button, cutting loose her parachute and activating the evacuation pod's hovercraft mode. The pod chair dipped instantly, causing her stomach to lurch. Seconds later, the craft righted itself. She pressed forward on the controls, hoping to out-distance her pursuit.

Johnny latched onto her evac pod the moment he spotted her. He sensed her weakness, her defenselessness. She was all out of tricks. All out of zombies. Finally, it was just her and him. He rushed in to finish it.

He bridged the distance between them much faster than she thought he could. Out of instinct, she tried to find his eyes. Not that hypnosis had ever really worked on Arthur's kid before. The most she'd managed with him last time was a post-hypnotic suggestion that he'd die if he didn't take care of his business in Midwich. Like his father, Johnny seemed to have some sort of, if not immunity, then some heavy duty resistance to hypnosis.

Johnny had no intentions of allowing Pandora another chance to hypnotize him. As he grabbed onto her pod, he carefully averted his gaze. This far off the ground, it simply wouldn't do to look this modern-day Medusa in the eye. She might not be able to turn him to stone, but she could potentially turn him catatonic long enough for him to drop like one. The fall might even kill him at this height.

Behind them, four evac pods popped out of the top of the *Grey*. Seconds later, their chutes bloomed against the morning sky.

Pandora drew a gun, knowing it wouldn't do any good. He ripped it from her hands with a thought, caught the bullet she'd hastily fired and brought it arcing around to her left temple. He let it hover there, rifling in place.

"You're beaten. Give up," he said.

"You won't kill me. You promised Jackie."

Two more evac pods shot out of the *Grey*. Twin parachutes blossomed. One of the pods cast off its chute and switched over to hovercraft mode as Pandora had, while the other floated gently earthward. Johnny kept an eye on the pod as it approached, hoping it wasn't another complication.

"Then don't make a liar out of me," Johnny said. "Set this thing down and give yourself up."

She glanced at him, not directly, knowing he'd see that as a threat, but enough to size him up. "You're every bit the Boy Scout your father was. I'll come along quietly," she said, demonstrating her sincerity by bringing the craft into a landing pattern, "but know this: you're making a huge mistake. A war's coming between them and us. It's inevitable. They can't allow us to exist as free agents. We pose too great a threat."

"And you think anything you've done in the last 24 hours actually helped?" Johnny asked. "If they figure out people like us were behind this chaos, all their worst fears will be confirmed. They'll hunt us down. Make lab rats out of us. Make weapons of us. And wipe us out if they can't! You may've doomed us all."

She set the pod down. "No, you poor deluded boy, I've given us a fighting chance. There will be no grey area now. No one begging for peace and compromise when there can be neither. No one waiting for it to pass over. No one asking for understanding and patience while they swallow up our forces with every passing hour and turn them against us. No, the sooner this war begins, the better our odds of survival. Are you sure you're on the right side?"

"Yeah, well, good luck with the war and all. You're doing a bang-up job so far."

Trager's pod landed nearby. Mike hopped out of his pod and trained his weapons on Pandora.

"Now what?" Johnny asked, letting the spinning bullet he'd been threatening her with fall to the ground. In the distance, he could hear helicopters approaching and the sound of tank treads rolling into town.

Trager heard it, too. "Looks like somebody called in the cavalry."

Johnny frowned. "Then I better hurry." Once the military moved in, they'd lock down everything. Take away everything. He needed to act quickly before his window of opportunity closed.

"What? Where are you going?"

"I just have one last thing to take care of. Can you handle her?"

Trager whipped off his tie and used it to gag the hypnotist. "Sure."

67 – We All Have a Choice

The *Grey* blasted the SuperBig Mart's neon sign, clipped the tops off trees and utility poles, then tore through the burnt out area that used to be Archer Lane before Cougar's fires had consumed and leveled almost everything. The silver saucer churned into the asphalt, plowing the street up in great gouts before finally skidding to a shuddering halt in the church parking lot at the end of the street. The saucer's silver metal all but kissed the base of the steeple, but Soul's Harbor towered over it, wounded but victorious.

Johnny landed a short distance away from the crash. He trudged across the smoldering, broken wasteland, past the burning pyres of perfect homes and Archer oaks. Wearily, he stopped to rest on the front steps of Soul's Harbor. He stood there in the shadow of the saucer – or perhaps the church. As he scanned the horizon, he saw them: tanks, trucks, helicopters. The US military would swarm this scene within a few minutes. There wasn't much time.

Bounding with superhuman skill, he lighted atop the *Grey* and slipped back inside through an evacuation port. Everything was dark inside. The emergency lights were gone. The screens were blank. The exposed wires showed no evidence of life. Everything was tilted at a crazy 60 degree angle. He used electromagnetism to hold on and move about.

Undeterred, he switched his vision into the infrared. He'd hoped the ship still had power, that he could replay his dad's lost message, the one Pandora had confirmed was waiting for him when they entered the cockpit. He deserved that, after all he'd been through.

Or maybe he didn't. Maybe this was his penance for his mother's death.

He spotted the key, lying discarded. Whispering a prayer, he placed the key in the socket and turned it.

Nothing. A dead end. And soon the military was going to confiscate the saucer and take it far, far way, where he might never see his father's last message. Worse, it could've been erased in the crash. He needed power.

He placed his hands on a console and charged up his bioelectric field, hoping to jump-start the craft. The console sparked and spat, but the lights remained off.

Johnny held his head in his hands, utterly spent.

That's when the lights flickered on and voice beyond the grave called his name.

"Johnny..."

He lifted his head. A projector beam stretched across the room. Its intended angle was askew, knocked out of alignment by the crash, but though it fell across multiple surfaces, he still recognized his father's face.

"If you're listening to this, then I have to assume I'm no longer around to tell you myself. I've decided there's something you need to know about Titan and about yourself. But the boy upstairs isn't ready yet. I could never place a weight this big on shoulders so small and still call myself a good father. But one day, this day, you'll be ready. You deserve to know the truth." Johnny noted his father's basement study in the background.

"You're already so smart. I did some tests and, well, you're going to find out that you can do things that no one else can do. You're gonna have questions. I'm sorry if I wasn't there to answer them for you. It might freak you out a little at first, but don't be scared. God gave you these gifts for a reason. The point is, when you've seen people do the kind of stuff I'm talking about - shooting flames, moving stuff with their minds, lifting dump trucks, mind control – you can't help but wonder: are these people still human? Or are they something else?"

Arthur Lazarus picked up an all-too-familiar Bible. "You know by now that I believe this is God's revealed Word. And it says that everything was created in six days and that man, though he's fallen, was created in the image of God. It also says that there's nothing new under the sun."

John Lazarus smiled faintly as he listened to his father. It was like hearing him talk in the living room, guileless and unapologetic. Johnny had never fully bought into his father's faith. He'd always strongly suspected there must be a God. Only an idiot would think otherwise. The guys who claimed that all of the order, beauty and information in the universe just happened to come together in progressive orders of complexity from nothing by undirected specious processes… well, that took a lot more faith than he'd ever had in anything.

"According to the Scriptures, man and the animals were created after their kind," Arthur said, "and they were told to be fruitful and multiply after their kind. The idea of created kinds implies that we'll see variation, even speciation, but that a dog will remain a dog and recognizably so, be it a wolf, an English bulldog or an Australian shepherd. The same applies to humans. Even if we can bend the path of a bullet with our minds, even if we can heal from things that would kill the average person, we're still only human. No genetic information has been added, as evolution would require. The genetic potential was always there and has turned up from time to time, though we attributed it to more superstitious causes.

"Some people think that those of us with these abilities are somehow better than everybody else, more evolved, but all humans are fallen. We're still sinners in need of a Savior. Still humans made in the image of our Creator God, Who loves us despite our sin.

"We all have a choice, Johnny, whether we can sing or draw, whether we're gifted with intelligence or empathy or the ability to move things with a thought. We can use it selfishly or we can do what we do for the glory of God. We can use our abilities for good, to help others and point them to God. But you should know by now that a corrupt tree cannot bring forth good fruit. If you haven't already, you gotta get your life right, Johnny. You gotta repent and believe in Christ's resurrection. Because you can't do this alone."

"Just remember," Arthur said, taking off his glasses to stare solidly into the camera. "God made you the way you are and He loves you. I love you, son."

"Arthur! Dinner's ready!" Kate Lazarus called off-camera.

A moment later, a younger version of Johnny echoed his mother. "Daddy! Come and eat! Mom made sausage and eggs. We're having a breakfast dinner!"

Arthur laughed, replacing his glasses. "I gotta go, Johnny. Duty calls. Love you."

Johnny breathed out a shuddering sigh as the projector beam flickered out and his father vanished. He could hear the National Guard bearing down on him. They had the saucer surrounded. He couldn't be here when they decided to poke around and see what was inside. Grabbing the key, he put the chain around his neck and launched back out of the *Grey*.

He lighted atop the saucer for a moment, eliciting cries of alarm and wonder. And drawing the inevitable swarm of gunfire. With a tired scowl, he bent the bullet stream away from himself and bounded away. A trio of helicopters immediately gave chase. Johnny kept ahead of them, avoiding bullets the whole way until he managed to slip out of sight for a few seconds.

He stopped running, turned invisible. Waited for them to pass.

68 – Aftermath

Trager sat on Ness' old porch swing, listening to the rhythmic squeaking of the metal chains upon which it hung. It wasn't easy to convince himself that the events of the past two days had really happened. He took a glass of iced sweet tea from Emily on a proffered tray, but only to be polite. He preferred unsweetened tea. "Thank you, dear."

Ness' cabin afforded a grand view of Midwich, what was left of it anyway. Surveying the destruction from up here – Titan, Archer Lane, most of downtown – it just didn't feel like they'd beaten her. It felt very much the opposite. Having been turned into her mindless weapon for most of the night didn't help Trager's mood much.

Ness felt no need to suffer tea under any circumstances. "No thank you, but I'll take some coffee if you've got it ready. A burner should be able to handle that, right?" As she ran off to fetch some, Trager shot Ness a withering glance.

"What?" Ness asked.

Trager knew why he was in such a grouchy mood. Gage had to be taken to the emergency room due his extensive injuries. It looked like he would pull through, but, knowing Ness, he probably felt guilty for even allowing his great-nephew to come along for the final showdown with Pandora.

"Be nice."

"I am being nice. I'm always nice."

"Ness."

"Yeah, well, fine, but mark my words: you can't never trust a pyro. Cougar's proven that often enough."

Trager didn't deign to respond. Of course, Cougar did tend to make more enemies than friends. They hadn't seen the pyrokinetic since he fell from the saucer, but eagle-eyed Ness swore he wasn't in the Plaza when Titan Tower fell.

"Did you catch the headlines?" Ness asked, changing the subject. "*Flying*

Saucer Gets Religion. That's what they came up with. There's pictures of that thing parked at Ed's church all over the internet."

"I read it," Trager said. "Ed himself is on page 6. *Local Pastor Cleared of Meth Charges, UFO Church Reaches Out to Disaster Victims.*"

"Meth charges?" Ness did not look amused.

"Nobody will remember that this time next year. All they'll remember is the saucer," Trager said, sipping his tea. A photo on page 4 caught his eye. The caption mentioned that several residents had reported seeing a "flying man" on Halloween night. The picture showed a deniable blur of a human figure, which Trager nonetheless recognized must be Johnny's silhouette.

"They're blaming pretty much everything on aliens," Trager continued. "Little green men are not only getting credit for stuff that actually happened, they're making up new stuff to go along with it. Government agents, men in black, tons of UFO sightings. They've even connected *el chupacabra*, Bigfoot, and that Mothman thing with this nonsense!"

"A little misinformation goes a long way," Ness said. "Where is Johnny anyway?"

"He had a meeting, but he should be here any moment."

John Lazarus sat across from Weasel Hopkins and Jackie Holloway in a booth at the Midwich Diner.

Jackie's face was hollow and tear-streaked, her eyes red-rimmed. Johnny kind of knew how she felt. Her father was dead… and her estranged mother and grandfather were responsible. They hadn't recovered Curtis Holloway's body yet. They were still sifting through the rubble of the Titan explosion. The Tunnel hangar was clogged with rock and debris. There was simply no way he could have survived. It hadn't been easy news to deliver. Weasel and Jackie had gone off alone together for a while after Johnny told her the bad news. They'd only just returned.

They were waiting for Titan's elusive Director, Charles Huxley, who'd requested the meeting and arranged it through Mike Trager. Presently, a man came to their booth and slid into the seat beside Johnny. The same man who'd been at his house just before Cougar burned it to the ground.

"Thank you for meeting with me. I wish it were under better circumstances. My condolences, Miss Holloway," he said. "I knew your father."

Jackie stared daggers at him. She'd made it pretty clear that she blamed

Titan for her suffering. Titan was connected with the abandonment of her mother, the death of her father and possibly concealing the existence of a twin brother from her. The only reason she didn't electrocute him on the spot was because Weasel had made her promise not to. They needed to know what Titan wanted from Johnny.

"Anyway," Huxley said, "I wanted, first of all, to thank you for your efforts to save Titan and –"

"Skip it," Johnny said. "What do you want?"

He paused, sizing Johnny up, then shrugged. "Have it your way. First, you should know we won't be rebuilding the Titan complex–"

"Good riddance," Jackie said.

"– but the offer I made you earlier is still on the table: a job, a home, a scholarship at Kaukasos College," Huxley said. "You upheld your end of the bargain. You stopped Pandora for us. Titan will uphold its end. And we need you now more than ever."

"I have a few questions," Johnny said.

"Of course. I'll try to answer them to the best of my ability, if you don't mind answering a few questions for me in return?"

Johnny and the others exchanged glances, then nodded agreement.

"My father left me a key to the *Grey*–"

"Yes. The key unlocks a recording your father made for you." Huxley opened his briefcase and handed Johnny a DVD. "While you can't access the *Grey*, this is a recording of him making the recording he left for you." In response to their unasked question, he added. "We have a lot of embedded cameras in this town."

Johnny kept his expression guarded. Charles Huxley obviously didn't know he'd already seen the recording and that he knew about the hovercameras at Titan's disposal.

"Where is my mother? Where are you holding her?" Jackie asked.

"She's safe. As are all of the other Indigos we recovered."

"When can I see her?"

"I'm afraid that's out of the question. She's too dangerous. All human contact has been forbidden."

"But she's alive?" Weasel asked, correctly reading Jackie's anxiety.

"Of course."

"Did you know about my brother?" Jackie asked.

"Pandora took Jack when she disappeared years ago. Curtis prevented her from taking you as well."

"Why didn't he tell me?" she asked. "Why didn't I remember I had a brother?"

Director Huxley offered her a quick, false smile and shrugged. "I wouldn't presume to tell you Curtis' motives for keeping the truth from you. I suspect he believed he was protecting you somehow. As for why you don't remember your own twin, well, given your family history I think you already know the answer to that question."

"Were all of the gammas destroyed?" Johnny asked.

Charles Huxley shot him a look that betrayed his outrage, but covered it quickly. "Most of them were destroyed. The gamma program has been discontinued."

Johnny didn't trust himself to speak. Huxley was lying to him and he knew it. Of course, Huxley couldn't know he'd read the Kaukasos file. What else was he lying about?

"Why did you build a flying saucer in the first place?" Weasel asked.

The Director grinned. "Mostly because we thought it would be cool. Besides it made for a good cover story, one most folks would dismiss out-of-hand but would also sate their desire to dig further. Folks figure once the UFO nuts get involved, there's no way you'll get past the hoaxers, wild speculation and mad conspiracy theories to get at the truth about any alleged super-humans. In fact, that's why we called you Indigos in the first place: we figured associating you guys with aliens and 'Star Children' would throw any serious investigation well off the scent. And we were right. It's a waste of their time to bother. They just put it in a box labeled: One of Life's Little Mysteries."

Johnny frowned. That didn't make sense. Why would Titan spend millions of dollars on that technology just to throw folks a red herring? There had to be more to it.

"And where is it now?" Weasel asked. The military had airlifted the saucer out of Midwich practically right after the now infamous photograph was taken.

"Safe. Speaking of which," Huxley said, turning to Johnny, "your father may have built the *Grey* but that key was not his to give away. I'll need you to hand it over."

Johnny stared at his proffered hand. "I don't have it on me."

"Where is it?"

"Safe."

Weasel cut in. "Did you guys have anything to do with Roswell?"

"Maybe. OK, last question."

Johnny didn't hesitate. "Kaukasos College."

The Director nodded, his demeanor more eager. "Kaukasos is our most valuable asset. If you accept, Kaukasos will become your new home. As you must already suspect, in addition to being an accredited university, it's also a proving ground for other Indigos. It would give you the chance to explore your abilities in a safe environment and exchange information with others like yourself." He took a deep breath, then pressed his point, "Which brings me to my last and more pressing question: Are you in?"

"So what was your answer?" Trager asked after Johnny finished relating the details of the interview and his suspicions to those gathered at Ness' cabin.

"I don't trust Titan," he said. "They've given me little reason to. Huxley lied to my face about the gammas. Something's definitely going down at that college. If I can get close enough, I might be able to stop it."

"Do you think that's wise?" Trager asked.

Time to clear the air. "Look," Johnny said, "I realize that, despite everything we've been through, you're still a company man, through and through... but I'm also aware that you recently found yourself zombified, stripped of free will. Did you like it?"

Trager shook his head. "'Course not."

"So you recognize that mind control is just wrong," Johnny said. "Well, Titan plans to turn their gammas into little super-powered point-and-shoot robots. Are you seriously OK with that?"

Trager sighed. "I'll help you stop the gamma program, just so long as we keep in mind that Titan is not the enemy."

"Fair enough," Johnny said, reaching out to shake Trager's hand.

"So I take it you said yes."

Johnny nodded.

"You sure this is what you wanna do, kid?" Ness asked.

"Somebody's gotta stop them, but I can't do this alone." He wasn't sure yet where he stood with God, but his dad was definitely right about his needing help.

"You don't have to," Emily said, giving him a hug.

Her embrace was like a warm blanket on his soul. He honestly thought everything was going to be alright, just so long as Emily stood with him.

The words of Destiny Pascalé insinuated themselves into his thoughts. *We're married. We have a child. We love each other.* He shook his head to dispel the troubling worries that accompanied the memory.

Glancing over her shoulder at the others, he asked, "What about you guys? Can I count on you?"

Curtis Holloway grinned as, one by one, those Johnny had assembled pledged their support for his cause. "They've got heart," he said, setting down his binoculars. "You gotta admit that."

"You could join them," Jack Holloway said. "They could use you."

"Why, Bubby? Because I can take enough bullets to kill an elephant and be fit as a fiddle the next morning?" Curtis asked. He gratuitously tossed back a can of beer. His healing ability was the entire reason he could drink so freely without worrying about burnt-out brain cells and a pickled liver. Truth be told, it took a whole lot of beer to even give him a small buzz. In other words, a side effect of his healing ability was that he couldn't get drunk. His non-existent alcoholism was just an act to fool Titan and the powers that be that he was a ruined and pitiable drunk and certainly no threat of any sort. "No, they can handle this without me. We've got more important things to take care of."

Earlier, Gage, Ness and himself had been thrown clear of the blast that leveled Titan, but somewhere during the trip down, Gage lost his grip on Curtis. He blacked out after that.

When he came to, he was sore and stiff, but all of his wounds had healed. A talent he'd kept hidden from everyone, except his estranged wife. Maybe that's why she left him behind to die in the hangar tunnel, knowing he'd probably survive after all. Then again, if Gage hadn't gotten him out of there in time, Curtis might have been cremated beyond his ability to regenerate. Overall, he suspected Hope wasn't really in complete control of herself. Her twisted father had hypnotized her. Curtis had to believe that. Otherwise the plan was doomed to failure.

His son had been staring at him, waiting for him to come to when he awoke. Jack only sat apart from his father out of habit, not because he had to. He had to maintain his distance with most people. Curtis, Jackie and Hope were all immune to his field of disruption. He'd always suspected it was a genetic quirk.

"You should've at least told Jackie you survived," Jack said.

"I done told you, Bubby. Too risky. I mean, it's your plan an' you can do what you think is right and I'll respect that," Curtis said. "But you came to me 'cause you know I can do this sort of thing and you know I'm good at it. I didn't come to you with this. You sought out your dear ol' dad out of your own sweet accord to recruit me for this mission of yours. Besides, you know as well as I do, everybody has to think I'm outta the picture if we're gonna pull this off. Especially your Sissy."

"You're right, but I don't have to like it."

"I'm right there with you. And for the record, I hate what it's gonna do to her. But if we fail, they'll be nothing to tell."

Father and son stared at one another, grim but resolute. Both were thinking about the flip-side of the coin. Yes, they would die if they failed, but if they succeeded they would finally have their family back.

69 – For Sale

The film froze on a snapshot of John Lazarus. The movie began to fade as the camera zoomed in on his face. It continued on until only one of Johnny's golden eyes was showing. A logo superimposed itself over the image: two hands cupped together offering a stylized tongue of flame. Beneath the icon were the words "Prometheus."

A round of polite applause ensued when the lights came up and Charles Huxley walked onstage followed by a spotlight. Huxley was holding a rolled up comic book in one hand. "Amazing! Right?" he asked, knowing he had his audience in the palm of his hand. "Most of you have never seen anything like it. Well, not outside the Saturday morning cartoons or the local comic book shop," he said, unfurling his *Mann from Midwich* comic and waving it around. "Am I right? By the way, the events in your complimentary *Mann from Midwich* comic – based on actual events. One of our very first super-powered prototypes, what we now call Indigos. We've learned a lot since Hugh Mann."

Huxley rolled his comic back up and used it to point to the screen. "Our Indigos can do things that we've only dreamt possible: toss around telephone poles, deflect bullets, ram through buildings..."

The screen behind him showed Bantam and Freight Train Farley.

"They can dodge bullets and fight with preternatural reflexes that any martial artist would envy..."

Jennifer Winters replaced the muscle mutants onscreen.

"Better yet, they can bend the path of an enemy's bullet and use it against them!" he said, as Mike Trager, Hillary and John Lazarus appeared onscreen to another round of enthusiastic applause.

"And all the rest," he added, as shots of Emily, Cougar, Jack the Disruptor, the Anarchist, Jackie Holloway, Ness and Destiny Pascalé dotted the screen. "We have flame throwers, invisible girls, people who can predict the future, shoot anything they aim at and, well, even hypnotize entire towns."

Photos of Pandora and Silas brooded behind him for a moment, then everything faded and the Prometheus icon returned.

"So what do you think?" he asked. "You've seen them in action. You've seen what they're capable of. Imagine an army of Indigos at your command. Imagine what a superhuman sniper like Ness would be capable of. Someone who'd make Vasily Zaytsev look like a kid with a popgun. And forget the Marines. Send in some bulletproof muscle mutants. Wouldn't you like a spy with Jackie Holloway's ability to blend in? Yes? And it just keeps getting better and better! The military applications are endless. You know it. I know it. But... there's just one little problem, isn't there? Come on. I know one of you is just dying to say it."

"How do we control them?" someone with a thick Bolshevik accent asked.

"Bingo," Huxley said. "He hit it right on the head. Who wants a gun that might just decide to shoot the guy pulling the trigger one day?" Charles Huxley gave them a sly I've-got-a-secret wink. "We've got you covered. How many of you caught what was going on down in Gamma Lab there. Remember that? That was a teaser. I've got someone you need to talk to."

A new spotlight appeared at the edge of the stage and a tall, stout man in an expensive suit appeared on cue. He was carrying a black parasol. As he approached, Huxley remarked, "My associate Dr. Ernst Dobzhansky is from the *nefarious* Parasol corporation." He feigned being frightened. "By the way, let's see a show of hands: How many of you were impressed with the latest results of the Hive program. Superb work, Dobby."

The man with the parasol bowed graciously. "Our Hive drones are the perfect soldiers: oblivious to personal discomfort, they feel no fear, no remorse, no pangs of morality. They always follow orders. Perfect shock troops. But we can do better!"

"Better?" Charles Huxley asked.

Dobby grinned. "Better. Combining the perfect control of our Hive drones with the awesome abilities of the Indigos, gammas are the perfect bio-weapon. The Parasol Hive chip puts you in complete control of your gamma. You can even turn it off and on whenever you want."

"Think about that," Huxley said. "You can have your very own super-powered sleeper agent go online at the push of the button or via a simple phone call. Your gamma doesn't even have to know he works for you."

"And the Hive chip still works on non-super powered soldiers. After a simple implantation behind the ear, you can switch them on and off at will," Dobby said, snapping his black parasol open and shut playfully for emphasis.

"What about Pandora?" someone asked. "If she's out there, she's still a threat to all of us."

"All the more reason to have more agreeable Indigos at your own disposal," Silas Darling said as he walked out on stage from the opposite side of the stage Dr. Dobzhansky had entered. "Oh, don't be alarmed. I won't make anyone cluck like a chicken. Not tonight."

The audience laughed, albeit nervously.

"I assure you that my daughter is also completely under my control. I've finally discovered the cure for the strong-willed child: hypnosis!"

"Does this mean there's no secret plot to take over the world?" Huxley asked

"*I'm* not taking over the world anytime soon. I'm retired, for crying out loud. But maybe you better ask this lovely audience of yours if they're planning to pick up where we left off," he suggested with a sly wink.

"Well, we couldn't legally endorse that sort of thing," Huxley said, "but I can't help thinking… you know, gammas and Hive drones would definitely be a step in the right direction for those with… such ambitions."

"I think we've said too much," Silas said. "In fact, I think it's high time we gave these ladies and gentlemen the opportunity to place their bids. In your information packet, you'll–"

"What about John Lazarus?" someone shouted from the back. None of the presenters onstage could see him on account of the blinding spotlights.

"What about him?" Huxley asked.

"John Lazarus nearly brought your super-powered freaks and your zombie soldiers to a standstill… and he's just a kid," the stranger said. "So what are you going to do about John Lazarus?"

"The Lazarus boy is unique," Silas said. "And I should point out that despite his formidable skill, if we're completely honest, well, he survived mostly on luck and pluck so–"

"Why is he still walking the streets?"

Charles Huxley held up a hand. "We have further plans for John Lazarus, plans we think will usher in a very exciting new area of Indigo research. And I think our core customers will really appreciate the applications."

"Which is what makes letting him go free so he can wreck your future plans seem so counter-productive," their critic said.

There was an uncomfortable pause. The presenters exchanged glances.

Silas grinned. Charles Huxley shrugged. Dobby scowled.

Silas answered. "Merely counter-intuitive. Destiny Pascalé's powers are genuine. She predicts the future with a high degree of accuracy, better than anyone else we've ever tested. We call her the Oracle with good reason. Her prediction was that letting Johnny go at this point will make him more malleable for what we have in mind for him in the future."

"And you trust her?"

"Implicitly," Silas said. He waited expectantly, but the other didn't have anything further to say.

Taking advantage of the lull, a younger man in the front of the audience asked, "How can I get one of those flying saucers?"

Someone with a Texan accent hollered, "Put me down for three!"

As the audience laughed, Huxley squinted against the spotlight. His interrogator seemed to have left.

"All interested UFO enthusiasts should give my secretary a call to schedule an appointment," Huxley said. "I can't make any promises but, well, God bless capitalism. I'm open to discussing new opportunities. But right now, it's time to place your bids!"

Huxley peered into the back of the auditorium one last time, frowning with implacable concern. What had all that really been about? Shrugging it off, he grinned at his audience, ever the showman.

The man Charles Huxley was searching for took the nearest elevator, making his way to the rooftop. He peered across the city skyline, nodding his head. Taking a deep breath, Hillary ran across the roof and bounded skyward.

70 – The Bravest One

Brad Farley stepped out of the cab and stood on the curb, building up his resolve. This was the right thing to do. He was convinced of it. But a part of him would rather face a thousand Bantams than the wrath of his father – and his daddy wasn't going to like this one single bit.

Everything he'd been taught growing up was a lie. You couldn't judge people based on the color of their skin. Last night, he'd fought and nearly been killed several times by people with the same shade of melanin as himself. Evil was in every man's heart, no matter what shade they came in. In that regard, everyone was the same. Brad wasn't sure what the remedy was for the human condition, but he knew it wasn't hate and prejudice.

He'd experienced first-hand last night that people hate what they fear. Pandora was so busy trying to convince everyone that she was better than everyone else – more evolved! – and Brad Farley thought he knew why. She knew she was different and she was so afraid that people would persecute her for it that she convinced herself that she needed to persecute them instead. She was so afraid they would go on a witch hunt that she gave them tangible reasons to launch one. She subscribed to his dad's idea of winners and wusses, whether she realized it or not, but maybe there were no winners when you thought that way. Bottom line: she was afraid of non-Indigo people, so she hated them and set out to dominate them – just as his dad's fear and ignorance led to his prejudice against pretty much anyone who didn't share both his skin color and his twisted ideology.

He took a deep breath as he walked up the steps of the local Y, which had been converted into a refugee hotel for those left homeless from last night's events.

"You sure you wanna do this?" Alyshia asked.

Brad took her hand and involuntarily looked down at her stomach, though she wasn't yet showing. He wasn't sure what kind of world he was bringing this child into, but he knew he'd do everything he could to protect that gift and to avoid making the same mistakes his father did. Of course, he had no idea how he was gonna do that, but he smiled despite himself.

"What if he disowns you?"

"You have to fight for the things that matter."

Hand-in-hand, they opened the doors and took the first step in their new life together.

A SNEAK PEEK AT JOHN LAZARUS: MANN FROM MIDWICH

1 – MIA

Graham Lazarus dashed along the top of the burning zeppelin, trying desperately to outrace the explosions that were gutting the Nazi vessel behind him. Things weren't exactly going according to plan. The *da Vinci* was parked near the airship's rudder. The autoprop's rotors were already warming up. If he concentrated hard enough, he could probably see the look of accusatory terror on the pilot's face. Avery Winters, an irritable fellow most folks called Jughead, was always complaining that he cut things too close. Not that any of this had been his idea, mind you.

Suddenly, he heard the keening whine of incoming aircraft. He didn't even have to look to know what was zeroing in on him. When he'd read the intelligence reports, he'd had trouble believing that the Germans had actually developed the sort of top secret weapons they'd been sent to seize. The one that had them all talking was the possibility of seeing a bona fide Nazi flying saucer. Disc-shaped, jet-powered Coanda-Effect Vertical Take-Off landing aircraft, to be more specific. They were fast, but not very maneuverable. Unfortunately, most of them carried some sort of directed energy weapon that shot bolts of destructive lightning at the invading Allied forces. Bursting out from behind a row of lumbering zeppelins, they'd surprised the Allied forces. Moments later, the sky was filled with falling, disintegrating aircraft. Captain Lazarus and his crew had been forced to make their jump early. Even as their chutes opened, German planes, saucers and ground-based flak crews began cutting down the invasion force. He'd lost track of his men during the descent. Most of them were probably dead. Except Harley, of course.

The *da Vinci* had been maneuverable enough to avoid destruction thus far, but it was a sitting duck right now. Jughead seemed to have come to the same realization, because he took off at that moment. The rotored vehicle dipped down out of sight. If it was anyone else, Graham would have despaired, but that crazy pilot had never let him down before, so he kept running, never giving up the hope that his friend would find a way to get him out.

The saucers strafed the surface of the zeppelin with more traditional weaponry, hoping to cut him in half, but he kept just ahead of the line of fire. Graham couldn't spare more than a glance, but he knew they'd come back around for a second pass. Sure enough, the Nazi saucers banked hard and circled toward him. The zeppelin continued to explode in sections, causing him to wonder whether he'd be roasted before he ran out of road or whether the saucers would have their way with him. The saucer pilots laid down a hard line of fire. Their tracers made it clear they were a lot more dedicated this time. He didn't dare stop, but it looked like he was going to dash straight into a hailstorm of bullets. He could almost see the lead saucer's pilot grinning with cruel anticipation.

Suddenly, an Allied *Mustang* whipped into view, guns blazing. Cutting across their flight path, the fighter plane tore both saucers in half. Flame and shrapnel rained down upon the surface of the balloon. Concentrating hard, Graham Lazarus used psychokinetic power to shield himself from the raining debris. It was difficult to do while still running, but there was no time to slow down with the zeppelin destroying itself on his heels.

Not that it mattered. Graham was out of runway. With a foxhole prayer, he readied himself to leap off the zeppelin. At that moment, the *da Vinci* rose into view. A ladder hung from its underside.

Grinning like an idiot, Graham dug in and leapt for the swinging ladder. Even as he grabbed it, Jughead began climbing back and away from the exploding zeppelin. As they rose, Graham got a good look at the giant aircraft as it crashed into an exploding apocalypse. It was hard to believe he'd escaped. Of course, it wasn't his idea to land on top of the zeppelin to begin with. His parachute had gotten shot up on the way down, so it was either use his kinetic powers to land safely atop the German ship or plummet to his doom. The zeppelin had come under attack from Allied planes and begun its explosive swan song only seconds after his landing. It was a stroke of pure luck and a testimony to the effectiveness of Nikola Tesla's radio wristwatch design that he'd caught Jughead's attention in time for a rescue.

As the zeppelin showered its burning wreckage on the ground, the full measure of this mission's chaos unveiled itself before him. Nazi super-panzers, monstrous tanks towering several stories over the soldiers in the field, slammed the approaching Allied ground forces with mortar shells. Saucers, zeppelins and more traditional aircraft engaged in dizzying dogfights, causing the skies to rain blood and fire. Bullets, mortar, grenades, flamethrowers and discharges from energy weapons few had ever suspected even existed crisscrossed the battlefield from heaven to earth. If that wasn't bad enough, foo fighters ping ponged across the heavens, disrupting electronics and interfering with the ignition systems in nearby planes, causing them to tumble from the skies. Foo fighters were a form of ground-launched self-guided jet-propelled flak mine. Intelligence reports called them *feuerballs,* literally fireballs, but everyone else just called them foo fighters. The device looked like a glowing tortoise shell set spinning like a Catherine wheel. Despite their wild airborne antics, they never seemed to crash into any other objects. In fact, foo fighters tended to spook if fired upon, as Jughead demonstrated when one got too near their craft.

At the top of the ladder, Graham gratefully accepted the hand of the *da Vinci*'s gunner Ness "Bulls-eye" Harper.

"You lost, Killjoy?" Bulls-Eye asked as he pulled him aboard.

Graham rolled his eyes. The nickname Killjoy was misleading at best. If anything, he was always getting in trouble for trying to have fun. It was just that he and the US military had different ideas as to what fun might entail. Anyone else would have been court marshaled by now, he suspected, but the brass tended to cut folks like him, people with extraordinary abilities, a bit more slack than others.

Still, it was hard to find any humor in the scene below. You wouldn't know it from the full tilt battle in progress, but this was supposed to be an easy mission. According to the briefing, they were supposed to arrive in overwhelming force, subdue the remnants of a fleeing Nazi army and seize a whole lot of experimental weapons. The war was over. Hitler was dead. This was just a mop-up. They were here to claim the spoils of war, particularly something the Nazis called *die Glocke*. According to Allied intelligence, the German Bell was the only project they considered War Decisive. Put simply, they couldn't afford to let the German Bell get away. If it was really as dangerous as the Allied scientists suspected it was, it would give the Third Reich the means to snatch victory from the jaws of defeat.

SS General Hans Kammler, Hitler's Number Three Guy, was determined to escape them and for good reason! Kammler had designed the Auschwitz concentration camp, right down to the gas showers and crematoria. He was in charge of the Nazi special weapons research division. He'd escaped them at Mittelwerk, an underground weapons factory where Nazi scientists were developing the V-1 and V-2 rockets and jet engines, among other things. The factory used slave labor from a concentration camp specifically built for that purpose. Kammler was a madman who assembled his slave labor force by means of specious mass arrests, worked them to death under hellish conditions, shot and tortured them for sport, and used them for experimental fodder as well. A part of him wanted personal vengeance for the awful things he'd seen and heard about back at the Mittelbau-Dora concentration camp.

"Where to?" Jughead asked over his shoulder.

Graham didn't answer immediately. He was looking for his objective amidst the maelstrom. "There!" he shouted above the wind, pointing to a runway being guarded by the Nazi super tanks. An enormous Junkers Ju 390 transport plane was taxiing into position. "Kammler's on that plane. He's trying to sneak our target out the back door."

Jughead nodded, then dove sharply. Graham held his breath involuntarily and grabbed onto a handle to keep from falling out of the craft. Their crazy pilot's skills were legendary, but having a front row seat to his extraordinary abilities wasn't exactly easy on the stomach. He bobbed and weaved, avoiding flak, falling debris and other aircraft in his mad race to reach the Ju 390 before it took off.

To anyone on the ground, it probably just looked like they were falling from the sky. Somehow Jughead pulled them out of the dive. Graham thought he was going to vomit for a moment as they leveled off and headed for the fleeing aircraft. A couple of oversized tanks and a squad of soldiers stood between them and their objective. Each tank sported three barrels. Graham had never seen anything like these monsters.

"Harley made it," Bulls-eye called to their pilot.

"What? Where?" Jughead asked. His eyes were nearly as good as his reflexes, which was saying a lot. Of course, no one could best Ness Harper's eagle eyes.

"The tank to the right. You owe me a dollar."

Sure enough, a figure was climbing up the super-panzer. Panicking German soldiers were firing upon him with everything they had, but he seemed no more bothered by their bullets than a cloud of gnats. He tore the vehicle's hatch completely off its hinges and leapt inside.

Graham could imagine the sound and flurry of activity inside the tank when Harley descended into the metal bowels of the beast. Their berserker never wore armor. Not even a helmet. The over-muscled brute didn't need it. Graham tried not to think about what Harley was capable of in close quarters. War was a nightmarish enough business as it was.

Moments later, one of the super-panzer's turrets spun around to belch destruction on its unsuspecting twin. In due course, Harley emerged from the first tank with a wicked grine. He was covered in blood. He dropped a handful of grenades down the open hatch for spite.

The *da Vinci* flew between the ruined metal colossi and over the Junkers Ju 390. The six engine heavy transport plane was now in position for takeoff. Jughead set his autocopter down directly in its path. Bulls-eye took a bead on the pilot and shot him through the transport's cockpit. The craft taxied off course for a moment before the co-pilot recovered. Machine gun fire and the distinct possibility of being crushed by the enormous transport forced Jughead to lift off again.

"Get us above it!" Graham ordered.

Jughead grimaced but dutifully brought the *da Vinci* to hover over the Ju 390. They immediately took fire from the transport's two dorsal guns. Graham mentally redirected the bullet spray from one of the guns, while Bulls-eye took out the other gunner. Still, the *da Vinci* took significant damage. It shuddered and threatened to stall. Jughead managed to keep his bird in the air, but only barely.

Jughead glanced back at Graham with a scowl. "Whatever you're planning, now is the time."

Graham nodded. He leapt out of the autocopter while Bulls-eye took out the other dorsal gunner. He landed roughly atop the aircraft, but managed to hold on. He watched for a moment as the *da Vinci* pulled up and away. Smoke was pouring from the bottom of the craft. Still, he knew they would cover him for as long as they could.

A top hatch opened and three Nazi soldiers emerged. Normally, Graham would've simply tossed them overboard, but he was momentarily stunned by their appearance. Hair. Fangs. Claws. He'd thought Nazi werewolves were a rumor. The first leapt at him with a guttural roar. Graham came to his senses in time, tossing the hairy fiend off the aircraft with kinetic force.

The next slammed into his chest, knocking him onto the wing. Graham bounced from the force of the werewolf's blow, nearly skidding off entirely. As he got to his feet, both remaining werewolves bounded toward him. One raised a sub-machine gun. Graham mentally tossed him into the other. Both tumbled and rolled off the wing. Graham noted that they were completely human-looking when they bounced off the runway.

He heard a single shot. Another Nazi slid off the fuselage of the Ju 390, having been picked off by Bulls-eye as he was about to shoot Graham unawares. Graham breathed a thank you to the *da Vinci*'s gunner.

Graham felt the heavy transport rising. Holding panic at bay, he headed toward the hatch and hurried inside. He was immediately met by a Nazi soldier with a knife. Graham ripped the blade from the other's hand with a thought and sent it into his chest.

The vessel began thrumming with power. He'd been on transport planes before. It didn't feel right at all. He hesitated, wondering whether it would be more prudent to abandon his mission.

Then the walls began to glow with a bluish light.

Bulls-eye Harper gaped in alarm and wonder as a blue light began enveloping the Ju 390. "What is that? What's happening?" he asked.

Jughead didn't answer. He was frantically trying to reach Graham Lazarus. "Killjoy, get out of there. Captain Lazarus, do you read me?"

Suddenly, the sky seemed to light up brighter than anything Bulls-eye had ever seen. The transport plane shrunk to the size of a dot and the space around it seemed to stretch and pull around that point. Everything was eerily still for one single second. Then an electromagnetic pulse exploded out from the space that had once been occupied by the Ju 390, a wave of energy that knocked planes from the sky and men off their feet.

The da Vinci tumbled through the heavens, eventually coming to crash near the wrecks of the super-panzers. If it hadn't been for their phenomenal healing powers and reflexes, neither of the autocopter's occupants would have survived. As they crawled out of the wreckage, each man searched the skies for any sign of their friend.

But the sky remained empty.

2 – Full Moon

"Pack your silver bullets, Johnny," Mike Trager said when he answered the phone. "We're going werewolf hunting."

"Are you for real?" Johnny asked. He fumbled around in the dark for his alarm clock. 2:13 AM. "Do you realize what time – Wait, did you say werewolf?"

He sat up on his bed, grabbed his pants off the bed post and began pulling them over his boxers.

His roommate grumbled in his sleep and buried his head under a pillow. Nocturnal by nature, Weasel Hopkins usually went to bed around this time, but he'd been on a non-stop video game spree over the past few days. He'd crashed a few hours ago and wouldn't be getting up anytime soon.

"You have less than five minutes to get out of your Scooby-Doo pajamas and be outside your dorm. This is not a drill."

John Lazarus groaned as Trager hung up. Ever since he'd signed on with Titan Biotech, he'd been at Trager's beck and call. The funny thing was that if you asked anyone, Trager didn't work for Titan. He was just the local high school football coach. Just like Johnny was just your average college student. If anyone knew what they really were and the extent of their involvement in the events that had rocked Midwich a year ago, they'd just freak.

People couldn't handle the truth. They suppressed anything that was too big or too uncomfortable to accept. Folks preferred their fictions, which made it easy to cover up Titan's involvement in the events of last fall. Right now, they were rebuilding, satisfied in the knowledge that Midwich had suffered a terrorist attack by radicals opposed to Titan's mission of improving the world through green fuels, bio-crops, and pushing human potential through medical breakthrough, genetic research and social reforms. West Virginia was coal country, so the media had given a lot of play to the green versus fossil fuel angle.

Internet speculation centered more on the flying saucer seen in connection with the Midwich "Night of Terror." There were a couple of videos floating around online of a bona fide 1950s UFO rising over Titan just before their research complex was blown sky high and a cellphone snapshot of the crashed saucer parked in the shadow of a local church. Another cellphone video clip showed a man flying into the heavens after the saucer. The Flying Man of Midwich had been the subject of a lot of speculation. The UFO nuts were having a field day, connecting the Night of Terror to the Mothman, *el chupacabra* and the Men in Black. Skeptics were saying it was an elaborate Halloween hoax and that the footage was obviously as fake as the Bluff Ridge Bigfoot film, which had Bigfoot hunters saying that it might be authentic after all. Bottom line: the crazies had descended upon Midwich like buzzards and there was an honest-to-goodness UFO festival scheduled for this Halloween on the first anniversary of the saucer crash. They were calling it the Flying Man Festival.

The truth was almost crazier than the things they'd imagined.

Minutes later, Johnny was dressed in a T-shirt, a black hoodie and jeans. Trager pulled up in his brand new Victory Red Hum-V, a replacement for the vehicle he'd lost when someone tore it in half atop the very saucer whose existence the local skeptic's society was doing its very best to deny. Johnny touched the key he always wore around his neck, a subconscious affection. A key to the *Grey* itself, if he could ever find it again. The National Guard had carted it off minutes after it had crashed.

Johnny hopped in and buckled up. "Are we it?" he asked, noticing the back seat was empty.

Trager nodded.

"So what's this about a werewolf?" He tried to sound casual, but he was seeing horror movie images that were all hair and fangs.

"The full moon brings out all the crazies," Trager said, "but we've received reports of a wolfman leaping through the trees an hour away from here. We've actually been tracking his progress over the past week or so. There've been a flood of reports of a large bear, large wolf, wolf standing on its hind legs,

Bigfoot, werewolf… stuff like that. We've narrowed down his range and Huxley has given the go-ahead to pick him up before he does any more damage."

Charles Huxley was Titan's CEO and not exactly one of Johnny's favorite people, but the man had brought jobs, jobs, jobs to Midwich, WV, so no one would hear a bad word about the man. Johnny forced himself to think about their target.

"So what's he done? Has he attacked anyone?"

"He's robbing convenience stores. The security video we got off his latest theft convinced us we needed to move in. Got your i84?"

Johnny pulled the device out of his pocket in reply. His late father, Arthur Lazarus, was the genius behind the i84, a Titan agent's exclusive access point to their top secret database and Argus, the surveillance satellite they maintained in geosynchronous orbit over Midwich. It also gave them access to the myriad Orwellian cameras the corporation had built into the city. Johnny flipped his on and immediately found the new file Trager had sent him.

The video was the typical grainy gas station variety, but he had no trouble making out their werewolf's big furry face. "That's not a mask?"

"Keep watching."

The wolfman threw the cashier, a man easily twice his size, out the front glass, then leapt behind the counter. He stuffed handfuls of cash into his pockets, then hopped back over the counter. He swiped some beef jerky and a bag of chips on his way out. The thief paused in the doorway suddenly, then glanced over his shoulder at the camera. Without warning, he bounded toward the camera, leapt high up and apparently destroyed the offending device. The wolfman's enraged fanged face filled the screen before the video went to snow. Johnny jumped back from his screen despite himself.

Trager stifled a chuckle. Poorly. "That got me, too," he said when Johnny shot him a withering glare. "So what do you think?"

"Hairy. Super strong. Big teeth," Johnny said. "Not a bear. What am I supposed to think? It looks like a werewolf."

"Werewolves don't exist."

"But we've always had legends about werewolves."

"Legends, yes. Based on something, yes. The biggest lot of them are probably based on big wolves or bears."

"What about the rest of them?" Johnny asked.

"Well, there's hirsutism."

Johnny nodded. He remembered reading a book about werewolves that mentioned people who grew hair – a lot of hair – on their faces and bodies. In one case, the fellow made a living promoting himself as half-man half-lion. The picture looked like Lon Chaney's *Wolfman* or Michael J. Fox's *Teen Wolf*. "What about his strength?"

"You tell me."

Johnny gritted his teeth. Ever since he'd signed on with Titan, Trager had taken it upon himself to be his teacher. That in and of itself really didn't bother him so much. After all, Trager and his dad had worked together and he had a lot of experienced advice to offer. Still, his overuse of the Socratic Method was a little patronizing at times. Johnny forced himself to think it through.

The average Joe would probably decide that the thief was in costume and makeup or that the film was a hoax, because werewolves don't exist. A cryptozoologist might be willing to consider the idea that he was looking at a werewolf, a Sasquatch or some other cryptid, until he saw "Bigfoot" raid the cash register and snag some munchies on the way out. Johnny's experience taught him there were other possibilities.

Johnny and his friends were Indigos and they could do things that nobody outside of a comic book do: move things with their minds, leap tall buildings, bend the path of bullets and a whole lot more. His girlfriend could make toast without a toaster. Weasel's girlfriend could choose to be completely invisible. He was one of the few who knew that Midwich's Halloween Night of Terror involved a super-powered battle between Johnny and his friends and a woman who'd hypnotized half the town. And yes there had been a flying saucer involved.

"He's either an Indigo with a body hair problem, an Indigo disguised as a werewolf or the real McCoy. Couldn't you have convinced Ness to come along on this one?"

Ness' nickname was Quatermain. Like his namesake, the Indigo sharpshooter never missed. He couldn't help but think that ol' Ness and a box of silver bullets would solve their problem pretty quickly.

Trager shook his head. "Past his bedtime and he doesn't work for us. You remember what he said. If it doesn't involve Pandora or the gammas, don't bother asking."

Johnny scowled, looking at the road ahead. They drove for a while in silence. For the most part, they were surrounded on either side by thick woods. Occasionally, the forest broke to a view of old farmhouses and fields. The full moon washed these nightscapes in a ghostly light that made the forest's shadows darker still.

"This is a dumb plan," Johnny said into his commset. Minutes ago, Trager had dumped him off in the middle of the deep, dark woods armed with a flashlight. People like Johnny didn't really need weapons any more than they needed a flashlight. If he so desired, he could will himself to see into the infrared and effectively give himself night vision.

According to Trager they were at the center of their wolfman's pattern of activity. He was probably around here somewhere, but Johnny was starting to worry that Trager had sent him on a snipe hunt. Did he really expect to find a werewolf out here?

On cue, he heard a howl.

"Relax," Trager said. "Just a coyote. You should be coming up on a field. There's an old farmhouse our target could be using as home base."

"Or he could have checked himself into a motel somewhere with the cash he stole."

"Quit complaining."

True to Trager's prediction, the forest broke and he came to a field bathed in moonlight. A sagging, clearly abandoned two-story house and an equally condemned barn stood at the other end of the field. Johnny crouched down at the forest's edge and switched his vision to see into the infrared. Extending the range of his vision to match an eagle's, he immediately saw something out-of-place in one of the house's second story windows. A wolfman was staring at him across the field.

"Somebody's home. Second window from the right," Johnny said. "I think he's spotted me." Their target darted out of view, retreating further into the room. "Yeah, he's ready for company alright."

"Go in," Trager said. "I'll cover the other side of the house to prevent his escape."

"Here goes nothing," Johnny said. Taking a deep breath, he dashed across the field as quick as a flash. He rested with his back to the house's siding, waiting for his accelerated breathing and heartbeat to return to normal. Once he'd sufficiently recovered, he willed himself invisible, a trick he'd picked up off an electrokinetic. Basically, he used his own electromagnetic field to bend light around himself like the aliens in the movie *Predator*. You could still see his outline if you really concentrated, especially when he was moving. Hoping this trick would give him a slight edge over their target, he stepped onto the porch and pushed the door open.

The door burst back shut, knocking him down in the process. So much for the element of surprise. Johnny became visible again as he rolled to a crouch, ripped the door off its hinges with a thought and sent it back at his opponent. The wolfman growled, pushing the door off his chest. He and Johnny rose to their feet slowly and at the same time, their eyes locked.

"Get out!" the wolfman roared.

Johnny stared at him calmly, but his heart was thumping in his chest. He was after all unarmed and standing not ten feet away from a very angry werewolf. "No."

The other barred his fangs in what Johnny supposed must be a smile. "Did you know I can hear your heart racing? Smell your fear? I know you're afraid."

Johnny smiled in return. His target was talking instead of attacking, which meant he wasn't quite sure he could beat him. That door must've hit him pretty hard. "Who are you?"

"You want to know my name?"

"Yes."

The wolfman blinked. "Creech. Edgar Creech."

"I'm John Lazarus. I need you to come with me."

"Where?"

"To a place that helps people like us."

"You're with Titan, aren't you?"

Even before Johnny could think to answer, Creech did a back flip that landed him halfway up the stairs. Johnny bolted after him, but he could tell right away he was dealing with the acrobatic variety of muscle mutant. He'd tangled with a martial artist with this variant of the gift before. He'd had trouble keeping up with her movements. As he reached the top of the stairs, Johnny watched the wolfman as he bounded down an upper story hallway toward a large picture window.

"Trager, he's coming your way!"

Creech burst through the window in a shower of glass. He bounced off the door of Trager's Hum-V which was hovering at the second-story window. The car's hovercraft technology was a company perk, so to speak. Creech fell to the yard below, but quickly scrambled to his feet and headed for the barn.

Johnny burst out the window after his target. Having seen Creech crash into the Hummer, Johnny opted to jump onto the roof of the flying car before hopping to the ground.

"Did you actually think that would work?" Johnny asked as he slipped into the barn.

"You'd be surprised how often it has," Trager said. "Careful in there. He's a slippery one."

Johnny searched the barn with his night vision, but the werewolf was carefully hidden from view. The moon shone through a giant hole in the roof.

Rusting farm equipment hung from the beams. He listened carefully, isolating Creech's heartbeat. The sound was coming from somewhere up in the loft to his–

He sensed the pitchfork's flight before he saw it. With his amplified hearing it sounded like a 747 rushing at him. Using his telekinetic abilities, he stopped the pitchfork in midflight just inches from his face.

He heard the wolfman curse.

"That wasn't very nice," Johnny said. Spotting a broke-down tractor, he hefted it up into the loft. Creech dove out of its path just in time and tried to flee. Johnny picked him up mentally and brought him back. He kept him hovering there, bathed in moonlight. Creech struggled against the invisible hand that held him.

"Let me go," Creech said.

"But you'll just run away again."

"This isn't a joke, man! You have no idea what Titan does to freaks like me."

"Then why were you drawing attention to yourself by robbing gas stations in that get-up?"

"This isn't a costume. This is my face! You think I can get a job looking like this?"

"Maybe we can help you with that," Johnny said.

"I've seen the kind of help Titan gives," Creech said. "No thanks."

A shadow fell over the barn interior as Trager's hovercar came over for a better view. Trager didn't hesitate. Drawing a gun, he fired a tranquilizer dart.

Edgar Creech went limp in a matter of seconds, but not before he managed to utter two simple words.

"Titan lies."

Read the rest of

John Lazarus: Mann from Midwich,

the thrilling sequel to Johnny Came Home, in 2013!

Legends arise. Dark forces gather. Heroes unite.

ABOUT THE AUTHOR

Tony Breeden is an author, creation speaker, apologist and Gospel preacher from West Virginia. He is the founder of DefGen.org, CreationLetter.com & CreationSundays.com.

Find out more about books from author Tony Breeden at
http://TonyBreedenBooks.com

Find us on Facebook at **http://facebook.com/johnlazarusbook**